The Anointed

Samantha Traunfeld

Cover Design by the author

ALSO BY SAMANTHA TRAUNFELD

The Legionnaire

The Blood-Cursed

To my favourtest cousin Catie, for getting me through this series.
You're the bestest.

NO KINGS

TRIGGER WARNINGS

Trigger warnings include: Fantasy violence, death of a fictional character, graphic depictions of violence, mentions of infanticide, mentions of possible sexual assault, mental breakdowns, panic attacks, psychopathic leaders and religious fanaticism.

I

SAIDEN

SAIDEN AND HER FRIENDS DIDN'T NEED TO CHASE ANYONE AS THEY returned to the channel between Taezhali and the island of the severed key. They were running away. Every time they rested Saiden worried guards would appear, swarming them from the rear, ready to pull their scarcely gained freedom away from them.

The thought of their destination offered no comfort. They were making their way back to a country and a situation they wished they could avoid. Back to Kaizia. Danger surrounded them no matter which direction they turned, but only one path called to Saiden. Only one set of wrongs were hers to right.

Saiden vowed to fix the mistakes she had made helping to place Revon on the throne. She would see peace and order returned to the only place she knew as home.

The fact that they weren't chasing anyone did not make the trip through the desert hills any easier. Somehow despite the fact that they all had considerably more training, only Eleni made it through the day without complaining.

They were better prepared this time too, so at least when they rested, they had tents and thick enough sleeping mats that the sand shifting didn't wake them. Or maybe that was a sign of how exhausted they really were. There was enough food to satisfy their hunger, and enough water to keep them hydrated under the unrelenting sun.

As they packed up their belongings from the night before, Saiden took stock of her friends. Their skin was deeply tanned, saved from blisters by Loralei's healing talent. In fact, the disgraced queen only interacted with them to give nightly sessions of her healing power. Otherwise, she kept to herself. No amount of prodding had made her speak.

Saiden didn't know how to handle that situation. Whatever tattered bond remained between her and her Queen was making her uneasy; pulling at her, deep in her gut.

"So we're here now," Mozare said sidling up to Saiden. He seemed off too. Between his brush with death and Ilona's distance, Saiden couldn't exactly blame him, but she missed the days of their easy friendship. "What's your plan?"

Saiden pulled the coin she had tucked tightly under her leather vest and flipped it between her fingers. For a talisman slipped last minute in to her palm, the gift from the captain had turned into a lifeline of sorts.

Cassimir smiled when he saw it. "I was wondering what he gave you. Now the plan starts to make sense."

He was behaving exactly as Saiden expected him to. "My plans always make sense."

He leaned into her, pressing a kiss into her hairline. "Of course they do. When you take the time to actually make them."

She couldn't argue with him there. Her life had been so full of unknowns recently that she'd gotten into the habit of rushing into things. All she could do was hope she'd have enough time to successfully reach the end. Preferably while still mostly intact.

"This time I had a plan going in. Your sister helped."

Eleni smiled sheepishly when they both turned to look back at her. They had used the same magic Eleni used to send letters to Rhena, back in Kaizia, to get word to the captain that they were going to be needing his services. She'd spent the journey hoping he'd be there when they walked into town. They hadn't had time to wait for his reply.

She strapped a pack to her back, checking that it was resting tightly against her spine. Even though they weren't running, she didn't think this was the time to get lax. Not with everything they still had to face.

2
MOZARE

MOZARE DIDN'T UNDERSTAND WHAT HAD GOTTEN THEM ONTO THE SHIP, why the captain felt indebted to Saiden and Cassimir, or why they were suddenly taking up an entire deck, albeit a small one, for their passage back to Kaizia.

He only understood that Loralei wasn't speaking to him. Hadn't really spoken to any of them since Saiden had freed him from the Emperor's executioner. And he couldn't figure out why.

As the others filed out of their shared living space, Mozare grabbed her arm, keeping her from following, doing his best to be gentle when he knew everyone's skin was worn from days under the hot desert sun.

She didn't turn to look at him. He didn't try to make her. Now that he had her to himself, he wasn't sure what he was going to say.

Indecision robbed him of all other choices, leaving him with only her name. "Loralei," the whisper of a dying man breathing through his teeth.

She still didn't turn around. "What do you want from me?"

"I want you to talk to me. I want you to look at me. I want to stop feeling like you're running away from me when you're right here in front of me."

Finally, she turned to look at him, and he wished she hadn't. He could feel the cracks spreading over his heart with a single glance at her cold, sad eyes.

But he had already broken her heart hadn't he? It was only fair that she did the same.

"How can I be around you? How can you expect me to be around you after what you did?"

"All I did was try to save your life." He didn't want to feel defensive. He didn't want to be having this conversation at all. He wanted to wrap his arms around her and forget about all the terrible things that had happened to them while they were being held captive by the now dead Taezhali prince.

"You sent me to get help. Why didn't you wait for me to come back? Why didn't you trust me?" That was the heart of their problem wasn't it. She didn't think he trusted her.

"You didn't hear what he said. No matter where we went he was going to keep coming for us. I couldn't let him hurt you."

Loralei's voice broke as she yelled at him. "You hurt me. How can you not see that?"

"I saved you. How can *you* not see that?"

Loralei wrapped her arms around herself, and his heart cracked a little more.

"I've lost everything and everyone who ever mattered to me. What meaning would my life have if I lost you because you were so ready to die to protect me! Because you think I would ever *choose* to have you die for me?"

He couldn't answer her. He'd wanted to have this conversation. But faced with everything he had unwittingly done to Loralei while trying to love her, he couldn't find the words.

"How long are you going to use me to make yourself feel better about your rebellion?" She whispered the words, as loud in his ears as if she were shouting.

"That's not..." He didn't want to lie, but he didn't want her believing that. He knew he only had once chance at this, and he still couldn't think of the right thing to say.

"I can't be here, can't be with you, if all I will ever be is a reminder of what you've lost. Of the mistakes you need to make up for." Tears started to fall, tracking through the coating of dust that covered all of them. "I want to be loved wholly. As my own person. I'm tired of being a symbol for everyone else."

Loralei fell in on herself, crumbling to the floor and there was absolutely nothing he could do. He was the reason this was happening in the first place.

Her heartbreak was entirely his fault.

3
RHENA

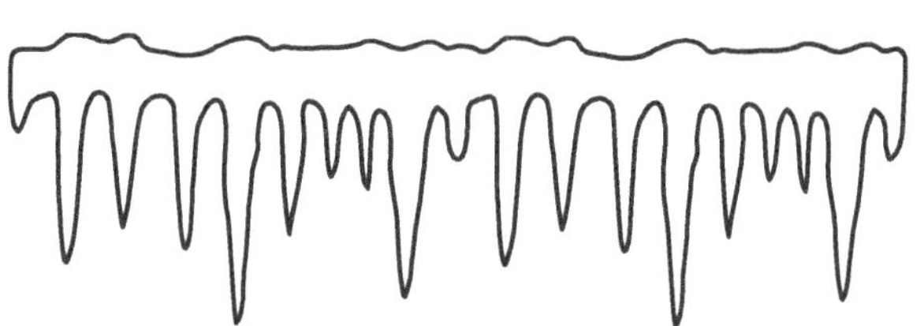

RHENA HAD NO IDEA WHAT SOMEONE DID TO HELP WANTED CRIMINALS GET back into the country. She wasn't sure if Saiden wanted her help to begin with. She would have asked if there was something she needed right? Her letter had been brief, and there certainly hadn't been any instructions.

It didn't stop her mind from circling over and over, thinking of everything that could possibly go wrong while Saiden and Mozare tried to get back into Kaizia. And there were so many different ways things could go wrong.

But she knew Saiden and Mozare. Knew there were so many outcomes where things went right, and she would be reunited with them in a few short weeks.

Now it was a waiting game. Her rage demanded action, but after everything that had happened to Talon, and his warning about her being followed, she was more hesitant to try. Shame burned through her. She should be doing more, but the thought of enduring the same punishment, having her skin slowly peeled from her body in sections, often left her paralyzed.

Talon was only now getting back on his feet, and his punishment had happened over 15 days ago. Even god-gifted healers could only do so much. His body needed time to heal the trauma on the inside as well. At least, that was what one of the healers told her the umpteenth time she had tried to gain access to his healing room.

She was taking a huge risk every time she went to talk to him, but she couldn't let him think he was alone. Not when he had gotten caught trying to help her. Not when they were fighting the same fight, and she was so lost. But Revon doubted her loyalties-rightfully so-and her insistence on visiting Talon repeatedly couldn't be making things better.

Even with all the negatives, Rhena couldn't stop thinking about him. He was only one year older than her, they were in the same recruitment class after all, but she'd never taken time to think about him before she'd threatened him that time in the barracks hallway. She only knew he was life gifted because he'd told her in the hospital.

The fact that Rhena hadn't known he was fighting on the same side made her nervous too. She had no way of knowing if she was judging people correctly, if she could make good guesses at people's intentions. She hadn't had nearly enough training in her solitary year in the Legion. Especially after her friends had been forced to leave and training had turned over to Revon.

In the end, Talon was the one who found Rhena. She was eating in the mess hall, feeling eyes watching her from every direction, when she saw him enter the room. It was the first time she'd seen him around other legionnaires since his punishment, and no one wanted to be around him. She went to rise, it wouldn't be the first time she sat at a table that everyone avoided, but Talon shook his head, not making eye contact.

She did her best to keep from obviously tracking him, but she kept him in view through her peripheral vision. In his fingers, there was a small square of paper, and then with a twirl as he walked through the line, the paper was suddenly gone. She tried to mask her shock, she couldn't let anyone see her reactions to him. As soon as he was seated she stood. As nonchalantly as she could possibly manage, Rhena rejoined the food line.

Talon sat down at a table all by himself. It wasn't the best choice, if he isolated himself too far, he would only look more guilty, but sitting with her wouldn't lower any of Revon's suspicions. As smoothly as she was able she grabbed the piece of paper from a small crack in the cement as she passed it and slipped it into her waist band.

For the rest of the meal, she was waiting for someone to notice. For someone to storm into the room and demand the truth about her allegiance. Rhena was starting to sweat despite the chilling effect of Ilona's gifts on the air directly around her. Panic made the ice on her knuckles crack with every spoonful, but she did her best to act as if it was normal.

As they all exited the mess hall, separating to head off to their next tasks, Rhena tried not to look too eager as she searched for somewhere hidden to open Talon's note. Once she was mostly sure no one had followed her she pulled the scrap of paper from her waistband, the parchment almost hot against her freezing skin, and opened it.

After months of waiting for Saiden's letters, seeing someone else's handwriting was slightly jarring. "Meet me between the blacksmiths and the butcher tonight after nightfall." She didn't like the immediate thought that popped into her head that this might be a trap. That maybe after such a severe punishment, Talon was prepared to do anything to avoid another one.

But at the same time, she wanted to think he was on her side because she was so tired of being alone.

Talon was waiting for her exactly where he said he would be, and as far as she could tell, no one else was waiting with him. There were faint lines over every inch of his skin, a reminder of trauma he would never outlive. She thought they were a sign of everything they were fighting for, and she desperately tried not to cry thinking about the pain that caused them. Together, they would stop this from ever happening again.

Rhena wanted to hug him, but they'd only really interacted twice before. The first time she'd had her blade at his throat so she didn't think they were at the hug phase of their relationship. But she was still glad he was here, and as whole as he could be. That would have to be enough.

"You wanted to see me?"

"You came to visit me. You're the only one who came to visit me. Why?"

Rhena took a moment to think about her answer. She hadn't been entirely sure of what had made her keep going to the infirmary time and again. But she wanted to give him an answer. "I wanted to see if you deserved it. Because everyone deserves to have their own side to the story."

"You already said you don't think anyone could deserve this."

"But Revon thinks you do. And the enemy of my enemy is my ally." It felt like something she could hear Mozare say, and that thought warmed her slightly. She could still feel the ice crawling down the back of her hands.

Talon snapped, and a small fire lit at the end of his thumb. The space around them settled, warming so that it matched the rest of the space around them. "I'm not done fighting." He said. She wondered how long he'd argued with himself to be able to admit that. She wasn't sure she would have been strong enough to try again after what he'd endured. "And I think we have a better chance of making it out of this alive if we do it together."

She couldn't agree more. "Was there something you wanted to do tonight? You didn't want to meet just to have this conversation, did you?" Rhena liked having confirmation that they were still on the same side, but they were out after curfew, and that was putting them at a greater risk of being caught. They didn't have to explicitly be committing treason. Being out here was bad enough.

"I have something you might be interested in seeing.

4

LORALEI

LORALEI DID NOT WANT TO SPEND GODS KNEW HOW LONG TRAPPED ON A ship where she couldn't escape him. She could barely stand being trapped in her own skin. There was absolutely no way she could avoid him, and the painful reminder that she couldn't be with him, no matter how her heart ached at the separation.

She couldn't handle being with someone who always had one foot stretched into the otherworld, ready to die at any moment. For her. As if she could ever shoulder the weight of his death on her conscience.

Despite all the time she'd spent in the tunnels at the palace, for the first time in her life, Loralei was starting to feel claustrophobic. She wasn't sure how she was going to survive this trip, isolated from the rest of their group and trying to heal her broken heart.

She'd rather have another broken spine to fix.

Unfortunately she'd learned long ago in a different life where she'd been free that wishes rarely came true for people like her. Only now was she beginning to understand that, while she had escaped the dirt she'd been born in, she had traded it for a gilded cage.

She felt her brain spiraling around the thought that all she had ever been to her advisors was a pretty bird for them to preen and prune.

Someone they could use to manipulate the people of Kaizia for their own selfish ends.

It didn't take long for her companions to leave her to her solitude. They weren't sure what to do with her anyway. No one knew how to deal with the rage and guilt that swirled beneath the surface of her skin. She didn't.

She found a dark spot in the ship, though if *he* decided to look for her the dark certainly wouldn't stop him. But at least the non-gifted people crewing the ship wouldn't see her completely break down.

Although she didn't board the ship with any weapons of her own —all her pilfered weapons from her life as a bandit had been confiscated by Akil—she'd managed to steal a short cutlass off of an unsuspecting pirate.

She sat now in the dark, twirling it, the point pressing into the flesh at the tip of her thumb. She couldn't feel the pain, and it didn't matter either, not when her power healed the wound before a drop of blood could fall from her finger.

The fact that she was so much of a freak that she couldn't make herself bleed did not help the spiral going on in her mind.

Loralei leaned forward and the long locks of her hair brushed against her knee, and an idea popped into her head. She didn't give herself enough time to consider what she was doing, pulling the hair tight with one hand and running her stolen knife through the strands.

She hadn't known she was crying until she felt her tears soaking into the dirty fabric of her loose Taezhali trousers. She'd need new clothes soon, she couldn't stand the way she smelled anymore, but it wasn't her priority right now.

"Want a hand with that?"

Loralei should have been able to feel Saiden coming. Her powers were so strong now she was practically a beacon. But she had been wrapped up in her own turmoil, leaving herself open to danger.

At least she wasn't Mozare.

What was Saiden thinking about her right in this moment? At one point Loralei had ruled over her—Saiden had been her subject. Now, she was witnessing every crack in her armor.

Oh, how the mighty had fallen.

Saiden reached out a hand for the blade, her skin warming Loralei's where it briefly made contact. She hadn't realized she was shivering, despite how warm the ship still was.

Without saying anything else, without poking at the weaknesses she was leaving out in the open, Saiden simply kneeled behind Loralei and began lifting sections of her hair to run the blade through them. In a distant part of her mind, Loralei wondered why she hadn't switched the blade out for one of her own.

"Have a lot of experience with this kind of thing?" She tried to joke, but the words sounded hollow to her own ears. She didn't know how Saiden and Mozare managed to joke at times like this.

"I am accustomed to cutting my own hair. There aren't a lot of people that want to touch the marking of the gods. Not when it's the symbol of my curse." Saiden hadn't stopped referring to herself as cursed, despite the fact that she had survived the unleashing of her powers when no one in recorded history had ever done so. But Loralei wasn't able to have that discussion right now.

"I needed to feel in control of something." Loralei finally confessed when she thought the silence would consume her whole. "Nothing in my life has ever been my choice. Before him." Loralei didn't need to say his name for Saiden to know who she was talking about. "And then he tried to leave me behind like that was ever the choice I would make." She did her best not to shake as Saiden finished up, keeping her tears as under control as she could manage.

"It's okay to be out of control. And it's okay to look for ways to take it back wherever you can manage it." Loralei wasn't sure how the words made her feel. Not when everything had been numb for days and she couldn't find herself. Still, she was silently grateful Saiden had climbed into the dark with her.

"We'll have to trim it again in the light." Saiden wasn't trying to push her out of the hold, but Loralei still tensed for a brief second imagining walking out there without her hair to hide behind. What would the others think? What would they say when they finally saw her like this?

Saiden placed the knife somewhere out of reach behind them. Despite how tight the space was, she sat down next to her, their legs pressing against each other from hip to ankle. She didn't speak, but Loralei didn't need her to. She needed someone to sit with her in the dark and wait for her to be ready.

When her tears had finally dried, she wiped her hands on her pants, although they were both so dirty she wasn't sure it made a difference, for her hands or her pants. Then she stood, Saiden quietly unfolding next to her, and prepared to step back into the light.

She was surprised to the sun was setting as they walked back on deck. The pirates seemed wary of them, though she wasn't entirely sure why. She knew Saiden had a history with these men, however brief, but they didn't know what to make of Loralei. Two stopped at the sight of them, but Saiden smiled.

"Mason, Finlay, never thought we'd meet again."

The two men smiled back. Mason's smile really lit up his whole face while his friend's was more a contented grin. "Glad you managed to get your girl back." Finlay spoke.

"May I introduce you to Loralei." Saiden gestured to her.

She laughed when Mason curtsied over dramatically, a sound that shocked her own ears. She could already tell she would like him; though she didn't mind the toned-down demeanor of his friend either. "If you think of something that needs extra hands let us know. We'd love to be of help."

Normally she might have resented that Saiden had spoken for them both, but somehow her friend knew exactly what she needed. If she had something to do, like the time she'd spent in the kitchen during their stay in Taezhali, maybe she could keep herself from going absolutely mad.

5

MOZARE

THE ONLY SOUND IN MOZARE'S EARS WAS THE THRUMMING OF HIS OWN blood. He couldn't hear the ocean, could barely feel the way the waves rocked under his feet. His shadows wrapped around him with a vengeance, and everyone around him on the boat went out of their way to stay as far away from him as possible.

Not that the ship had enough space for them to truly avoid him. If he wasn't careful, the ship would be at the bottom of the sea when the new power he'd grown during Akil's torture cracked the vessel in half. Even now, the strength of it surged right under his skin, waiting for him to let his guard down.

He couldn't let everyone on this ship die because he didn't know how to love her correctly. He didn't know how to do this riotous feeling in his chest justice. Not when there was so much history between them. Not when he had betrayed her before he'd ever considered loving her.

Mozare's hands were shaking so much they looked fuzzy with the the constantly reforming tendrils of shadow emanating from them.

A hand grabbed his shoulder. After everything they'd been through, his first instinct was to reach for an ax, prepared to swing back and remove those hands from whoever they belonged to.

But Cassimir had his other hand rested on Mozare's harness before he finished the thought. His friend knew him too well, despite how short they'd actually been acquainted. But he was also in love with Mozare's best friend, so maybe they all knew each other better than Mozare realized.

"Take a deep breath with me."

"If I breathe too deep, my chest will crack open and all of this," he vaguely gestured to the gathering shadows, "will consume everyone here."

"You control them, not the other way around. You are hurting, but you don't want to pass that to anyone else. You know that. So, breathe with me." Cassimir used the hand on his shoulder to turn Mozare around. He didn't seem afraid that he could get hurt as he grabbed Mozare's shadow clad hand and pressed it to his chest. Mozare didn't understand what he was doing until he felt Cassimir's chest expanding under his fingers.

He tried to match their breathing, and to his surprise, found that the shadows on his fingers began to slowly unravel, settling back into the place inside him where his powers rested.

"Let's talk about it." Cassimir said. Despite his gentle nature, he wasn't really giving Mozare a choice. Probably for the best, if he had a choice Mozare probably would have continued to run from this pain until it completely ate him alive.

"She hates me because I tried to save her life."

"By sacrificing yourself for her?" There wasn't judgement in his voice, he was simply clarifying the circumstances. Mozare still felt like the words were blades, each of them drawing blood, but none of them enough to be fatal. Just enough to leave him bleeding.

"I didn't have a lot of choices while your cousin was holding us hostage as his test subjects."

"Can you imagine what it would have been like for her to live in a world where she was only alive because her love was dead?"

Mozare froze. He hadn't wanted to die for her. He wanted her to escape the darkness so she could live in the light. Loralei deserved to be shrouded in sunlight at every minute.

"I've already lived in a world where I was alive because she was dead." True he hadn't loved her when he believed her to be dead, but he had suffered from the guilt of the rebellion. He suffered from it still, though he didn't want to admit it. Then he'd have to face that all of his actions since stemmed from that one decision.

He had orchestrated the plan that had gotten her removed from her throne, that nearly killed her. Because he hadn't taken the time to see the world from her eyes.

The same way he was right now.

He betrayed everyone he cared about at some point or another, and he was nowhere close to making amends. Realization began to dawn, that he was not the only person in his life anymore. He had been blinded by his own feelings again. Every decision, every time he thought he had found the correct path it was because he thought he was doing what was right. But he'd never asked himself who it was right for.

His legs gave out underneath him, nausea rising in his throat that had nothing to do with the tides beneath him. Not that he had a lot of experience being on ships, this was a first for him, but his world rocked harder than any stormy sea could.

Cassimir was too smart to be with them. In the back of his mind, Mozare wondered what exactly had brought this man into their lives. The rebellion didn't seem like enough of a reason for the gods to grant them such a sage friend.

His friend sat down next to him, all the words he needed to say floating around them as Mozare kept trying to process his own faults. But staring into the abyss was going to kill him, friends or no.

And he couldn't go off into the darkness until he managed to fix things. The right way this time.

6

RHENA

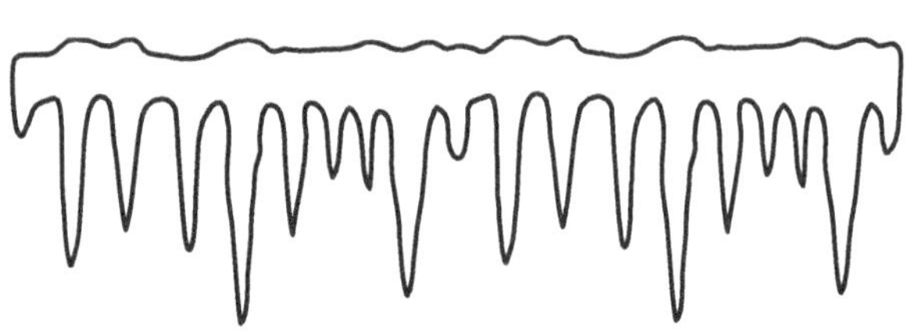

RHENA WASN'T SURE WHERE TALON WAS LEADING HER, BUT SHE FOLLOWED him anyway. Maybe it would get her killed, and maybe it wouldn't, but at some point, she had to trust someone. If this was the path fate had set for her then so be it. She might be young, but she already knew that no one escaped their fate, no matter how they raged and fought against it.

When Talon led her into a dark alcove in an unexplored part of the castle she was half convinced he was leading her into a trap. "Rhena you need to breathe. If you get too much colder you're going to pass out, and I can't do anything to help with that."

Right, because she'd completely forgotten that he was regulating the temperature around them so her cold snaps didn't alert anyone to their presence. Rhena closed her eyes, taking three deep breaths, the shaking in her hands slowing. The small bit of relief allowed her to pull some of her power back into herself. Talon gave her a thumbs up, but then she heard Revon's voice, and no amount of deep breathing was going to get her powers back under her control.

Talon turned, pressing her into the wall and pressing his body over hers. The pressure settled her in her own skin. "It's not a trap. Can't you feel the magic here? I think he's doing some shady ritual, but I'm unable to sense it because he wouldn't be calling on Keir."

Of course not; Revon had been gifted by the goddess. Although, his gift was small if Mozare was correct, which she never doubted. That was why he'd needed her, to feel for Ilona. She closed her eyes again and waited to feel the goddess's hand press to the back of her head.

She opened herself to the feeling. Rhena had been so closed off recently, so afraid of her power giving her away whenever it wasn't under her control. It felt freeing now to let go, to let Ilona back into her mind.

Until she felt the power coming from the room. Whatever they were doing in there, it was a perversion of her gift, it was wrong. The sensation was oily on her skin, and even her gifts recoiled from it, the space around them becoming stiflingly hot as Talon's powers were no longer covering her own. She wasn't sure what was going on, but whatever it was, was making Ilona angry.

Rhena didn't want to feel her anger anymore.

But now that she was open to her goddess, she didn't want to cut herself off from her either. Something pulled at her. She took a step out of Talon's arms, trying to find a vantage point to poke her head around the corner and look in at whatever was going on beyond their sight.

Rhena hadn't known there was such a large area of open water in the palace, but maybe there hadn't been one before. At least no one had told her about it. Revon was standing just beyond the edge of the water, shirtless with some unknown marking painted over his skin. Laying in the middle of the small lake was Revon's newly appointed general, who Rhena was pretty sure was entirely naked, though luckily, she couldn't see him well enough to know for sure.

The goddess nudged her again, commanding that they bear witness. Talon's warmth was at her back now, keeping her grounded as her fear spiraled out of control.

"What do you think they're doing?" He asked her.

She was worried for a brief second that they might be heard, but the two men seemed stuck in a trance, their spirits farther away than their bodies were.

"I don't know. But she is not happy about it." Rhena didn't dare invoke the goddess out loud. She wasn't entirely sure why, but she didn't think it was right to speak her name in this audience. "This can't be good news for our cause." She was sure now that they were on the same side.

"What do we do about it?" They were trainees after all.

Rhena wasn't sure she had the answer either. But she knew who might. They just needed to wait until her friends made it home.

7
SAIDEN

A FEW DAYS LATER SAIDEN AND LORALEI SQUARED OFF AGAINST THE DECK of the ship. They had to be careful of their surroundings—the captain had already given them as much room as he could spare, and the last thing either of them wanted was to accidentally injure one of the crew members.

Luckily, she'd had enough foresight to recruit the boys to referee their sidelines. She'd almost regretted asking Mozare when she saw the way Loralei's posture had gone rigid at his approach, but she wasn't going to ask him to go away now, when they needed him.

Especially when neither of them would tell her what was going on between them. After saving Mozare from execution, she had expected a lot more explanation of what had happened to land them in their position in the first place. But then they were being forced to leave. All she had gotten was an emotionless retelling, broken into pieces between the two of them. She wasn't stupid enough to think that was all that was going on, but she wasn't unkind either. She wouldn't push either of them to talk about it until they were ready.

Instead, she'd offer a training session to Loralei to support her, and help burn off some of the restless energy coursing through them all. After everything they had gone through together, she owed the queen that much. She wasn't trying to make up for the past, they had all made their mistakes, but she wanted to learn from them and do better.

Saiden wasn't sure which of them would have the advantage. She'd had years more training than Loralei, but that was skill. Loralei had gained a mastery over her powers, which Saiden understood to have grown during their time in the southern kingdom. She couldn't say the same thing about her own gifts.

Yes, she had managed to reach a place where she wasn't constantly battling against the strain of her power, but she didn't wield them nearly as freely or competently. Though they were also in the middle of the ocean, so she wasn't sure if Loralei's powers were accessible to her out here.

They were about to find out. She'd spent so long analyzing the pros and cons of her position, that she'd missed when Loralei stepped towards her, palms directed towards her face and sparked a bright swath of light across her vision.

Saiden had to close her eyes against the brightness, at the same time fighting the flare inside her that was her own power calling to its likeness. She didn't know what could happen if she let them out onboard the ship, and she wasn't willing to risk the lives of everyone on board to have the advantage in a sparring match.

Only her training kept Loralei from knocking Saiden completely to the ground with her next move, swinging for Saiden's legs. She jumped, taking the rocking of the ship into account as she landed on the railing.

"Careful Saiden," Cassimir called out to her. Distantly she could hear Mozare laughing. "One wrong step and you're going for a swim."

"She's hot headed enough to be fine in the water," Mozare called. She didn't bother giving him a response. Couldn't have answered him even if she wanted to, because she was too concerned with dodging Loralei's offensive maneuvers.

Whatever had happened in the dungeons while she and Cassimir had gone off to rescue Eleni, had magnified her powers significantly. Without even a hint of earth, Loralei grew vines, launching them at Saiden's wrists and ankles, trying to tie her to the rigging.

She jumped, reaching for her one remaining kindjal blade after having lost one in order to escape the Isle of the Severed Key. Swirling the blade between both of her hands she managed to fend off most of the vines advances, but even she wasn't fast enough to fend off Loralei, when she slipped behind Saiden and got a blade to her throat.

Even with the direct threat, Saiden smiled. She was proud of how far Loralei had come since the days when she had demanded Saiden train her. And she had to admit she was relieved she wouldn't feel as responsible for Loralei in the fight to come, not when she could handle herself quite well.

Mozare clapped, but Loralei ignored him, removing her dagger and placing it back in the sheath resting against the light layers of her skirt. Saiden didn't bother trying to figure out where she had managed to get a skirt like that aboard a ship mostly crewed by men. Loralei had a talent for getting anything that she put her mind to, Saiden seriously doubted clothing was outside the realm of her ability.

"Want to go again?" She asked. Her skin glowed in the late morning sun, but she had barely broken a sweat. The Queen still looked as regal as ever, even with the shorter hair and pirate clothing. It had been a surprise when Saiden had found Loralei sawing at the long locks of her hair, but the desperation in her face when she'd seen Saiden made her quietly sit down and help to even out the cut.

Now, Saiden didn't see desperation. She saw ferocity, the kind that had been hiding in the queen all along, suppressed by politics and her advisers' expectations.

Saiden didn't bother with a verbal reply, she simply jumped forward, one arm striking towards her in a tight fist, the other holding the blade. She didn't give Loralei enough time to determine which hand was the bigger threat. She was almost close enough to make contact, when one of Loralei's vines pushed its leaves out far enough to shield her from the blow.

That was new. She didn't think her powers were strong enough to enhance living organisms. Then again, none of them fully comprehended the lasting impact that weeks of torture had wrought on her and Mozare.

He was the next thing on her list to worry about.

Right now, she was more worried about the blade swinging

towards her eye. If Loralei didn't want her to see today, she was doing an excellent job trying to remedy that situation. Saiden ducked fast enough to avoid temporary blindness, but she could've sworn a few red hairs fluttered to the deck around her.

She grabbed the rigging behind her, and as Loralei lunged in for her next attack, she swung herself up into the air, using her surroundings to her advantage and positioned herself behind Loralei. She used enough of her power to wrap ice around the queen's feet, keeping her from turning to meet the next blow, and wrapped her arm around Loralei's throat in the same kill position she'd pulled on Saiden.

"A tie then, it seems." Eleni called from the sideline. She wasn't sure when Eleni had joined them. She had been below deck, doing her best to be helpful, when Saiden had suggested the sparring match. Now she stood on Mozare's sideline, the captain's son Nico next to her, his face pale and sweaty.

Saiden's heart sank in her chest. She didn't like seeing that look on anyone's face and started mentally preparing herself for bad news.

As he forced himself to address them, Nico looked rather seasick, despite having spent most of his life aboard the ship. "I want you to teach me how to fight."

8

Mozare

Next to the skinny boy, Eleni spoke up. "We actually came here together because we've both decided that we need lessons, and it seemed easier to ask together." Mozare wasn't sure what she was talking about at first. He already knew that Saiden had made training one of the stipulations to her agreeing for Eleni to accompany them.

He took in the odd pair. Eleni already knew them. She had no reason to be nervous about initiating a session, despite how intimidating Saiden and Loralei's sparring had been. But Nico, he was new to this. And based on what Saiden had told him about their journey across the channel, Nico had a good reason to be a little awed by the lot of them.

Mozare was honestly surprised that he hadn't noticed the boy's behavior when the two first approached. There was a unevenness to his stance that had nothing to do with being on the open ocean, and the boy was wringing his hands so hard he was sure to give himself skin burns. Until he noticed Mozare watching him and violently shoved his hands into his pockets.

He smirked. If he couldn't talk to Loralei, which she had made abundantly clear she didn't want him to do, he needed to find something else to make the time and his unbearable proximity to her pass by easier. Training someone new, someone who looked like he'd never handled a weapon in his life, that was something he could do in his sleep.

Mozare turned to Saiden. "I get the kid. You and Loralei can work with Eleni." Even saying her name was hard for him, piercing in to the ever widening cracks in both his heart and his armor. He needed to set a quick boundary, before any of his meddling friends could suggest a different arrangement.

Saiden gave him a funny look that years of friendship told him meant that they would absolutely be talking about this later. Then, locking arms with both of the other women, she effectively split their training area in two.

He turned away from them, doing the mental acrobatics necessary to turn off his sense to Loralei and her movements. It was one of the hardest things he'd ever had to do. But he understood the pain he had caused her, and he never wanted to do that again.

"So what do you know about fighting?"

Nico shrugged. His face had a red tint to it that had nothing to do with being in the sun.

"You've seen others fight. Why haven't you learned yourself."

Mozare had a feeling the other boy wanted to shrug again, but he had turned on his instructing face, the kind that told his students he wouldn't put up with petty bullshit. He wasn't going to teach Nico if he couldn't understand something about him first. That was the exchange.

"Did you know I was born on this ship?" Nico shook his head like he was trying to set the memory loose, "No of course you don't. That was a stupid question. Anyway, yeah, I was born here. Every single one of these people have seen me grow up from just a wee babe. They've never seen me as anything more than a child. Why should I have a blade, when one of them could always protect me?"

Mozare saw some of the pieces of the puzzle start to click in to place. He could feel the resentment underneath all of it, of a boy not yet old enough to be a man, convinced that was what he wanted to be. But there was love there too, for the family who'd raised him.

He tugged one of the longer daggers from the collection strapped across his chest. His axes were on his back, he would be getting them rehandled as soon as was safe to do so, but he wouldn't have shared those anyway. Flipping the blade so he was holding it by the point, he offered it to Nico.

Mozare kept a close eye on the way he grabbed for the blade. "It's a tool, before it's a weapon. Use it wisely and it will never have reason to do you harm."

Nico started nodding emphatically, and Mozare tried to hide his flinch. He wished they had something safer for him to start off with. Despite his little speech, he was still worried about the pirate boy hurting himself. Or more specifically, he was worried about facing the captain's wrath if his son got hurt on Mozare's watch.

"You'll start with the basics." Mozare showed Nico how to spread his feet, doing his best to adjust for the constant movement of the deck under him, and led Nico through a set of motions ranging from defensive to offensive techniques. This was his element, he felt most comfortable with a blade in his hand, teaching others.

He was barely thinking about Loralei, though a small nagging part of his brain wanted him to turn and see how the women were doing. He managed enough self-control not to completely embarrass himself in front of the group of pirates gathering to watch them. If he faltered, Nico could bear the consequences, and he was done pushing his problems on to other people.

He would find a way to fix this. Not only his relationship with Loralei but the damage done by the rebellion he'd helped lead. He needed time to figure it all out. Time he felt distinctively slipping away from him as Kaizia grew ever nearer.

9

RHENA

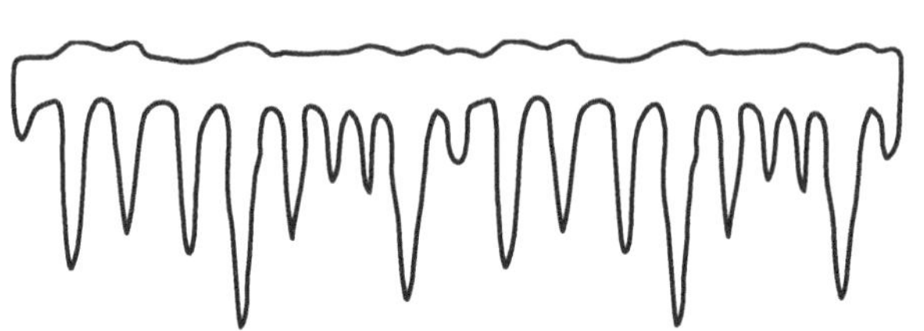

RHENA DID HER BEST TO STIFLE HER SURPRISE WHEN REVON WAS STANDING at the front of her training room. Sessions like these weren't mandatory under his command, but they were highly recommended, to the point they may as well have been. Even without the pressure, Rhena would have made sure to show her face.

Being a spy was all about appearances anyway. She might be a terrible spy, Talon had caught her after all, but that wasn't going to stop her from fighting for her beliefs. And to fight, she needed to be alive and well, not holed up in some infirmary.

Running into Revon had her second guessing her priorities. Maybe this time putting herself out there was also going to put herself in danger. She didn't need to be the next gifted soldier he decided to use as an example.

Not that she could really back out now, he'd already seen her. If the hesitation in her step hadn't already damned her, turning around and running surely would. It took every ounce of will in her body to keep herself in the training room, and to keep ice from forming along the windows. They were reaching the cooler months, but a sudden frost would have been a dead giveaway as to how she was feeling.

She gave a short bow to her king, and joined the lines of soldiers getting ready for training. She couldn't see Talon among them, but she wasn't sure she would have been brave enough to approach him if she had. It was probably for the best that he didn't make it to this class.

Next to Revon, one of his newly promoted generals stared at them with a mean slant to his smile. Rhena didn't like the energy she felt radiating from him as he took in the gathered crowd of recruits. The hair on her arms was raised, and the voice in the back of her head which she'd always attributed to Saiden's training was screaming at her to get as far away from him as possible.

Instead of the training weapons they kept in the barracks, dull or wooden weapons intended to keep them from doing serious damage, their instructor began to pass out freshly sharpened short swords. The weight was the same as the sword strapped to her back, and yet she couldn't shake the feeling of wrongness.

"Partner up." She knew this would happen, it happened every class, but the instructions still shook her. Rhena turned to the recruit next to her, bowed, and put herself into a firm stance. Lari was the same age as Rhena, and the paleness in her normally warm cheeks told Rhena she wasn't the only one afraid of what this training session meant for them.

At their general's command, they placed their blades against each other's, and waited for further instructions, but the only thing their new general said was, "fight."

This was new. She'd sparred before, but training sessions were usually more controlled, their guidelines more rigid. It was about learning, not practicing.

Then their king started speaking. Anyone who stopped moving was reprimanded by the general as he passed through their ranks, some more vigorously than others. "You are soldiers, not puppets. If you are going to be good fighters you will have to learn instinct, not the repetition of basic movements. Draw first blood from your partner, and you can go. Bleed, and you'll have to fight again."

The blood drained further from Rhena's face. This wasn't just sparring. These were war games. Rhena's stomach was sick, and she had to fight the urge to vomit in the training room. Some of the recruits in her class weren't even older than nine yet, still children. She was still a child in most people's eyes. What good would pitting them all against each other do?

Unless there was an ulterior motive. Her brain started racing. Of course, he would have a reason to shift their training to something more dangerous. It wasn't about fighting. This was all a test of loyalty. He couldn't have soldiers that valued each other's safety over the sanctity of his orders.

He wanted to break them.

Rhena wasn't sure what the best track for her to take was. She could beat her partner, get herself out of this ridiculous exercise and possibly prove herself to Revon at the same time. However, she risked unknown consequence of being at the top of her class. What if he decided to put her in the field? What if being too good brought her attention that got her caught?

She couldn't work through all the different scenarios in her head fast enough. Blocking Lari's strikes was almost second nature, all her training with Saiden was paying off, but one misstep, one haggard glance at the general, and then pain seared through her.

Rhena dropped her blade to clutch at the bleeding gash in her arm. Lari's sheepish expression varied between disgust and pride. Sure she had cut one of her fellow recruits, but this meant she didn't have to move on to the next round. She believed herself to be safe.

"Cheap shot." Revon called from the front. She couldn't tell who he was more ashamed of. "You certainly should've been able to block that, Rhena. Where's your head?"

She couldn't tell if he wanted an answer, not that she could have answered truthfully without condemning herself. Blood seeped through her fingers, her revulsion made worse when the general came to her with fabric scraps and began to wrap the injury. She should've expected there wouldn't be healing between the fights, but she would have rather lost the arm entirely than let the general touch her bare skin.

Everything about him felt off, deep to the core of his power. The parts of her that normally flourished in the presence of the god's gifts flinched away from this man, coiling deep in her belly as far as it could get from him. It was a very bad sign when even the goddess began to press against her consciousness, her warnings a whisper as loud as a scream.

The other matches took longer than the one she had lost to Lari, but not by much. She should have been embarrassed by this fact, but all her brain could focus on was the tally of victors to losers. She needed to know who she would be fighting next.

The bandage tied around her arm had stopped the bleeding, but there was no way she would be able to use the arm to fight now. Not against any opponent with even the most basic sword skills. There was barely enough strength to lift the fallen blade from the ground, the first swing would've knocked it clean from her hands again.

Others joined her against the wall, sporting injuries that ranged anywhere from shallow cuts to far worse than the burning slice on her arm. She didn't know what Revon hoped to gain by putting them all in the infirmary, but he was certainly getting a glimpse at his most ruthless recruits.

She didn't want to be one of them. Of course Rhena was a soldier and she knew what that meant for her life. She'd never forgotten the fight in town with the Enlightened where Saiden had killed to save her life, but she didn't think they should become heartless. And that was exactly where Revon's training was going to lead them.

Revon celebrated every gruesome win, slapping his soldiers on the back or shaking their hands. Revulsion turned her stomach, but she couldn't be sick. Even if her injury could be to blame, it was too risky to be anything other than stoic when Revon was watching. If she was too obviously against his policies it had the potential to put many people in danger.

She still hadn't figured out a new way to undermine him. Even in her fear her mind had been racing trying to think of something she could do from the inside. She wasn't going to risk freeing more soldiers, not when doing so could force Talon to endure more of Revon's cruel justice. But she wasn't prepared to give up yet either.

Finally, when her name was called again, she pulled her hand free of the bandages on her arm. She covered the fabric in a thin casing of ice to keep the pressure on it. She might not be doing the right thing, Revon certainly hadn't prioritized field medical knowledge during his short reign, but she also couldn't fight if there was blood flowing down her arm.

Rhena did her best to keep her breathing even as she walked to the center of the room. They weren't all fighting at once this time, these next rounds were a show for the king and his general. He wanted to see them bleed. To watch as he bred darkness into their souls.

She wasn't going to let him win hers.

She pushed herself into a correct stance, unused to fighting with her non-dominant hand. Surely Saiden would've gotten to this in their training if only Revon hadn't tried to turn her into a mindless weapon. Rhena let that rage simmer under her skin, pushing herself further through the motions of her fight.

It wasn't that she wanted to win. She didn't think winning at this point in the game was the right move. But she couldn't have Revon thinking she wasn't putting her all into the fight either. Not when she was at the top of many of his suspect lists. Talon had told her as much all those nights ago when she first visited him in the infirmary.

The boy she was fighting was lankier than she was. She could see every opening in his technique, all the sloppiness in his form. When their fight had gone on long enough and she was starting to doubt his ability to actually win by his own merits—even with her lackluster attempts at defending herself—she kicked out her leg and swept his feet out from underneath him.

As he was falling to the ground his sword arced up and cut into the wrist of her already injured arm. She hissed at the pain, though she managed to keep her sword pointed at her target sprawled out on the floor. "Ah so you've won boy." Revon said, pushing between them. The only reason she lowered her sword was because she couldn't imagine the punishment for accidentally threatening their king. Not when he was already on the war path looking for traitors.

Revon reached out, offering to help him back to his feet. When the boy was almost standing again, Revon pulled a small blade that had been concealed within his robes and sliced him across the face, just below his eyes. "But what a sad victory it is. Seconds from a true death strike, and you decide to cut her wrist. You're dismissed."

The boy, Rhena finally realized she didn't even know his name, didn't bother to press a hand to his face as he turned and nearly ran from the training hall. He let his blood flow freely, the red a sad mimicry of tears none of them could shed.

Revon grabbed for Rhena, and she had to force herself not to pull her injured hand from his grasp. He held a hand out to the general, who passed him another piece of fabric. Revon leaned in conspiratorially as he wrapped the new injury, her blood quickly soaking the cloth. "In my mind you are the victor. Everyone watching could hear mother death call for him. Next time, you finish it."

For a brief moment, shock covered her face, but as the king backed away, Rhena did her best to school her features into the guise of the obedient soldier. Let him think she'd follow his orders. She knew there was no way he could force her to kill for him.

He'd have to kill her first.

10
SAIDEN

THE SUN WAS SETTING WHEN SAIDEN AND LORALEI BEGAN THEIR TRAINING session with Princess Eleni. Even after their fight, Saiden could still feel tension rolling off Loralei in waves. She secretly worried about the damage all that anger must be doing to Loralei's spirit. She also hoped that she could manage enough control for their training session to be productive.

Eleni wasn't like them. She wasn't born to be a fighter, which meant they couldn't approach this the way they might a normal training session. She'd had her education with the priestesses in Taezhali, despite not having joined the order. Discipline wouldn't be an issue like it could be with new recruits, but violence wasn't in her nature.

Giving her a weapon might make her too nervous to actually use it. Something they couldn't have if they were heading into what amounted to an open war zone. Not when she'd promised Cassimir she would do everything within her power to keep his sister safe.

Saiden started off with very basic training, going over some body mechanics with Eleni. Using her and Loralei's own movements, she showed the princess how she could use her size to her advantage. You didn't always have to be scary to survive, sometimes being smart was enough. Especially if the people you're fighting underestimated your ability.

When Eleni spoke up, her words unnerved Saiden slightly. "When those men took me, they dragged me from my room. They ripped my prayer scarf away and used my hair to keep hold of me." Despite all the consideration Saiden had put into this training, she hadn't considered the trauma Eleni still had to face.

The fear that clouded her friend's eyes broke her a little. Even though it was unusual for her, she stepped towards the princess and wrapped her tightly in her arms. She was shaking, and Saiden cursed herself again for not thinking of the mental toll training might have on Eleni.

Loralei spoke from behind them, but Saiden didn't think Eleni was ready to stand on her own yet, so she didn't let go entirely. "The way you take yourself back from them is by learning. You perfect these techniques and you'll know no one can ever do that to you again."

Her words were hard but not unkind. And they were true. She had seen the reclaiming through Loralei's own training—she had made herself more than a queen to be protected. She was fierce within her own rights now, a warrior like the rest of them.

Saiden knew that Loralei would never let herself get hurt the way she had been when Revon had snuck up behind her and plunged his blade through her spine. Now, she wouldn't have to do it all alone.

When Eleni's shaking had subsided a bit, Saiden talked Loralei through her changes to their lesson, and the two of them set to work making Eleni feel strong.

11

LORALEI

OBVIOUSLY LORALEI HADN'T KNOWN THE TWO PIRATES SAIDEN HAD BEEN excited to see on board the ship, but she quickly became grateful for their company. After her conversation with Mozare, she felt even more isolated from the group. They were his friends first after all, how could she impose on their company when she had ended things between them?

But these men weren't part of that, and their constant flirting and games were the boost to Loralei's self-esteem she hadn't realized she needed. Plus, she got to be useful when she was with them, taking part in whatever shifts they'd been assigned for the day. After spending weeks in the kitchens in Taezhali, Loralei never wanted to go back to idleness.

And when they were done for the day, Finlay and Mason always invited her to their card games.

She had never played cards before setting foot on the ship, so when she had won the first night, everyone had chalked it up to beginner's luck. When she had continued to win the next night, and the night after that, people began to suspect her. Not that she minded. This was something entirely her own, and it was time that luck was actually on her side. Even if her luck towards everything important still sucked.

The cards made sense to her. Finlay and Mason played what the other men called a "bastardization of fortune's hand", a card game where the object was to always keep your cards higher than the rest. A person with fortune's hand could choose to eliminate another player, wiping their score for the round or save themselves. The winner was whichever player managed to make it to the end of the game.

The betting was complicated, and she'd had to hear the rules a few times before she had understood them entirely, but once she started playing it had all come easily.

After a long day on deck tending to the captain's men, Loralei was ready for the lively card game that would keep her mind from racing to darker places.

Except that, this time, when she stepped foot in the hold where they normally set up their table, Mozare was sitting there along with the men. She saw him right away, her eyes still drawn to him despite her every attempt to pretend like he didn't exist.

And he knew it too. He tried to hide the smirk on his face, but she knew him well too. Had spent a long time in those dungeons studying his face for any signs of change that she could read him as easily as a book.

He knew exactly what he was doing by being there. She had half a mind to turn around and find somewhere else to spend the evening, to show him that he couldn't control her, couldn't manipulate her into talking to him. But this was her fun, and she wasn't letting anyone else dictate that for her.

If Mozare wanted to play games with her, she was going to show him how good she was at winning.

She had already made it clear to both Finlay and Mason that she wasn't interested in romantic attachment, and they hadn't seemed to mind, so she didn't feel guilty when she perched herself on Finlay's lap and reached an arm over Mason's shoulders.

Finlay was by far the more cuddly of the two, but she knew where Mason's boundaries were, and she was sure that he would be okay with the casual contact.

She smiled up at Mason and hoped beyond hope that he would go along with her ruse. Her heartbreak already felt so close to the surface, she couldn't bear for any of them to have front row seats to it.

When Finlay wrapped an arm around her, she felt herself relax, "here to be my good luck charm lass?"

"Someone has to give you some luck mate, you've thrown away every coin you've earned so far." Mason's gruff voice spoke from next to them.

Loralei did her best to put on her court smile, the one that had fooled everyone into thinking her the obedient, docile queen, and placed a hand against Finlay's face.

"It's really the least I can do, considering everything you've done for me." She let the innuendo hang in air, not caring what the other men would think of her. She only cared that Mozare thought she was moving on without him.

She was hoping he would storm out, but when the room remained unusually silent, she finally turned to look at him again. His hands were clasped tightly together on the table as someone began dealing the cards, shadows haloing his fingers.

His face burned as he stared at her sitting in Finlay's lap, and she waited for him to explode. She didn't think he would ever hurt her, but every person had a limit to how much they could tolerate, and Mozare was quickly approaching his. Especially as Finlay swept her shorter hair over one shoulder and rested his face in the crook of her neck.

She didn't take her own hand of cards, instead she lifted Finlay's set so they could both look at it, hiding Mozare from her view. She had no doubt his eyes were still locked on them, she didn't need to see him to feel his burning gaze.

Loralei was the only reason Finlay won any of his money back. As rounds passed it became more and more clear that Mozare was a terrible gambler, doing outrageous things that even she couldn't understand, and quickly losing all the money he had brought to the table.

When the other men were satisfied with their winnings, or tired of losing, they called the game off for the night.

Finlay gently lifted her with him as he went to stand, and she did her best to stay close to him, despite every fiber of her being wanting to be alone, to cry and scream and rage at what her life had turned into.

"Did you get what you wanted?" Finlay asked her, leaning close. For someone who'd had no prior warning, Finlay had done an amazing job keeping up with her deception, and even now looked like a lover sharing secrets.

She wasn't sure how to answer his question. Yes, she had managed to get under Mozare's skin, but was that truly what she wanted? She couldn't even tell anymore. Once her desires had been so simple, now everything was a tangled mess, both in her head and in her life.

She settled for simply shrugging her shoulders. "Thank you, either way. For playing along."

"Not much would force me to push a pretty girl from my lap. Especially when she's in need of a friend." Loralei could tell he was flirting with her, but more than that she knew he meant the friend part. She'd never really had friends before, and the thought of Finlay being her first friend went far in warming the all consuming cold that had taken up residence inside her.

She pressed a kiss to his cheek and watched as he departed, slapping backs with the men whose money she'd helped him steal.

Loralei had assumed that after her show, Mozare would have taken the first opportunity to get far away from her, until she felt his fingers wrap around her bicep.

"You can play whatever games you'd like. You can't push me away. I will never stop fighting for you."

Mozare was gone before her own reply was even past her lips.

"It shouldn't have to be a fight."

12
SAIDEN

While Loralei and Mozare played cards, and Eleni was off somewhere being useful to the pirates, Saiden took the opportunity to have a quiet dinner, her and Cassimir. With all the chaos in their lives recently, they'd barely had an opportunity to spend any time together.

Saiden could still barely wrap her mind around the declarations they'd made to each other aboard this very ship. This ship, where a dock above her she had almost lost him entirely.

The food was much better now that Eleni had taken to helping the men in the kitchen. Even though her talents didn't compare to Cassimir, who had no doubt given suggestions to the chef regarding tonight's dinner if the smell was anything to go off, she did at least keep things from being flavorless.

As long as the ship's cooks kept things from burning, they could make quite the team.

Cassimir wrapped an arm around her shoulders, though she wasn't quite sure how he managed without also spilling his dinner while the ship rocked beneath him. She should know better than to question his will, especially when it came to her.

She smiled up at him, and the smile he gave her in return lit up the inside of her chest.

"You're glowing my love." He spoke, the whispers a gentle caress.

She looked at her hand, not entirely surprised to see light actually radiating from under her skin. This time, she wasn't afraid of it as she reached into her powers inside her and wrapped the light around Cassimir as well.

Saiden could see what he meant about glowing. It wasn't just the way he was wrapped in her light, but the contentedness of his features. He reached between them, placing both of their plates on the bolted down table, and gathering her into his arms.

"I would bask in your light every day of my life, and find that life very well lived." He spoke, pressing his forehead against hers.

Saiden felt her cheeks blush, but didn't have time to think about it before Cassimir was pressing his lips to hers, enveloping her in everything that was their love. His warmth was more comforting than anything she could've conjured herself. Gradually she let her own light recede, so she could bask in the radiance that was purely Cassimir.

When a few minutes had passed with no end in sight, Saiden gently detached herself from Cassimir, doing her best to have even footing as she walked over to their bunk. The food might be better with some Taezhali spices, but nothing would save it if they let it get too cold.

When he smiled at her though, nothing else mattered. She wasn't something to be feared anymore, she was his.

13
RHENA

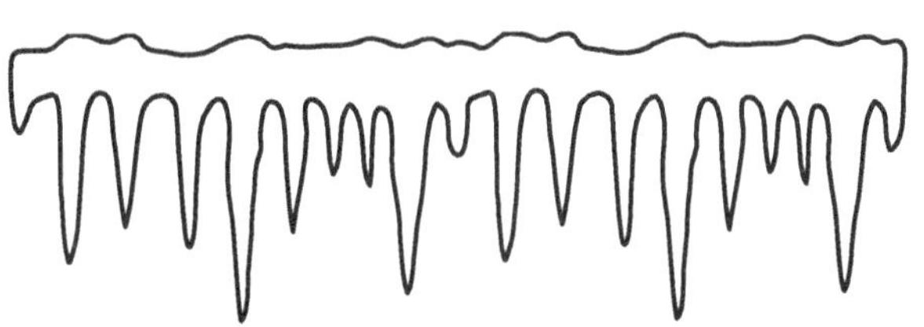

RHENA WAS TRYING TO BE USEFUL. SHE KNEW BEYOND A DOUBT THAT something weird was going on in the palace, and she didn't want her family to come home only to be blindsided by some power they couldn't even guess at. She couldn't let Revon get the upper hand, no matter how much it scared her to be looking for him. No matter how the general's touch still lingered on her skin, weeks after the training session where he had first touched her.

She wanted to vomit at the thought, a chill cooling the air around her. She wished Talon were here with her so he could balance her again, but he was stuck on night guard. If she couldn't get her power under control she was going to end up like Talon. Rhena pushed herself back to her training with Mozare, trying to remember a calmer time when they were all still together. She needed their presence at the back of her mind to give her enough courage to take her next step.

Not that she had an exact plan in mind. That was probably part of why her hands were shaking the way they were. She wasn't prepared, and she wasn't nearly experienced enough to be able to make it up as she went. Not when there was so much at stake, not only for her own life, but for her friends as well.

They were on their way back. She kept the sentence on repeat in her head. She didn't need to do anything right now, she needed information. That was easy enough. She needed to watch, and listen. She could manage something that small.

From what she already knew about Revon he spent most nights hiding out in the archives, absorbing everything he could, or running his bizarre experiments. She should have tried to find somewhere to hide in there, but she hadn't thought that far ahead.

She was relying on him being consumed by his work, buried in his texts, and her footsteps being quiet enough they wouldn't draw his attention as she found somewhere to conceal herself. Rhena didn't know if that would be enough, but she didn't dare pray when summoning the goddess could ruin her.

As she was braving herself to take the first step into the room, someone grabbed her by the scruff of her neck, the big hand so hot against her chilled skin it felt like it was burning her. Ice spread on the floor underneath her, until the hand on her neck was the only thing keeping her standing.

"Keep your head down and don't say anything." He whispered in her ear, and she could've sworn she recognized his voice, but all she could think was how grateful she was that it wasn't the general's hand around her throat.

"My king," he spoke again, a few seconds later. She fought with her entire being to shove her powers back inside her as Revon spoke.

"Are we having a problem here?" He sounded disinterested in the way only a man obsessed with power could be. As long as they were in the palace they were under his control. She knew that was why he had moved the legion here instead of keeping the old barracks running.

"You know recruits my king, they aren't the best at doing what they're told. This one was supposed to be back with my food, but she must have gotten lost. Nothing a few lashes won't solve." She wasn't sure what game her savior was playing, but at least that the chill in the air could be excused as her fear at having displeased a fully-fledged Legionnaire.

"Of course. I'm glad you're seeing to her discipline." Rhena felt his eyes on her, and hoped with everything in her that Revon didn't realize it was her.

"Thank you, your majesty."

Rhena felt him bow, the hand still on her neck forcing her to bow next to him. They stayed that way as Revon's footsteps grew quieter in the distance. *She hadn't been caught.* At least she hadn't been caught by him, but she had no idea what this new problem meant for her.

The hand on her neck finally released, and she turned, placing her hands, palms facing the floor, out between her and her savior. At least, she was still hoping he was her savior. She lifted her eyes and got her first look of the man that had kept Revon from finding her.

She'd seen him before, but right now, with the adrenaline coursing through her system, she couldn't quite place it. It could very simply be that she had seen him around the Legion before. His powers called out to hers, finally easing the chill in the air. She wasn't used to that.

"I know you. You used to hang on to that blood-cursed bitch."

The words rang through her head, and finally everything clicked into place. He was the legionnaire Saiden had been forced to duel what felt like a lifetime ago now. *Oliver.* But he had helped her. She couldn't make up her mind about what she thought he stood to gain from it.

He whistled, and his partner turned the corner. She reached out her hands, resting one against each of Rhena's cheeks. Suddenly another power coursed through her, one different from her own, but complimentary. This girl's gifts must've come from Keir and she could feel their soothing warmth relax the tension in her muscles.

"What did you just to do me?" Rhena asked, and though she should have heard a tremor in her voice, should've been worried about whatever was being done to her without her consent or understanding, she was finally calm for the first time in months.

"That's my gift," she answered voice smooth in the air. "I heal the mind. It's not as showy as healing the flesh, but it's still important."

Oliver rested a hand against her back, "the flesh doesn't matter if the mind is broken. We saw that with the girl." He wouldn't speak Saiden's name, but Rhena knew that was who he was talking about. It's all anyone seemed to be talking about these days.

"She's not mad." Rhena wasn't sure why she had admitted it. She still didn't know these two, definitely shouldn't have trusted them with information so sensitive to the success and welfare of her friends.

But they didn't look angry when she said it. Oliver simply turned to his partner, a mix of something between wonder and aggravation crossing his face. "Of course she would survive that curse Melana." The words were too loud considering they were hiding. But I guess she was supposed to be getting reprimanded so maybe no one would think twice if they overheard them in the hallway.

Melana didn't look so convinced. "How do you know that? You watched the same brutal execution that we did." Of course she had. Revon made his public displays of Saiden's power mandatory for all of them to attend. The vision of her cruelty, of her emptiness, still haunted Rhena's nightmares.

How much was she willing to share with them? The only memory she had of them was Oliver challenging Saiden, and almost killing her in the duel to run a simple mission. She had nothing to go on besides his brutality and his quick thinking today with Revon.

"I don't know you. How can I trust you?" Not how do I know I can trust you, because she was certain Oliver would tell her she couldn't.

"Good question." He reached out a hand, wiggling his fingers. "Give me your hand."

"Oliver." Melana's tone sounded like a warning. "This is serious."

"You know what Talon said. He wanted this." *Talon.* What did Talon have to do with anything?

"He's a child, and so is she." Rhena wasn't good at guessing people's ages, but she doubted the pair could've been that much older than Saiden or Mozare.

"There are no children in a war zone. Especially not gifted ones." He turned back to her. "Do you want to trust us?" She desperately wanted to say yes. She wanted to have someone to rely on again so badly, that the ache of it in her chest never dulled. She loved her friends, but they were too far away to do anything right now. And she needed help. She was certain now that there was no way she could do this on her own.

She grabbed his hand with her own. "Listen kid," he said negating his own commentary. "This is serious magic. Neither of us can speak of this deal again without sending death hunting. And she can be a cruel mistress, never forget that." Ice had returned to her veins.

"This will keep you safe from possible betrayal." Melana's words tried to push through the anxiety buzzing in her ears, but barely managed. She had to hope she wasn't in way over her head again.

Oliver drew his finger between their hands, and black lines similar to Mozare's shadows spiraled onto their skin. Rhena watched, slightly mystified as they sank into her skin. "I will speak no word of what is spoken here to another," he recited and the tendrils grew bold, "nor do anything to otherwise harm Rhena." *He knew her name.* She hadn't expected that.

The lines sunk into her skin as he finished speaking, and inside her next to the well of power that housed her own gift, she could feel their bargain take root.

"When Saiden escaped, she wasn't kidnapped." She could feel the bargain inside her wrapping the words in their magic even as she spoke them. "Mozare and Cassimir brought her to the southern kingdom."

Oliver looked like he wanted to smack himself as he spoke. "They figured it out. I don't know how, but they brought her out of it. They're coming back."

Melana and Oliver turned to look at each other. There was nothing but hope on either of their faces now. No matter how much he hated her, Oliver must've seen the same truth that Rhena knew deep in her soul. They had a chance now. Because of her.

14
SAIDEN

SEVEN DAYS INTO THEIR JOURNEY, ILONA'S PRESENCE AT THE BACK OF Saiden's mind sent her reeling from sleep. She still hadn't gotten used to the idea that they could present themselves like this any time they wanted. The feeling was strange, like she had grown a new limb and wasn't quite sure what to do with it.

What she did know was that the goddess was alerting her of coming dangers. She could feel the truth of it all the way to the tips of her toes. If she was getting a divine warning, she wasn't going to sit around and wait to find out what was coming to kill her.

She would hunt the threat down and eliminate it.

She frantically started shaking her friends an effort to rouse them before danger struck. Cassimir had already started to wake, her absence tipping him off to something being wrong.

"What's going on?" He asked her, watching as she woke Mozare last, and their friends began to groggily pull themselves from their bunks.

"Something bad is coming. I can't tell you what." Her panic only worsened as she tried to explain her feelings to Cassimir. She knew he trusted her. He wasn't going to be the one she had to convince. They were on a ship full of non-believers and she needed them to have faith in her in this moment.

The only good thing about wearing her hair loose was that she could pull at the strands in her anxiety, racing over every thought in her brain. She was overwhelmed, simple enough. After spending so much of her life in danger she couldn't bear to witness anything happen to the people she cared about.

"Breathe Saiden." Cassimir was holding her hands. She wasn't sure when he had moved from their bunk, but he was standing in front of her now, and he had pulled her hands out from the snarls she had inflicted on her curls. Another warm hand grabbed on to her shoulder, and she knew by touch alone that Mozare had pulled himself from the bed and was standing behind her, ready to catch her if she fell.

"What do you need us to do?" Loralei asked. She hadn't joined the huddle, but her words were supportive, nonetheless.

"Can either of you feel what's going on?" Saiden didn't know if this was a stretch. She hadn't had enough time with her powers to really understand how everything about divine connection worked.

"I can feel the goddess. Something must be wrong with the sea." Mozare spoke.

"That's quite a jump." Eleni said, although she had mastered the ability to sound calm while questioning him.

"Water fits under her control. That's why Rhena's gifts from Ilona manifest in ice. We're surrounded by water, so I don't think it's as much of a stretch as it might've sounded."

Mozare was so sure of himself, and Saiden, being as new to her powers as she was, had to trust that he knew what he was talking about. Their group filed out of their sleeping area, Cassimir's hand never straying from her back as they all followed her above deck.

The wind whipped her face as soon as she managed to push the heavy wooden door open, lending credibility to Mozare's claims. Men raced aboard deck, and as she tried to walk against the gusts of wind she marveled at their ability to do so.

All around them gear and sails were being tied down, everything loose on deck was either secured to a railing or thrown below. Whatever they were witnessing, this ship had seen it before, and they were prepared.

"It won't be enough. All these men will die."

She didn't want to hear Ilona's voice in her head, and certainly didn't need her omens. Even she could see that this storm was only beginning. At the helm of the ship, the captain directed his men, arms swinging as if he were conducting music in the greatest hall of Kaizia.

When he spotted them, he yelled. Saiden was surprised they could still hear it above the raging of the storm. "Get back below deck. You don't have enough experience to get through this without getting yourselves and my men killed."

Saiden was faced with a decision. They could go below deck and hope that the gods favor was enough to keep them alive. But she'd be dooming these men to certain death. She caught a flash of Nico's face through the soaked tendrils of her hair, and realized her mind was already made up.

She couldn't let these people die. Not if there was anything she could do to stop it.

But her friends needed to get below deck. She couldn't look at Cassimir, not when she knew he would fight her on the decision to put her own life at risk. Instead she turned to Mozare. He was still her partner, even after everything they'd gone through. She didn't need to speak for him to understand what was going through her head.

He simply nodded. The look on his face was torn between worry and anger, but he didn't try to stop her. Whatever influence Ilona held over them, he must've known this was the only chance they had.

In a rush of movement, Mozare grabbed Cassimir, wrapping thick arms around his chest. He pulled him through the door Saiden had wrestled open, sending the rest of their friends stumbling back through as well, She only wished she could've kissed her love, in case this was the last she would see of him.

But now wasn't the time to think of death, even if its mistress still pressed at her consciousness.

Now was the time to fight for life. Not only her own, but the lives of everyone currently on board this ship.

It took Saiden much longer to reach the captain than it would've for his men. She couldn't take the winds, and she'd never really developed her sea legs, but she didn't have time for that now.

Once she was close enough to the captain to capture his attention he started shouting at her again. "I told you to get back below deck."

Saiden didn't have time to fight him. He'd seen her bring a man back from the brink of death. She needed him to trust that power. "Every man on board this ship could die if I listen to you." Her voice didn't carry as well as the captain's, but she could see he had heard her nonetheless.

"You don't know that."

"I don't know the seas as well as you do. How likely does a ship this size survive a hurricane when it's on top of them." Because she'd finally realized that was what they were facing, the outer rim of a hurricane quickly spinning towards them.

Saiden could tell by the look on the captain's face that the odds weren't good, even before he opened his mouth to answer her. "It's unlikely."

"Get your men below deck. I think I can save your ship."

The captain took a long moment to look at her, a battle of its own raging across his face before he called the order out to his men. Saiden watched them, at the same time sizing up the vessel and deciding on where she was going to make their last stand. It might be a battle against nature, but it was still a battle, and that was where her brilliance shined.

The captain swept the deck, helping anyone knocked around by the storm back to their feet and corralling them all through the doors leading below deck. She hoped none of her friends tried to make it back outside. The wind whipped violently at her, the force as strong as any blow she'd ever felt.

Saiden began the process of reaching for her power. Without Cassimir, without her friends, she didn't have a safety net—she'd need to do this all on her own. She was only shaken from her trance when a pair of rough hands grabbed for her ankles.

Disobeying her orders, the captain was still on deck, and he had grabbed her before a wave had crashed over the edge, knocking them both a few inches sideways.

"What are you doing out here? You'll die."

"This is my ship. If someone is fighting for it, I'm going to be right beside them."

Saiden couldn't argue with him on that point. The ocean raged beneath them. She could feel the ship cracking under the pressure. They had only a few moments to change their course, or they would be ruined.

"Get yourself tied down. I can't be sure what will happen when I use this much power."

Saiden returned to the well of power inside herself, and pulled at the energy she could feel coming from the ocean. She was the master of her powers, and with enough strength, she could tap into the waves and use them to protect them ship. Wind whipped at her face, her hands, pushing and pulling her in every direction.

It was too much of a distraction being tied to human flesh. The thought should have terrified Saiden, but from within the depths of her powers she couldn't remember how to be afraid. Light poured from her body, but she no longer had the ability to see it. She was only her power and strength and the storm.

She pushed herself to become the ocean. With the powers inside her, life and death swirling around each other, if she pushed far enough she could feel everything about the water around them. Her skin became coated with the rage of the waves, and each of her breaths was the flutter of fins trying to outswim the storm.

Saiden lost herself to the feeling of it all. But she wasn't overwhelmed. She felt strong, her power finally listening as she wove the waves into patterns that kept them steady against the rising tides, pushing the storm from the ship in every direction.

She did her best to tune into the groaning ship as well, even as the heartbeat of the ocean around her tried to steal her attention. Except for Rhena, all the people she loved most in the world, were depending on her to save them. She needed to feel them too.

Deep enough into her powers now, Saiden was able to use Keir's gifts to feel for their heartbeats. It was such small magic. And inside her, the power started to grow a mind of its own. It would be all too easy to pull on their life forces, to tug at the blood in their veins. If she had been weaker willed the power might have won.

She didn't have enough experience for this. She pulled away from them, wrapping them in the light that had saved Loralei and Mozare from her powers when the crowned prince had cornered her in the hallway. Even if she lost herself, she wasn't going to lose them. She'd never sacrifice anyone else, not while she still had herself to give.

Maybe that was what she needed; to remind herself what there was to lose. She had a family, a real family for the first time in her life. If she didn't have them, she never would've survived her mother's death. Never would've had a chance to save this ship and all the other innocent lives on board if her love for them hadn't helped her to get some control back after her curse had been released.

She was a force strong enough to fight a hurricane. The gods had imbued her with enough power to change fate. They both pressed into her consciousness, taking her further away from her body. She should've been afraid. Saiden should've remembered that she couldn't trust them to care about the things that she cared about. But after being away from them for so long, and now being so close to their power, she couldn't fight them. She didn't want to fight them.

The storm raged, but their ship moved as if sailing across the smoothest seas. They were immune, protected. The chosen of the divine. She wasn't going to let fate hurt them again. Not while she lived.

15
MOZARE

ALTHOUGH MOZARE AND CASSIMIR HAD BARELY STEPPED ON DECK, THEY were both soaking wet, water running in rivulets down Cassimir's face. Mozare pushed his hair out of his eyes, he desperately needed a haircut. Prison would do that to a man.

Cassimir swung at Mozare the second the door was closed, and Mozare couldn't even blame him. He would've done much worse if the positions had been reversed. He lifted an arm to block the swing , but he wasn't going to fight back. Not when Cassimir had every right to be angry, and not just with him.

Mozare could see that Cassimir was angry with Saiden too. The desperation in his face flavored by the anger. Neither of them thought she needed to face this alone, but Saiden was stubborn, and she deserved to have a partner who trusted her gut. Cassimir turned around and pounded on the door, helplessness sinking through the rest of them in heavy waves as vicious as the ones outside.

He could hear the ocean rage against them. He didn't know what Saiden felt in the storm that he couldn't feel. What their goddess didn't show him. Even without her wisdom, he could feel her presence all around them, could practically taste the way death hung in the air.

"Why would she do this?" Cassimir turned back to Mozare. "Why would you let her risk herself out there all alone?" Mozare was already starting to ask himself the same questions, but he tried not to let his doubt erode his belief in her.

He'd lost one religion already. He wouldn't lose faith in her.

"I trust her." There wasn't more to his explanation. Saiden had given him the look that told him she had a plan, and he trusted her instincts. He wasn't going to fail her now, when she had put her trust in him to get the man she loved to safety.

Cassimir slumped against the door, the fight going right out of him. Mozare knew there wasn't a point to his fight, but something soured in his stomach to see the other man so defeated.

"What if she overwhelms herself? What if she can't summon enough power to do the job and she dies? And *we all die*, alone and separated from each other?"

Mozare didn't get the chance to answer before Eleni was crouching down beside her brother, her mostly dry clothes soaking up water everywhere she touched him. "She couldn't have done this with us up there. She needed us to be safe enough that she could give herself entirely to the wind." He wasn't sure how Eleni had come to feel so certain in her answer after knowing them for such a short time. But somehow her words must've made sense to him, because despite their size difference Cassimir sank into his sister, sobs racking his body.

All Eleni did was hold him, rubbing one hand in circles over his back.

Inside his own head, Mozare's own turmoil over leaving Saiden behind ran rampant. There was no one here to comfort him the way Eleni did for her brother. Saiden was his family, one of only two people he could give the title to, and she was risking her life out there without anyone to watch her back.

The screaming of his brain only stopped when a thin set of fingers wove between his. His skin froze at the contact. His entire body tense as if moving might reveal that it had all been a trick of his mind.

"I still can't stand you. But she's my friend too. I don't want anything to happen to her." Loralei's voice was soft, but he could hear the tremor behind it. She didn't argue against the fact that Saiden needed to do this alone. He suspected that of all of them she was able to understand that the best.

The words weren't forgiveness, but he could see a bridge opening between them, the possibility for reconciliation lurking in their future. It was a hope he couldn't afford to let go of. Not if they were going to make it out of this mess alive.

Loralei led him by the hand until they were seated next to the siblings, and Mozare rested his other hand on Cassimir's shoulder so the four of them were connected. Because that was what Saiden did for them, she connected them. Together they would weather whatever storm came.

And they would all fight. For her. Because she knew they could make it through this.

16
SAIDEN

In the eye of the hurricane everything was silent. The waves returned to their gentle rhythm lapping against the scarred ship hull, and the sky cleared. The power buoying inside Saiden began to settle again, and her feet came back to rest against the splintering wood of the deck.

Logically, Saiden knew this was only a brief respite from the danger that would face them today, but the pause gave her a moment of hope. She had been able to control her powers enough in the first part to keep the ship from breaking entirely under them. Maybe this was something she was actually capable of doing.

The captain stood at his spot at the helm, legs wrapped in thick corded rope. Even from across the deck she could see the same hope beginning to bloom on his face. This ship and his crew meant so much more to him than Saiden could even imagine. In the grand scheme of things, her stake in this fight was much smaller than his.

He still thought she could do it.

Her powers rose in her chest again, her confidence bolstered by his belief. He'd already seen her powers once, when she had brought Cassimir back from the brink of death. This was on an entirely different level.

This was what she thought it might feel like to be truly Anointed.

She didn't let the thought take up too much space in her mind. Already she could feel the winds rising again, the anger of the sea pressing against them, indignant by their ability to survive her wrath.

The ocean knew nothing of true wrath. Not when it was incapable of love or loss. She did not doubt that the sea was mighty, but it fought only for destruction. She fought to protect. And she was not going to fail her friends again. Not when she finally had the power to do something about it.

She pushed back against the wave. She wasn't going to let the ocean continue to rage around her. She was going to stop the storm. Power flooded her veins again. Saiden could feel Ilona and Keir through the tips of her fingers, but in this moment, flooded with both of their gifts, there was no desire greater than hers.

But even Saiden had her limits. And her body was still mortal, even if her gifts were fully divine. She could not hold on forever.

She had used every drop of power in her body to keep the ship afloat. This time when her body came back to ground it did so with a crash, the waves still pushing at the ship violently, though without enough force to do significant damage. The storm was gone, but it would not let her forget either. It would not go easily.

Her body rolled with it, and now that she could feel it again, she wished she couldn't. She had figured that burning through her power would feel a lot like her life had before her mother's death, but this was so much worse. There was a hollow void inside her chest that nothing could fill, and her body was all too aware of the loss.

She knew she couldn't hold on to consciousness much longer, but the sight of the captain walking towards her on deck planks that didn't break was enough for her. The ship rocked again, and as Saiden lost herself, she was pitched over the side and into the ocean below them.

17
CASSIMIR

THE ONLY REASON CASSIMIR COULD SIT STILL WAS BECAUSE, WITH HIS BACK against the door, he felt as if he could sense some of what was happening on the other side. He couldn't feel Saiden, certainly not the way Loralei and Mozare could with their divine connections, so he was forced to take whatever scraps he could get.

The vibrations that had been racking his body slowed. As soon as he had felt that first sign that the storm had ebbed he was on deck, and there wasn't a thing in this world or the world beyond that was going to stop him. Not when Saiden was out there in who knew what condition.

He only needed to open the door a crack to see Saiden's body roll off the side of the ship. Cassimir's brain took a minute to recognize that she wasn't fighting it, she had given in to the waves.

No.

She was unconscious, and as her body hit the water, he couldn't be sure if he was screaming. The world around him had no sound, his ears consumed by the ringing of bells. His friends pushed out the door behind him as he finally got his body to start moving.

He tried to run towards her, but the distance felt eternal. No one was holding him back, but somehow he still couldn't reach her. His clothes soaked again in the lingering rain, weighing him down, his heart beating in his throat as the seconds ticked by in his mind.

With a rope tied around his ankles, Cassimir watched the captain dive over the railing of his own ship, plunging into the waves after Saiden. Or her body. He wasn't even sure she had been alive. He couldn't imagine how much power was required to stop a hurricane.

His brain flipped back to their escape from Kaizia, to the weeks she had spent trapped in her own mind. She had only surfaced once to fight Loralei's bandits before dropping back into an exhausted, comatose state.

His fingers were cold, his skin gone numb as his entire body went into shock. Mozare passed him, no judgement for having frozen, as he chased after the captain to help pull them both back on board.

Saiden looked pale in his arms, her body limp. He couldn't tell if she was bleeding, not with the way her hair hung in wet tendrils on her washed-out skin. That damned curse. He'd never hated her hair before, but now he couldn't stand the sight of it.

The captain laid her down on the deck of the ship she'd managed to save.

"Any of you gods-blessed know a magical way to get water out of lungs?" He didn't think the captain was insulting them, but he didn't know the man well enough to read into what he was saying. Cassimir didn't understand how the captain himself didn't have a way to deal with this, he made his entire living on board a vessel that was always a breath away from sinking.

But the captain was paralyzed too. They all were, looking at their savior reduced to an empty shell. She would die if they couldn't figure out a way to help her.

Eleni. He'd almost forgotten his sister was on board with them, but she was already in motion. She was always so prepared in these kinds of situations. She kneeled beside Saiden, and he suddenly remembered how much training their mother had passed on to her about the priestesses and their ways. The magic of nature, something that didn't require a gift, something any ordinary person could learn.

Knocked from her stupor, Loralei went to kneel down next to her. "I'll keep an eye on her vitals. I can't heal her until the water is out, otherwise I could do more damage." Loralei stuttered out. Cassimir didn't think she even understood what Eleni was going to do, but she was trying to help which was still more than Cassimir himself had managed to do.

He finally forced himself to move, kneeling across from Saiden, holding her hand between both of his. If this was the only thing he could do, if he could only serve as a reminder of what she had to live for, at least he was fighting for her.

Mozare rested a hand against his shoulder. He didn't have any gifts that would help, not if they were keeping Saiden in this realm, as desired. So, the two of them waited, watching their women as they performed a miracle.

Cassimir heard his sister speak their sacred language, but even he didn't know what she was saying. He hadn't been privileged to the priestess training. He watched her as she hovered her hands over Saiden's chest, slowly extracting the water from her lungs so she would finally be able to breathe again.

Loralei didn't move her fingers from Saiden's throat, though he doubted she needed to touch her to feel her heartbeat. She never wavered, never flinched. He did his best to remain confident that his sister knew what she was doing. That she could save the woman he loved.

And he begged in every language he knew, to every god of the known universe to let her live. Their story couldn't be over yet.

Cassimir flinched as Saiden coughed, turning to her side to expel the remaining water in her lungs. He wanted to pull her into him, to cover her in kisses, to remind her how much she was loved. But drowning wasn't the only death Saiden had escaped tonight, and the strain of exhausting her powers was pulling at her. She barely had the strength to squeeze his hand before she was pulled back under.

But she would live, and for now, that was enough.

18
SAIDEN

SAIDEN COULD FEEL HER BODY THROWN OVER THE EDGE OF THE SHIP, BUT there was nothing she could do to stop herself from being carried over the railing, she couldn't even get her arms to reach out for something to hold on to.

Her body was exhausted, every muscle strained from what she had forced her powers to do. She didn't regret it, her only thought as she went over was the hope that she wouldn't die. That she would see her friends again and apologize for scaring them.

Consciousness floated around her, but every time she reached for it, it slipped through her fingers. Her body felt weightless, and something at the back of her mind told her this was a good thing. It felt right to be suspended like this, something finally calm around her. These waves weren't angry, not the way they had been in the storm, but there was no escaping them either.

When the gods came to her, they didn't bother taking her somewhere new. Saiden was too tired to even open her eyes to see that they were not physically with her either, not the way they had when she'd called on them in Kaizia. They couldn't reach her here, so far from their borders.

But they could still speak to her, especially when she was so weak she couldn't fight back against the intrusion.

"That was magnificent." Keir said, though his voice lacked the enthusiasm that might have come from a human. He recognized she had enacted a miracle, but it wasn't all that special because they expected that from her.

"You performed excellently. Better than we could have expected." Ilona agreed.

When Saiden finally managed to push words past her lips her voice was nearly unrecognizable to her own ears. "What do you mean performed?" Sometimes their riddles were too much for her, and her brain was already so fuzzy she couldn't think about anything too complicated.

"That was a test dear." Keir answered for her. He tended to be the more straight forward of the two. Saiden almost wished this was another riddle. Otherwise she would have to face the ugly truth he was giving her.

"A test? You sent a hurricane to test me? You put all those lives at risk so you could *test me?"* If she'd been in her real body she would've been yelling. She hoped that in whatever way they managed to connect to human emotion they could feel hers.

"You must know that we needed to see your power work, being bound as long as you have, we needed proof."

"How ironic you would require proof of me."

In her current state, she could not fight the gods, though she could feel their grip weakening. She stopped listening, sinking back into the silence of a dreamless sleep. Her friends were still waiting for her on the other side of this test, and she needed to get back to them.

19
LORALEI

LORALEI WAS SITTING AT SAIDEN'S BEDSIDE WHEN SHE FINALLY WOKE UP, three days after the hurricane had passed. They had sailed right through it, safe because of Saiden's protection. She wished she could've seen it. It must've been something to behold. But now, her friend was barely hanging on, and Loralei couldn't stand to be away from her.

The only thing she could do for Saiden now was sit by her bedside and monitor her vitals. She couldn't find anything wrong with Saiden that needed to be healed. She had to assume that Saiden had burned herself out, and now her body was waiting for the power to be replenished.

When she blinked her eyes open, Loralei was torn between joy and an overwhelming desire to scold Saiden for not caring about her own personal safety. They wouldn't get through these next months without her—certainly couldn't go up against the man that had attempted to kill Loralei without a care. She was terrified thinking of it.

She couldn't bear to be alone anymore. Not when she was responsible for her own feeling of isolation. She wasn't going to fix things with Mozare anytime soon, there was too much pain there, but at least she could learn to be a good friend.

"What happened?" Saiden's voice cracked as she tried to speak. It brought Loralei back to the day they had all first arrived in Taezhali, and the haze that had consumed Saiden on their journey finally began to lift.

"You saved the day of course. Real dramatic. Oh, and then you pitched yourself overboard and had to be rescued by the dashing captain. He looked quite magnificent pulling you back on board, although he is a bit old for my taste." Loralei was rambling, and she wasn't entirely sure why.

"Loralei, the slower version." Saiden pressed a hand against her head as she tried to sit back up in the bed. When she flinched, her arm giving out, Loralei tumbled forward to catch her before she could do any real damage to herself. Not that she couldn't heal it, but it was always better to avoid the damage in the first place.

"What do you remember?" She asked, instead of starting another rambling explanation that wouldn't make any more sense than the first.

The smile on Saiden's face was sheepish, "not much admittedly."

"That can happen when you use a lot of power at once. I barely remember the days I spent trying to heal my back."

She hadn't been trying to make the mood any worse, it was a sick room after all, but she could feel the weight of her words settle over both of them. She changed the subject. "It would've been a lot easier to tell you what you'd done if you hadn't had Mozare locks us all below deck first. The captain is a bit tight lipped on the whole thing. I think he was waiting to see how the story ended before he decided how he wanted to tell it. He'll be happy to see you're still among the living."

"And you?"

"And me?" Loralei turned Saiden's question right back on her.

"Are you glad I'm still in the land of the living?"

Loralei's brow furrowed with the words. "Of course. I don't dream of your death Saiden. I have plenty of actual enemies to wish death upon."

Saiden tried to laugh at her words, but something in her still hurt, and she curled up on herself. Loralei reached out, placing one palm on Saiden's forehead, the other reaching for her wrist.

"How are the others?" Saiden asked. Loralei wasn't entirely sure who she would want to hear about first, so she decided on a collective answer.

"They're all waiting for you to wake up, while trying to figure out our way back in to the country and keep themselves from crowding your room." She saw a question on Saiden's face, but it didn't make it past her lips, and Loralei didn't want to push her. "In fact, a few of them will probably be angry I haven't already gone to fetch them."

Loralei stood. She didn't need to specify who, they both knew Mozare and Cassimir could be equally hot-headed, especially when it came to Saiden's welfare. She started to turn away, but Saiden grabbed her, a surprising amount of strength in her grip for someone who could barely hold herself up.

"I'm glad you're here too." Loralei knew she didn't mean on the ship. She didn't have words, so she simply nodded, and when Saiden finally let her go, she went off to find the others.

Luckily for her, their three companions were all together training aboard the main deck, so it was quite easy for her to round them up. Cassimir had dropped his weapon the first second he had seen the queen, and the rest followed him back below decks without her even uttering a word.

Only Eleni really acknowledged her, a simple squeeze of her hand that meant more to Loralei than she was sure the other woman knew. After all, Loralei been keeping Saiden alive all this time, even if she hadn't let the others know exactly how close they had been to losing her.

She didn't crowd Saiden, not when her bedside was full of other people hugging her, and laughing and crying with her. She didn't need to be beside her. Saiden looked up, watching her lean on the wall opposite her. Saiden knew what Loralei had done for all of them and she was grateful for it.

20

RHENA

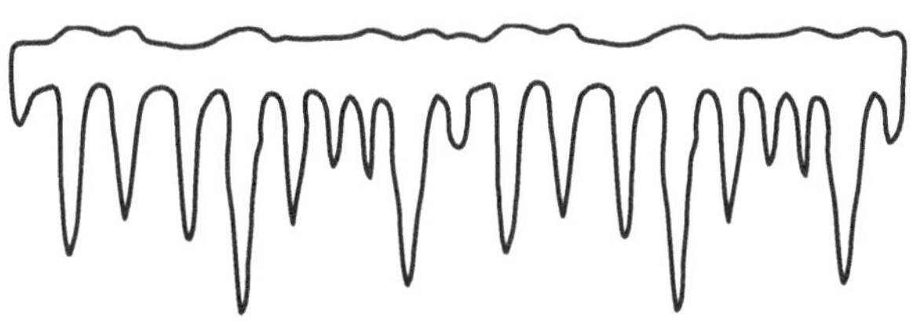

RHENA WAS SURROUNDED BY OTHER LEGIONNAIRES AT HER NEXT MEAL, AND could not shake the feeling of unease coursing through her. She didn't know these legionnaires, she'd had very little time for socializing in general and spent most of her time with her own recruit class, so she didn't know the older soldiers. She was only grateful that the number of bodies in close proximity to hers were enough to keep the ice in her veins from lowering the temperature in the space around them.

Looking around the hall, she was trying not to be obvious in her search for a friendly face; both to keep her table mates from feeling insulted, and so she wouldn't bring suspicion towards them. She needed someone to ground her. She didn't think she would be able to do it on her own, not with all these people around, more than she'd ever seen in the mess at one time.

Revon made sure they took the time to prioritize their diets, which she knew didn't come from a sense of responsibility for their well-being. He needed his soldiers prepared when it came time to fight. Even still, it's not like they were on a set schedule. The dining area was spacious, and the kitchen well staffed, so there was a large window of time for them to get their food.

This set up worked well for Rhena, because she could avoid the lunch times when most of Revon's minions were in the hall and keep herself from drawing any more attention from them. Until today, when every walk by the hall had proven to have more and more people in the hall. Eventually she decided she needed to sit down and eat. Otherwise, even extended hours weren't going to give her enough time for her meal.

She didn't like being pressured into making decisions, and this felt worse. Something was clearly going on here, and with Revon's increase in punishments, Rhena couldn't help but be worried about what she might witness.

Or be subjected to.

There was still a very high probability that Revon would decide she was a counter-revolutionary and have her skinned alive like Talon. Or worse. She didn't want to think about some of the other things he'd done while she waited for her friends to make it back here.

Rhena knew she had been right to be wary when Revon marched in, his general and the other newly appointed members of his inner circle preceding him into the crowded room. She wondered how many were like the general now—participants in Revon's awful experiments to gain more power. She didn't want to think about that either.

Behind him, she also saw Oliver and Melana enter the room, though their presence did nothing to soothe her mind at this point. She was so nauseated she almost wished she had skipped lunch.

"I'm glad to see so many of you gathered here." Revon began. Something must've kept them all in the mess hall long after many had finished their meals, though she couldn't pick out the strands of magic that might've done so. "Because today you will find your place among my ranks."

Rhena didn't understand what he meant, and by the confused faces around her she wasn't the only one who didn't get his meaning. They were all legionnaires by right of their gifts, given by either Keir or Ilona. That was how it was supposed to work.

"Not to fret my children." Revon continued. "The legion welcomes any gifted who wish to serve the crown, but I need the powerful among you by my side in the darkness that is to come." Rhena hated listening to him speak about darkness as if his every step didn't hide them all from the light.

As if he himself had a divine claim to them.

Rhena froze as the full force of his words hit her. Revon wanted more pawns for his experiments. He wanted more of them to submit so he could grow their power. Rhena didn't want it to be true, but the proof of his trials was staring them in the face, even if she and Talon were the only ones who would see it.

She didn't bother looking for him in the crowd, not when she could feel the general's eyes tracking her. Everything they'd done recently, the duels to first blood, the longer patrols, the rigorous training sessions, it was all a test for this moment. Revon wanted something better than his divine soldiers, and he didn't care what he had to do to get it.

Rhena's panic spiraled out of control, ice cracking against her knuckles and storm clouds gathering overhead. The legionnaire next to her must have felt the rise in her gift, because she closed a hand around Rhena's wrist and squeezed. She didn't know this woman, and the woman refused to look at her, but she kept a tight hold on her, until all Rhena could focus on was their skin pressed together, and her powers calmed.

She shouldn't have been grateful, a stranger's help always came with a price, but she was so desperately grateful. This woman, who she didn't even know, had probably saved her. And she couldn't even thank her by name.

Revon's super soldiers spread through the crowd, directing them into lines, moving them by force if they took too long to follow the orders. She didn't want to obey, but she couldn't let them touch her, so she followed the rest of her table into the closest line and waited to see what test they would go through next.

The room around them filled with various manifestations of gifts. Shadows lurked in every corner, and every step Rhena took threw her into a new climate. Light blinded her, and the only thing that kept her from falling when vines grew under her feet was the same woman who had saved her earlier resting a gentle hand against her spine.

With every person ahead of her who was dismissed from the hall,

Rhena's own panic grew. She couldn't see what they were doing to the legionnaires at the front of the line to make their powers unleash so brutally, and she wasn't prepared to find out what it would do to her own out-of-control powers. She knew that she had run out of chances to be saved, no one was going to directly step between her and Revon if something went wrong with her testing. No one would dare.

She could admit that she wouldn't be able to stand up to him, not after seeing the number of soldiers he'd defiled for his own gain.

Rhena finally saw what they were doing when there was only one person left in front of her, and her lunch almost made a reappearance on the back of his legs. One of the new guards pushed up the soldier's sleeve, sliced into his skin and waited for the cut to bleed. Then the guard cut into their finger, and dripped their own blood into the cut.

She didn't understand the fundamentals but something in Revon's experiments made this new kind of soldier a catalyst for the powers of other people as well. The life gifted man in front of her held a small flame in his hand, and they watched, taking a few notes before the second soldier healed the scar. Rhena didn't know if that left their blood inside or not, but she didn't like the thought of being tainted like that.

She was unsure if Revon had specifically been watching her, or keeping an eye at the front of every line, but as she stepped up, he clapped his hands and the entire hall froze, the silence deafening.

"Rhena dear. I am excited to see these results. After all, the two traitors took so much interest in you, they must've seen something in that power. And now, you have the opportunity to serve your country in a way that would make the goddess proud."

It took every ounce of willpower to keep herself from making a face as Revon invoked their goddess. She stepped up, trying to keep herself from bolting from the room. She wouldn't have made it far anyway, not with all the people crowding the entrance.

If Revon hadn't brought the crowd to a stand still she may have been able to get through this without the fanfare, but now every eye in the hall was plastered to her, and waiting for her results.

She held out her non-dominant arm. No way was she going to purposely let anyone put her at a disadvantage when she was surrounded by enemies. That was Mozare's voice in her head, asking her who had the advantage. It certainly wasn't her. Even if a few of the soldiers in here might have been on her side, she doubted enough of them would come to her aid for it to make a difference.

The woman cut into her arm, and her partner let his own blood drip into the wound. Rhena's powers rose unbidden, even worse than the lack of control she had when her emotions were high. This was wrong, and she knew everyone else undergoing this test had to have felt that too.

Ice covered the entire floor. Not a single one of the soldiers tested so far had the same reach. As storm clouds crackled in the sky above them, she could see the pure glee cross Revon's face. While they were watching her powers swirl around the room, she took the control she did have, and froze the drop of blood still sitting in hers. Even if the healers sealed the wound, she'd be able to retrieve it later. She wasn't going to be sullied with whatever unholiness Revon had inflicted upon them.

Not if she had a choice.

"Thank you for your participation my child." Revon said, and she didn't like the way he dragged the sentence on. He dismissed her, but she felt his eyes linger on her long after she had left the mess hall.

21
SAIDEN

SAIDEN SAT ON THE DECK OF THE SHIP SHE HAD SAVED AND TRIED TO ignore the stares of the men working all around her. She knew they thought they were being discreet, but everywhere she turned another pair of eyes were watching her. It had been bad enough when she had saved Cassimir after pirates had ambushed the ship, now these people were looking at her as if she were divine.

She did not want or need this attention from them.

Especially not while she was trying to do a training session of her own with Eleni.

"You still need to learn to control your power." She was saying, when Saiden finally managed to concentrate on their conversation again, instead of her audience.

"I stopped a hurricane, with my powers. I never could've done that before."

"You passed out for three days afterwards, so I'm not sure we can consider that as having control over your powers."

Saiden knew Eleni was correct, but it didn't stop the feelings swirling around in her chest. She was proud of what she had accomplished, she had saved all of them, but she had also put herself in a very dangerous position. If she fought like that in a battle she would get herself killed.

She didn't admit it out loud, but she straightened her spine, and waited for Eleni to continue with their lesson. Despite not being gifted herself, she still had the most potential for helping Saiden. Mozare and Loralei, though they meant well, were too blinded by what it was like for them to understand it was different for her.

Eleni had a more neutral approach to helping Saiden manage her powers, based on the laws of science her people had discovered. Saiden couldn't use her powers without giving of herself. Without training, the toll would eventually claim her entirely.

"You can't draw from the universe without returning something to it. Your gifts may be granted by gods, but they are made of the energy of this world. Like everything else, they're a limited resource.

"Okay so how do I fight without losing myself?" They didn't have enough time to build a foundation. Saiden needed the rapid, battlefield version of this lecture because they were heading straight into war; sailing closer and closer to it every minute aboard the pirate ship.

"I'm not entirely sure yet." Eleni admitted. Saiden would always appreciate her friend's honesty, but sometimes she wished the other girl would lie. Just a little bit. "But I think part of your problem is that you're going in so hard to accomplish large tasks, that the power has control over you, and not the other way around. The stakes are so high whenever you've been able to fully tap into yourself that you've been okay with letting big waves of it crash over you. Now try something small."

It kind of made sense. The two times she'd fully given in to her powers consciously she'd brought Cassimir back from the brink of death and stopped a hurricane. But she hadn't been able to maintain the light when they'd rescued Eleni. The stress of the two more dire situations had made it easier for the power to channel through her, but they had come at a much higher cost.

Then she'd grown the orange sapling and it's fruit while waiting for Cassimir to wake up and that had felt as natural as breathing. But everything was easier with him. She couldn't rely on that safety net during battle, not when the general in her head was telling her there was a very good chance they wouldn't all make it out of this alive.

Saiden nodded, rolling her shoulders, and trying to trick her muscles into relaxing while her brain spiraled. Eleni reached over, and rested her fingers gently on top of Saiden's upturned palm. No pressure, just the gentle reassurance that she was still there. Settling back into herself, Saiden counted her breaths, and then hovered her free hand over the boards of the ship right in front of where they were sitting.

One thing she had discovered on this journey, which she hadn't had time to fully appreciate on their last trip, was that nothing on board a pirate ship ever truly dried. Not her skin, her clothes, or her weapons, which she found herself constantly polishing in an effort to stave off rust. But neither did the boards of the ship, though she realized they had to have been treated with something to keep the water from damaging them at sea.

Slowly she centered her focus down into the wood, into the trees that had been cut down to be fashioned into paneling and the droplets of water that clung to it no matter how sunny it got. The two things fell in separate domains, water in Ilona's territory and earth in Keir's. Gently she started to pull them apart, dragging the water out with her consciousness, collecting the droplets under her hand.

Eleni giggled and Saiden was finally brave enough to open her eyes again, not even having fully realized she'd shut them to begin with. All around them, tiny droplets floated above the ship deck, a rainstorm in reverse. Part of her wanted to frown, the acknowledgment that she still hadn't been completely in control of her powers gnawing at her. But the rest of her was relieved she'd managed any feat of magic without feeling as though she would pass out.

She continued, gathering the water in tighter, so that the individual droplets became streams she could weave around them. When the boys popped their heads out to check on them, she sent darts of it to splash them. Saiden and Eleni couldn't contain their laughter at the soggy frowns on both of their faces as water dripped from their hair.

"That's clever." Cassimir complemented her, before kneeling down in front of them and shaking the water from his hair onto both her and his sister. She laughed again, but kept a piece of her focus still holding on to the water she'd collected, running her streams away from the ship and back into the ocean.

"That was really good sahadi." Eleni complemented, a smile as wide as her brothers splitting her face. "More practice like that and I think you'll settle into a better equilibrium."

Saiden smiled, even as she felt her face warm. She wasn't used to this kind of praise. Nakti had tried her best to raise her well, but she had always been a soldier first, so her praise had been harder to win, not as easily given as it was here. Her heart ached a little at the comparison, at how much she missed both of her mothers.

Eleni had never let go of her hand, and she squeezed Saiden's gently in hers now, no doubt reading her every thought as it flicked across her expression. "Want to see what else you can do?"

22
MOZARE

AS HIS HOMELAND SLOWLY APPROACHED ON THE HORIZON, MOZARE found himself wishing for another storm to overtake them and push them back out to sea. Not because he wanted to see the toll it would take on Saiden again, but because dread had been his constant companion every day since the lookout had first spotted Kaizian shores.

They had spent every free minute training, Saiden and her powers, Eleni's ability to defend herself, Loralei's new mix of combat style. Mozare and his suppression of his emotions.

He still didn't know if it would be enough for them to get through this fight together. He didn't even think of wishing they'd get through it unscathed, only that they would survive enough to heal on the other side of things.

Mozare watched as his friend disembarked the captain's ship, keeping one eye on them while the other watched for patrols. They had done their best to pick somewhere abandoned, but none of them were quite sure how paranoid Revon had gotten in the time they were gone. They couldn't trust any of their training, or the insight they had about how things were run now that he was king.

Saiden stayed on the ship the longest of all of them, Cassimir only a few steps ahead of her. Of their group, she had the most history with the captain, and a lot of responsibility and debts had passed between the two of them. The nosy part of him wished he could've heard their conversation, but he wasn't willing to risk their security to eavesdrop.

Loralei joined him on the beach. They weren't back to where they had been before everything had gone wrong, but the hurricane seemed to have done them some good. At least she didn't seem to outwardly hate him as much as she had.

It wasn't much progress, but he wasn't in the position to scoff at any kind of progress no matter how small. Not when it came to her.

He hated being here, hated it even more because he knew he was the reason this country had become the hostile place it was now.

His whole body was tense as he stretched out every one of his senses, physical and gifted, to search for scouts. He didn't have the ideal gifts for feeling human life around them, but he needed to do something, because letting his brain spiral was only going to make it harder for them to go unnoticed.

Even the focus required wasn't enough to keep his shadows from pooling in the divots of his knuckles. Instead, he set to patrolling, hoping to at least keep his panic to himself as everyone else dealt with feelings about returning to Kaizia as fugitives wanted by the king.

Except this wasn't a return for all of them. Eleni had never been there before, didn't know what his country was capable of when things were good. He heard her soft footsteps trailing behind him, and found that he didn't mind she had chosen to come after him. At least Mozare still had someone who thought he was worth chasing after.

"Tell me what's going on in your head right now." It was a different approach to his panic than the one he had taken with Loralei during the ball, or had tried to exercise on himself during the days of Akil's torture. Instead of focusing on the good, Eleni wanted him to face the bad head on.

"What's the point in returning here, when I'm the one who ruined it in the first place?" He didn't have enough sensibility to lie, or enough forethought to keep silent.

Eleni rested a hand against his bicep, the touch so gentle he flinched. Mozare almost wished she would slap him, because at the moment he thought it would be a lot less jarring. Because he was already so raw, that any touch sent his nerves into overdrive.

"And what purpose does that thought have?" she asked him.

Mozare froze, and even though his mind was spiraling, he kept track of what was going on around them. He wouldn't get her hurt because she was trying to help him. That much he was still capable of. At least for now. He had no doubt that if Revon caught them he wouldn't be capable even of breathing for much longer.

What purpose did his thoughts have? He'd never really put much into the purpose of his thoughts. He was a man of action, not some scholar, and definitely not any kind of philosopher. But if he was going to be trapped in a nightmare of his own making, he may as well consider its purpose.

"Torture probably." He suggested, after the silence between them had grown deafening.

"And why would you want to torture yourself by subjecting your mind to these patterns of negative thoughts?"

It didn't take long for him to answer that question. "Because I deserve it." Even though he felt the truth of it down to his bones, his voice still broke as he answered Eleni. He crashed down to the beach, and she gently sat next to him.

"No one deserves to be an unwelcome guest in their own head. There is nothing you could have done to have earned that kind of suffering." Mozare heard the words as Eleni spoke, understood the sincerity in her voice, and yet still couldn't believe her. She didn't know the things he'd done well enough to understand that this was exactly what he deserved.

In all honesty, he probably deserved even worse.

"Bad things happen in the world, and sometimes we are part of them. Did you think you were doing a bad thing when you started this?"

Of course not. He'd been young when he'd first met Revon, and their new king had taken advantage of that and the rage he'd felt, and used him for his own purposes. And Mozare thought the gods were giving him a way to return balance and order.

He couldn't have been more wrong.

"I can see the wheels turning in your head. Maybe you think I'm wrong, maybe you're fighting everything I'm saying to you, but at least you'll have my voice in your head too, when your negative thoughts get too dark."

Eleni was so different from the rest of their group. She wasn't a warrior in the same way they were, but she could fight the battles they didn't have the tools for. She'd helped Saiden start to connect to her powers and gain control, convinced them that she could make a difference here.

Helped him, even if he wasn't sure that she was correct, because at least he could hear the people coming towards their ship.

Mozare stood, grabbing Eleni, and pulling her back towards their friends, her words wrapped around him like a bandage barely keeping him from bleeding out.

23
SAIDEN

SAIDEN AND CASSIMIR WATCHED FROM THE EDGE OF THE SHIP AS THEIR friends departed. Along the edge of the boat, the pirates had lined up to bid them farewell, a far more spectacular goodbye than they had gotten last time. Then again she hadn't fought a hurricane for them last time. Now, she was a hero of sorts, though she wasn't sure she was comfortable with that title either.

The captain waited for them above the gangplank that would put them back on home soil. Saiden hadn't been sure until this very moment they were even going to make it home, and now that they were here, she wasn't entirely sure how she should feel about it. Her home had brought her so many memories of pain, but it had also brought her the little family she held so dear.

She couldn't decide if it was a place she loved or one she loathed. Wasn't sure she would ever be able to pick one side or the other.

Saiden didn't know the proper way one dealt with a captain of a pirate ship. There had never been formality in their relationship, so now she was stuck watching as the odd assortment of pirates escorted her from the decks of the ship.

The captain flipped a coin in his hands.

"I'm not sure I've ever escorted a crew off my ships that I wished would stay." The captain began, and the wistfulness of his voice seemed out of place. "You were useful, the lot of you. If your attempts to fight for your homeland fail, which I somehow doubt they will, you will always have a place among my crew."

Cassimir collected a few coins from the pouch at his waist and handed them to the captain. "Thank you. Both for getting us here safely, and for your offer. We won't forget it."

The captain accepted the handful of coins, counted them, and then offered them back to Cassimir. "Seems an awful lot of money for a one way trip to your deaths." Saiden could tell he was hiding something behind the words, but she didn't know the captain well enough to determine what it was.

Cassimir didn't seem to understand the pirate's motive either, but he took the money and slipped it back into his pouch. A minute passed without any words spoken between the three of them, until the captain held out his hand again, the coin he had been flipping tucked between two fingers.

"This is a magic coin. Earned it in a bet. Speak into it and I'll hear you. If you request my aid, I will come. I may not be able to fight this battle with you, but I believe you'll survive it. If you need assistance in the future, I owe you my allegiance."

Saiden repeated a different version of the captain's own words. "Seems an awful high debt for a pirate to offer strangers."

"No price is too high for the life of a child. You've saved him twice now, as well as my crew and my ship. There is no debt too high in my mind."

Saiden understood the captain in a part of her soul that didn't need words. She simply nodded, and slipped the coin in tight between her armored jacket and the thin shirt she worn underneath.

"I hope the day never comes, but I will be honored to carry this with me." She tapped the spot against her chest where the coin rested, and bowed her head to the captain. Each of his crew in turn bowed their heads at her. Nico stepped from the crowd, a crooked smile over his face, and waved goodbye.

Saiden expected to feel the slide of sand under her boot as she took her first step back on Kaizian soil. Instead, the entire world around her shifted, pulling her away from the beach, away from her friends, and from Cassimir, who only seconds ago had his warm hand pressed to her back.

Suddenly Saiden was far away, wind whipping at her skin again as if she were back in the middle of the hurricane. Except cold seeped into her bones, and when she finally opened her eyes, all she could see around her were snowcapped mountains.

She had never seen snow this pure and white, and in her leathers, she also knew she wouldn't last long on this mountain. Saiden tucked her hands under her arms and waited. This wasn't new to her, she knew who had summoned her here, even if she realized they shouldn't have had the ability to do so without her willing it.

"You are right child." Ilona's chill voice did nothing to warm her shivering body. "We shouldn't have been able to call you. But as you grow more powerful, your connection to us does the same."

"We missed you." Keir spoke, but even his words lacked their lyrical quality. His white cloaks were thicker, the collar edged with furs. His ivory skin glinted, almost blending into the snow.

"What do you want from me?"

"My dear, such a harsh tone." Ilona chided.

"Did you not also miss us child?" Keir asked, but Saiden couldn't tell if he meant it or not.

"Why would I miss you?" Saiden had spent so long living in the shadow of what should've been a gift, tortured herself with raw power and risked hurting everyone she cared about. "Why would I care for you at all. You have done nothing but make my life hell-and used me to hurt the people around me."

Ilona did not take well to her anger. "You think you know what you're talking about, but there is no guarantee that the life you would have led without us would have been any better."

"At least it would've been mine."

Saiden hadn't even realized she'd been feeling these things until she had been given the chance to confront her gods. Considering their normal roles during these meetings, she was surprised by how little Keir was speaking.

"You think your life would've been better. Then go live it." Keir tried to stop Ilona, but a wave of her hand, and Saiden's mind was sinking inside itself.

24
RHENA

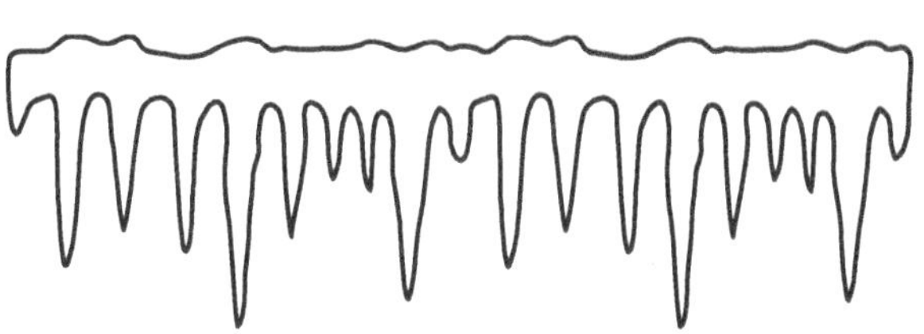

RHENA HAD A CLOTH WRAPPED PACKAGE ON HER BED, AND A NOTE FROM their King that said she had been invited to dinner with him and a select group of Legionnaires whose progress he was quite proud of. She'd nearly thrown up at the sight of it, knowing that Revon or one of his henchmen had been inside her quarters.

She remembered Saiden getting her own package just like it, and the vile dress she'd been forced to wear when Revon had still given regular state dinners. There hadn't been one to her knowledge since her friends had fled the country, though if Revon was spending his nights experimenting it was really no surprise he was too busy to host banquets.

It made this dinner all the more intimidating. She was far too young to be getting this much notice, but she wasn't stupid. She knew this had to do with his tests. Both the weird assessments during training, and the show she'd unwillingly put on in the mess hall a few days ago.

Rhena wasn't sure what part she was playing in this game, but she certainly hadn't been given a rule book. And she wasn't sure she would make it through tonight if she was forced to sit with Revon and his abominations. It was even worse, if her instincts were correct, his invitation could be dangerous.

She would rather die than let him experiment on her. Even though she knew the grief her death would cause her friends, she wasn't afraid to face it. She only wished that she could see them again.

Saiden's voice rang in her head this time. *Remember to look at it from every angle. Only raise your sword if it's your last resort.* She had a feeling that death might be her only option tonight, either by her own hand or branded as a traitor. With her show of power earlier, Revon might want to keep her alive, punished brutally but still breathing, but she wasn't going to let him.

The small mark on her arm from where she'd carved out the soldier's frozen blood was a good reminder of the pain she was willing to go through to stay out of his mess.

She slipped the dress from its wrapper. It wasn't nearly as bad as Saiden's had been, but then again, she didn't have anything to hide, not like Saiden's tattoos. With all that Revon preferred to dress himself in black and white she didn't miss the fact that her dress was blood-red. The color of Saiden's curse. It was a reminder and a warning wrapped in pretty ribbons.

The dress itself was simple, although the ribbons that tied up the bodice were something she'd probably need a second set of hands for unfortunately. The fabric grazed the floor, something about them having her exact height measured made it feel like there were eyes glued to every inch of her skin.

Across her collarbones, was a delicate piece of gold vining, and at her neck it held a thin piece of the red fabric that would hang behind her like some kind of cape. The vines were taunting her, and she had no doubt that choice had been made on purpose. Revon was too cunning for something like this to be accidental.

Every scrap of this dress was a threat. He was prepared for her to step out of line, it was almost like he wanted her to try. But he'd underestimated her, because threatening her with this dress showed Rhena his hand. All she had to do was keep from falling into his trap.

In the end, Rhena hadn't needed anyone's help to get her dress on, she'd strung the ribbons to her bed post. She didn't want anyone else in the small amount of space that was dedicated to her.

The red of the dress made her want to cry. She missed her friends so desperately, but she needed to be strong a few days longer. Then they would be here, and she wouldn't be so alone. The gold vines sat almost high enough to look like the collar Revon had forced Saiden to wear after killing Magdalena, and that was enough to set rage burning in her veins. There would be no chill coming from her tonight, as long as she could feel the metal collar with every breath.

Once the dress was finally on, Rhena gave herself one more moment to breathe where no one was watching her, and then she stepped into the hallway, squaring her shoulders as if she were preparing for battle.

In a way this was battle, one small battle in the grand war they were waging. She was a small piece of the bigger puzzle, but she was ready to do her part.

She was surprised to see Talon step out of his room as she passed it, his neatly tailored black suit detailed with swirls of red that matched her own dress. Rhena wasn't sure if this was a theme for the evening, or if perhaps they were being singled out. It couldn't have been good for her to be matching Talon when she had been going out of her way to avoid being seen with him.

The two of them must've resigned themselves to whatever was to come at the same moment, because when Talon stuck out an arm for her, she rested her hand in his elbow and they headed to Revon's private chamber. At least, if they were walking into a firing squad they could face it together.

But as they were getting closer to his rooms, they were not the only ones adorned in blood. Every one of Revon's guests tonight had something red in their outfits, though none as pronounced as Rhena and her solid red gown.

Sometimes it was easy to forget that she was a child, but compared to the others in the room, it was clear she was. She was reminded of the days when she would try on her mother's wedding dress, the hem trailing well past her feet. She hadn't been with the legion all that long, but, still, her childhood felt like a lifetime ago. She supposed war did that to memory.

There was very little socialization going on, despite the number of legionnaires gathered. At least they weren't the only ones feeling apprehension at tonight's invite. She didn't recognize most of them, though across the room she swore Oliver's bulk stood out among the guests. She didn't want to look like she was trying too hard to find allies.

She needed to be more prepared to face down her enemies. Even without others by her side.

Revon finally joined him, three of his new soldiers filing into the room with him. He wore another one of his split suits, Keir and Ilona's colors spilling into each other, stitched together by red vines.

He smiled at her when he noticed her watching him, and she blushed as she turned away from his gaze. She tried to pretend like she was involved in one of the scarce few conversations going on around the room.

She knew that Revon didn't believe it, but she was going to hold on to her lie like a lifeline. Revon clapped his hands again, the same way he had in the mess hall, and like it had before, the room went silent.

"Thank you all for coming." He started, as if any of them really had a choice. When their garments had been hand delivered with the invitations. "It's important in these trying times to remember that our gods have not forgotten us. They have not left their favored children behind. Like before, when resistance has risen, the gods have given us the means. To that we should all be grateful."

His soldiers started clapping at his words, the applause slowly spreading to the rest of them. She wondered if they had taken the time to rehearse this before, or if they were all prepared to eat up whatever he had to say.

"In the times of old, when darkness and immorality tried our countrymen, the gods did not forsake them. They made us, the gifted, and granted us the right and power to protect their lands." She couldn't tell if he was waiting for something, or pausing for dramatic effect. "And when the gifts were not enough to drive evil from our country, they created the Anointed. For a time, I thought they had given us Saiden for that purpose, a weapon in their hands to drive out the darkness."

Rhena tried to hide her shock at hearing him speak her name. He knew someone must've been watching her, waiting to see how she'd react. She kept her eyes glued to Revon waiting to see where the rest of this speech went.

"But I am not a man who can't admit his own faults, and I am certainly not wise enough to know the gods' way. Her presence here was a test, and her absence has made us stronger. The gods have given us a way to strengthen ourselves. And I have chosen you to be the next to earn this new gift."

Rhena's stomach dropped, and she was suddenly glad he had chosen to give his speech before dinner was put out on the table. She wasn't sure she could've kept herself from being sick if she had eaten.

"Of course, some of you are too young to undergo such a rigorous process." She hoped desperately to fall into that category. She hoped Talon would also fall there. "In the meantime, you will take on the responsibilities of those partaking in the ritual. That means extra watches, extra patrols, but nothing you can't handle. That is how we will bear the weight of our promise. And how we will reach a new day."

Rhena noticed the woman from the mess hall who'd saved her, standing with another woman, and she could feel her even from a distance, their gifts in alignment. She knew there was no possibility the two of them fell into the 'too young' category, and that made her want to cry. She'd felt camaraderie with that woman, and there was no way for her to repay that favor.

Only the rage that simmered inside her kept her from doing anything she couldn't take back.

They all finally sat down to dinner, though as courses were carted through the room, the best she could manage was a few bites before she'd push the food around her plate, hoping her neighbors didn't notice her lack of appetite. The only people still talking at the table were those Revon had already gifted, but she was grateful the room wasn't silent.

It would be all too easy to become lost in the silence completely.

25
CASSIMIR

One second he had been walking behind Saiden, and the next, he was forced to drop their things so he could catch her as her body went limp and she sagged past the end of the gangplank. Mozare had been watching their exit, and rushed to their side as she fell, keeping her head from hitting the railing.

His sister stood by the queen, the fear on her face palpable. Loralei gave her shoulder a squeeze before pushing herself between Mozare and Saiden. He knew Mozare meant well, but if anything, Loralei was the one she needed right now. She was the healer.

Loralei pressed a hand over Saiden's head, and the other over her heart. She leaned towards Saiden as if she was listening to something. Loralei hissed, pulling her hands back from Saiden's body as if they'd been burned.

Cassimir was torn looking between her, and watching the breath in Saiden's chest rise and fall. "What happened?" he asked, his voice frantic. He had already spent enough time with the group that, for the most part, he didn't resent them having power he wouldn't have.

At this moment, however, he wasn't sure what he might've given up for a fraction of their power. For the smallest ability to help Saiden right now.

No one answered him. "What is going on? You're going to tell me. Now." He hated the hardness of his voice, hated hearing himself like this. But fear had broken him, it broke him a little more every time he saw Saiden brush against death.

Loralei didn't speak to him, she turned to Mozare. "Did you feel that too?" He didn't appreciate the way they were so in sync, leaving him out of whatever understanding they were reaching. He didn't need more things in his life to complicate it. Cassimir was ready to yell at them again, when his sister pressed a hand on his shoulder. She had always been the calmer of the two of them.

He looked up at her, his arms wrapping more tightly around Saiden's body as she began to shiver. "Trust them. They love her too."

Cassimir didn't think the others could hear her over the waves, she'd spoken so quietly. Mozare and Loralei were staring at each other, and he wished he could tune in to the conversation silently going on between them.

When Mozare finally spoke aloud, Cassimir suddenly missed the silence. "The gods have her. Ilona is angry, I can feel it. She's not even pressing into my mind, I can't hear her, but I can feel how angry she is."

"Keir isn't happy either. Why would they be angry with her?"

Neither of them seemed to have an answer. In the end, Eleni was the one who finally spoke, voicing the words that had the potential to damn them all. "Because Saiden is angry with them.

INTERLUDE

Saiden woke up in a cottage that had never been more than the setting of her hazy childhood memories. But she wasn't a child anymore, she was grown—her body the same as the one she distantly knew waited on the beach of her country's borders.

But her mind couldn't really hold that thought, not when she could look down at her fingers, her untattooed fingers, and register the soft sheets around her legs. Someone was in the kitchen, the tell-tale clanging of pots and pans announcing their presence.

Saiden reached for a blade, but no matter where she looked, she couldn't find one. She should've had one by her bedside, she couldn't remember the last time she had gone to bed without tucking a blade within her reach, but now there was nothing.

She panicked. Her brain couldn't reconcile the two lives fighting for dominance in her memories. Saiden pulled her legs free from the blankets, and then startled herself when she noticed they weren't covered in scars. She pulled at the sleeves of her shirt, but there was nothing underneath but smooth tanned skin.

Every mark of her history, every difficult thing she had lived through had been erased. She wasn't sure what that left her with.

When she finally caught a glimpse of herself in the mirror, she froze again, a scream building in her throat. Her hair, the hair that always marked her as something other, was the same brown as her mother's. She ran her hands through it, but no matter how hard she tried, how hard she pulled at it, the locks wouldn't go back to their red.

This time she did scream. Something fell to the floor in the kitchen, and footsteps came closer to her room. *Her room.* That's where she was, though she only now realized it. Why would she forget her own room? She suddenly couldn't remember the answer.

The fluttering scraps of fabric that separated her room from the rest of the house were pushed to the side, and her mother's face came into view, flour sprayed all over the apron she was wearing to protect her clothes while she made dinner.

Of course, her mother was making dinner. Her father was going to be home any minute. It was silly that she had fallen asleep in the first place.

"Another nightmare my Maus?" Her mother asked, forgetting about whatever she had been working on to take a moment to sit down with Saiden. "I thought they had been getting better."

"I don't know Mama. I feel lost a little. It must've been a nightmare."

Her mother wrapped one arm around her, pushing back her hair, her brown hair, while she rocked them slightly back and forth. Neither of them cared that flour slowly drifted off her mother and was coating everything. There was warmth in her chest that Saiden had been missing, though she couldn't remember a time when her mother's hugs hadn't been a short distance away.

The door to the house opened, a loud thing with rusty hinges and her father's boots stomped their way through the hall. "Where are my girls?" Saiden laughed, although warning bells chimed in the back of her memory. No matter how old she got, she never got tired of hearing her father come home and ask for them.

But his voice made her mother nervous. She couldn't tell why, until she realized there should have been another pair of boots stomping next to his, a little bit quieter. Her brother Waylen should've been coming home too.

After all, she had been on the early shift at the mines, that was why she could get her nap in. He was set to be coming home with their father after a long day in the mines. Her mother quickly rose from the bed, Saiden hurrying after her to see what had happened.

The man in the kitchen almost looked like a stranger to her, but she could see the way his face was lined with agony.

"Where's Waylen? Where's our son?"

"He's gone Maggie." Saiden didn't know what made her feel worse, the fact that her beloved brother was dead, or that she didn't seem to remember ever having a brother in the first place. Both feelings were quickly replaced by rage.

She knew the people in charge of the mines hadn't been careful enough. They kept pushing the men farther into the caves, not caring that they were moving too deep too fast for anything to be stable. And now her brother was dead because of it.

Detached, Saiden watched her mother crumple to the floor, her father rushing to catch her. She had the sudden desire to know him better, though the idea was so foolish she quickly dismissed it. Of course, she knew her father, and she was going to get revenge.

She might not have power, she was a village girl after all, but rage went further than most people gave it credit for. Saiden grabbed one of her mother's cooking knives, the weight of it so familiar it almost gave her pause and rushed from their house.

No one stopped her. No one even glanced twice at her. Why would they, when she had been a background character to all their lives.

Only the foreman stopped to take her in. She probably looked insane, half-dressed and clutching a kitchen knife so tightly her knuckles had gone white around the handle of the blade.

She swiped it across his throat before he had a chance to call for help. The only thing her mind could focus on was getting to the men responsible. She didn't need to hurt anyone who was in the same situation as her, forced to work in unsafe conditions when the opposite meant certain death.

Saiden killed, or at least greatly maimed three more of the men before she was detained. She hadn't expected to get that far. They relieved her of the dripping kitchen knife, one guard holding on to each of her arms as they lifted her from the mine tunnels.

Her parents were watching from outside, horror clear on their faces. Saiden's mind repeated one solitary thought. *It doesn't matter—they're already dead.* Despite seeing them there, her brain wouldn't stop screaming the phrase over and over.

There was no need for a trial, the evidence of her crimes was clear in the red spatter now coating her hair. When she caught her reflection in the guard's blade, she thought she finally looked like herself again. She finally woke from the illusion as he pulled his blade across her throat.

26

LORALEI

Loralei watched as Saiden jolted awake, the second time she had been left alone this week to tend to her friend in her unconscious state. She desperately hoped, though she wouldn't voice it aloud, that she wouldn't be left in the position again.

Not because she didn't care about Saiden, but because watching someone with the power to stop a hurricane unable to keep herself conscious was absolutely terrifying. Especially when they were following her into war with very few allies.

Saiden cried, not in a loud way, but the way Loralei had when she'd realized everything she'd lost after Revon had stabbed her. This was the way a person cried when everything they loved and held dear was taken from them within a single moment. When the grief consumed so completely that the mind could barely tolerate it.

Loralei couldn't watch it. She pulled Saiden to her, half in an attempt to comfort, and half in an attempt to block the look of raw grief on Saiden's face from her view.

"What happened?" Loralei asked, her voice the best impression of soothing she could muster given the circumstances.

Saiden didn't answer, shaking her head against Loralei's chest like she was trying to clear it free of a nightmare. Loralei didn't try to ask her again, she simply sat with her friend and let her cry.

When the rest of their crew made it back to the cave they were sheltering in, Loralei could see how their faces tore between relief and distress. Saiden was awake, but she hadn't spoken a word. All she could do was stare into the cave. Loralei had tried everything she could think of to get her to speak, but nothing had worked. Instead, she had elected to sit next to her, and wait for reinforcements.

Mozare didn't seem like he knew what to do either. From what Loralei understood of their relationship the roles were usually reversed, and while she had no doubt Mozare cared as deeply for Saiden as she did for him, he seemed wholly unprepared to be on this end of the emotionally vulnerable spectrum.

Loralei huffed. If Mozare wasn't going to be helpful he was a hindrance, and he was better off somewhere else. She grabbed his arm, slightly surprised that he didn't try to fight her as she pulled him out of the cave and back on to the beach.

"I have no idea what I'm supposed to do in this situation." Mozare said, his skin quite a few shades paler than it normally was. It took him a moment to finally look up at her from where he'd hunched over on the beach, and she braced herself for the look on his face. It was a different kind of heartbreak than what connected them, but it felt equally as damning.

"You're coming with me."

Something different from despair passed behind his eyes, so brief Loralei didn't have time to analyze it. "Where?"

"We can't stay in a cave. Not when we don't know where the king's..." She paused, the word sour in her mouth, "...men are." She finally finished. They used to be her men. And now, she wasn't sure who she could trust, though she did have a few ideas.

She didn't know if she should explain her thoughts to Mozare. Loralei certainly couldn't blindly trust Mozare, but she didn't want to spend time talking about it when she needed to be doing something. Anything. As long as it got her out of the suffocating misery of being back in this country, stuck in this cave with Saiden and her nightmares. She knew that made her cruel, but sometimes that's what life did. It had a way of ruining even the best things.

And she had been far from the best, or even decent, of that she had no doubt. She had not needed to fall far to reach where she was now.

But even though she might not have trusted Mozare if their situations were reversed, he seemed to trust her. Either that or he saw something on her face that told him not to push the situation, Loralei wasn't sure. He simply adjusted the straps on the harness keeping his axes tight against his back, pulled his hood up over his head and motioned for her to lead the way.

Now that she had the control she so desperately wanted, her idea felt feeble. As if fighting to prove it's worthiness would've made it more concrete. She wasn't making sense, even to herself at this point.

She pulled the cloak one of the pirates had added to their supplies and wrapped it tight around her. Following Mozare's lead, she pulled up the hood, covering the uneven length of her hair. Mozare said something to the rest of them, but the buzzing in her ears was too loud for her to hear it.

Loralei left the cave behind, saying a prayer to anyone who might be listening to protect the only people in her life that might still care about her. Mozare caught up to her in a few steps, his heartbeat tapping in rhythm with her own. She'd keep his heart tucked in next to hers so he couldn't give it away, wouldn't risk his life for hers again.

They were the thoughts of a madwoman, but maybe hanging on the brink of death had done something more to her than she'd originally realized. Or maybe she'd always been mad, and now she was finally free to live that truth.

"You don't have to trust me." Mozare said, and she tried to hide her flinch in the flutter of her cloak as she turned to face him again. "But could you please tell me where we're going? I don't think I can handle any more unknowns."

Loralei pulled him into an alley, giving her flashbacks of the men she had killed to save Saiden, a lifetime ago. She took a good look at him, possibly for the first time since he'd been kneeling on the floor of the emperor's throne room. His face was worn, tired lines creasing around his eyes. She couldn't bear to look at it for too long.

"I know someone who might be able to harbor us. These were my people once upon a time, and despite what you might think of me, I did try to be a just and kind queen." She tried to turn away from him again, but he reached out to grab her, fingers firm as they wrapped around her wrist.

"I was wrong." He didn't clarify about what, and Loralei wasn't sure that she could handle hearing the clarification anyway. Then he surprised her by letting go, letting her walk away.

She was careful to stay relegated to the shadows as she crept her way between the stacks of houses, avoiding the loud clashes of armored boots as they patrolled around them. It was a bit of a walk, but Loralei let herself settle into the silence, while her thoughts did anything but.

Loralei had seen this particular door a few dozen times, so it surprised her that when she found it, there seemed to be something different about it, although she couldn't tell what. Maybe she was the one who had changed, and it had nothing to do with the door, or the flowers that were painted on it.

She raised her hand to knock, and felt Mozare reach behind him, prepared as always for the worst to come. She had to shake the nerves from her bones before she could manage the faintest tapping against the door, the quiet sound echoing through her skull.

As the moment dragged on, she wasn't sure what was worse, the idea that Alisa would open the door with hatred in her eyes, or that she wouldn't open it at all. When the door finally opened, she braced herself for things to be even worse than her anxious thoughts could picture.

The door was barely cracked, Alisa peeking through to see who was knocking on their door at this late hour. Loralei took one last deep breath, reaching for her powers, before she looked up to face her, bracing herself for whatever might come.

Shock crossed the other woman's face, and she reached out to grab them both, pulling them through her doorway and slamming it loudly behind them.

"What is it, Alisa?" Her husband James called from the other room. Loralei hoped he was healing well without her visits.

"It's her majesty." Loralei didn't think the words were loud enough to travel to Alisa's husband.

She half expected the woman to curtsy with the way her voice was laced with reverence, tinged with disbelief. It wasn't every day you were face to face with a woman everyone believed to be dead after all. Suddenly Alisa arms were around her, and Loralei had to take half a step back to stop them both from tumbling onto the floor. Over Alisa's shoulders, she saw Mozare tense and relax within the span of a few seconds, watching the reunion, but still separate from it.

"We thought you were dead." James said, finally having joined them in the small kitchen space. He was still limping, the crutches he was resting on a few inches too short for his height.

"I have a favor to ask you." She said, unsure how to handle rumors about her death.

"Let me put on the kettle. I have a feeling this conversation will be easier with tea."

27
MOZARE

MOZARE WATCHED THE THREE OF THEM, AND DESPITE THE RELIEF HE COULD see etched across these strangers' faces, he could not get his muscles to relax. He wanted to trust Loralei, but they didn't have the kind of relationship he had with Saiden. One where he could read her thoughts and predict her moves going into battle. He was completely in the dark for the first time since he'd learned to control his own shadows.

He thought they would sit in silence while the kettle boiled, but Loralei surprised him again. She led the man of the house to a seat, although Mozare didn't understand why he would listen, aside from his apparent loyalty to Loralei's old title. "I kept a few things secret from you that you might want to know before you agree to hear me out." She said, and Mozare was sure he was the only one who could hear the tremble in her voice.

Loralei was so used to judgement that she now expected it from everyone at every turn. He wanted to put a hand on her shoulder, anything to reinforce that he was here for her, but he wasn't sure how much was too much. He would take whatever crumbs she was willing to give him, but he also didn't want to risk making things worse.

"It used to kill me, coming here and seeing you injured." She said to the man. "James, I wanted to help you so badly."

The man, James, interrupted her, "you helped every time you stepped foot through that door."

"But not as much as I could have. I was afraid then, of who I am. But I'm not anymore. And I'd like to help you now, if you'd let me." She hovered her hands over the injury in James' foot, although Mozare couldn't tell how old it was, his field training told him it wasn't healing well.

He was already far more familiar with Loralei's healing talents than he wished, so when the light began to steadily glow from the center of her palms, he felt the memory of that power across the scarred skin on his back. As she sat there, her focus completely centered on James, Mozare could see the man's shoulders begin to relax, the pinching in his face releasing.

James must've been in so much pain, and now, he was finally getting the relief he deserved. It was crazy that healers weren't more available to the public. But he couldn't afford to get lost in a mental tirade about what was wrong with their country. Instead, he kept his focus split between the couple, waiting for either of them to lash out at Loralei.

There were two obvious reasons he could think of for them to be mad at the Queen. On the one hand, she had once been Chosen, so they might find her gifts to be an abomination. On the other, they might hate that she had the power all this time to do something, but was too afraid. Either way, that anger could be dangerous.

But Mozare didn't see anger on either of their faces. James looked younger somehow, like a weight had been lifted off his shoulders. And his wife? Alisa stood in the corner, silent tears trailing through the cook ash on her cheeks.

When James stood from his chair without pressing on to the crutch, she cried out, racing to him. Mozare placed a single hand between his shoulder blades to steady the man against the rush of her weight, but he wasn't sure it was even necessary. It was more of an instinct than anything else.

He stepped back as James lifted Alisa, pressing his lips to hers as they shared a private joy. He felt bad about intruding, but they still needed the couple to agree to help them. At least, he assumed that was

Loralei's purpose in bringing them there. Part of him would've understood if this was enough for her though, one thing she could check off her unfinished business.

James placed Alisa back on the floor, pressing another kiss to her forehead, then Alisa moved to embrace Loralei. Despite how much he had been paying attention to the room, he had missed the tears tracing matching paths down Loralei's own face as the couple rejoiced. He filed the response away to take out later when he was alone and had time to think about it.

If he ever had time again.

Alisa kept Loralei close as she stepped halfway out of their embrace, neither of them seeming willing to release the physical connection. "How could I ever repay you?" Alisa asked, and Mozare heard all the emotions in her voice that he couldn't see on her face. The hopelessness, the fear, the lifting of those negative thoughts.

"I never want you to think you are indebted to me in any way." Loralei said, which shocked him a little. He certainly would have used the exchange to their advantage, pressing to convince the family to aide them.

But that was where they were different. Where he feared they were too different, and they always would be.

"But you need help, yes?" Alisa said, cleverness at the tip of her tongue.

Loralei nodded.

"Whatever you need, whatever we have, it's yours." James said. Mozare felt that everyone here knew intrinsically that Loralei would never take more than was absolutely needed. He disliked that he didn't think the same was true about himself.

He slipped out of the house, telling himself it was to keep watch for patrols, but knowing that he was lying to himself. If he stayed he was going to send himself right back to the shadows, and he couldn't afford to put them all at risk.

Clearly, Loralei was more than capable of handling the situation anyway.

She slipped out the door, a smile to her voice as she said goodbye to the couple, pulling her hood up to cover herself from nosy neighbors. "They're going to let us stay here. It's not a lot, but it's a roof."

He hated the defensive tone that had taken over her voice. He didn't know what to do to make things better between them, to get back to the ease they'd so briefly shared. But now wasn't the time for that either. Mozare was starting to wonder if he'd have time for any of this before he died. It didn't seem likely at the moment, given everything that was going on around them.

"Let's go get the others." He said, trying to leave.

"No wait," Loralei grabbed his arm, and the touch nearly broke him. "We should talk about Saiden first." She said, cringing as she spoke the words.

"What happened back there?" Mozare asked, trying to control the conversation.

"I don't know. Fear is a powerful thing, the same way we saw with them," she gestured to the closed door. "Fear can take control, can make a strong man break without a single sword. Can cut them down as easily as wind tears through a sail." There was a far-off look on Loralei's face, as if she drifted farther from him with every word.

Mozare couldn't stop himself from trying to get her back to him. "What are you thinking?"

"I know someone who deserves to be afraid. And I know the exact thing that will break him."

28
SAIDEN

EVERYTHING SAIDEN HEARD CAME TO HER THROUGH A FOG. HER HEARING should be fine, so the only thing she could blame it on was the ringing in her mind as she tried to process what had happened to her. What her goddess had done to her.

She knew Ilona could be angry and vengeful, but she had never known death's mistress to be cruel. Not like this. She had given Saiden what might have been a peaceful life, and then used it to remind her what it was like to live without power.

As if she hadn't been powerless all her life.

As if she wasn't already keenly aware of what it felt like to have no control over the things that happened to her in her own life. She'd had a family. She'd known loss. To give Saiden her parents back, to show her that she might have had a blood brother only to rip it all away from her, not only by waking her up but by killing Waylen when they knew how she would react.

She didn't know how to reconcile these gods to the ones she'd once served.

Loralei had tried to help her, but she didn't know how to put these terrible things into words. Not when Loralei had already dealt with so much pain. And, as the fog slowly lifted from her mind, she realized that was part of the punishment. How could she share imaginary pain with people who had bled and nearly died for her, without being weak?

How could she expect a nightmare to amount to anything compared to the actual horrors they'd faced?

Cassimir and Eleni sat on either side of her, and behind her she could feel Loralei drag Mozare from the cave, but she couldn't be bothered by any of it. The warmth of bodies pressed against her barely even registered. Her hands were still as cold as ice, despite how far she was from the mountaintops.

She didn't know how long they sat there in complete silence when she felt Loralei and Mozare return. Saiden didn't want to face them, Loralei specifically. How could she understand a grief so raw over a family that was already gone. One that had never really existed to begin with. The queen had lost far more than wishful thinking.

"I found us somewhere to hide out, tucked away in the city." Loralei declared. She was trying to take control of the situation, something Saiden might've done if her head weren't still locked in a far off hellscape.

"Do you think that is wise mistress?" Cassimir asked her. He had mostly stopped using the title with Saiden, but it normally made her smile when he used it to address Loralei. Now she couldn't feel anything.

"Let's go." They were the first words she'd said since waking, and they completely ignored Cassimir's concern. She didn't have time for concern, or for caution. She was already dead inside.

Her mind woke up a little more when she realized where Loralei was bringing them. It was smart, Loralei's devotion to her people would have gained her their respect in a lot of places they had traveled to for her charity days. This was the universe's way of returning that kindness to her.

Saiden had let her friends deal with their hosts and sort out living spaces, it wasn't like the people on Loralei's charity lists were living in big houses, most could barely afford the roof over their heads, but she couldn't be inside.

For the first time in weeks, Saiden twisted her hair back, pinning it so that once she pulled her hood over her head the red locks would no longer be visible. Most of the houses built in the winding streets of Norbury couldn't access their own rooftops, as newer houses had been built on top of the older ones. Saiden, however, had the luxury of staying in one where she could hide out up top and take in the setting sun.

It didn't take long for Cassimir to find her. She knew he would, and she didn't mind having him in her space. He sat down next to her, legs hanging off the edge of the crumbling rooftop. When he lifted his arm for her, she was quick to tuck herself into his warmth, despite the lingering heat from the day.

The city was so packed together it never really cooled, but Saiden could still feel ice burrowed in her marrow, a mix of shock and hypothermia from spending time on the mountain. Even if her body had never left the cave, the cold held on to her memory.

She'd had enough lessons tonight to know that memory could be a powerful thing, and if wielded correctly it was an even stronger weapon.

"What happened in there?" He tapped one finger against her forehead, leaving a spot where she could feel him even after his hand returned to his lap. "You were so far away."

"I angered the goddess. She didn't like that I was ungrateful of her gifts. I threw them back at her, and she decided to show me a world where I didn't have these powers." Saiden looked down at her hands, as if looking at them for long enough would let her see the tendrils of power buried deep inside her.

"What did it look like?"

"My hair was brown for one." Saiden laughed. She didn't mean to, and she probably looked crazy doing it. But the fact that her hair color was the first thing she brought up was slightly ridiculous. Everything else was going to hurt anyway, so she might as well laugh now while she still remembered what laughter sounded like.

"That must've been a shock." The way Cassimir spoke made her think he was smiling. But she knew if she looked at his face she would never get through the rest of it, and she needed to tell someone what her life might have been like.

"I had a brother." She choked trying to continue, and Cassimir ran his hands in circles on her back. She couldn't think. She couldn't breathe, not when she was focused on the loss of things she'd never even had to begin with. "My parents called him Waylen."

"What did he look like?" Cassimir asked, his words blending with the wind.

"I never even got to see him. He'd been killed in a mining accident. My father was coming home to tell us."

"And your mother?"

"The news ruined her. I've never seen her so broken, and we saw her after she'd been wrongfully imprisoned for over a decade."

They both waited in silence a little while, as if Cassimir knew she needed time before she could finish. "What happened next?"

"I tried to kill them all. I had no training, no powers. I took my mother's kitchen knife and I killed four of them before they managed to stop me. I woke up as one of them slit my throat. They made my parents watch. They must've been so disappointed in me."

Cassimir bent to place a kiss at her hairline. She hadn't realized her hood had begun to slip, but they were up so high she didn't think she needed to pull it back in place.

"The worst part of all of it was that the entire time I was in there my brain was trying to tell me it wasn't real. But I wanted it so bad that I ignored my instincts in order to chase this fake life." She didn't know if Cassimir would understand, but she desperately hoped that he would.

She didn't want to be alone in her grief anymore.

29
RHENA

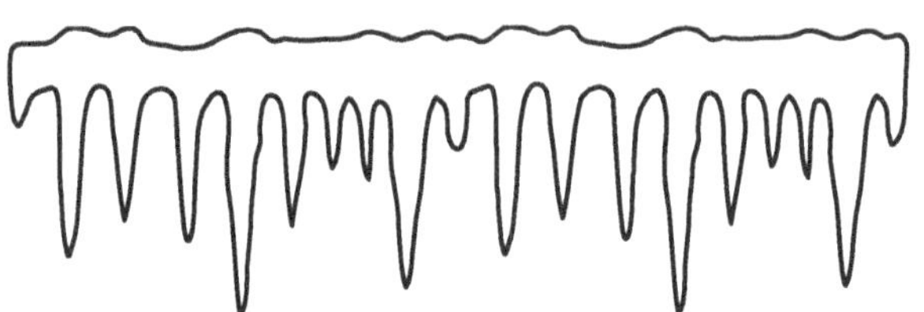

Rhena knew she was too young to be on patrol. At least she would've been, by the standards Nakti had set for the army when she'd been its general. Revon didn't seem to care if they died. He was simply culling the weak among them, even if it was a weakness that would disappear with age, proper training, and a full night's sleep in some of their cases.

She certainly hadn't slept through an entire night in weeks, possibly months, but Revon didn't care about sleep deprivation. Or arming children. Rhena was lucky that she had managed to get herself partnered with Talon. It was a risky move, with him being a pronounced traitor and her a suspected one, but she couldn't pass up the opportunity to get him away from the palace and as many spying eyes as possible.

And this was Revon's way of trying to get them to prove their worthiness outside of the pure strength of their individual gifts. The fact that she was with Talon was surely another test all on its own, to see if the two of them could be trusted—if Talon's punishment had been enough to persuade them both to see things his way.

Rhena wasn't naive enough to think that Revon didn't have spies following them, but he didn't know her well enough to be aware of the times she had crept through the city streets before, and didn't have a problem doing it again.

"Sai…" she began to say Saiden's name and then stopped. There was necessary risk and then there was foolishness. If they were being followed her name would be a dead giveaway that she was a traitor. No one but Revon had spoken her name since she had escaped all those months ago.

"My trainer told me the best place to find information was always going to be a pub."

Rhena could tell Talon knew who she was talking about by the way his face changed. They all knew, especially after Revon's announcement in the mess hall, how close she had been to Saiden and Mozare.

"That may have worked for them," he was being careful too. If anyone overheard them, they couldn't concretely tell who they were talking about. "But you look like a child, and I look like mincemeat. I sincerely doubt anyone is going to let us anywhere near a bar. Even the seedy ones out here."

He scrunched up his nose as they walked past a bar whose patrons smelled enough to cover the scent of beer leaking into the alleyway. She didn't like that he thought she looked like a child, despite still being one himself, but she didn't argue.

There had to be another angle, another way for them to get information that would help her friends, as well as something they could pretend was useful for their king. She also had a third goal, which was to keep Talon from getting into anymore danger. She knew how these streets could hurt you for being different, and her first experience with anything like a patrol had ended in bloodshed she didn't wish to repeat.

"Sometimes, people aren't the only ones who can give you information. At least not speaking to them in person." Talon spoke, and when he motioned for her to follow him, she did. She didn't know him well enough to trust him the way that she was, but war did strange things to all of them.

He wove through the streets, his mind working the same way as hers. If they had a tail, there would be no way of keeping up with them. Unless of course, Revon's new gifts allowed his soldiers to track their heartbeats, in which case no number of slanted roofs and thin passageways could hide them from their pursuers.

And Rhena watched as every once in a while Talon checked the cracks between bricks, and the holes where wooden walls had been chipped away by bugs and weather and time.

She didn't understand what he was doing, but she didn't dare ask, not when there were so many places for listening ears to be hiding. If she trusted Talon, now was the time to prove it.

When they finally stepped out from the stacks of houses and narrow alleyways, they were outside the temple. No amount of training or will power was enough to stop her from freezing at the sight of the Enlightened kneeling outside in deference. Her brain couldn't separate the sight in front of her from the cobblestones running red with the blood that coursed through her memories.

She grabbed Talon's sleeve, trying to pull him back the way they came, but he didn't follow. Rhena's panic built until finally the cold at his back made him turn to look at her. Whatever he saw on her face, he pulled her into him, and the warm feeling of his gifts wrapping around her helped to settle her.

Unfortunately, Talon wasn't the only one to notice her cold snap, and three pairs of Enlightened eyes turned to look at them.

"Gifted." One of them let out, bowing to rest their forehead against the cobbles in deference to them. The second followed, but the third didn't take their eyes off Rhena's face, and she knew the moment they recognized her, because fear took over the reverence on their face and they stood.

"You are sworn to the cursed one. Her hands have spilled Enlightened blood, and her curse disappoints our masters."

Talon stepped in front of her. She didn't want to be glad, but she was so relieved he was there to defend her. Rhena's hands were so frozen she didn't think she'd be able to grab for her own sword.

"Gifted shall never come to harm at our hands, for the gods act through us. We never meant to cause you harm." Were they apologizing?

The other two Enlightened sat back on their feet, still in prayer, but no longer with their faces to the ground. A second one spoke. "We feel the disturbance in the powers of our gods, we know what blasphemy occurs nightly and we know that the gods do not wish for this abuse of their generously given power. But we cannot stop it."

Rhena didn't realize that the Enlightened had the ability to sense their gifts, and certainly not to feel Revon's experiments. Especially when she hadn't felt them outside of the night he'd had the general in the body of water under the palace.

"This temple is a holy place, and here none shall be harmed." It was a truce of a kind, since Rhena doubted she'd ever trust the fanatics. But it was also an opportunity. As her brain raced, it finally clicked what Talon had been doing. He'd been searching for slips of paper the same as the one he had left for her in the mess hall.

"If what you say is true," Rhena began, hoping she had worked things out correctly in her brain, "then you can aid us. We know the blasphemy that goes on in the palace and we wish to see an end to it."

The words were dangerous to say out loud, but the way the Enlightened's face morphed, the dedication that now glowed in their features, Rhena knew her guess had been correct. And they needed whatever allies they could muster.

The Enlightened nodded at her, as if they were convinced that perhaps this was finally their path to the divine. "Collect any information that you can find, gather it here on our behalf. We need any information we can get on how to stop this from happening and how to fight back against it."

"Gifted one, it would be an honor."

30
Mozare

It was only right that Mozare went with Saiden to try and get word to Rhena. They were the ones she mattered to most. And he had been the one to ultimately make the decision to leave her behind when they had been forced to flee Kaizia with an unconscious, broken version of his partner.

Saiden had a plan. She hadn't told any of them what it was, but as he'd known to trust her on the ship, he knew to follow her now. She'd never needed to tell him what she was up to before. Saiden had never been the one keeping secrets.

She slipped through alleys they had once been tasked to keep safe, a phantom in a city that had never once welcomed her. And he kept her safe, the only reassuring thing about this city right now was that he knew they could rely on each other.

Saiden didn't even reach for her blades. Mozare couldn't tell if she was on edge, but he couldn't imagine feeling anything but tense. Even with their little sister waiting for them at the end of this darkness.

Mozare watched Saiden slip out from between the shelter of buildings, at ease as she blended into the tree line. Now he could call his shadows in fuller force, wrapping the darkness in between the tree branches to ensure they were completely hidden.

There was little woodland standing between them and the palace, and he could smell the smoke that meant more was being burned. He wondered which one of Revon's soldiers had been tasked with the destruction.

Saiden's shoulders stiffened as he tightened the shadows around them. He wasn't used to her being able to feel the power, he had spent so long separated from her. Now, he still wasn't sure how she felt about having the ability to sense him like this.

He couldn't imagine he would enjoy his powers if they had come at the same cost as hers had. Not when she'd had a mother who'd loved her, and had lost her after only just getting her back.

When Mozare realized how close they were to the walls of the palace he pulled his shadows back. Saiden did a good job keeping them out of sight of the watch towers even with the missing trees.

"So what now?"

"Do you know how paper is made Mozare?"

The question seemed so out of place, he didn't answer it. Whatever Saiden was thinking, she would either explain it to him, or he would see it for himself.

"It's just trees. Another part of this land." She pulled a piece of paper from her pocket, the edges worn. He could see traces of ink, but nothing he could read. That was good, because he would have felt awful for reading it if Saiden wasn't outright sharing it with him.

Saiden laid the paper on top of her open palm, the rose tattooed on her skin a bright contrast to the dull parchment. Then Mozare watched in awe as it began to fold itself up, tucking its corners until it was no longer a paper at all, but a small parchment colored bird.

Mozare was giddy with excitement, though he was careful not to be too loud about it. "How did you figure that out?"

"I was frustrated. I wanted to fly away from all this. And then," she motioned to the bird still tucked into her palm. He didn't need to hear the rest. Without complete control over her new powers, they had manifested her wish for her. At least they had tried, no one had been able to fly with their gifts to the best of his knowledge.

Even Saiden had only hovered in the middle of saving them from the hurricane, and that had been an unsettling thought all on its own.

"It's brilliant."

Saiden's smile was small, but he could see that beneath the apprehension for her gifts she was also proud. And maybe that was enough of a first step. Together they watched the bird take flight, its paper wings a little out of sync. Not enough that the guards would notice though.

Their little paper messenger sailed right over the guarded borders of their palace with ease. Now, all he could do was hope that it made it to their little sister.

31
SAIDEN

SAIDEN DID HER BEST TO LOOK CALM, BUT ONLY BECAUSE SHE DIDN'T WANT the others to keep coming to check on her. When Rhena hadn't met them in the place she'd instructed her to the day after the experiment with her power, Saiden had been nervous. Now, three days later, she was ready to storm the palace all on her own and kill anyone who tried to keep them apart.

She knew the feelings weren't rational, but they lit the pool of power in her belly in a way that made it almost seem possible. Only the danger it might cause to Rhena kept her tethered to her body.

If her friends weren't watching she would have paced, but she was trying to assure them she was fine. She didn't want them to know that inside her mind a monster pressed at the bars of its cage.

All she wanted was to see Rhena coming through the ruined remains of the forest that once grew lush around the city they'd called home. The ashes that returned to the ground and prepared it for new life. In her mind's eye she could see new plants take root, new life growing here. But only if they stopped this corruption from spreading further.

Instead of pacing, she kept herself and her mind occupied by lighting small fires at the tips of her fingers, and coaxing the flames to dance. They didn't hurt her as long as she remained focused on keeping the fire away from her skin. It was a good exercise in control, she reminded herself.

There was no use in creating an inferno if she couldn't control a single spark. Saiden wasn't prepared to give in to her powers again.

Not unless she needed them to save Rhena. She wasn't going to lose anyone else to the false king. He wouldn't tear anymore of her family from her.

When she could sense the rest of her group giving up hope for the day, she heard the smallest footstep settle in the ashes. There had seemed nowhere to hide, yet she hadn't caught sight of Rhena before hearing her. She knew the rest of them grabbed for their blades, they were still fugitives in a kingdom that wanted their heads, but all Saiden did was open her arms.

It might make her a more obvious target, but she also had her powers and her friends behind her. If this was a threat, they wouldn't get anywhere near her friends. Not while she drew breath.

Someone barreled into her chest, and Saiden wrapped her arms around Rhena, her smaller form shivering, whether from fear or the cold Saiden couldn't tell. She hadn't really noticed that the days were starting to get colder. The only thing that marked time passing for her were the orange shades burnishing the leaves of the few remaining trees around Norbury.

"I missed you little Maus." Saiden whispered into her hair. Tears soaked into the jacket Saiden was wearing, but she didn't care. She didn't even mind when the tears froze, the ice burning into her chest. She would hold Rhena as long as the younger girl needed. She would never get over the feeling of having her here again.

Mozare came over, wrapping his arms around the two of them, their little family reunited at last. She knew that she should've stopped to make introductions, but manners were the furthest thing from her mind right now. All she could see and hear and smell was Rhena, tucked in safe against her.

She dipped into the power inside her, grasping it where it had begun to settle, and let it course through Rhena checking for injuries.

Rhena started to giggle. "It's weird feeling you push around like that big sister." Tears lingered in her voice, but Saiden was also proud of the steadiness in it as well. "I never thought I would be able to feel you like this." She saw something weird flash over Mozare's face for the briefest moment, an agreement of sorts she didn't bother thinking too hard about.

"I had to make sure you were alright." Saiden replied. It was the truth, although it left out how urgently the thought had fought for attention in Saiden's mind.

"We've made some friends." Mozare spoke for her, saving her from having to make the introductions herself.

Saiden startled when Rhena took one look at the others and pulled her blade. But she was also somewhat proud of the way Rhena put herself between them and the fallen queen, blade steady despite its weight.

"Loralei is on our side little one." Saiden spoke, placing one hand on the flat side of the short sword and encouraging Rhena to lower the blade.

"Loralei is dead." Rhena put her blade away, but the skepticism never really left her face.

"The rumors of my death were greatly exaggerated." Loralei spoke, not at all fazed by having a weapon directed at her.

Rhena turned to hug Cassimir, though this one was brief, and he used the opportunity to introduce Rhena to Eleni.

"I am so glad we have made it back to you." Eleni spoke, and despite never having met before, Saiden knew she meant every word she spoke.

"You were the one who sent the letters?" Rhena asked with a curious tilt of her head. Eleni's smile was bright as she nodded. "Thank you for giving me that piece of my family."

"Did you bring your stuff?" Saiden asked, looking around. She must've dropped it somewhere when she'd run into Saiden. But as the delay of Rhena's answer grew longer and longer, she felt the chaos swirling in her chest get worse and worse.

Rhena didn't make eye contact with her as she shook her head no.

The panic that usually meant her powers were about to go haywire started to build under her skin. She didn't understand why Rhena wouldn't have brought her stuff.

She reached out to grab her, but the ice coating her fingernails made her pull back. Saiden could still feel the marks on her chest from Rhena's tears, she didn't want to risk hurting Rhena in the same way.

"Were you in danger? Were they chasing you?" Saiden finally reached for her blade, though it was more so she had something to do with her hands than because she needed it. Saiden was far too smart to have not realized what Rhena meant.

In the end Mozare was the one who had to say it out loud, because Saiden couldn't force her mouth to form the words. "You aren't coming with us."

Light pulsed from Saiden's body, a side effect far too dangerous when they were trying to hide. It only stopped when Cassimir wrapped himself around her from behind and she was finally able to lose herself in his warmth.

"I can make a difference if I stay." It's exactly what Saiden herself would've said, which is why it hurt her so much hearing Rhena say it. She had damned her when she'd agreed to train her. She should've never let her into their group.

Rhena grabbed for her wrist, and Saiden put all her effort into keeping herself from exploding, from hurting her.

"You're right little one." Cassimir spoke behind her. "It won't be easy, but it is very brave."

Saiden took another crumpled up piece of paper from her pocket, and let the power inside her tunnel into it, until a small paper mouse rested in Saiden's palm.

"Take this mouse. If you're in danger, release him and he'll find me. I will come for you." It was all Saiden could do. She would never deny Rhena her choice, even when that choice put her in danger. And if she wanted to think like a general, this was the better tactical decision.

She didn't have to like it though.

"I have something for you as well," Rhena said, reaching to her waist and unstrapping a worn leather belt that Saiden recognized as her own. "I found these, and knew there was only one place they could belong."

Rhena gingerly handed Saiden the kindjal blades she had left behind. The one piece of Nakti that she could still hold on to. A tie to another life where things had been so much simpler. When Cassimir stepped even closer behind her she didn't hesitate to rest her weight on him, to let him keep her steady when she didn't have the strength herself.

Mozare gave Rhena the same instructions Saiden would have if she'd been able to find her voice. "Don't be reckless. You can only make a difference if you live through this." He pressed a kiss to Rhena's forehead.

Saiden did the same, lingering before pulling Rhena against her. Cassimir hadn't let her go yet, which she was grateful for, so she was sandwiched between them, and was able to feel her heart fill for the briefest of moments. Every living person that she loved in the world was here in the forest with her. For now, that was enough.

She had to hope they'd get another moment like this.

32
LORALEI

LORALEI KNEW HER IDEAS WERE BORN FROM REVENGE, BUT IT HAD FUELED her for so long, it only felt natural. Every thought in her head had been colored by the scar on her back. It pulsed ever so slightly with each step she took on Kaizian soil, as if the mark itself remembered what caused it.

As if a piece of him continued to live in her after all this time.

She wanted to kill that piece. Almost as much as she wanted to kill the man responsible for putting the mark on her body in the first place. All because he had thought he'd make a better king for a kingdom that had once chosen her. This was her home, whether he wanted it to be or not.

That was the other thing she'd fight for. Her revenge needed satisfaction, but beneath it she longed for a home. She wanted to belong somewhere, and she wasn't going to let anyone take that dream from her.

Mozare walked through the forest with her, although she still hadn't told him what she was going to do. He didn't try to speak to her. Their relationship was slightly less tenuous after everything that had happened with Saiden, but she still wasn't prepared to talk to him in great length.

She certainly didn't want to talk about their relationship again. Once, on board the ship, where she'd been forced to break the few still beating pieces of her heart, had been enough. She wouldn't survive the conversation a second time.

"What exactly are we doing in the woods?" As they reached the burnt tree line it seemed Mozare's patience had finally worn out.

"I don't know what you're doing in the woods, but I'm committing psychological warfare."

Mozare's face scrunched up at her admission. She didn't know if it was because he didn't understand, or because he didn't like how openly she'd admitted her motives.

"You don't live with a small group of bandits without learning to make your target fear you. And what does Revon fear?" The question was mostly rhetorical, but she was still curious to see if he would try to answer it. When he didn't, she continued. "He fears losing his power. Over the kingdom, over his gifts, and over himself."

"And you expect to antagonize this man how exactly?" She didn't like his tone. He either thought she was stupid or reckless. It didn't really matter which, because she didn't care for his judgement and she didn't need his permission. This was her life, finally, and she was going to make her own choices.

"What better way to remind him of the threat of losing his power than to remind him of me? He thinks he did such a great job deposing me, but it was far too easy. Subconsciously, I have no doubt that he knows that, and he worries about the same happening to him. I want him to feel that pressure."

"You don't have to do this. You're being reckless." Ah and now he'd said it. "I don't think you're making good choices."

"Well at least they're mine." She pulled at the laces of her dress, trying to loosen it enough to stick one of her shorter blades under the fabric.

"You're going to haunt him naked?" Mozare's voice was distressed, she didn't have to turn around and see his expression to know his eyes were wide. He'd never even seen her naked, and now he thought she'd be roaming around in a state of undress. Stupid men.

"Of course not." She pulled a dagger out from a strap none of them knew about, she came loaded these days, and sliced the blade against her scar. It wasn't deep enough to do any real damage, but enough to bleed. As she pulled the strings of her corset tight again, she could feel the blood seeping into the laces. Enough to remind Revon of what he had done to her.

When her back felt thoroughly wet, she reached into herself with her powers and sealed the wound. She ignored the reminder of how it had felt to heal it the first time. She didn't want to let that pain in again.

Mozare looked like death when she turned back around to face him. She supposed the reminder of what had happened to her wasn't a pain he wanted to relive either. Studying his face, she couldn't help but remember the gentle trace of his fingers over her scar.

That was the world she wanted to return to. Where love didn't hinder, where it accepted her as the whole of her parts. And right now, Revon was the biggest obstacle to her returning to that world.

She didn't want to leave him like that, with the darkness chasing both of them, so before she could think about it too much, she pressed a chaste kiss to his cheek, squared her shoulders and set off towards her palace.

There were still entranceways to the tunnel she remembered that she'd never shared. Unless Revon had used his time as king to map them all out, she had a few choices on ways to get back inside. And she doubted he would want to get rid of paths that could help him escape when he knew his position on the throne was tenuous at best.

Even with the burned down forest, Loralei was able to trace her way back to the underground tunnel entrance. Somewhere along its path, this entrance used to connect to the old bunkers, the space the rebels had used to plot against her, but the path had caved in long ago. That was why they had moved the legionnaire barracks above ground in the first place.

She slipped inside, lighting the tips of her fingers in the gods glow so that she was able to see the space directly around her. If Loralei shone too brightly she'd give herself away. That at least was a lesson her advisors had taught her well, reinforced by the actions of every adversary she'd faced recently.

Even Mozare in a way. She shut down that line of thought before it could get too far. She didn't want to be reckless. She wanted to be useful, and she couldn't be useful if she was caught.

She slipped into her old room, keeping her gift open to the feeling of other people's heartbeats. It was a risk that made sense. Sure, someone might recognize that there was a gifted person in the room, but from what they knew from Saiden's recruit girl, the palace was full of gifted these days. She wouldn't stick out as much here as she had when she'd been the only gifted one in a very lonely palace.

Carefully, she moved through the room, taking in the enshrining of everything that had once mattered to her. They hadn't touched any of her things, despite the months that had passed since her supposed death.

Once she reached the lit hallways, it was harder to make her way. She could bend the light around her face to distort her features, but she didn't know which rooms Revon had decided to claim. Saiden and Mozare hadn't talked much about their life as Revon's generals, and she regretted not asking more questions before jumping into this.

But it was too late to go back now. Instead, she adjusted her plan. In every crack and shadowy corner, Loralei reached into the soil way under their feet and grew flowers. Not flashy ones like the ones she'd grown in her garden, but fragrant ones. She wanted Revon reminded of her at every turn, even after she'd made her way back to the relative safety of her friends.

When she sensed the heartbeats of three approaching soldiers, she tucked herself into a bedroom, hoping none of them were the current occupants of the room. As they passed, she felt lucky, but she knew all too well how fast luck could run out.

"The king summoned her. And she submitted, but her powers are different. The experiment isn't taking to her as well as the rest of us." One of them said as Loralei cracked the door open.

"That's why he needs the rest of us to get down to his rooms."

Loralei's luck seemed to be spreading a little further, but it might be enough to get her through this whole thing.

She didn't think any of them were life gifted, but it was hard for her to tell. She didn't have the kind of experience around other gifted people that Mozare had, so tracking gifts wasn't really something she was confident about.

Loralei didn't call on her own gifts though, just in case. She slipped her shoes off, tucking them into her corset laces so they didn't give her away, and put her years of sneaking through the grounds to use.

The three of them made enough noise that it was easy to follow even from a distance, making it that much harder for them to catch her. She tracked them far into the cellars, into rooms she'd barely spent time in herself. The space had always felt wrong to her, as if no life had ever belonged there.

She felt them stop, but with the room being so stuffy she wasn't able to hear them until they started coming in her direction again. Loralei ducked, shoving herself behind piles of old junk she couldn't identify and crossing her fingers they hadn't seen her. Peeking through a slit in the pile in front of her, she saw two of them carrying a limp woman between them. The third walked next to them, finger on her pulse. Definitely not life gifted then. When she concentrated on them, she finally connected to one, the woman they were carrying. While she was certain now that the three soldiers were gifted by Ilona, she also knew the woman was like her, gifted by Keir.

She had no idea what they were doing in that basement or what it meant for her and her friends. Her instincts told her nothing good was coming from that room. Loralei raked her brain for information, any kind of building plans or old maps from this part of the palace. She had one thing she wanted to do before she could leave.

Loralei wanted to see Revon. She wasn't ready to face him head on, and still wasn't entirely sure she could beat him in a fight. In fact, there was a fair chance she would freeze at her first sight of him, but she needed it anyway. Even if it was to prevent herself from freezing later, when there were more lives on the line than hers.

She'd already survived one death at his hands.

Now, she needed a reminder that for all that he had lived in her nightmares and terrorized her every waking thought, he was still a man. Which meant that he could die, and she would make sure it came to that, even if it killed her.

Loralei sent the silent words out into the universe, not foolish enough to pray them. She'd long ago given up hope that anyone out there cared about her. Not when they'd chosen her, gifted her, and then forced her to hide who she was.

She could only feel one heartbeat now in the room behind all the stone and broken masonry, so she risked it. Mozare's voice rang loud in the back of her mind, urging her to stop being reckless, to remember that there were people who cared that she made it back to them.

Loralei turned him off, although she couldn't fully clear herself of the feeling his reminder had left behind. It didn't change anything, she still needed this.

Silent feet carried her through the dank hallways, the chill sinking through her feet until midway up her calves. She wasn't sure she would've been able to feel her feet even if the stone wasn't as cold as it was.

Her hands were shaking at her side, but she didn't have enough control over herself to get them to stop. This man had done everything in his power to get rid of her, all for a throne and her kingdom. And she'd let him have it. She should've fought harder for her people.

For herself.

Now it was time to regain that power.

She slipped around the corner, knowing that she would see him when she did. He was kneeling above a shallow lake, one Loralei hadn't known existed there. She couldn't even begin to imagine how the water had gotten there, or what possible damage it was doing.

Now she began to wish she had brought someone else with her, because she was too far out of her depths to know what he was doing. She had a gut feeling that this was important, weighed down by the fact that she had no idea how she would explain what was going on.

Loralei took another step forward, and felt the stone crumble slightly under her bare foot. It wasn't much, but she froze as the sound rippled through the silence, and Revon's back tensed.

"You weren't supposed to come back." He said, something coloring his voice that she couldn't quite understand. Loralei didn't know if it was worse to answer him or remain silent, but the words were coming out of her mouth before she even had a chance to properly think them through.

"You weren't supposed to come for my power or my throne. But sometimes the choices we make come back to haunt us." If Revon had been stiff before, he was practically stone now. Before she had time to think, she turned, sneaking back through the paths, moving as fast as she could towards the closest exit to the palace.

She felt the moment he started chasing after her, and something inside her reveled in it. Even though she was the prey, the hunted, she was the one with the power now. He'd heard her voice and been afraid. But she still knew this place better than anyone.

She slipped into an alcove that hadn't been properly sealed when the renovations happened in the palace during her childhood and waited for Revon to pass. A rose cupped in her hand, she let its fragrance trail after him, giddy as she turned the other way and escaped to the outside world.

Darkness cocooned her, and she had a feeling it wasn't the darkness of a normal moonless night. She let herself fall into the shadow's embrace, because she could not fall into the arms of its creator.

33
Mozare

Mozare left Loralei at the palace despite his better judgement. He didn't want to let her go into that hell on her own, but he couldn't see any way to stop her that didn't involve physically restraining her. Not that he hadn't strongly considered doing that, he was just sure the resulting fight would end in their capture.

Walking back to their refuge, he knew that his anger and carelessness were as likely to draw unwanted attention as the fight brewing between them. He didn't want to be caught, but he was lying if he said he wouldn't go for a fight. The house they were hiding out in was too small for sparring, even up on the roof, so that wasn't an option right now.

No one seemed to be following him, and as he got closer to their home, his rage settled into his bones, and his mind finally cleared. He didn't want the family harboring them to come to any harm. Not after everything they'd done for them. He wouldn't let that happen.

As soon as he walked into the house, he knew Saiden could feel it. They'd been partners too long for her to not notice his restless energy. Cassimir on the other hand wasn't so adept at reading him.

"Where's Mistress Loralei?" He asked, unable to feel the tension in the room. Or trying to relieve it possibly, but Mozare couldn't tell.

"You need to get out some steam." Saiden said. It wasn't a question, but her interruption also meant Mozare didn't have to answer Cassimir's question so he was grateful she was taking charge.

"I'm game for whatever you have planned."

Mozare should've asked for clarification on Saiden's plans before jumping in head first. He wasn't sure how Saiden had managed to find clear space for this training exercise, but he'd learned long ago not to question her. Sometimes she was able to get things done that he didn't expect anyone else would be capable of doing.

If her mysterious ways did not include the occasional delirious loss of consciousness, he would probably be a lot more comfortable with it.

He walked until he was in the middle of the field. If something went wrong he wasn't sure there would be a safe distance for his friends to watch from. He did his best to calm his nerves before reaching into the well of his powers. He couldn't let what was going on inside his mind get out of control, or his powers would too.

Unlike the catacombs, death wasn't so prevalent on the field. He knew Akil had tortured and killed possibly thousands of people in his patched together laboratory, but it hadn't resonated with him so deeply until he felt the difference now.

Saiden understandably had a lot of questions after he had finally mentioned the gruesome truth of how they'd escaped the catacombs, that even Loralei's detailed recount still hadn't answered. He hadn't tried to do it again. Between the ship and the small apartments they'd been hiding out in, there was no way he would have risked it. However, it was an asset they couldn't resist exploring if they were heading into war completely outnumbered.

The corpses met his call with more hesitation this time than they had in Akil's hell hole. The vengeance those dead had craved had been a powerful motivator, and the fact that their souls seemed to have been resting peacefully made his conscience prickle with guilt.

Calling these soldiers took more focus, their bodies a mix of rotting flesh, bones and his shadow enhancements. They certainly weren't the prettiest of soldiers, but a lot could be accomplished with terrifying, and they fit that bill. If Loralei thought they could fight Revon by building on his own paranoia, the corpses of his victims would certainly go a long way. And it avoided putting anyone in real danger, since these soldiers were already dead.

"You talked to me about give and take, about balance. How do you balance this part of your powers?" Saiden asked. Mozare wasn't sure if she was asking for herself, or to remind him to keep his powers from going haywire. Either way, he had to pause and think about it.

"I think it's a sense of duty. I am here for a cause and these soldiers serve that cause. If I die, they can't continue to serve me and I can't continue to serve my cause. They need me to be alive as much as I need them to stay alive."

"So training serves that cause too right? Call them." Saiden made everything seem so simple. He hadn't needed logic to call his soldiers when he was stuck in the catacombs. He'd only needed to be full of love, haunted by the fear of losing it. And he had lost it anyway.

But if Saiden was using him and this experiment to understand her own combination of magic, he would try to put the chaos of it into words for her. To sink the fear he was once again feeling at the prospect of losing Loralei deep inside himself. Let them crack him open and see only his devotion and care for her spill out, leaving the ugliest bits of himself behind.

His conscious separated here on the field in a way it hadn't in Akil's tunnels, his sight coming from a dozen eyes, his arms moving with the weight of countless limbs. It spooked him for a second, and as he startled, the creak of bones played across the wind in a harrowing song.

Mozare tried to focus, tried to recenter himself in his own body, the pump of blood through warm muscle and the air in his lungs. Finally, he pulled his awareness from the corpses around him, Saiden's worried face centering in his vision.

"What are you feeling?" Saiden asked.

Mozare tilted his head to one side as he pondered the question, and the bodies around him that still had heads of their own copied him.

"This isn't like last time." He started. "I can feel each of them, when before they were my comrades in arms. Now they're a piece of me."

Saiden unsheathed one of her kindjal blades, the blue one Cassimir had gifted her in Taezhali, and without hesitation punched it through the face of the soldier nearest to her. Mozare flinched as if the blade had been coming for his own face, but there was no pain behind the blow. The rest of his soldiers shuddered, but they did not mimic the way he moved anymore. Whatever had been briefly connecting them, the blow had severed it.

Now he had his soldiers to command. He started small, and built his way up to an army. It was the only advantage he might be able to give them. And if Loralei was going to fight dirty, he would be in the dirt right beside her, fighting for their lives. For their love.

34

RHENA

WITH EVERYTHING RHENA HAD PUT INTO PLACE TO FIGHT AGAINST THE tyranny of Revon's rule, she should've felt more settled, but restless energy constantly coursed through her. Her powers were rampant, made worse by the new training Revon was requiring of those lucky few he'd selected to be part of his trials at some point in the future.

Their new trainers pushed her harder than she'd ever been pushed before. She worried every time that she wasn't ready to dig that far into her powers. Rhena saw what it meant to be lost to the gods gifts when she'd seen Saiden brutally kill that prisoner with no remorse. She feared that outcome more and more every day.

Now she couldn't sleep, could barely eat, was only doing enough to keep others from being suspicious of her. She didn't want them to worry about her health for fear that it would get her another audience with the king that she couldn't fake her way through.

She was getting worse and worse at keeping herself under control. Every day she saw the others following their orders and she wished to scream at them to do something, do anything to stop the horrible things going on in their country.

Rhena had gone back to sneaking prisoners out of the dungeons again. She was worried about Talon facing the consequences for her actions, but she'd made sure prisoners only went missing when Talon was on patrol and visible by others. She couldn't let him take another punishment he didn't deserve. The prison was cold in a way she was sure had nothing to do with her powers. Not that they weren't constantly at risk of betraying her secrets, but because even she was cold as she walked through the stone doorway into the space beyond.

She'd started three nights ago, on the evening her silent ally had been Revon's next choice for augmentation. Rage hadn't been enough to keep her focused, she'd needed purpose. And there was no purpose for her if she continued to act within Revon's expectations. The smells that filled the dungeon made her dinner rise in her throat, but she knew it was nothing that could be controlled. Revon didn't even have the decency to give them buckets for their waste.

Her friends weren't the only ones who could rebel. They were back in the country to fight, and she was going to help gather an army for them. Every single person, gifted or not could be the piece that swayed the war in their favor. It might not be the most impressive army, but she was still naive enough to think that being on the right side of the cause would help them gain more support.

She knew there were others who wanted to fight back, because despite her efforts, every night the cages in the dungeons were filled with more and more people. Some recaptured, some new, and even some Rhena were relatively sure supported Revon. He was a man made mad by a power he could barely hold on to, and he would kill whoever he needed to make his tentative grasp feel stronger.

Rhena had come to understand a lot about men in power in the last few months. Even with Loralei in the end, it seemed that too much power would drive them all mad. They weren't meant for this, gifts or not.

She froze out the first lock. It was sloppy, but she couldn't find a new set of keys she could steal, whose disappearance wouldn't be noticed. She hoped the guards would think they'd overlooked a gifted prisoner when they'd locked up this new group instead of considering the other possibility. Sometimes it was good that people tended to see what they wanted to.

"Anyone who's fighting this tyranny is free. You don't have a lot of time to get out of here before the next rotation of guards. Make sure that the healthy among you help the injured. We have to be better than our oppressors." She couldn't wait to see if they got out. Revon's guard rotations had become more sporadic, making her attempts more risky, but she almost liked the danger at this point. At least this was a risk she was chasing herself, instead of one that came from being alive.

Outside she heard something she hoped was the sound of desperate feet running. But then she felt it, the slimy feeling of the general's gifts brushing up against her mind. Her powers rose, preparing to defend her, even if her mind wasn't prepared to do the same. Not with all the innocent people who could become collateral between her and the general. Between her and whatever other backup he came with because she knew Revon wasn't foolish enough to send him alone, no matter what new abilities he might have developed.

She unfroze the rest of the locks in one blast of ice, hoping that she had enough control to keep any of the prisoners from being cut at the same time. Maybe some of them would fight on her side, maybe they wouldn't. But at least she'd done something worth dying for.

Rhena wasn't prepared to end things, not when there was a fraction of hope for her to get out of this. Her friends were back. She had to make it to them, and she'd be safe. She didn't want her death to fall on Saiden's conscience. She knew her big sister would carry the guilt the rest of her life if something happened and she wasn't there to stop it.

She pulled her sword from its sheath across her back and took two steadying deep breaths. Or as steadying as she could manage when she was up against an unknown number of more powerful assailants.

She flowed through the crowd of prisoners, but remained somewhat separate from them. It was as if the world itself singled her out for this fight. She hoped that meant she was capable of winning it.

At the worst, she'd put a dent in his numbers before she went out.

Who has the advantage? Mozare asked in her head. *I guess it depends on what matters more, numbers or skills?* She answered him. There was no doubt in her mind that they had the advantage overall, but there was still one thing going in her favor. Despite all the observation and testing she'd suffered through, she knew they would underestimate her.

Light flashed in her face as she stepped out of the dungeons, but she didn't need to see to feel the gifted soldiers Revon brought with him. She felt him too, surrounded by them on all sides, not bothering to get himself involved in the fight. All around them were halos of death, all the fallen prisoners who did not make it past the ambush meant for her.

She was starting to understand why Saiden carved death into her own skin.

Rhena closed her eyes, and let her instincts guide her. It was risky. She was taking a bet with the universe that Revon didn't have any ungifted men fighting for him. But she thought the odds on that were probably in her favor.

As one of his augmented soldiers stepped to her side, she feigned right, ducking down and rolling as she swiped her blade through the back of one of his ankles. It was dirty, but fights were never fair.

His body hit the floor with a wet thud, blood mixing into the puddle that already stained the floor. She didn't think he was dead, but he was down for now. A second soldier approached her, and Rhena took the offensive, slicing towards their chest before they could get a weapon aimed at her.

The light behind her eyelids began to fade, and she dared to open her eyes a crack. The hall was a bloodbath. The few tracks of footprints leaving the palace gave her hope, but very little.

Revon was watching her. He flicked his fingers, and two of the soldiers guarding him broke off from his circle and charged her. Rhena didn't dare move, she wouldn't give them any indication of what she was doing before they were close enough to share air.

Then she froze the blood underneath them. As both soldiers lost their footing she sliced into the chest of one, flipping her own weapon and using it to impale the second. Revon's face burned with anger, his meager shadow talents curling around his ankles.

"Enough."

All his soldiers stopped. The people still left behind didn't waste the opportunity, helping whoever they could to get out of the palace.

"Surround her, but do not raise your weapons against her. There is no where for her to run."

Rhena couldn't get her back to a wall, couldn't stop them from getting all the way around her, trapping her without even touching her. She wasn't skilled enough for this fight, the only reason she'd made it this far was because she'd been facing them while they were distracted by prisoners.

There was no one on her side here but her. She noticed with a mix of relief and worry that the woman who'd helped her was not among these soldiers. She hoped it wasn't because she was dead. Although death might've been a preferred alternative to whatever was waiting for her.

She put her sword back into its sheath. She'd worry about the blood soaking the blade later. Revon pointed to the general, and shadows crept from his hands, all of them watching as they wrapped around her body, pinning her arms to her sides.

When she'd seen Mozare's shadows, they hadn't been like this. They certainly weren't corporeal enough to bind a person, but what the general conjured now was inescapable. Fear struck through her, but her gifts felt lost to her. The power rested inside her, but she was no longer able to touch it.

"You thought you could let prisoners out every night and I wouldn't notice come morning that there was no one left to execute?" He finally dared to get closer to her, and she could see the way sleep less nights pulled at his features. "You think your friends can come back to my country, and I wouldn't know about it?"

Rhena tried to keep her features from confirming or denying his suspicions. He had no way of knowing they were back, she knew her friends were too careful for that. Slowly, without bringing attention to herself, she let the little paper mouse slide down her leg, hoping they were watching her too closely to notice the trail of blood that tracked behind it.

"I don't know how they've managed it." He said, pulling at the ends of his unkempt hair, "bringing the queen's visage to haunt me. I see her around every corner, catch the smell of her flowers…" Revon interrupted himself, as if he had said more than he intended. "You will be the price for their betrayal. You will pay for every deed in blood."

Someone hit her upside the head before she even had time to panic, and the world around her went black.

35
SAIDEN

SAIDEN GOT THE PAPER MOUSE, A LITTLE MORE WORN THAN IT HAD BEEN when she'd given it to Rhena, a little while before she saw the message Revon had left for her.

He hadn't specifically known who to leave it for. She didn't think he could guess that she was back; but Rhena's sword was left at the edge of the woods, a lock of her hair tied around the handle. It called to her as much as her name would have, and she knew exactly what the message meant.

Rhena was in danger. She was in danger because Saiden had allowed her to go back to the man who had viciously killed her mother in cold blood, so they had the chance at a little more information against him.

She'd been so foolish. Rhena was still a child, and while she was talented, talent wouldn't save her from his cruelty. Saiden still remembered the time she spent as his prisoner, both when he was a rebel and through the delirium from when she'd been a captive of the king.

Saiden didn't want to think about what he might be doing to Rhena. The thought of her living through a fraction of what Saiden had been dealt at Revon's hand made her blood boil, and sparks flicker at her fingertips.

Rushing home, Saiden shocked everyone by crashing back into the apartment they were hiding in, and risked getting stabbed by a variety of different weapons. When Mozare saw the blade in her hand, she saw the same fear bleed into his expression that was surely in hers.

"He has Rhena." It wasn't a question, and it didn't need repeating as they started strapping on their weapons.

Cassimir turned to Eleni, and she could see a different kind of fear on his face. "Don't worry brother. I'll stay here. This isn't the time for me to try and prove something." Eleni leaned in to kiss his cheek, before turning to Saiden. "I'll have medical supplies prepared in case you need them."

"Cassimir you should stay too." Saiden said. She didn't wait for him to ask her what she was thinking. Chaos was her strong suit, and she wore it well. "They know we're here, or they think it at least. Keep your sister and these people safe."

She could tell he wanted to argue with her, but whatever was on her face was enough to convince him it wasn't worth it. He stepped into her space, but she didn't feel crowded by him. Not even when he leaned down to kiss her in front of all their friends.

"Be careful my love." He whispered, a prayer shared between the two of them.

She couldn't promise she'd make it back, none of them could, but she could promise to be careful. She nodded and then kissed him again, letting that kiss tell him everything she couldn't say aloud.

Loralei and Mozare followed her out of the small cottage. In not asking them to stay behind they both must've figured she needed them, and as they ran towards the king, she told them her plan.

36
LORALEI

LORALEI TRAILED AFTER SAIDEN AND MOZARE, AND WONDERED BRIEFLY IF this was what her life might have been like if she'd never been chosen to be Queen. In Kaizia most of the gifted became soldiers in an army she was once able to claim. Would she have joined them if given the choice?

The only reason she was even considering it was to save herself from being terrified about what they were about to face. She and Saiden might have explored the tunnels lending them some familiarity now, but it was one thing using them to escape her would be assassins and another to use them to return to the palace where she had almost died.

Maybe she had died. She felt like a different woman from the one who'd been Queen. Even with the passage of time, as she stepped back on the palace grounds, she could feel the cool stone seeping through the soles of her heavy boots, welcoming her home.

They knew she belonged here, even if that wasn't the case anymore.

Mozare had given her a sword, and while she much preferred to fight with her powers, the stone might make vines hard to access. She doubted Revon had cared to tend to her gardens, he may have even had them burned so no one could use them to remember her by.

Saiden had Rhena's sword strapped to her back, so maybe they would all be using different weapons tonight.

You would think after weeks of sneaking into the palace to mess with Revon, this journey wouldn't take such an emotional toll, but it was different with Rhena's life on the line as well.

This was different than coming into the castle to drown Revon in regret. She knew at some point tonight it was very likely she would have to face the man who stabbed her clean through her spine. Who would've killed her had the gods been done with her.

And he could very well kill Rhena. She might not know the recruit very well, but she was important to both Saiden and Mozare, and she didn't want anything bad to happen to her. She wasn't sure the palace would survive the chaos Saiden might unleash if she had to witness it either.

The look Mozare gave her as they crept through the halls told her he was thinking the same thing. She didn't like that she could still read him like this, but she didn't deny that the talent had its uses.

Saiden's plan was vague, but Loralei was used to that as well. Saiden had a good mind for strategy, but when she was under pressure, she didn't always do a good job sharing those plans. All the better, Loralei was pretty sure she would have hated having any more advanced knowledge than she already possessed.

Of the three of them, Loralei wasn't entirely sure who was more determined to thwart the usurper's plans, but together, though their forces were few, they were formidable. It was foolish of Revon to challenge Saiden the way he had. He had given her the powers she wielded. He should've known exactly what forces he faced.

Although the idea to harm Magdalena had never even crossed her mind, Loralei understood exactly the kind of thinking that made Revon kill her to unleash the curse. It disgusted her how much she could understand it, even if she never would have made the same choice.

Despite the fact that she was as dangerous as her friends, they sandwiched her between them as Saiden descended into the tunnels first, leaving Mozare behind her to hide their tracks. Their footsteps reverberated against the wet metal walls. Loralei dragged one bare finger along the slimy steel, causing her to pull away and wipe the grime on her pants.

Loralei didn't know how Saiden could bear the stickiness long enough to guide them through the mostly dark tunnels towards the place she'd once called home. Their breaths echoed in the silence around them, but at least this time no one was chasing them.

They were the only threat in the sewers.

Finally, Saiden reached up and released a second hatch, a small shaft of light pouring through and setting her hair a blaze. She no longer wore the tight buns gathered at the base of her skull, although she still had it braided in case there was a fight.

Because they were very unlikely to get through tonight without a fight.

Loralei felt her powers rise in response to Saiden's. With a hand against her friend's shoulder; she lent Saiden strength as her powers searched the palace grounds. They would only have one chance to get to Rhena undetected. They couldn't risk going in the wrong direction.

It was strange to be so in tune with the powers of another person, especially when they'd both been restrained for one reason or another. With Saiden's powers bound and hers shamed, they never would've been allowed this intimacy. Now they could use it to save their friend.

Loralei felt Saiden's shoulder sag for the briefest of moments when they finally picked up Rhena's heartbeat. For Mozare's benefit, since his gifts did not allow him the same sight she and Saiden had just had, Loralei spoke. "She's in the throne room."

"He's there too." Saiden added, the hollowness in her voice betraying a rage Loralei knew far too well. She was familiar with that, had long since forgone other feelings to bask in the company of that rage. If nothing else could keep her alive, she could rely on her anger to make her fight.

Mozare placed his hand on Saiden's other shoulder, and she turned, but their contact never broke. With Saiden's power high under her skin they were a chain, a conduit.

A perfect balance. They were strong together, stronger than anything Revon could throw at them, she knew that. But they were broken too, each of them in their own way.

"She is ours." Saiden started, a snarl on her face that made her look wild. "He will pay for every drop of her blood spilled. I will take my revenge on him; I will make him suffer. And through all of it, I will smile. Don't follow me if you cannot handle that."

A smile cracked on Loralei's face, a feral reflection of everything Saiden still hid behind her mask. "We're done losing. We are done suffering."

Loralei waited for either of them to protest, but the time for words had passed. It was time for bloodshed now.

37
SAIDEN

Revon stood at the front of the throne room, and Saiden knew better than to ignore that fact. But she also couldn't deny that most of her focus was on Rhena; bloodied, bound and kneeling in the middle of the room. Even from a distance, Saiden could see the tears that tracked their way through the blood on her face.

Revon took them in, his posture rigid, and his face getting redder by the moment. "I don't know how you managed it you bloody witch." Saiden thought Revon would focus his anger on her, she was the one who had gotten away from him, but he had turned his attention completely onto Loralei.

After weeks of screwing with his head, perhaps he'd forgotten Saiden's own slights against him.

"And my prodigies. Come to beg? I would've given you everything. I would've made you powerful."

Saiden's powers flared. Her gifts wouldn't hurt Loralei or Mozare, so she didn't try to rein them in. Her time in Taezhali attested to that. Revon turned away from the light shining from under her skin, and she used his distraction to put herself between him and Rhena.

She turned to her friends. "You get Rhena out of here. Now."

"We can't leave you with him." Mozare spoke. The fear on Loralei's face echoed the words, but she couldn't speak. Saiden knew being face to face with Revon again must be horrific, but she was brave enough to endure it.

Saiden didn't know if she would have had the same strength. "Do it." She ground out.

Even if Mozare didn't agree with her, Saiden knew he'd do what she asked. He owed her that much, and they all owed Rhena for letting herself get into this danger in the first place.

Saiden let the full force of her light keep Revon from blocking their escape, and she ran, Rhena's sword in her hand until she'd forced Revon onto his back on the steps of his throne room.

"You wanted me to be a weapon. That's what you mean by power. I've sharpened my steel, but you are no longer the one who wields it."

Revon laughed, even with Rhena's blade pressed to his throat, he dared to laugh at her. "You think that I'm foolish enough to fight the god's Anointed warrior without back up."

Saiden flinched, and although she knew the sword she'd commissioned for Rhena was a strong weapon, it wouldn't be enough. Not as Revon's guards began to surround her.

She unsheathed the remaining kindjal blade from the set Cassimir had gifted her, and held the blade flat against her forearm, prepared to block whichever one of the soldiers dared to strike out against her first.

The only thing that made Saiden happy was knowing Mozare had gotten Rhena out. She only hoped the soldiers were too distracted fighting her for any of them to follow her friends.

She knew what it was like to defend herself against a dozen or more enemies at a time, but this fight was different. Here no one was guarding her back. Mozare had left her behind exactly the way she had asked him to, even though she knew he would blame himself for the rest of his life if something happened to her.

And the stakes had never been so high before. The first soldier struck out at her and she disarmed him quickly, running Rhena's blade across his stomach and letting his intestines fall out where they wished. She didn't have time for mercy.

Before, all she stood to lose was her own life. Death didn't scare her.

But now, people she cared about could be hurt and that scared her more than anything. She saw each of their faces as she sacrificed the lives of these soldiers to her cause. Rhena laughing in training when she finally mastered a skill, Mozare and Loralei, the way they had been together in Taezhali.

She swung her blade, trying to dip into her power and use it to shield her where her weapons couldn't. It wasn't easy, splitting her focus when she'd spent so much of her life training and honing her skills to be as sharp as her blade. She felt their swords connect with her, but didn't feel her own blood as the strength of her power sealed over the open wounds as quickly as they appeared.

Saiden was strong, but not even she could hold up that much power indefinitely.

Still, she knew pain, and heartache. She went into this battle royale of her own volition, knowing that every minute she spent fighting gave her friends another minute to get as far away as they could.

She hoped they never stopped running. Faced with the corruption bleeding through the country she'd once loved, she hoped with every swipe of Rhena's sword that they abandoned it to its own fate.

More footsteps sounded, reinforcements to join the storm of fighting and tangled limbs growing around her. She didn't think Revon would be able to erase the stain of so much blood this time, and the thought brought her a tiny piece of satisfaction. Let his people see the death and despair his kingdom was being built on.

Even though she'd tried her best, she couldn't stop her thoughts from turning to Cassimir. To the way her death would scar him. She hoped there was enough support between his family, and the small makeshift one she'd claimed, for him to keep fighting. Not for Kaizia, but for the happiness and peace he harbored inside himself.

As soldiers kept coming, she lost herself to the maelstrom of blades and the rising tide of her powers. Her thoughts faded to white noise, blood pounding in her ears. Her strength wavered, her knees giving out under her, still she fought, keeping their blades away from the fragile skin at her neck, making them pay for every drop of blood they spilled.

In the chaos, her thoughts scattered.

All she knew was she'd broken Cassimir's heart. She wouldn't make it back to him tonight.

38
Mozare

Mozare was holding on to Rhena as tightly as he could as he ran back out of the palace. He didn't like having to escape their home again, but Rhena was somewhere between conscious and unconscious, and he couldn't risk staying to fight.

Loralei was behind him, and by the sound of it, her vines were trapping the soldiers in pursuit of them against the walls. Mozare couldn't fight himself, not with Rhena in his arms, but he had a new power he could use.

He stretched his own consciousness into the space around him, and when he latched on to the feeling of death, Mozare pulled. Ilona's powers coursed through his body as the corpses came back, flooding to his side.

Rhena's hand clutched at his chest. Mozare gave himself a second to be distracted looking down at her as his own soldiers started to swarm the gifted ones following Revon's orders.

Weakly, she lifted a finger, and pointed at one boy in the group. Mozare should've recognized them after spending so much time training Rhena's recruitment class, but he didn't.

"Not him."

Mozare didn't know why she would want to save him, but he

didn't bother arguing. Through the power connecting him to his soldiers, he gave them the same order. Everyone else was fair game.

He flinched when a hand came up to grab his shoulder, but relaxed when a blade didn't follow it. "I have to go back for her. Is this enough? Are they enough to get you out of here?"

Loralei was angry, but he could see the fear that bled underneath the anger. And he knew exactly why she couldn't leave Saiden behind. He remembered the scar Revon had given her and knew she wouldn't let that happen to anyone else.

He nodded, and hoped that Loralei could see everything on his face that he wouldn't dare say out loud. He loved her enough to let her do this. He might have tried to kiss her, but Rhena shook against his chest, and the panic sent him running again.

He had his guards close in around them. They didn't need to take out Revon's forces, they needed to get out of the palace before Revon could throw any more unexpected twists at them.

Not that he trusted Revon's games to end outside of the palace walls. He clearly had no qualms using whatever he could to keep them under his thumb. He'd used a fourteen-year-old girl as bait for Ilona's sake. He couldn't remember what it had been like to trust him.

Mozare wasn't sure how he had let himself be tricked so thoroughly.

Rhena coughed into his chest, and he worried about the smoke beginning to cloud his vision. He couldn't panic now. Not when she was relying on him to get her to safety. His soldiers wavered, momentarily untethered before he could focus on them again.

He thanked his gods for the trials he'd suffered at Akil's hands, and then almost laughed. His life must've gone to complete shit for him to be thankful for the terrible things the prince had done to him.

But he would relive that torture every day for the rest of his life, to see Rhena safe and healthy and whole again.

She was shivering, but it wasn't cold. Mozare stopped to help, but even wrapping her in his jacket did little to stave off the chill.

Once they were outside the palace, away from immediate danger, he was finally able to send his soldiers back to their resting place. Only then did he realize Rhena's cold wasn't related to the temperature.

Elemental powers were tied to emotion, and hers had to be out of control right now. Until she got help, she'd never be warm again.

Mozare slammed into the room a little too carelessly considering he knew Cassimir was waiting on the other side expecting danger. He ducked in time to keep them from being impaled by the dagger Cassimir launched from his hand.

He couldn't tell if the siblings were swearing or praying when they started talking in their mother tongue. He was still so unused to hearing it, especially now that he understood how revered the language was to its people.

"What happened?" Cassimir finally asked, switching back to the language of the middle kingdom. "Where are Saiden and Loralei?" Mozare knew the panic on Cassimir's face was likely mirrored on his own. Mozare had secretly been hoping they would defy the odds and make it back here before him.

To make matters worse, he suddenly realized that leaving both of them to fight meant they didn't have a healer.

Their host started to clear off the table, giving Mozare enough space to gently lay Rhena on top of it. "I'll get supplies." Eleni said, already halfway across the apartment digging through their small stockpile of medicinal herbs. She was Rhena's best chance at the moment, but Mozare was not feeling hopeful.

They couldn't begin to understand the full depth of what Revon might have done to Rhena. And he remembered what she'd told them of another gifted boy, the one whose skin Revon had removed piece by piece.

He was not heartless enough to be grateful, but he was somewhat relieved that Rhena seemed to have escaped such a brutal punishment.

"The two of you need to leave. Everyone else needs to leave." Eleni said, returning so she could kneel by Rhena and dab her forehead with a rough cloth. "Let's not make things more difficult by crowding the room."

Mozare could see Eleni fingers tremble a little and wondered if she was nervous. If she needed them to leave to help Rhena he would, but that didn't mean he had to like it.

Cassimir clasped him on the back, and in silence the two of them marched from the house. He didn't need to ask where they would wait, Cassimir simply took the lead, showing Mozare a hidden path up to the roof. Together they waited, although he was unsure what news they needed to hear first.

All he knew was that he wouldn't sleep until he heard something.

39
LORALEI

LORALEI MAY HAVE HAD A SWORD, BUT SHE'D HAD HER POWERS FOR FAR longer, and she was not afraid of people knowing anymore. She was especially fond of the fear in Revon's soldier's eyes as her vines pulled them back against the walls, clearing the hallway for her and tightening against any who tried to free themselves.

This is what it meant to be powerful. She didn't need her crown, her advisors, or the love of her people. She only needed her friends and her power. And this was how she was going to save Saiden.

She knew that leaving Saiden behind would probably get her killed, so as soon as she saw that Mozare would make it out with the girl, she'd been ready to turn back. Even if that meant coming face to face with the man that haunted all her nightmares.

Saiden had fought through worse, and if she could do it, then Loralei could at least try.

She didn't have to touch the doors to open them. She simply remembered the way the gifted had barged into her room when they were attempting to kidnap a scared queen, and did the same.

Except she wasn't the scared queen anymore. When she opened the door, she swung her sword towards the first soldier who dared to approach her, taking in the layers of fighters surrounding Saiden in the middle of the room.

Amidst all the bloodshed, Saiden's hair was no longer recognizable. But Loralei didn't need the marker to see her in the crowd. Bodies fell around her in a macabre dance, leaving Saiden in a channel of corpses.

Another hurricane, tinted by blood.

Loralei did not hesitate to fight through the men. Anyone with the audacity to attack Saiden, now fully endowed with power by their gods was a foolish mortal indeed. Especially when she knew that Revon had prattled on about the Anointed in his rhetoric against her reign.

It wasn't enough for her to come into her powers. Not if she wasn't going to be a weapon for Revon's cause. Saiden being Anointed meant nothing to him, if that power was not on his side of the war.

These people did not see the ugly truths about their King that she was privy too, but maybe it was time for her to change that.

Ideas burst to life in her mind, but she couldn't let them stay, not when a distraction could cost her a limb. She sent a light beam towards her blade, blinding the man to her right so she could stab the soldier on her left.

She caught the moment that Saiden realized that Loralei had come back for her. Something like relief passed over her face, mixed with fear, and tracks of blood dripping from a wound on her forehead.

Maybe if she'd had more time with her powers she could have healed it on her own, but in the midst of the fight, Saiden seemed to rely only on her legionnaire training, which had never failed her before.

It wasn't going to be enough now. Loralei could already see the way Saiden's strength flagged as she blocked a strike, her return a second too slow to make impact. Loralei tunneled into her own power and hoped that the improvements Akil's torture had given her held up under the stress.

All around her, she grew her vines thorny and tight, building a tunnel that protected her as she charged through the gathering forces. All this effort for one girl, yet Loralei understood why Revon put his soldiers at risk for her.

She might have done the same if their positions were reversed.

When she finally made it through the melee, she did not dare grab Saiden. Not when she could feel the other girl's powers swirling around her without any sign of use. "Saiden it's time to go. You cannot win this fight today. And we will certainly be far worse off if we die here tonight."

She watched as a detached version of Saiden re-sheathed her blades, although she only felt reassured when Saiden finally rested her hand in Loralei's upturned palm.

Loralei did not give her a moment to reconsider, she pulled, knowing Saiden would have no choice but to follow her. She did not care about the men hacking away at her work, not when a few steps could free the two of them from it entirely.

Behind her, she finally felt Saiden's power focus, the shell of it disappearing from around her, and pushing itself against the same walls Loralei was building. *She was fortifying them.* Loralei didn't realize this was something she could do.

Her powers, once they were gone from a plant, could do nothing to protect it from storms, or even another gifted. She had never felt another power building atop her own. She had not thought that kind of collaboration to be possible. It was another thing she would have to think about when their lives weren't in imminent danger.

She wondered if they would ever stop being in constant danger. At the moment things didn't really seem like they were working in their favor. But she would never doubt, until the day she died, that the fighting kept her alive. Gave her purpose.

Even though this had once been her kingdom, Lorelai had no idea where to run. She hadn't been chased through these streets since she was a small child, and the dangers she'd faced back then had been mostly imaginary. Now she ran from the very real threat posed by Revon's men.

In a twist from their normal roles, Saiden ran in front of them, and Loralei wasn't sure how she felt about the legionnaire trusting her to watch their backs. Maybe she was exhausted, or maybe she expected to be charging into the danger. Either way it made Loralei feel like more of an equal, instead of a liability the rest of them were always watching out for.

All the energy in her body was pushing her to go faster, stopping her already exhausted muscles from giving up. Despite her dislike of shoes, she was grateful for the tight-laced boots Alisa had made her borrow. The streets were littered with broken glass and wooden splinters. She was having a hard time understanding how the streets had gotten so bad in a few months.

She didn't like it when she finally realized the direction they were heading. Although even Loralei had to admit that it made sense for them to run towards the cemetery when they needed somewhere to hide. The mismatched stones crowded the lot, giving them ample hiding places.

Saiden crumpled behind the headstones, and Loralei could feel the exhaustion set in when she reached out to her with her own powers. Between the fight, and the way her power had swelled trying to protect her it was no surprise.

Loralei was shocked, however, when Saiden began to speak. "I didn't think I could feel that rage. What it must be like for you to face him, after what he did to you? All I could see was the way he'd cut my mother's throat."

Loralei tried to speak, but her voice was trapped. She hadn't been around when Saiden's mother had been killed, but she mourned the woman all the same. After all, Magdalena was the closest Loralei had gotten to a mother's love as well, even if the love had never been for her.

"She never even got a proper funeral. There's no grave, I don't even know what they did with her body." Saiden whispered

"I know what it's like to be lost completely." She didn't miss the hardness on Saiden's face, but she didn't stop either. "Your mother isn't gone because you still love her. And Cassimir and the other idiot, and even Rhena, they all loved her. And when we get this country back, we can make sure her sacrifice is honored."

Tears traced Saiden's cheeks. "I didn't forget you."

Loralei shouldn't have been shocked, but part of her was. She hadn't expected a single person to mourn for her, even when they'd truly believed her to be dead. Rising, Saiden reached for her hand again, and Loralei was startled by how much warmer Saiden's skin felt against her own.

She didn't try to stop Saiden from taking her wherever they were going. Loralei was past the point where she worried about Saiden wishing her harm. She knew that Saiden had never truly wished her harm in the first place, though it hadn't really registered in her mind until very recently that the betrayal she'd felt had been a lot more complicated.

Loralei did wonder briefly how much time Saiden had spent in the cemetery as she expertly guided them through the mismatched rows of headstones, avoiding cracked graves and littered pieces of broken marble. Like the rest of their city, things in the cemetery were crowded, building over top of each other and encroaching from every angle.

Still Saiden's footsteps didn't falter until she reached a solitary headstone, oddly alone despite the clear lack of space for burials. Then she read the epitaph on the grave and understood exactly why the single grave stood alone.

Our beloved general, fallen before her time. May she rest forever in Ilona's peaceful embrace. It wasn't a grand stone, but they both knew it didn't need to be. Nakti wasn't the kind of person to flaunt her status above others. She'd been proud of the work she did, of the service she'd given to her country.

Loralei grabbed Saiden's hand, squeezing gently. A silent understanding passed between them that she doubted many other people could grasp. She didn't let go when Saiden started moving again, leading her around the corner.

The grass here had overgrown its neighbors outside of the small plot for the general's grave, and Loralei had a hard time understanding why Saiden was kneeling there, and not in front of her adopted mother's burial site.

Her confusion deepened further when Saiden took out the small, bejeweled dagger she'd acquired during their time in the southern kingdom of Taezhali and started cutting through the overgrown grass. Part of Loralei hated to see the plant die, even if most people considered it to be a weed, but the curious part of her far outweighed any outrage she might've felt otherwise.

Eventually, Loralei gave in to her own exhaustion, kneeling next to Saiden and finally seeing the small stone she was cutting the grass away to uncover. It wasn't large enough to be a formal grave marker, yet the sinking feeling in her stomach was telling her that was the exact intention behind it.

"My mother gave this to me, to mark your death." Saiden started, pausing to clear the grief from her throat. "Because I hadn't realized that my grief over Nakti and my guilt for your death had been tied up in each other. There was no healing from one without acknowledging the other. I couldn't let the feeling of pain in because I thought I deserved far worse."

Tears were streaking down Loralei's cheeks again. She was so tired of crying, of grief. But there was something about these tears, shed over the land where her first friend had mourned her, that was healing too. "Sometimes I still think I deserve worse, that all of this is because of me."

She knew Saiden didn't say it to detract from the moment, but to show how deeply she'd truly been affected by the idea that she had failed Loralei.

For once, the queen took a page out of their book, Saiden's and Mozare's, and tried to lighten the situation with humor. "I guess it's a good thing I didn't die then."

Saiden had a funny look on her face as she turned to face Loralei, which made her think she might still need some more practice before she should try joking during a serious moment again. Instead, she drew Saiden into her arms, the blood clinging to both of their skin momentarily forgotten in the reconciliation.

Loralei had already forgiven her, but this felt like a new start. One she was going to fight tooth and nail for.

40
CASSIMIR

CASSIMIR SAT ON THE ROOF NEXT TO MOZARE, THE TWO OF THEM FACING the palace where it rose above the rest of the city. They both stood to lose their love tonight, yet he couldn't have felt further from the other man than he did in that moment. At least when he had been inside, Cassimir and Eleni had been able to sit vigil the way they would have back home.

He didn't know how they prayed in the middle kingdom, and it seemed too late now to try. He wasn't sure he wanted to pray to any power, divine or otherwise, that allowed the kind of pain he had seen on young Rhena's face. He might not be as close to her as the others were, but she was like a sister to both Mozare and Saiden, and he already knew that Saiden's family was his.

Cassimir owed Rhena the same protection he would give Saiden, if only because she wasn't there to protect the young girl herself.

"Saiden gave us time to get her out." Mozare finally spoke, his voice a boom destroying the pretense of peace between them. "She's going to die in there."

Cassimir didn't like the finality he heard in Mozare's voice. Didn't want to hear the words spoken into the universe, or for anyone out there listening to make them true.

"In my kingdom, we have certain customs," he started awkwardly, unsure how to broach the topic. "A certain set of prayers meant to guide the lost home, Eleni and I were working our way through them when you came home, but I was going to continue here on the roof, until our women make it back safely."

Because Cassimir knew they would make it back. Saiden would make it back to him. She'd never break a promise like that, not with him. It was the only thought that kept him on the roof, instead of charging through the streets to rescue her himself.

Without taking his eyes off the tallest spire of the palace, Cassimir knelt, the uneven roof tiles rough against his knees even with pants between the skin and stone. At first, he spoke the words under his breath, his language a foreign sensation on his tongue so far from his homeland. He felt Mozare's hand on his shoulder, before he got down on his knees, and Cassimir reached out to hold his hand.

Mozare might not understand the words, could not speak the prayers himself, but Cassimir felt the enormity of the moment, felt Mozare's will join his in carving a path home for the people they loved. That was all it took, the words weren't important, the language never mattered. It was love that connected all of them, and love that would guide their friends home.

He wasn't sure how long they knelt there, attention torn between the spires of the palace and the streets below them, before he heard the subtle sound of footsteps. His knees burned where the gravel had burrowed its way into the muscle, but the pain was nothing compared to the tightness of his chest with every inhale.

Cassimir ducked low, concealing himself behind the wall, waiting to celebrate their return until he was certain they were the ones who'd made it to the safe house, and not any of the king's men. They couldn't afford for their nerves to give them away, or let their eagerness to be reunited put the others at risk.

A tendril of a vine snaked out from the cluster Loralei had started to cultivate for cover wrapping tightly around his wrist, the touch so similar to Saiden's fingers he could feel tears welling up in his eyes. He looked at Mozare and knew that they had both come to the same conclusion. Words never passed between them, they simply rushed to the rickety ladder, their speed making the risk of it falling from the side even greater than normal.

Neither cared. Cassimir had half a mind to simply jump from the roof top and deal with whatever injuries he may sustain later. But he was too wise to let himself give into the impulse, no matter the strength with which it raged through his system. He didn't know if either of them would be up to healing anyone, and he would never put himself above Rhena if their abilities were weakened. Better not to risk the injury.

Cassimir hurried behind Mozare, neither of them being as cautious as they should have been. When he finally caught sight of the girls, all he could see was the blood that soaked every inch of Saiden's skin. He wished for a touch of her power, the ability to reassure himself that it wasn't her blood, that she wasn't going to die a few steps away from him.

Fate couldn't be so cruel.

They rushed to their loves, pulling them into an embrace between them. Limbs tangled, and he wasn't entirely sure who he was touching, and it didn't matter anyway. The relief that coursed through him at seeing their faces, both of their faces, nearly brought him to his knees right there.

Cassimir let go, tucking a blood hardened lock of Saiden's hair back behind her ear so that he could look into her eyes. They all had their fair share of blood on their hands, but he could see the guilt in her features, the grief caused by so much death. It would take a long time to outlive that grief, but all he was asking for was time. Together they'd figure out the rest of it.

Saiden pressed in close to him again, and he didn't care that she was covered in blood. "I kept my promise." She said, the words a sigh against his chest that he'd almost missed.

He kissed her forehead, the blood flaking from her skin against his lips, a covenant and a sacrifice all in one. A reminder of how easy this life is to lose.

"You did. I never doubted you."

Over her head, he could see Mozare hovering awkwardly near Loralei, unsure how to share his own concerns and relief with her. He hoped they'd find their way back to each other eventually, but it wasn't his place to pry. If any of them were going to meddle in affairs of love, he would leave that to his sister.

Cassimir met Loralei's eye, "you are alright?"

She patted herself down, glossing over the rips in her garments where she'd either been injured or grabbed, and looked back up at him, a smirk hiding deeper feelings. "Seems I've made it out in one piece." He knew there was more under the surface. It was the same complicated cocktail of emotions that this fight brought out for each of them.

Tears streaked paths in the blood and dirt caked on her face, but he didn't bring that up. Cassimir didn't think he was the right person to press that issue either. He would bring it up later when he and Saiden were alone so she could make the decision for herself.

"How's Rhena?" Saiden pushed away from him, already heading for the door to the cottage. He didn't try to answer her, she would see soon enough. Cassimir simply followed after her. He always would.

41
RHENA

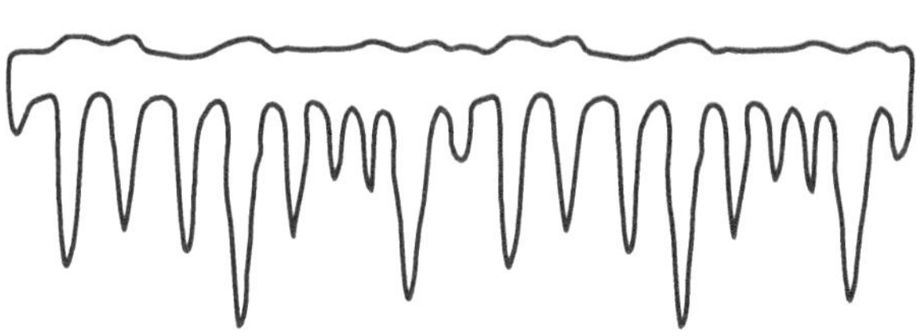

RHENA KNEW THAT HER FRIENDS TRUSTED ELENI, AND FROM WHAT SHE knew of the Taezhali healer, she trusted her as well. But it didn't change the fact that she barely knew her, and that what she wanted most in the world right then was to be sitting with Saiden and Mozare. Preferably while he told them stories and Saiden braided her hair.

There was more to her injuries than what appeared on her skin, and no medicine was going to fix that. She was terrified, and so long as she was terrified, she was also going to be freezing. She had tried the whole way back to the crew's hiding place, wherever that was, to calm the frigid storm of her powers and welcome a brush of warmth back to her body, but she had failed.

The warm cloth Eleni pressed to her forehead felt like a gift from the heavens.

When she pressed two more warm cloths to the insides of Rhena's wrists, she could feel her body begin to register warmth again. The feeling spread through her fingers and up into her chest. It wasn't the same as truly being warm, but it was enough to fight the numbness that had begun to frighten her.

Unfortunately, as the numbness receded, it was replaced by pain. Revon hadn't done nearly as much damage to her as he'd done to

Talon, her family had gotten there before he'd had the chance to use her as an example, but he'd still used his time to remind her of the cost of disloyalty.

Not that Rhena considered herself to be disloyal. She simply wasn't loyal to a broken king. She would never serve a fractured throne.

"I need you to walk me through what happened." Eleni spoke, her voice like a lullaby. "And I need your patience. I need to remove some of your clothes, and that might not be comfortable."

Rhena turned her head enough that she could look Eleni in the eye. This discomfort in her voice made Rhena pause. Something lying underneath her words that Rhena was not clever enough to figure out on her own. She must've given her a funny look, because Eleni opened her mouth as if to explain something, when there was a commotion outside.

"Give me a blade." Despite her injuries, Rhena did her best to sit up. The boys were outside, and if they were already engaged in a fight, she wasn't going to sit there like she couldn't defend herself. And she had no idea if the princess knew how to fight. She might be the only one inside the house capable of defending them, even if her capabilities were questionable in her current state.

Eleni didn't hesitate to hand her a weapon from a pile they must've collected since coming back into the country. No way they could've made it back carrying that much steel. Whatever she heard outside scared them both, but she would not waver.

Saiden was the first through the door, and only the shocking red of her hair kept Rhena from striking out at her. Instead, she dropped the weapon, which sounded louder as it hit the table and then the floor than it probably was. Saiden didn't give her time to get up from the table, not that she thought she would be able to. She could already feel her strength dying, now that she realized they weren't in any immediate danger.

Sure, bad things waited for them outside these walls, but for now, they were all together, and they were all safe. She couldn't really ask for more.

What did shock her, was the fact that Saiden was crying. Rhena had never seen her older sister cry, and she wasn't quite sure what to do.

"I'm so sorry little Maus." Rhena ignored the pain that came from Saiden wrapping her up in her arms. "I never should've let this happen to you."

Rhena wasn't sure how she was supposed to answer that. She knew, as she was sure the rest of their friends knew, that it wasn't Saiden's fault. But Saiden still felt guilty.

Thankfully, she was spared from trying to piece together a response when Loralei and Mozare stepped into the room, crowding the already small kitchenette. "Why don't you let me help with those injuries Saiden." The queen did a good job of sounding both firm and kind, though Rhena supposed she shouldn't really think of her as the queen anymore.

Saiden only backed off when Mozare stepped behind her, pulling his partner into his arms instead. The look on big brother's face was very out of character, and Rhena wasn't the only one feeling a little lost in it all.

Loralei replaced Saiden, perching gently at the edge of the table as if she were a bird, ready at any moment to fly away from them all. Then she offered Rhena a hand. It wasn't anything special, but Rhena could feel power brewing under her skin.

Relief flooded Rhena when she touched a finger to Loralei's hand, her power searching through Rhena's body looking for injuries to heal. The skin she could see through the rips in her clothing started to knit itself back together. Rhena's mind occupied itself wondering if this was what it looked like when the healers regrew Talon's skin.

"You're very good at this." Rhena said, and then stopped herself from saying anything more.

"Considering I shouldn't have these powers at all, they do tend to come in handy." At first, Rhena thought the older girl was mocking her, but when she finally met her gaze, Loralei winked, and Rhena knew she was forgiven.

Not that she was quite sure what she needed to be forgiven for. The feeling was welcome all the same. The lady of the house, Rhena still hadn't been formally introduced, handed them all wet rags, giving Saiden two, so they could start scrubbing the blood from their skin. Rhena hoped for a shower, but she'd never lived in the city, and she didn't know if the house could manage the water needed for that.

Saiden wiped a swath of blood away from her eyes, and it finally clicked how much blood was covering Saiden's skin.

"How did you make it out of there?" She asked, her voice a mix of incredulity tinged with the smallest bit of fear. Not of Saiden, never of Saiden. Simply of the darkness that was required from all of them to survive these days.

Saiden gave her a weak smile. "I think that is a story for another day little Maus. It is time for all of us to rest." It took the words leaving Saiden's mouth for Rhena to finally realize how they all slumped against whatever furniture they could lean on, careful not to get blood anywhere it might stain.

"You're right, of course."

"I set up another bed roll in the room where you're staying." The lady of the house interjected again, worn hands holding a thread-bare knit shawl tightly around her shoulders. "It's going to be a tight fit, but it's the best we can manage."

Saiden went to reach out to the woman, and then thought better of it. "Thank you Alisa. We are indebted to you."

"There's water outside to get properly clean, and then it's off to bed with all of you." She didn't think the lady—Alisa—was much older than her friends, but Rhena didn't miss the motherly tone to her voice. By the tears gathering at the corner of Saiden's eyes, Rhena doubted she had missed it either.

Cassimir stepped towards Saiden, letting her lean her back against him to rest her weight. "Thank you. We'll do our best not to disturb you again tonight."

Their host spoke one last time, foot perched on the bottom of what looked like a rickety staircase. "I think peace in our land is worth a little lost sleep. If this is what I can contribute, I do it gladly."

42
SAIDEN

SAIDEN NEEDED ANSWERS, AND SHE WAS PREPARED TO GO STRAIGHT TO THE source. A few days had passed since they had rescued Rhena, and Saiden was feeling restless. After the gods had spent so long barging into her life whenever they felt like it, she figured it wouldn't matter if she went to a temple to gain access to them. With her friends guarding her back, she knelt in the middle of a dark alleyway, rested both of her hands palm up on her lap and waited.

They took their time, she didn't know if they had other things to do with their existences or not, but she felt they were making her wait as a power play more than anything else. They knew she finally wanted to speak to them, but they weren't going to let her summon them at will.

But Saiden was patient. She had time, and she wanted these answers enough to stay here until they came to her.

Her assumptions were proven correct when they finally appeared, summoning her back to the deck of a ship, anger on both of their immortal faces. "You think you have a right to summon us?" Keir asked, deceptively calm. The fact that he was asking instead of Ilona, who was normally the hotter headed of the two, was not a good sign. Not when he sounded angry himself.

"I need answers. You are letting the kingdom you are supposed to protect go to ruin. Why?"

"What do you expect us to do, child?" Ilona finally asked, but her voice was no longer calm. It was low and so quiet Saiden almost hadn't heard her. She was an explosion bubbling up. Saiden knew she should've been more careful, with everything they'd forced her to live through recently, but she was perhaps being a little hot headed as well. She wanted to know she was heading in the right direction. She needed a way out of this that kept her friends safe.

Their fight with Revon was far too close a call for her comfort.

And if there was anyone who could give her concrete answers it should be the god and goddess who ruled the realm. They had deigned to call themselves protectors of the land, and she was there to demand they live up to it.

"Protect them. You sit up here separate from those you call children, and yet you claim the land as your own. The people who've sworn their allegiance to you die in this brutality but you don't lift a finger to help them."

"We don't lift a finger to help them?" Ilona asked, pushing against Keir as he reached to restrain her slightly. "What do you think our gifts are for? What do you think you are for?"

Saiden didn't have an answer for that right away, but she didn't think they were going to give her time. "There is a war going on."

"Since the beginning of man there has been war going on." Keir answered. "Do you think we do not get prayers from fighters on both sides? How should we satisfy you all?"

"Or do you simply get to choose for us, because you love your friends so much? You do nothing with the gifts we've given you, and then you complain." Ilona added.

"You've given me a curse. This is too much power."

"It is not. You haven't burned through it." Keir argued. "You would have died if it were too much." His answer was far too simple. It lacked human nuance. They could watch the humans all they liked, but they were still too different to truly understand them.

"What am I for then?" She turned Ilona's question back at them.

The question that had never left the back of her mind. Why did so many people die, for a chance that she would live?

Ilona didn't answer her straightforwardly, but turned it around and asked Saiden another question. "You see how we surround you with strength. Why else would we do that if not to see you crowned?"

Crowned. They wanted her to be queen, like the Anointed of old? She wasn't made to be a queen. "Maybe because I was the only one of your freaks to survive infancy. What about Loralei—she was your queen chosen?"

"The chosen monarch was never a tradition rooted in our magic." Keir answered. Ilona had taken to pacing about the deck after Saiden's blunt answer. Perhaps she didn't like thinking about all the babies that had been killed because of their foolish mission to continue making Anointed children.

"What do you mean?" She tried to keep her attitude out of it this time.

"Just because a human claims they are invoking our will, doesn't mean they actually are. Especially when it involves that much pomp and circumstance." Keir spoke, but Ilona stood right behind him, nodding her head.

"I should be queen because *you* chose me?" They both nodded. "You gave me this gift before you even knew what kind of person I would be."

"It is a risk." Ilona admitted, "although we do have some control."

"You have control over my life, but can't help me?" She was furious, her rage roiling the sea around them. She'd never felt this kind of power in an interaction with them before. She'd certainly never affected her surroundings this much.

"It's all about balance."

"I could've ruined your kingdom as queen. You chose me as a baby!" Saiden didn't understand how they couldn't see how reckless their choices were.

"We knew exactly what kind of queen you'd be. Before those non-believers interfered with our gifts." Keir spat at her. This was dangerous territory now.

"In fact," Ilona started, pulling her hand through the air. Keir didn't try to stop her this time. "We'll show you."

Distantly, Saiden felt her body slump against the ground.

INTERLUDE

Saiden woke as the curtains in her room were pulled open, light shining over her still resting body. She saw her hands first, skin unmarred by tattoos or scars. She did not want to do this again, to live another life that was not hers because the goddess thought she had some lesson to learn.

At least this time she understood she was partially responsible for getting herself into this mess. Too quickly she settled into this life and forgot the one she was leaving behind.

Her lady's maids swarmed into the room, each of them carrying a different garment for her to wear. This was an important part of her daily routine. How could she have forgotten? Behind them all came her mother, and she didn't really understand the feeling welling up inside her that made her want to cry.

"Good morning my little Maus." Saiden sat up fully, the silky fabric of her nightgown sliding against her skin. "I think, for today you should wear this one." Her mother chose for her, and Saiden had never been more grateful for how well her mother could read her. She must've understood that Saiden was feeling off this morning, and Saiden was so lucky she was there to help her fill in the gaps.

She stood, and two of her attendants rushed to her side, as if this was unusual. She'd climbed out of her own bed before. "Do not worry so much." She said, "I can manage this much without getting myself hurt."

Both ladies curtsied. "We know your majesty." They said in unison, before one began to speak on her own. They'd called her your majesty, but it felt strange hearing those words, instead of being the one saying them; but that didn't make sense. "After everything with the rebels, we've been so worried about you."

Saiden was lucky because she knew that they truly cared for her. They considered her feelings and well-being as more than the figure-head of her country.

Her mother spoke when Saiden couldn't. "Her majesty appreciates your concern. Would you go gather some breakfast? I can help her into her gown. And I will call if we need any assistance." Her mother smiled at them. She treated all of Saiden's staff as if they were her own children. Ever since they'd lost her father, she knew her mother had relied on having something to do to keep herself going.

The dress her mother had chosen for her was stunning, although she had the luck of being able to say that most days. This one was a smooth black fabric that bled into red the same shade of her hair at the hem. It would suit her quite well, although she had no doubts the dress her mother had chosen for her would.

They were quiet as her mother helped her get the dress on, the straps wrapping the bodice hugging the softness of her curves. This wasn't a warrior's body; she had people that fought for her. She fought for them on the political side, by making alliances with neighboring countries, and planning for the future of her people.

She was surprised to see how long her hair was when she finally sat down in front of her vanity. Although she really shouldn't have been, it wasn't any longer than it had been the day before. And it was as red as the day she'd been born.

Her mother helped braid the top of it leaving most of her hair free to flow and mix into the fabric of her dress' bodice. "There are suitors lining the hallways already." Her mother spoke, breaking the silence. "I suggest, in light of today's executions, you choose to dismiss them."

Saiden listened to her mother on the rare occasion she gave her advice on matters of the court. She might be Anointed, but her mother was still older and wiser. She would dismiss her suitors. If they were unwilling to be courteous then she didn't want them attempting to win her. Not when she had executions to oversee.

Wait. *Executions.* She didn't remember why she had executions to oversee today.

"It's okay love, it's okay to forget. You've been through quite a lot." Her mother continued to run her fingers through Saiden's hair, more to soothe than to style, since she was already done with her braids. "With the rebel attacks it's no surprise you're going into shock. It's a lot to ask you to take on. But it's important that your people see that you are strong and well. They need to feel secure in your position. Then you can rest."

She nodded at her mother in the mirror and then smiled when she pressed a kiss to her cheek. This slow morning had been exactly what she needed.

After breakfast, Saiden did as her mother had suggested and dismissed her suitors so that she was walking down the hallway with only her general at her side. Nakti was a wise woman, and she was glad to have her as a leader of the Kaizian military.

Nakti guided her to the hall, pausing at the bottom of the stairs to her dais so she could take up her post. Saiden had enough power that she didn't really need the defense, but it felt like it looked more appropriate, so she'd never sent the general away. Let the people who meant her harm underestimate her own ability to defend herself.

Her guards brought in the two prisoners, roughly depositing them on the stone floor in front of her. Even Saiden flinched slightly at the sound of them making contact with the stone.

Words rose to her mouth without much thought. "You have been accused of treason, and of operating within a rebellion that intends to do harm to the kingdom of Kaizia." She introduced the trial. "How do you plead?"

Both prisoners looked up from the floor at the same time, and the sight of their faces made Saiden freeze. She knew those faces, but she couldn't place where she had seen them before. The boy was dirty, but his eyes were clear, his black hair shaggy and hanging in his face. The girl beside him was surprisingly clean, considering their stay in the dungeons. There was a smile on her face despite Saiden's accusations. She saw a memory of that smile somewhere else, after she'd heard a joke she didn't want to laugh at.

"Who are you?" She asked without meaning to. The others gathered to witness the trial stared at her. It was completely out of the norm for her to disrupt the proceedings of a trial, but she couldn't go on without getting an answer.

"We're traitors." The boy said. She knew that voice. She had spent years listening to it, she was sure of it. "Isn't that what you've said your majesty?" She could feel her powers rising in response to the drawl of his words, and she didn't want to stop them. Maybe this was some trick, and her body was trying to warn her. The gods, protecting their Anointed child.

She didn't trust it though.

The girl hadn't stopped smiling. She stared at Saiden with unrelenting confidence, despite the fact that she was kneeling in front of her, hands and feet chained together by white cuffs. *She remembered wearing cuffs just like them once,* she thought, though hers hadn't been entirely white. Then she saw the black cuffs on the boy's wrists and the feeling of certainty hit her even harder. She tried to call on her powers, they didn't belong in chains, but nothing came to her.

Saiden wasn't able to reach the power inside her, no matter how she tugged on the cords of it. It wouldn't come to her.

Executioners came forward, mistaking her rising as a sign to proceed. As they lifted their weapons, Saiden tried again, calling every drop of power she knew lived inside her.

But in this version of her life, she failed. And she was forced to watch as Mozare and Loralei's heads hit the floor.

43
MOZARE

MOZARE WAS BARELY FAST ENOUGH TO CATCH SAIDEN BEFORE HER HEAD hit the ground, and only because his powers rose inside him in response to the goddess's rising anger. Whatever Saiden had done in the world she met them in, he didn't think it had gone the way she had planned. He didn't think she would've gone into the world, especially in some back alley, if she knew it would end with her being knocked unconscious.

Not that any of them could really plan anything when it came to their deities these days. They were fickle beings, and trying to force them into anything was more likely to backfire than get them anywhere.

He let Cassimir take over holding her, as a silent agreement went on between them that they needed to get her back to the safe house where they weren't so vulnerable. Cassimir carried her fairly effortlessly, despite Mozare knowing how heavy she was strapped with all her extra weapons.

They were all carrying more steel than they used to, but that was the world they lived in right now. Because he had given the throne of their kingdom to a mad man, wrapped in a bow. He'd never outlive his guilt if something happened to any of them because of it.

That was what he had to live with now, the certainty that this hardship was his fault. He scoped out the path in front of him, doing his best to keep himself from sinking so far into his mind that he conjured his shadows, locking them all in a storm of his own anxiety.

Being trapped in the dark wouldn't help them get Saiden home.

He focused on her wishing he had the ability Loralei did to sense her heartbeat. Then he could keep a monitor her even as Cassimir carried her, but he didn't have any power to rely on here. All he had was his wit and his blade, and his brain wasn't the sharpest of the two.

Loralei was leaning against a building around the corner from the house where they were staying, trying to look casual as she kept an eye on the comings and goings of a town she used to rule. He didn't think she looked as discreet as she probably did, but he was inherently biased. He would notice her anywhere, in any crowd or any life.

She was too bright for this dark world.

When she saw them, she sighed. "What happened to her this time?" A few months ago he might've been offended by her casual tone when his best friend was injured, but he knew she was as worried about Saiden as he was, she just showed it differently.

They didn't stop long enough to let Loralei search Saiden over, since they were still vulnerable. She simply walked beside Cassimir, one hand hovering over Saiden's prone body and the other over the weapon strapped to her hip.

Loralei knew exactly how dangerous her city could be. He remembered the way Saiden had mourned when Loralei had killed the men who'd attacked them, but if he was honest with himself, he thought she'd made the right choice. In her place, he probably would have done the same.

That was part of healing, he'd realized. Noticing how much they were alike, how their brains worked so similarly. If he'd been king, would she have risen against him? He'd never know, but he doubted he'd ever stop asking himself that question.

Mozare, Cassimir, and Loralei finally made it back to the house, though as Mozare held the door open for him, Cassimir refused to bring Saiden inside.

When she noticed no one followed her, Loralei poked her head back out of the doorway, "What is it?"

"Look at her fingers." Cassimir said, adjusting her in his arms so that they could get a better look at her hand. Wrapped between her fingers, shadows danced, the same as Mozare's own. But where his were completely black, Saiden had Keir's light braided through hers.

If she hadn't been unconscious, it would've been a beautiful sight. But the fact that her body was calling on her gifts when she wasn't even awake was terrifying. He'd never heard of something like that being possible, but they already knew that Saiden was capable of things no one else had ever done.

And that meant this was dangerous. Without Saiden's morals, without conscious judgement, Saiden's powers could do a lot of harm. And they were surrounded by innocents. He couldn't let her harm anyone else when he knew that guilt would plague her when she woke. Because she was going to wake up from this, even if he had to fight the goddess herself.

They took Saiden up to the roof. Cassimir went first, Mozare behind him, prepared to catch them both if Saiden's powers really ramped up. And Loralei was behind him. He wished he could get a glimpse inside her head and see if she was panicking the same way he was.

He didn't know if her training as queen helped her remain impassive, or if she knew how to get them out of this, but he was jealous of how calm she remained.

Loralei grabbed his wrist once Cassimir was settled on the roof, pulling Mozare back down a few steps so they could watch Cassimir with Saiden but not be spied on as they spoke. "What happened? I thought this had stopped happening."

What was he supposed to say. "Saiden decided she wanted answers, so she sought them out." He didn't dare speak their names out loud, not when he could already feel their presence bearing down on them.

"Why the hell would she do that? You'd think she liked this." Loralei huffed. He had to admit he was glad to see that she was shaken too. He should've talked Saiden out of going to them after how cruel the gods had been to her recently. But he didn't want to go against her.

He hadn't been a good partner to her the last time he'd gone against her and look where that had landed them. This whole time he'd been trying to make it up to her, and he still failed.

"It's time for one of you to fix this," Cassimir said, pulling at his hair. Mozare couldn't even begin to imagine how frustrating it must be to constantly feel like there was nothing he could do to help. At least Mozare had his power to fall back on when Saiden was pulled into these nightmares by their gods.

And Loralei, of course she was the most capable of helping, with her healing ability. Mozare looked to her, but he could see the frustration at the corner of her eyes, the weight of constantly needing to figure out how to fix her.

Saiden's powers continued to grow, and he worried about the damage she must've been doing to their hideout, especially when so many of the house pressed in on theirs. Eleni finally joined them, the clamor on the roof growing loud enough to get her attention.

She knelt next to Saiden on the bed of vines her powers were growing in her unconscious state, tucking pieces of her hair behind her head. Every single one of them watched her, waiting to be given a task or some kind of instruction on what they should do if they wanted to help her. Because they wanted to help, they just didn't know how.

"Listen to me sister. We did not come back here so that some divine power could take you from us. There is a world we are fighting for, and you are going to see it come about." The words were so soft, they were almost carried away on the wind. But he saw the way Saiden seemed to react to them. Her powers still ran rampant, but vines had slowed their rapid growth.

Rhena came up last, and Mozare was grateful when Cassimir grabbed her, keeping her from getting too close to the swell of Saiden's power. It was already too strong. He could feel time slipping away from them. If they didn't do something soon to get Saiden back he feared she'd slip into her gifts completely, returning to the haze she'd been in when they'd left Kaizia.

"This is overwhelming her." Eleni said, and although it felt obvious, there was also something relieving about having someone else speak the words spiraling in his thoughts out loud. Identifying the problem had to be the first step towards fixing it.

"What do we do?" He asked. They shouldn't have been looking to her, but Mozare didn't miss the fact that they all turned to Eleni as he asked his question.

"Everything is about balance. Without somewhere for all this excess power to go, she keeps channeling it back into herself. She needs somewhere to put it." The words were simple, but it was hard to imagine a way to do what Eleni was saying. They were way out of their depths here.

He looked up, but prayers were lost on him. Mozare would never ask his goddess to interfere when she was the reason Saiden was suffering in the first place. That was how he finally caught Loralei's eye, an idea blooming to life between them.

"We're the vessels." He said, and Loralei's expression stayed stone. She didn't flinch, didn't shy away from what he was saying.

"We have to be. Who else could it be?" She asked, resignation lacing her words. Mozare remembered that day in Eleni's gardens where the two of them had held on to her, and Saiden had finally tapped in to her powers. This had to be the same.

He couldn't let them fail her.

Loralei stretched a hand towards him. "Together?"

Mozare didn't speak, placing his hand in hers as his answer. Together, they stepped in front of Saiden, passing through the dome of her gifts as they grew around them.

They knelt in sync, neither letting go of the other's hand. Mozare took a deep breath, and then together with his love, grabbed one of Saiden's shoulders. He felt the second her magic began to funnel into him, the invigorating feeling of being connected to the whole world without ever leaving the roof.

Loralei was glowing, and he did his best to wrap their rooftop in his shadows so their light show didn't alert the palace. It was more difficult than he'd like to admit, taming the maelstrom of his gifts laced with the strength of Saiden's overloading magic racing through him, but he managed it. He wouldn't fail them.

The well inside him overflowed with Ilona's gifts, but he held on because he could see Saiden's powers pulling back into herself. Could feel Loralei's hand tighten in his as the flood slowed to a trickle.

Mozare couldn't tell if he was faint or electrified when Saiden fell out of his grasp. Eleni caught Saiden's head in her lap, a sprawl of red hair spreading out like blood. Loralei fell into him, and he relished the contact, even as he felt guilty about taking something he didn't think she wanted to give him.

Saiden spasmed, and he couldn't tell what was happening now. Her power didn't spark, he couldn't see anything wrong with her. Didn't think either of them could handle any more of her gift.

Thankfully she settled again, but unrest still roiled under her skin. And because it was under her skin, it was under Mozare's as well.

"Fight for us." He said selfishly. "Fight, because we aren't ready to be without you. Because we are not prepared to grieve for you." Tears laced his words, but here amongst his family he didn't care about weakness. He cared about Saiden.

He saw her lips move, but could barely hear the sound of the words as she spoke. "I'm not going anywhere you idiot."

44

LORALEI

LORALEI WATCHED CASSIMIR TAKE SAIDEN FROM HIS SISTER AND FELT THE tension melt into palpable relief on the rooftop as she spoke the one sentence before curling into Cassimir's chest and going to sleep. It was very different from the oblivion she'd been pulled into by the gods. As Saiden slipped away, her heartbeat finally settled, and Loralei could feel the moment her powers finally calmed again.

"That was reckless." She said, cutting through the relief her friends were feeling. Someone had to talk about it. They were going into war, they couldn't afford to lose the only one of them who might have a chance at actually stopping the devastation plaguing their country.

The excess of Saiden's power roiled under her skin, pushing her rage even further. They couldn't keep doing this to each other and to their kingdom.

It was time to put other people first. They couldn't impulsively think about themselves. They were six people with the fate of an entire nation in their hands. There was no time for impulsive decisions that prioritized their own rage or desire for justice.

Her people deserved to be free first.

Loralei couldn't be the only one who thought that way. Not when she was the only party innocent of bringing this regime about. Well, her and Eleni, who'd still been in Taezhali when the rebellion had taken over her throne.

Maybe she was angry too.

She let go of Mozare's hand, pulling back into herself, reconstructing the walls she'd let down in order to help Saiden.

The look on Mozare's face wasn't too far from anger either, but she doubted it was because they were of the same mind. They never seemed to manage to be on the same side anymore, even though she had once thought they would die for each other.

Maybe fate would still give them the chance.

"It was reckless, but that doesn't mean she was wrong." He said, gritting his teeth through the words. She couldn't tell if it was because he was trying to keep the words in, or because there was more that he didn't want to say.

"How do we win this fight without her?" She asked him, her anger poisoning every word. She put her arms out wide, trying to stretch her fingertips to every corner of her country. "How do we save them without her?"

Loralei was yelling, even though they needed to stay unnoticed. Despite the eyes that were watching, bouncing back and forth between the two of them. She knew they had an audience, but not even that knowledge could stop her from raging.

She had been angry for far too long, had kept it all buried inside her, letting it fester. "We can't afford to lose her. The rest of us, we don't matter. She is the only one that can win this war. Saiden. No one else. The only reason the gods had given her these powers is to fight his depravity." She didn't need to say his name for them to know who she was talking about.

"She can't win this if she has to sacrifice everything that's important to her. It's not winning if she loses herself." Mozare didn't yell, which made it feel so much worse. His anger seethed, a slow burning you couldn't feel until it was too late.

Hadn't Loralei given herself up for this fight? For the kingdom? Why couldn't she expect that the rest of them would have to make sacrifices too? It wasn't fair. She'd given up everything she'd ever been as a child.

Had she ever found herself again?

Maybe it wasn't fair for her to expect others to be ready to make the same sacrifices that came second nature to her. But it didn't feel fair to her people either, that they suffered because of choices a few soldiers made for them.

There was no reality where she could balance the two.

"We're probably going to die. The world will survive our loss, but not her's." Her voice was quiet this time, defeated. The same voice that had spoken to Rami when she thought she would lose Mozare to the emperor's justice.

She rose and left the others to their rejoicing, tainted now by the anger that still festered inside her. Loralei couldn't be happy with the rest of them, so she'd take herself out of the equation until she could board the anger back up inside her and hide behind her mask again.

For a minute she thought no one would follow her, tucking through the hidden streets of a town she knew by heart. She loved this town and its people, and every broken thing in between.

"How can I live in a world where you don't?" Loralei jumped when she heard Mozare's voice behind her, shocked and annoyed in equal measure that she hadn't heard him coming up behind her.

"You expected me to do the same." Her voice was hollow now, and somehow that felt like an improvement to being so angry. Because she'd rather feel nothing, than be a creature consumed by rage. "This world doesn't need me."

"I need you."

"And I should care about that why?" The words were cruel, the taste of them bitter in her own mouth. She knew that she was trying to hurt him at this point, even though no amount of pain she could inflict on him would fix what she was feeling inside.

Loralei wouldn't turn her head, couldn't force herself to look at him. She didn't need to anyway, she already knew exactly what she would see on his face. The disappointment…the sadness. She couldn't bear the weight of anyone else's grief. Not when she was already drowning in her own.

Thankfully, or maybe not so thankfully, Eleni saved her from having to continue the conversation. "You both need to come back up here."

Panic sat heavy in her chest, but she didn't hear it in her voice, so it couldn't be something about Saiden. Eleni cared too much about her to be that cavalier if she were in any kind of danger.

Loralei climbed the ladder back up to the roof, Saiden's hastily grown vines already wilting around the perimeter. She could feel Mozare's warmth as he crowded the ladder behind her, despite the fact it could barely support the weight of one person.

It was a reminder that their conversation wasn't done, and she hated that.

Saiden was still curled up in Cassimir's lap, but Eleni was standing at the edge of the roof, eye on the horizon, tension in her posture once more. Rhena stood next to her, and even though Loralei wasn't blessed by the goddess, she could feel the spark of Ilona's power and the cold chill in the air.

"What is it?" Mozare asked, climbing over the roof behind her, far too close. She couldn't think with him so close to her.

"Something seems to be on fire." Eleni said, arm lifted to loosely point in the distance.

From the corner of her eye, Loralei saw Cassimir shake Saiden awake again, her rest denied because there were bigger concerns looming over them once again. Mozare joined the others at the edge of the roof, but Loralei couldn't move. Her feet were frozen to the ground, so stuck she might have been able to convince a non-gifted that she had the goddess's gift of ice like Rhena.

"What's even in that direction?" Mozare asked.

This time the void of her voice was born of pure fear. "The orphanage."

45
MOZARE

MOZARE DIDN'T KNOW WHAT ORPHANAGE LORALEI WAS TALKING ABOUT, and he was relieved Saiden asked her first. "What do you mean?" They kept looking between the fire in the distance and Loralei's face, now a few shades paler than it had been.

"Do either of you know what happened to Cara's siblings?" Mozare had known the children, in the time when he'd served beside Cara in the rebellion. Had taken care of them on occasion, when Cara had been serving as their insider in the palace, staying close to Loralei.

Saiden and Mozare stared at each other. To be honest, after the way everything had worked out, he'd hadn't really thought about them again. Saiden hadn't even really known them, so she had no reason to consider the children, but Mozare should've been better.

"How do you know the orphanage is where the fire is?"

"What better way to get back at us then burning it down and blaming us?" Loralei asked them, but he knew the question wasn't meant to be answered. "What better way to turn people against us, to encourage them not to fight, than if they think we burn children in their beds?"

Mozare felt panic creeping in, but his path here was clear. They could stop this if they were fast enough. He moved towards the ladder, and Saiden tried to follow, but Cassimir had to catch her when she swayed and almost fell back over.

"Sai, this one isn't your fight." He said, leaving no room for argument. He hoped his efforts to fix things gave him the right to make those decisions again. "We'll make this right."

Saiden must have realized she'd be more of a hindrance than a help, because she sat back down without a fight, but pointed over to Cassimir. "Take him then, get any injured children to the healing tents and Eleni, Rhena and I will make our way over there."

He knocked their foreheads together briefly, then he and Loralei raced over the edge of the roof, a vine extending behind her so they could slide their way down. They weren't far enough from the ground to be in serious danger, but they also didn't have time to waste on their own injuries. He heard Cassimir behind them, but didn't turn around.

They didn't have time to be slow. They navigated through the alleyways, each of them pushing themselves as far and as fast as they could go. He didn't know where they were going, he wasn't even aware there was an orphanage near the capital, but he trusted Loralei. As they neared the fire, he could smell it, and even though it was nighttime he could see smoke in the air.

"There are children over there." Cassimir pointed out, and Mozare finally noticed the small group of children huddled by the edge of the forest.

They stopped long enough for Mozare to take control of the situation. "Can you get them to your sister? Make sure you really think about it." He didn't want Cassimir in this alone if he didn't think he could handle it. Cassimir looked at Mozare and then at the children.

"I can take them. Go help get anyone else out." He clapped Mozare on the shoulder and turned towards the children in the woods. Mozare knew if anyone could calm them and get them to safety it would be Cassimir. He had a comforting way about him.

Mozare and Loralei continued running. They had no choice if they were going to make it in time to make a difference.

They got to the orphanage, and the smell of burning overcame him. It consumed every one of his senses, his eyes watering as he tried to lift his shirt to cover his mouth and nose. Loralei bent over, tearing the hem from her skirt and giving him a piece to tie around his face. "I need you to trust me…" she started, and he wasn't sure if she was out of breath from running or from nerves. Surely, she could heal any strain as it came?

He could still feel Saiden's burn off coursing through him; there was no way that Loralei couldn't feel it too. His instincts were telling him he was going to need it.

"I need to go in, I can feel for their heartbeats. And I need you to stay out here so the children I free have someone to protect them. I'm trusting you to be here for them. We don't know if whoever did this is still out here, waiting to finish the job. We can't put these children's lives at risk because of our actions. This is where our choices matter."

He remembered their conversation in Taezhali. *Choice is the thing that makes us into monsters.* His choice here was easy. "I trust you." And he did. What she was saying made sense, it was the decision of someone used to delegating. To ruling. He could finally see how a crown would have suited her.

Loralei looked surprised at this answer, but she didn't hesitate, tying what was left of her skirt at her waist so it wouldn't trip her up, calling the gods light to her fingers and heading into the fire. His panic rose, but he knew she could do this. When Loralei put her mind to something not even their gods could stop her.

Besides, she'd already defied death once.

After inspecting the area and picking somewhere safe to lead the children, Mozare finally saw the first of them running out to him. He should've done something more with the time he'd been waiting, but fear had paralyzed him.

He checked them over for injuries as best as he could, despite being death-gifted, all legionnaires were still required to learn basic field care in case of injury. He had started carrying some first aid supplies so he didn't have to rely solely on Loralei's healing. He put them to use, wrapping what he could with the bandages he had, ripping up his shirt to use when he ran out of those.

It wasn't his best plan, but doing something with his hands kept him from running in after Loralei. As the stream of children started to slow, the older children helping to carry the smaller ones, he had to fight more and more to stop himself from going in after her.

No one came to attack them, which was probably the only good thing going for them. Despite that, he was still on such high alert that he nearly reopened Cassimir's stomach when he returned, but was happy to let him escort the next group of children back to Eleni's healing tent.

Mozare continued to wait. A little girl came out crying in the arms of a boy who was probably getting close to being too old for this place. He went to Mozare, "She said she'll be out to you soon." The boy said, coughing as he tried to speak. Mozare reached out to him, taking the young girl from his arms.

The boy was bleeding and Mozare was out of bandages now. The wound in his arm looked deep, with one hand pressing the girl to his chest, he stripped off his belt, letting his weapons and other tools fall to the ground. He needed to stop the bleeding enough to give Loralei time. Then hopefully she'd have enough power left to heal him before he passed out.

He didn't know what to do with a child, but as the boy sat, Mozare rocked her in his arms, and exhaustion seemed to pull her under. He couldn't let the boy to sleep though. Sleep was bad for anyone in his condition, Mozare understood that much.

"What's your name?" Mozare asked. He needed conversation to keep him awake, and Mozare could provide that. The distraction wouldn't harm him either. He appreciated the message Loralei had sent through the boy, but it didn't do much to assuage his worry.

"I'm Simon." He hissed, and Mozare's panic focused, zeroing in on Simon.

"Are you hurt anywhere else Simon?"

"No just my arm."

"Can you tell me what happened?"

"I was trying to get Zeli out, she was too scared to go when the other kids in her room left, but the building is in really bad shape in there. A beam broke, and when I covered her, it sliced into me."

"That was incredibly brave." Mozare answered. He was in awe of this child, who had lived with so little, putting himself at risk like that.

"If the little people don't care the world goes to shit." He answered. Mozare could tell by the practiced way he spoke the words through his pain that he'd spoken them often. They resonated with Mozare in a way nothing had in a very long time.

Finally, he saw Loralei heading out of the building, soot covering her from head to toe, but otherwise uninjured. Until she collapsed to the ground, and Mozare's panic skyrocketed again.

"Stay here Simon, we'll be right back to help you." Mozare didn't even bother trying to put Zeli down, the girl clung tightly to his neck even in sleep, so he raced to Loralei's side with her in his arms.

Loralei coughed again, and Mozare didn't understand. She should be healed; she should've had no problem going into the building. He'd only let her go in without him because he thought she was going to be okay.

Mozare knelt beside her, carefully balancing Zeli against his side and reaching for Loralei. He cradled her in his arms, completely desolate, lost on what he should be doing.

"I'll be fine. Just a little smoke in the lungs."

"Can't you heal it?" He knew his voice was too desperate for him to ever pass it off as calm. He didn't even bother trying to hide how worried he was. Not when he'd forced himself to let her go in there alone. He trusted her, but he didn't want to see her injured either.

"Need to save my strength for the children." She coughed again, but even he could tell that every word sounded stronger. She jut needed to rest a minute and breathe the fresh air. Mozare didn't even think before pressing a kiss to her brow. He was so happy to see her, dirty and sweat stained as she was.

She didn't stay with him long, but he felt something shift between them in those moments, a healing of something broken. He wouldn't get his hopes up, would never dream of pressuring her if she wasn't ready to forgive him, but he'd hold on to the feeling anyway.

"Simon could use your help over there. He's bleeding quite a bit." Mozare didn't want to admit that he'd briefly forgotten about the child.

"Then let's see what we can do." Loralei tried to walk but her steps were shaky. He reached out, grabbing on to her elbow, and though she was too stubborn to admit she needed help, she leaned into him.

They made their way over to Simon, and considering his injuries it was surprising that he didn't fret or cry, he simply sat watching them. Loralei knelt next to him, and Mozare was half convinced it was because she could no longer stay on her feet. Even if she wasn't injured, the adrenaline had to be wearing off at this point.

She placed her hands over Simon's injured arm, and Mozare watched as the skin knit itself back together. He adjusted Zeli in his arms, re-sheathing his weapons. Simon had piled up the things that had fallen from Mozare's belt, and Loralei bundled them all in the singed fabric of her skirt.

They walked together to the healing tents, taking their time despite Loralei's desire to help the other children and find Cara's siblings. None of them wanted to risk injury as shock and exhaustion set in. They didn't have enough strength to push themselves any faster than they were.

Mozare hoped their efforts had been enough. He had never been active enough in the government to know about an orphanage, so he had no way of knowing how many kids there were, or if they'd managed to get them all out.

How many of Revon's men lurked in the shadows watching as they set those children's home ablaze? The idea of killing children, even as a way to turn people against his enemy never would have crossed his mind. It was abhorrent, and he didn't understand anyone who could follow a man who would order such a thing.

But he'd followed him once too. Been lured by pretty words and the idea of a better future. He'd let that man manipulate him into doing terrible things, so how could he judge others for falling into the same trap?

The little girl in his arms wiggled again, and he didn't even think before pressing a kiss to her forehead. She could've died tonight, this pure small creature, innocent in everything. Her blood was almost on his hands.

Shadows snaked around him, rising to meet his panic, and he worried he would scare Zeli, would push her from his arms. But she was only curious, sleepily pressing a finger into the darkness as it moved to weave around them both. She didn't flinch or shy away from him, and it helped the storm in his chest settle a little. He doubted it would go away for a long time, but he didn't mind having something else to focus on.

When they got to the tent, he pulled back the flap, relief flooding him as he saw Cassimir walking back and forth between the rows of children, mostly helping to calm them after what they'd gone through. He couldn't see a lot of injuries, but Eleni seemed to be tending to the children who needed it, Saiden in the back corner with two children tucked on to her lap, all three of them sleeping.

Two little ones charged Loralei, and Mozare tensed. Logically, he knew they were children, but it was only the child still clinging to him that kept him from drawing a blade to defend her. Instincts were hard to outlive, especially when the world gave him every reason to mistrust people.

He saw the tears in Loralei's eyes that she was trying to hide from the children in her arms. He assumed they had to be Cara's siblings, and he felt the tears in his own eyes gather as well. They may not have saved the country yet, but they'd still managed to do good, and that was all he could hope for.

46

RHENA

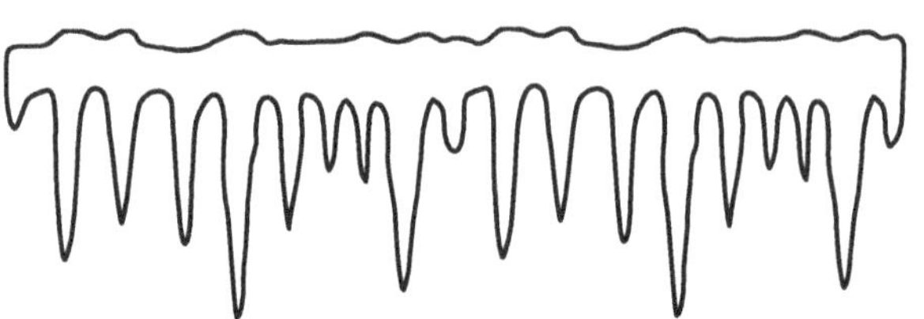

IT HAD TAKEN RHENA A FEW DAYS TO SLEEP OFF THE EXHAUSTION. Between her own rescue, and helping the children who escaped the orphanage fire, she hadn't had a lot of time to process. But now that she was finally settling, she needed to update her friends on everything that had happened since their last meeting. It had almost been harder to reach them since their arrival, since magic no longer seemed to be an option.

And things had been happening so fast at the palace, that she'd been solely focused on her own survival; she hadn't been able to think of another way to get word to them. Now she felt like she had a lifetime's worth of information to tell them.

Rhena made her way up to the roof. She'd only been there a few days, but she'd already realized they had staked it out as their space. They were making do with what little they had. It was better than living in the palace when Rhena hadn't even trusted her bedroom to be hers alone.

Saiden and Eleni were huddled in the corner, possibly meditating, but Rhena wasn't entirely sure. She couldn't feel the goddess anywhere near the hovel, so that was probably a good sign, but she didn't trust that instinct. She couldn't really trust anything these days. Except her friends.

She had never stopped trusting them. Not when they'd led rebels against the queen, and not when that rebellion turned out to be the wrong choice. Sure, she wished they had included her in these life changing decisions, but she knew that she was a little sister to them. They didn't want her carrying the weight.

Rhena could see the guilt of it every time she made eye contact with Saiden, and she wanted it to go away. She could fight with the rest of them. This was her home too, the only one where she'd ever truly belonged. It was time for her to fight.

"We need to talk." She didn't know why her voice came out barely above a whisper, but it didn't matter because Saiden heard her anyway. She suspected her sister had known she was there the whole time but was giving her space. Eleni on the other hand jumped a little when she heard Rhena.

"You've scared me." She said, pressing a hand to her chest. Rhena wondered if it was a show or not, but she didn't really know Eleni well enough to guess one way or the other. Eleni looked back and forth between them, and stood. "Should I go get the others?"

"That would be helpful. Thank you sahadi." Eleni smiled down at Saiden and moved to head off the roof and gather the rest of her friends. "I'm glad to see you walking about little Maus."

"I'm surprised I'm alive." It was a harsh statement, but she'd felt how close death had been to her, and she hadn't thought she would escape it. Saiden's face paled, and she stood, closing the distance between them so she could wrap Rhena up in her arms.

She hadn't realized she was shaking. The space around them wasn't any cooler than it had been when she'd come up, so at least her powers seemed to be in check. The shaking must've been nerves. Or maybe relief. Either way, as Saiden held her tight, she gave herself time to be weak. She had people to help protect her now.

Footsteps stomped up the rickety ladder, far harder than they should've given the rusted metal's condition. Then a second pair of arms wrapped around her from behind, and her gift reached out to him. *Mozare*. He had mostly carried her from the palace, but she had missed his hugs more than anything.

As far as she was concerned, her family was back together again.

When they finally let her go, they didn't stray far from her side, each of them sitting down beside her as they gathered into a small circle so they could listen to what she had to say. And that meant it was time for her to speak.

This time when she shivered, the icicles on her fingertips proved it was her powers shifting the temperature around them. She didn't want to have this conversation. She didn't even know where to start.

Saiden grabbed her fingers, ignoring the way the ice froze their skin together. "We're here. You're safe now. I promise. I won't let anything happen to you again."

"Remember." Loralei spoke up from across the circle, "we're the ones he's afraid of. We have that power. I won't ever let him touch you." She barely even knew Rhena, but Rhena knew what had happened to the once queen, and she believed every word Loralei said.

"Revon, he's found a new way to reinforce the powers of his gifted soldiers. Anyone with real promise. I don't know how long he's been experimenting, but he finally succeeded a few weeks ago with his new general. It twists the power somehow. I can't explain it. It feels wrong."

Slowly, Rhena started to regain the ability to bend her fingers, which is when she realized that Saiden was using her own gifts the same way Talon had used his to keep anyone from detecting them by her cold snap.

"What happened to Talon?"

"To who?" Mozare asked.

"The boy I told you to spare. Do you know what happened to him?"

"I didn't touch him. But I'm also not sure what's happened little sister." Mozare looked at her with a look of pity she didn't want.

"If he's okay, he would've sent word through the Enlightened." Saiden's hands tensed in hers. "We couldn't use a pub to get information." Rhena explained. But she understood what Saiden was feeling. The last time they'd face the Enlightened together, Saiden had been forced to kill one of them to save Rhena.

Mozare answered for her. "That's sound logic, even if it might feel risky to us."

Rhena valued his praise. They'd been her trainers after all. "I need to go see them."

"There's no way you're going there alone. Not when Revon is probably hunting you." Saiden didn't leave any room for arguments, not that Rhena was planning on arguing with her.

"We should go there too. They have the best archive outside of the palace," Loralei added. "We need information and as unfortunate as it is, they are probably our best opportunity to get it."

Saiden's own fingers started to glow, and it made Rhena feel a little better that she wasn't the only one who still didn't have her powers under control. She didn't let go of Saiden's fingers, she held on the same way Saiden had for her; without hesitation.

They were making moves, even if they were in the shadows. And Rhena finally felt like she could see a way out.

47
SAIDEN

SAIDEN HATED THE IDEA OF VISITING THE ENLIGHTENED. POSSIBLY HATED IT more than sneaking back in to the palace. She'd been so conditioned to the hate that the Enlightened had for her, that she wasn't sure she had enough control over her powers to face them again without hurting them.

She didn't want to be a weapon, no matter whose hand wielded it.

But Rhena needed this, and Loralei thought it would get them the information they needed. So, she strapped her gear on, covered her head in one of Eleni's spare headscarves, and started to move through the city, keeping between houses and trying to avoid the sound of Revon's patrols.

Every step towards the temple set her heartbeat soaring. Only her need to protect her friends and the discipline Nakti had drilled into her kept her from completely spiraling out of control. Even still, her fingers kept shifting between light and shadows, sometimes disappearing completely from her sight.

She didn't want to think about it, so she pulled her sleeves down to cover her fingers. It's not like she wasn't used to having to hide her skin. That wasn't out of the ordinary, though she was mildly surprised by how the action helped soothe her nerves.

Mozare led their group, while she took up the rear, Rhena and Loralei sandwiched between them. The siblings were protecting the safe house, although Cassimir had hated being left behind. Normally she would've put herself up front because it was the most dangerous spot to be, but she couldn't rely on her senses, when each of their heartbeats rang in her ears.

The best thing about her gift was being in tune with her friends, but, it was also torture. She knew that Rhena's heart was beating as fast as her own, and that Loralei's was too calm. She'd never really dealt with the Enlightened in her life in the palace, and Saiden wasn't sure she knew what to expect.

She hoped this went better than it had last time. In front of her, Mozare motioned for them to stop, leaving them behind so he could cross the road and watch the pathway from the other side. It was smart, but Saiden hated that he was out in the open. She didn't like anything about this.

But they needed answers. And her attempt to get them last time had come at too high a cost. This time, she hoped they wouldn't have to pay. She wouldn't let any of them pay it. They were the one thing she would never be willing to sacrifice. Not for anything. If they had to live the rest of their days on the run, if they never freed Kaizia, she'd be fine. As long as she had her family.

It was a bitter truth she hoped she never had to face.

Mozare had Rhena cross, Loralei keeping watch on her side as the youngest of them put herself at risk. But she crossed with no issues, and Loralei followed close after her. When Saiden was the only one left, she began to cross, but both of them had missed the guards coming.

She saw Mozare's face pale, but there was no going back. She pulled her weapon, motioning for him to stay hidden where he was, weapons concealed. She could handle a few guards on rotation. But as she watched his face, it suddenly shifted, fear and confusion mixing on his face.

Saiden moved into a stance, ready to attack whichever guard turned the corner first, until she realized what made Mozare's face change like that. Not only were patches of her hands completely missing from view, she couldn't see her arms at all. Or her feet.

Whatever her powers were doing, they had completely blocked her from sight. Saiden took advantage of the camouflage. She wasn't actively controlling it, and she didn't know how long it would last. As she ran, she felt Eleni's scarf fall loose from her head but she didn't dare pause to grab it.

The guards turned the corner, her scarf floating in front of them, but they didn't charge her, and as she crossed into her friends, the magic keeping her hidden from view died out. Mozare grabbed her, pulling her deeply into their nook as the guards marched by.

She understood now what Rhena meant about their gifts feeling wrong. She didn't have a lot of experience around gifted people, but even her limited understanding could tell there was something off about them.

"What did you do?" Loralei asked, her voice a harsh whisper.

Saiden looked at her hands again, and they were completely back to normal. "I-I don't know."

"We can figure that out later. We need to keep moving." Mozare's voice was calm, but she knew it was a facade.

From their hiding spot they were close to the temple, and thankfully made it there without any other issues.

The Enlightened gathered around the temple did not enjoy seeing her. She'd briefly forgotten that she'd lost Eleni's scarf and now her unbraided hair fell free around her shoulders.

"The Blood-Cursed one is not welcome here," one of them said. "Her binding is an offense to the gods."

"We do not welcome any without the gifts in the temple." Another added.

Saiden stepped inside anyway, and as her friends stepped in behind her and closed the door, she flooded the room with shadows. Once she knew every person inside the temple was paying attention, she lit Keir's light in her hands, haloing herself in its glow. As she adjusted to the dark, she could see the Enlightened around her dropping to their knees.

"You cannot discredit the gods' gifts." Her voice didn't sound like her own. "Nor the vessel who wields it."

The few who had remained standing dropped to the ground in reverence, and she flinched at the sound of their bony knees hitting the stone. This was not what she wanted either, but she felt like she lived a life between loathing and reverence now. She was never free to be her own person. Even though her mother's death had allowed her gifts to manifest, she would never outlive her curse.

But she had bigger things to worry about than a few bruised knees. The world was falling to pieces around them. She wasn't going to stop and worry about damage to a few religious fanatics who had on many occasions wished her dead.

Saiden didn't have time for old grievances either. They had come to the Enlightened for a very specific reason, and she trusted Rhena's instincts when she'd enlisted their help, even if she would never trust them herself.

"You honor us with your presence, Anointed one." One of them finally spoke. The words made Saiden shiver, the sensation of the gods in her mind finally leaving her be. She didn't trust them either at this point.

Rhena stepped out from behind her, and it was odd, to see the anger bleed into their faces, and yet not directed at her. They honored all gifted, but now Saiden was something special, something more. It made her skin crawl, like she desperately needed a bath. She wasn't even sure why they were angry.

A growl had escaped her before she'd even felt her own rage bubble through her, and she saw them all flinch, eyes gazing downward as if they were not worthy to look at her. Saiden wished they would go back to hating her.

"I came to you, for your aid. There was a boy with me, has he brought you any news?" Saiden was proud of the careful way Rhena asked her question, too concealed to give away any information to an eavesdropper lingering nearby.

"He brought you this letter, your little man of scars. Left it in our care." One of them pulled a slip of paper from the crease of their robe, and handed it to Rhena. Saiden couldn't see what it said, but Rhena clutched it to her chest tightly, so she hoped the news was good.

"We have another reason to request your aid." Saiden started again, "but we need your discretion first."

"We would never do anything to put the Anointed one," with hesitation they added, "and her friends, in harm's way. Your fate rests with those whose power is greater than our own."

Saiden didn't miss that they never claimed that fate would lead them somewhere good. Just that they wouldn't interfere.

After a tense moment, the Enlightened motioned for their small group to follow them beyond the prayer rooms, to what Saiden imagined was a small living area for those who tended to the temple.

They all crowded into a small room, not much bigger than one of the private prayer stalls Saiden usually used when she came to the temple. She may not have been welcomed in the past, but she'd been devoted to her prayers regardless. The four of them, plus three of the Enlightened, pressed in shoulder to shoulder, the warm breath of each exhale stirring someone else's hair.

"In what way can we aid you?" The eldest of the Enlightened finally asked after silence had clawed itself into the room.

"We are dealing with someone who intends to bastardize the gods' gifts." The words were disjointed coming from her, she didn't have the skill for politics and manipulation. She much preferred to be straightforward. "We need to stop him."

"Explain this to us, and we will see what aid we can offer you."

Saiden bristled at the command in the Enlightened's voice, but didn't have a chance to react. Rhena launched into the same explanation she had given them, but instead of confusion the Enlightened reacted with fear. They knew exactly what Rhena was talking about, and that it was a terrible thing.

"We have a ritual in our texts that mirrors what you are saying the false king is doing. It has never been successful with our more radical siblings." Saiden really did not like the idea of even more radical Enlightened. "We will give this text to you. It is the only thing we have that might help you to stop him."

At least they agreed on that. Revon had to be stopped.

"We have something else for you. Something that was entrusted to our care a long time ago, for a situation like this one, where you were unbound."

Unbound. A world where her mother was killed, that's what that meant.

"Who left it?"

"You're General Mother." A smile cracked the Enlightened's face that broke something inside of Saiden. *Nakti.*

Mozare voiced the words she could barely think to speak. "Nakti knew your mother was alive." He sounded as stunned as she felt.

"That can't be right. Why would she have let Magdalena rot?" Loralei added.

Saiden was shaking, despite the body heat raising the temperature in the small room substantially. "It's not like I can ask her. I buried her." Her hands were shaking, the Enlightened looking on with a mix of reverence and fear across their faces.

What was faith without terror?

"She gave us a memory, to share with you when the time was right."

Saiden couldn't speak, didn't know how to answer that. Thankfully Mozare could speak for her. "So, you're going to tell us a story?"

"There are many things about your gods that you still do not understand child." Mozare tried to argue, but the Enlightened elder didn't let up. "You can't argue when you've come for our help."

The tension in the small room continued to grow. "Your general had a gift for memory manipulation." Someone finally handed the leader a small bauble, and they held it up for inspection.

"She took these from your minds, but I can give them back."

Saiden should have taken more time to think about it, especially given how often she had been unconscious of late. But she didn't have the willpower to deny another memory of the woman who raised her, no matter how she feared it would hurt her.

"Do it."

"Lean your head back, and when the power comes, do not resist it."

48

LORALEI

LORALEI DIDN'T LIKE SEEING THE ENLIGHTENED PUT SAIDEN UNDER THEIR trance. It felt far too similar to what the deities had been doing to her lately, and she didn't like it when anyone played games with the people she cared about.

She took advantage of the cracks in the floor, pulling vines up from the earth and wrapped them around the necks of the Enlightened who did this to Saiden. Loralei still wasn't sure if they were truly friend or foe, and considering their track record recently, she preferred to play things safe.

"See I understand the whole, 'use any magic we can' but I want answers. Easy, non-convoluted straight forward answers. What is that bastard doing to the gods gifts and how do we put a stop to it?"

"There is no way to kill a god." One of them said in a sing-song voice. She supposed now that she no longer wore a crown, she had lost all her bargaining chips with these fanatics. That was fine, if she had to draw blood to get answers it wouldn't be the worst thing on her conscience. She doubted she'd even lose sleep over it.

Though she was cutting off their air, they still continued to tease her. "Not even an impostor. Sometimes it's not the skin that matters, it's what's within."

"I told you I wanted straightforward answers," she crouched down so she could get in their faces. "I promise you I am no longer a woman to be fucked with."

"A sorrow shared is a sorrow halved. A joy shared is a joy doubled." These Enlightened were lunatics.

One of the others, one of the witnesses, came forward, palms raised towards her. "His majesty is practicing a very old ritual, one where power exchanges hands, and in doing so grows. It was outlawed long before the first Blood-Curse was enacted because the exchange warped the power and was very unstable. And all the power could be reduced by the death of one partner."

There. She thought. *Someone who understood how this whole thing worked.* Loralei felt the heartbeats of the Enlightened grow faint as they passed out, and she finally pulled her vines away.

"Is he a god or not? Because I plan to kill him like any other man. Preferably with my own hands, and I'd like to know what I'm getting into." She didn't care who bore witness to her rage, she had earned it. Fought for and against it. After everything she'd lost, her rage continued to be hers alone.

"The only beings who reach close to the divine are the ones like her," they motioned towards Saiden's unconscious body, her upper half supported in Mozare's lap. She didn't even think to be jealous of them. Not when she cared about them both so much it hurt at times.

She loved them both too much to think anything of their closeness.

"What is the point, if not to reach divinity?"

"Unstable power is not necessarily weak power. Sometimes the brightest flames are the strongest. They tend to burn out much faster than any other."

"They're limitless then?" She wanted them to speak plainly, because she couldn't risk misunderstanding.

"Not limitless, because the power needs a source, it feeds on them, instead of divine energy within. The records say it burns the souls away, until there is nothing left but a husk of a man. But the burning feeds another purpose too. It feeds the one who conducted the ritual. And if this false king is not using his own powers, if he's relying on others to use the gifts he gives them, he will build a well unfathomably deep."

She didn't like the words coming out of this Enlightened's mouth, but at least they were straight forward. They'd always understood that coming back here meant Revon was their enemy, their first target. But now they understood how much more was at stake than their kingdom. If Revon ran out of volunteers, if he started forcing people to complete his ritual, he'd be sending them all to their graves.

Loralei didn't want any more of her people to suffer at the hand of that monster. Saiden shook in Mozare's lap, tears streaming down her face, but her powers weren't out of control. No shadows wove through her fingers, no flame threatening to set them alight. She bore grief on her features, but it was normal sadness, the kind every living being must endure.

"How do we stop him?" It was truly the only question that mattered in the end. There was no way he could live, not when he did so much damage to everyone around him.

"Kill him. Kill the source. It should stop the rest of them. Restore peace, it is what they have chosen you for." The Enlightened turned between the four of them, looking each of them in the eye, other than Saiden who was still stuck in a memory. "The gods would not have put four powerful people together, would not have led you all to each other, if this was not the path you were meant to be on."

It was meant to be helpful, to reassure them, but to Loralei it felt like another curse.

49
SAIDEN

SAIDEN WAS STUCK IN A MEMORY. SHE ALMOST WOULD'VE THOUGHT THE gods had gotten ahold of her again, except that this felt different. Instead of being thrust into another version of her life, she was a spectator of her own past. Watching a smaller, more innocent version of herself.

She had no memory of this moment herself, hadn't even realized that it had been missing until the Enlightened had pressed their fingers to her brow and given the memory back to her. And now she was watching herself, short red ringlets still loose around her ears, as Nakti brought her to visit the temple.

Even if it was fake, the memory hurt her all the same. To know that time had been stolen from her, time she'd spent with Nakti, when she'd been given so little of it. Both of her mothers had been torn from her, their deaths her fault. She'd never outrun that guilt.

But she suspected that wasn't the lesson she was meant to be learning here. She tried to focus, but tears clouded the already hazy vision in front of her. It seemed to wait, the memory still until she was ready to witness it. Saiden wasn't sure if that was a good sign or not. She certainly had no reason to trust the Enlightened.

Nakti, however, she'd trusted her entire life. If this memory had been taken at her request, Saiden had reason to fear what she would discover. But she craved the memory, the time, more than she was afraid of it so she cleared her eyes and watched her younger self walk in, hand wrapped in Nakti's.

The Enlightened at the front of the temple began to bow to her, until they saw the little girl walking with her. They ran and gathered behind the altar, as if they'd need tons of stone between them to be safe from a child who looked like she could barely carry her own weight. Saiden barely remembered being that small, that frail. She'd started training only a few weeks after arriving at the legion, and she had the muscles to prove it now.

"Why have you brought the cursed one to these hallowed halls." They screeched. Saiden as she was now had long been familiar with their fear, but as a child it had all still been new to her, and she'd tucked herself behind Nakti's knees to try and shield herself from it.

"You deny your god, you sully his name, when you bring her kind into his home."

"You would do well to keep your mouth shut." Nakti answered them, a steel in her voice usually reserved for the battlefield. "For you know nothing of my god or this child."

The Enlightened didn't seem to be expecting this and drew back as if each word were a knife thrown in their direction. She saw her younger self peer out at them, torn between her own fear and her wonder at this woman she barely knew protecting her from them.

Saiden had so very few people in life at that point. And the only ones who'd ever protected her, were her parents and this soldier. She wanted to be exactly like her. That Saiden did remember. The way she had revered Nakti from a young age for standing up for what she believed in. But she hadn't really realized how much she had been standing up for her.

"What do you want Blessed one?" They finally asked, retaking their places behind the massive stone altar. Saiden knew this place so well now, but she hadn't then. She watched herself take in the black and white monuments with awe. Before she'd ever had the chance to glance upon her deities faces, this is what she had known of them.

Black and white stone, and the fear of their followers.

"I seek your knowledge. Wisdom that has long been left in your hands to guard and to share where you see necessary."

"What do you wish to know?" She couldn't tell if the Enlightened were truly happy to share their wisdom, or if they only hoped to get them out of the temple as fast as possible. Because even the child version of herself had been able to see that Nakti wasn't leaving without the information she had come for.

As a trained Legionnaire she would have no trouble getting it out of them another way.

"Why has the child not manifested her gifts?"

"Are you sure you do not already know the answer to that my dear Blessed?" The Enlightened answered, a coy smile on their face.

"I was there when it happened." Nakti answered, her voice quiet, as if she hoped to keep the memory of her parent's death from touching the child behind her again. But watching, Saiden knew exactly what she meant. Nakti thought she had watched Saiden's parents die in their raid. And she had seen her father die, his blood pooling as red as her hair on the floor of their small kitchen.

But now Saiden knew that her mother had not died.

"For both? Or just the one. Because we have reason to think that our little queenling has a new prisoner in her dungeon."

"It's true then?" Saiden's voice layered over Nakti's as they asked the same question. It startled Saiden, the motion rippling the edges of the memory.

"You had doubts? In your own general? What a poor soldier you must make."

"Every good soldier knows to trust their gut. If that leads to doubt in others that is not a failing in me." Nakti answered them.

"Good child. Trust those instincts. They will serve you well."

"Her mother is alive then?" Saiden froze, but in this in-between dream world she had no room to panic. *Nakti knew.* She'd let her mother rot for all those years in that dank prison cell and for what? So, Saiden could become a monster, a weapon for other hands to wield?

She made it even worse when she spoke again. "The girl cannot know."

"We know of your gifts general. The ones you hide behind your healing talent. Would've made an excellent spy, but you chose the blade instead. An interesting choice when you had so many options left open to you."

"My choices are my own. You don't have to remind me of my gifts. I know how rare they are." Neither the version of her that stood beside Nakti nor the one who watched them knew what gift she was talking about. She'd always known it was strange Nakti had risen to her position with such a strong healing talent, but she was a powerful warrior, so Saiden had squashed her own doubts.

She should've trusted her gut.

Nakti started to turn and then hesitated. "And if her gifts are freed? If I can't keep her safe?"

"Pray." One of the Enlightened answered, as if every prayer they sent skyward was answered by benevolent hands. Nakti didn't seem to like their answer either. When she reached for her weapons, the Enlightened raised their palms towards her, begging with their expressions for her to avoid harming them.

"There is one thing. If the cursed one comes into her reckoning. If she can accept and maintain the flow of power within her she can outlive the release of her curse. But this has never been done. One would have to be incredibly strong-willed, and have something equally potent worth fighting for, or we surmise the powers will overrun them. That is the only true safety you can offer her. Train her well and on the day her gifts are released she can fight to maintain her own soul. Otherwise, she will become a vessel destined to crumble and falter."

Nakti didn't appear to like that answer, but she didn't draw her spear. She simply picked Saiden up, though she was really too old for that at this point, steeled her shoulders and marched out of the temple. She must've used the time to take Saiden's memories, because this entire day was gone. She only remembered walking past the temple with Nakti, never going inside.

Waking from this dream was not as difficult as escaping the gods' clutches. Once the memory was done with her, it simply let her go, allowing her to wake up as she would from any dream. Except she knew there would be no forgetting this. Not the memory, and certainly not the betrayal it had revealed to her.

50
Mozare

Mozare and Saiden didn't talk as they walked into one of the solitary prayer rooms. He hadn't spent much time in this temple, not when there had been space on both the legionnaire barracks and the rebel base set aside for devotion. He hadn't needed to. But the space was familiar to him all the same, especially as he entered the prayer room and felt the goddess press into his head.

He denied her again. It was becoming all too easy to simply push her back out of his thoughts, denying her the right to speak to him. He wasn't hers to control, and Mozare had bigger things to worry about than whatever riddle she had for him.

If Mozare couldn't fix whatever had happened in the memory the Enlightened had revealed to Saiden, he could at least be there for her now in the aftermath. Loralei finished her torment of the Enlightened, and then she and Rhena stepped into the small room as well.

The space was far too small to house all of them and their assorted weapons, but none was willing to step out. Not when something important had happened, and Saiden was the only one who could tell them. He was hoping the information the Enlightened had given her was enough to give them some sort of advantage because they were sorely lacking in that these days.

He couldn't let Revon win this fight. Not when he'd given him this place and the power to corrupt his kingdom. Not when there were people who still needed to be freed from him.

"So," he was and wasn't surprised that Rhena was the one who finally broke the tension between them by speaking. "What happened?"

"Did you know that Nakti had a gift for manipulating memory?" Saiden directed her question at Mozare, but it wasn't as if the others couldn't hear, crammed into the space as they were. "It's very rare."

"It's barely even recorded in the archives as an existing gift." Loralei threw in. He wasn't entirely sure if it helped the situation, but he appreciated that she was trying all the same. This already felt wrong, and if this was going where he expected it was, the whole thing was going to be a very hard loss for Saiden.

"I didn't know." He answered truthfully. Mozare was so glad this wasn't knowledge he'd had before, because he wasn't sure Saiden could've handled another betrayal after whatever she'd learned about Nakti.

Luckily, he somehow hadn't screwed things up too badly, because Saiden didn't even hesitate to believe him. He wished the warmth in his chest wasn't accompanied by guilt for all the things he had lied about though.

"What memory did she take from you?" Loralei asked, her tone gentle. They all knew this wasn't something that would be easy to talk about, and he was grateful she handled Saiden more gently than she had the Enlightened.

"She brought me here when I was little." Saiden sounded lost within her own mind, and he couldn't stomach the feeling that she was lost to him too. "She didn't understand why my powers hadn't manifested when she thought she'd seen the soldiers kill my parents."

"But your mother hadn't died." Loralei answered her and Mozare watched the exchange between the two of them, feeling suddenly unwelcome to this memory that had tied the two of them together long before they'd ever met.

"And she knew." Saiden's voice cracked, and he could hear her heart breaking behind it. "I don't know how she could have kept that from me."

A single tear traced its way down Saiden's cheek, and he would have done anything to stop it. He wasn't the one in their partnership who was good at fixing these kinds of things. He didn't have any kind words. He didn't even move, not when she wrapped her arms around herself, and not when Loralei tucked her into her own arms, trapping Saiden's tears between them.

"It's a shame you can't ask her." Rhena said, and he cringed a little. Reminding Saiden of the general's death at her own hand seemed cruel at this moment when she was already so vulnerable, but it didn't make her shrink the way he thought it would.

Saiden's face lit up, and Mozare couldn't track the change in her attitude. Not when she'd been so down before. She was never one to switch so easily. But she was also staring at him, and if he was honest, it was starting to unsettle him.

"Could you call on her? Long enough for us to have a conversation?"

Mozare didn't like this question, but he didn't want to disappoint her either. "I-I I mean probably? I suppose it's not that different." He'd spoken to the dead before, at the beginning of his training. But he was worried about the changes Akil had forced through him, and what it meant for his skills. Loralei was staring at him too, but he avoided her gaze. This wasn't going to be comfortable for any of them, but for Saiden he at least had to try.

If it didn't work, they could say they tried, and he hoped that would be enough to offer her closure. He couldn't stop thinking about how hard it was to live with divine powers and then still not be able to do anything to help. He wanted to help her.

"I think if we're close to her, I should be able to do that." He tried to sound more confident than he felt, but the huff he heard come from Loralei made him think he was failing miserably.

He was so tired of failing his friends. He was finding his way back to himself, back to the kind of person his friends could rely on. That was all he wanted now.

"We'll go to the cemetery then. It's the only place we can be close to her without access to the palace." Loralei added again. Mozare almost didn't hear her. He was busy trying to paint the bigger picture in his head. He had only fragments, and they weren't worth much to anyone.

"Should all of us go?" Saiden asked. He couldn't tell what she was worried about, or more specifically who among them she didn't want coming to the cemetery.

"Someone has to keep an eye over you two. We have no idea how this attempt will play out. And we aren't sending Rhena back to the safe house on her own. Not while he's hunting her." Loralei said, and the matter seemed settled. He certainly wasn't going to argue with her when he agreed with everything she was saying.

An Enlightened called to them from outside the room. "There are soldiers gathering nearby. It is time for you to leave."

Shit. They didn't have time to fight Revon's men and they couldn't let them find out who they were using to get information. A spy network didn't work if you couldn't have reliable sources and drop off points.

"Loralei, take Rhena, try to leave out of the back." Saiden started.

"There will be no leaving that way." The Enlightened answered in response.

Fuck. "We have to go now. The longer we wait and try to figure out a plan, the more likely it is they'll catch us. Time to pray, while the gods might still be listening."

51
SAIDEN

Saiden, Rhena, Loralei and Mozare were cornered. She knew that Rhena was a good fighter, but she was still the youngest of them, so Saiden was careful to shift her body so that she was in between Rhena and the large majority of the king's forces. They were too far from the palace to be worried about these fighters, but Saiden would rather err on the safe side of things.

She could see Mozare do the same, each of them splitting off to tackle a larger portion of the troops, and Saiden said a quick prayer to whoever was listening that Rhena would be able to handle whoever slipped through them. Between her power, which she was already better at controlling than Saiden, and her blade, Saiden figured she stood a good chance.

She no longer worried about Loralei. Between her freedom to use her own gifts now and the rage behind her eyes any time they encountered a contingency of Revon's forces, she knew her friend would be fine. Loralei turned her back to them, trapping Rhena in the middle of a protective circle and preparing to defend their backs.

Saiden was full of rage too. Enough that fire danced in her hands, though she was hesitant to let it go. Her control over her powers was limited, though improving, and the town was too congested for her to risk hurting anyone else.

Her brain flashed between the present and the last fight she'd had outside the temple when she'd been forced to kill one of the Enlightened to save Rhena. She had the strangest feeling however, that whatever their previous acrimony towards her, the Enlightened were on her side more now, than ever. She wasn't sure it was a feeling she liked, more like a thousand pairs of eyes on her, hoping that she'd fulfill some magic destiny she wasn't sure she understood.

She shook off the feeling they were watching her, doused the fire dancing between her fingers and pulled two throwing knives from the straps on her thighs.

"We don't want to harm you." One of his soldiers spoke breaking the silence.

"The weapons don't make that very clear." Loralei answered, her voice steel, as sharp as the blades in Saiden's hands. "Maybe you could have invited us for dinner. Would have been a much better introduction."

Their sarcasm was wearing off on her, and Saiden's brief glance at Mozare revealed the pride on his face for it. She almost smiled, she might've if her brain wasn't still racing with new information.

"You dumb bitch." The guard spit at them, and Saiden could almost feel the saccharine smile she was sure was glued to Loralei's face. The rest of his men, because he was obviously the one in charge, started to spread out around them.

The one next to the commander grabbed his arm, and she watched his face transform at the contact. "Remember the girl." Saiden assumed she was talking about capturing her, possibly so Revon could get his hands on the full force of her unbound powers, but they turned and stared at Rhena and that possibility was so much worse.

Saiden stepped in front of her, completely tucking her little sister behind her and out of sight of these horrid creatures who must've been out of their gods-damned minds. There was no world where she would ever let Rhena put herself in that kind of danger ever again.

"Why are you hiding her?" The man asked again, his grin splitting, the scar on his face pulling his features and distorting them. "Don't think she should get a peak at her own handy work? If the girl wants to fight a war, why don't you let her fight?" Pride surged through Saiden at the scar on his face, especially now that she knew Rhena had given it to him. Because she knew that something like that never would've happened if he hadn't been threatening her in the first place.

He stepped forward and she growled, pulling her arm back so that she could throw her blade if he dared take another step. Her skin crawled with even the smallest change in proximity, and she could feel how wrong the power inside him was. How corrupted Revon's experiments made them.

She knew the rest of them could feel it too.

Saiden wasn't sure what the signal had been, but all at once, Revon's soldiers charged them. She'd been outnumbered in a fight before, she and Mozare had survived worse odds, but she'd never felt this panicked before. Saiden hadn't had something she'd die to protect then, but she had a family now that needed her, and she wasn't going to let them down.

Behind her she felt Loralei's vines grow, and she matched that power, the vibration of Keir's gifts singing to her in a melody she'd never heard before but seemed familiar to her all the same. Her own vines spiraled out, the same as the ivy tattooed on her skin, growing at her command, wrapping around the ankles of the soldier who'd interrupted the conversation as their leader charged them.

Saiden threw both her knives, but shadows pooled, strings of them knocking the knives off their paths. She hadn't realized the shadows could be solid enough to interact like that, and her own lack of knowledge frightened her.

But Saiden didn't have to rely on her gifts. Not when she'd spent the vast majority of her life training. Not when, despite her downfalls, Nakti had been her mother, as much as Magdalena had been. She had given Saiden a power all her own the moment she'd placed a blade in her hand.

It wasn't forgiveness for what she'd done, but as Saiden pulled her unmatched kindjal from the sheath at her back, calm settled over her, and it was almost understanding. Saiden pushed forward, far enough that the man wouldn't get close to Rhena, but close enough that his men couldn't use the distraction to get around her.

She spread her stance and let her weight fall into the balls of her feet. Sometimes battle was as much a waiting game as it was a flurry of motion. She wanted this man off balance as he approached her. Wanted him to doubt every one of his footfalls.

Behind her, she finally heard Rhena pull her blade from its sheath, but she couldn't afford the distraction of looking at her. Not as every step brought this vile man closer.

When he was a few step in front of her, Saiden turned, looking like she was giving him an opening to Rhena, before she slipped in and grabbed his arms, flipping him back, and away from her in a macabre dance. Using her free hand, she slipped between them and sliced a line down his arm. The grin that broke on his face should've scared her, no one in their right mind smiled when that kind of pain was inflicted on them, but she was too deep in the battle to allow herself even a moment's fear.

She pushed towards him, and even this masochist stepped back at the approach of her blades, though his shadows rose to fight her off. It was unsettling, and she knew that this was not a fight she'd win on steel alone.

Saiden let her mind drift back to Keir's melody and pulled on his light, letting every tendril of his shadows burn away under it. If he wanted to hide behind his power she was going to make that hiding spot feel very small. Doing her best to trust the power inside her, she renewed her attack on him, slicing her blades towards his chest, flipping one so she could stab down towards his heart.

Even with the experiment, he was still a man. Still flesh, and that meant he would still bleed like any other man.

That was the thing she focused on as he finally drew a blade of his own, letting his shadows pull back around him like some kind of armor. She wasn't sure how much that would do for him, but she'd fought enough knights to know where armor was weak. Quickly, she re-sheathed her kindjal and replaced it with a stiletto from her jacket sleeve.

Light still burned in her hand from where she'd repelled his shadows, and as she grabbed her blade, it coated the metal. She used her kindjal to deflect his blows and when she finally got close enough, she struck him where normal armor would have a joint.

Blind rage burned over his face as he hit the ground, and Saiden turned to face the next opponent. She didn't understand why fighters weren't swarming around her when she was so used to being the main target of any conflict. But her friends were dealing with most of Revon's men, a wall of thorns between Rhena and those Loralei was fighting, keeping her more sheltered from the fight.

Saiden couldn't have been more grateful to her for taking care of the people she loved. She rushed to her side, standing between her and Mozare so the three of them formed a veritable barricade between the attacking soldiers and Rhena.

Mozare's axes swung through the air, landing in one soldier's face as he went to strike Saiden. She ran past pulling the blade free and tossed it back to him, a silent thank you on her face she knew he could read.

Two of them charged her at the same time, and Saiden used her powers to blind one of them while she punched her blade into the throat of the second, blood coating her fingers. She was careful not to drop her blade as she pulled it free, spinning to stab the blinded opponent.

Between the three of them, they quickly dispatched their enemies, though they were all quite bloody by the end of it. She didn't like leaving their bodies out in the streets, but they didn't have a lot of choices. Not when any moment could bring more soldiers to them, and the three of them were exhausting their combined strengths.

Rhena had a dead man at her feet. For a moment Saiden panicked, adrenaline spiking and her powers going slightly haywire at the thought that they had missed someone. But as she stood in front of Rhena, checking over with her hands and her powers she couldn't find any injuries.

She would've hugged Rhena if she weren't covered in blood, but she settled for squeezing the hand still firmly wrapped around her blade handle. Saiden took the blade from her hand, cleaning the blood from it on her pants before giving it back to Rhena to resheathe.

"We need to get back." Loralei was thinking the same thing Saiden was, she was sure of it. Even without the same training, she understood the danger. She and Mozare were standing together, and Saiden was sure if either of them had been injured Loralei would've already taken care of it.

They raced back to the safe house, all of them on high alert waiting for another ambush to find them. They made it back without any other problems, and were greeted with fresh towels and soap by Alisa. That woman was a blessing.

"We can't go back to the temple." Saiden said. Rhena looked shocked but Saiden couldn't tell why. "What's wrong little Maus?"

"Talon is supposed to leave me information there. What if he's in danger?"

With hands scrubbed free of blood, Saiden cupped her face, "We'll do what we can for your friend." But she didn't make any promises. As much as she wanted to help Rhena's friend, she wouldn't choose him over any of them if it came down to it. And if it did, she hoped Rhena came to forgive her for not being able to do everything.

"You stay here. I need answers, and I'm taking Mozare to the cemetery to get them." They knew what she was talking about, but Cassimir turned into the room in time to see them all covered in blood and talking about leaving again.

"What happened? And where are you going? Are you hurt? Are any of you hurt?" Her heart bloomed at his worry for her and for their friends. She walked up to him and pressed a shallow kiss to his lips, careful not to press into him and stain his clothes with blood as well.

Saiden started retelling, but at the tension she felt behind her, she decided to pull Cassimir into the small space the women had claimed for sleeping. Cassimir stood next to her as she pulled out fresh clothes but turned as she began to change. She gave him a brief summary of everything that happened in the short time they had been apart.

"And now, I need Mozare to call on Nakti so I can get some answers. I need to know how she could let my mother live in those conditions when she knew what it meant to me to think they'd both died for me." Saiden paused a moment as she realized that, while her thoughts might not have been true when she was a child, she knew now both of her parents had died for her.

"Let me come with you." Cassimir said. She touched his shoulder once she was done dressing and he turned to face her, grabbing her elbows so she couldn't look away from the fear in his face. Fear for her, fear something would happen to her when he wasn't there to do anything about it.

It was the type of fear they were all quickly getting used to, the kind that crept up on you and then never went away. It was the vulnerability of loving. She wouldn't change it for anything, even if she hated seeing it on his beautiful face.

This time when she went to kiss him, she leaned into him with her whole body. He wrapped his arms around her and she reveled in a warmth that was all desert sun and peace. "I can't come,can I?" She both loved and hated that he already knew her so well.

"I need you to stay with Rhena. She just killed a man. I need you to sit with her, so she can find peace again. The way you help me."

Because they weren't really in another room, Loralei joined in on their conversation. She hoped Rhena hadn't been listening. "Don't worry lover boy. I'm going with them. Can't let all the time I've invested into patching them up be for nothing."

She knew Loralei was forcing calm into her voice. Knew because it's exactly what she would've done if the situations were reversed. But she didn't call her on it. Their grief was so entangled, that she didn't mind Loralei coming with them. It seemed to make sense to her.

Cassimir pulled her back into him for one last kiss before he reluctantly let her go, letting her leave because he trusted her to fight to get back to him.

And she would. She would never stop fighting to get back to her family.

52
CASSIMIR

CASSIMIR WAS CONFLICTED ABOUT BEING LEFT BEHIND AGAIN. PART OF HIM hated the constant fear every time he said goodbye to Saiden, watching her walk out that door and spending the entire time wondering if she would survive to come back to him. At the same time, she'd asked him to look after Rhena, a girl as close to a sister to her, as Cassimir's own sister was to him.

That meant something to him, and he wasn't going to take it for granted. He wouldn't leave Rhena reeling on her own. He remembered what it felt like to take his first life, would never outgrow that horror. Cassimir wasn't going to make Rhena go through that alone.

Eleni was already sitting with her, helping to scrub the blood from under Rhena's fingernails, singing something off key under her breath. Cassimir left them for a moment, turning back into the women's room so he could grab her some fresh clothes. He handed them to Eleni and waited in the other room for her to help Rhena get cleaned up.

"Miri, you can come back now." Eleni called in to him, her voice loud enough to travel through the thin walls of the cottage. He turned the corner, and Rhena was still staring into space, the blank expression on her face making him nervous. He was afraid he wouldn't say the right thing, that he had been the wrong person to leave behind.

Carefully, he sat down next to her, a little bit behind her. Almost immediately she turned into him, moving in between his bent knees so that she could press her face into his chest, heartbeat rattling under her ears.

It didn't take long for him to feel the tears bleeding into the fabric. Cassimir bundled her into him, feeling some relief that the shocked numbness was cracking, letting them get through to everything underneath it.

Eleni stood, pressing her hand into his shoulder. "I'm going to make some tea." He saw everything she wasn't saying on her face, and nodded. This wasn't about them, but it was good to know they were on the same page anyway.

Cassimir ran one hand through her hair, the other rubbing gentle circles into her back. It was one thing to soothe Saiden, to ground her, but Rhena was so young. She wasn't seasoned the way Saiden was. Her life hadn't seen nearly as much pain.

He wished he could take this away from her. But that wasn't their reality anymore. Her youth wouldn't save her, but he would be there in the aftermath, because she was part of their family.

Cassimir let her take as much time as she needed, he would've stayed there all night. But after a little while, Rhena pulled away rubbing the cuffs of her sleeves at her eyes. The skin was red and puffy, pain laced through every inch of her expression.

"I don't know what to do with all of this pain." She said, her voice harsh and breaking. It broke something inside of Cassimir, but he did his best not to let it show, not to give her anymore pain that she was already burdened with.

"It's not easy." He admitted, trying to find the balance between honesty and compassion. "The world is going to throw a lot of pain at you, and it's not necessarily fair, but it is true."

Rhena wiped at her face again, an angry swipe of her fingers that pulled at the tears. "But there's a lot of joy there too. You can't forget about that. War is a dark place. But you don't have to be a dark person."

"I killed someone today."

If she were older, he might've told her that the man she'd killed wouldn't have hesitated to take her off the board. But those weren't the words he thought she needed right now. "You did. Don't let him take anything else from you."

Rhena turned away from him, and he thought for a moment that he'd ruined everything. He heard her sniff, and then she was leaning back in her arms, and he was pulling her tight to him again. "I don't want to give him anything."

Cassimir squeezed her tight, "you are still the person you were before this. I wish I could say that it wouldn't happen again, but I want you to know I'll never lie to you."

"Was it hard for you?" Rhena didn't need to clarify her question.

"Of course."

"Do you ever get past it?"

He almost regretted saying that he wouldn't lie to her. It would have been easier to say that he had, but it wouldn't have been honest. "It's lived with me every day since. But the pain of it isn't so intense now. It's more a reminder to live a life worth that sacrifice."

He hoped he was making sense to her. She nodded against his chest, her breathing still uneven, but not the same racking sobs it had been before. Eleni came back, gently settling down in front of them, a warm mug of tea in her hands.

She pressed it into Rhena's grip, tucking a strand of the younger girl's hair behind her ears. Eleni didn't know battle the way the rest of them did, but she'd seen the aftermath more times than he could count.

"Sometimes, you do what you have to in the moment in order to survive. And then, you take the time you need to forgive yourself. The rest of us will still be here, no matter how long it takes."

Rhena sipped her tea, curled up between them, and Cassimir hoped it was enough to soothe the broken edges of her spirit. Even if it was only an opening so she could find her own way to making peace with it.

53
MOZARE

MOZARE AND LORALEI FOLLOWED SAIDEN. A SILENCE HUNG BETWEEN them that had nothing to do with their own problems, with the fight they still hadn't gotten past, but with the fact that neither of them knew what to say to help Saiden. The revelation that Nakti had kept Magdalena separated from her daughter and Saiden from her mother was a hard one for him, he couldn't even begin to imagine what it felt like for Saiden.

Finally, Loralei broke the tension, but only to whisper harshly to Mozare, not to fill the full silence between the three of them. "I am only here because I think you're going to screw this up. Consider me backup for when everything here finally goes to hell. Between the three of us it seems incredibly likely something will go foul."

Mozare was glad that they had left Rhena in the relative safety of the cottage with Cassimir and Eleni. He was even somewhat glad that they'd been forced into the fight if only so they could bring her back where she was more protected. He knew the siblings didn't like being left on guard duty again, especially Cassimir, but this was something the three of them needed to do on their own. At least that was what he kept telling himself. He didn't know how Akil's experiments might have affected his ability to communicate.

Being able to call those corpses to life was new, but he didn't want Nakti's corpse to rise. He was pretty sure that would traumatize them all further, he wanted to give Saiden a chance to get some answers.

Saiden needed to talk to her. They needed answers, and they didn't have time to find them another way. It just meant he had to figure out how to dip into enough power to talk without fully calling her here.

For Saiden, he was willing to try about anything. After everything she'd gone through and had to deal with, the least she deserved was some answers. And, since he was the one searching for them, it would hopefully prevent her getting trapped by the gods again.

At least, that's what he was hoping for.

They followed Saiden all the way to Nakti's gravestone, the two of them watching for danger even though he was pretty sure Saiden didn't care. She was too stuck in her own mind.

That was fine. He had her back and he always would. It was about time he repaid all the trust she'd put in him.

Loralei stopped a distance away from Nakti's solitary grave, putting a hand on Mozare's arm to stop him too. "I'm going to go stand up there." She pointed to a higher peak in the rolling hills of the cemetery. "I'll keep watch. Do not push yourself, if you can't do this you can't, we can't have you die either. I was wrong when I said Saiden was the only one we need to get through this."

He wanted to kiss her and scream in equal measure. It was an incredibly frustrating way to feel because he could do neither. He bottled both of those feelings up and shoved them back inside his chest, locking them away for some future day where he could finally take them out again.

Instead, he thought of her position. She didn't have military training, but if Mozare had been the one to pick somewhere for her to stand, he would have picked the exact same place she had. He was proud of her, for how far she'd come, for how much she was willing to do for them and this fight.

He wanted to say something to her, say anything. Because they had no idea when the last time they would see each other would be. He couldn't risk leaving things unsaid this time. He opened his mouth and closed it, then opened it again but still the words wouldn't come out.

Loralei turned away from him, but not without saying one last thing. "I know." She did not give him time to try again, she simply moved into her position and left him to follow Saiden to the hill. He did so slowly, the pain of his own grief threatening to bury him right beside Nakti on the hill.

When Mozare reached Saiden they sat at Nakti's grave nearly in unison, some combination of their training and their years spent together making them act in sync. "What if the answer is harder than the question?" Saiden asked him, whispering quietly as if voicing the words would make the fear worse.

"You'll never know unless you try." He whispered back, her own fear only serving to call to his own, a mirror into his own twisting insides.

Saiden sat straighter, steeling her spine, shaking the thoughts of despair from her mind. He could see everything on her face, every tiny twitch telling another piece of the story. They knew each other better than anyone else in this entire world. He could do this for her.

For Saiden. For her, he would try anything.

He gave her his hand, and she latched on tight. They both needed the reassurance, the weight, their heartbeats pressed against each other. He was running on pure instinct, and the gentle press of his goddess against the back of his mind.

He pressed his other hand into the dirt in front of them, and Saiden copied, some instinct or divine power pressing into her head telling her to do the same. Then he opened the well of his powers and called out to the piece of it that could communicate with the dead.

Mozare called on Nakti with a heart full of love. His love, the love she had shared with Saiden, the love she gave every new recruit that walked through the doors of the legion. He gave that love to the earth in payment, to guide Nakti here to them. Then he sat with Saiden, and hoped it was enough.

The wind around them quickened, but they sat still against it, neither willing to move even an inch and risk something happening to the spell. Only Saiden's hand in his own reminded him that he was still alive despite the death that surrounded them.

Between one blink and the next, Nakti was seated in front of them, her visage a mirror to the way she looked when she was alive. There was no blood on her armor, she was whole again. Saiden cried next to her, but when she tried to reach out, she was unable to touch Nakti.

Her body wasn't here. But her spirit still smiled at her daughter. "Hello my child. Do not cry, I am at peace." Even though she was not here, Nakti still reached a hand towards Saiden, a mimic of wiping at the tears spilling freely down Saiden's cheek.

54
SAIDEN

"I NEVER THOUGHT I'D GET TO SEE YOU AGAIN." SAIDEN SAID, THEN SHE choked, the words clogging in her throat. The pain pressed against her ribs until she could feel every place they would crack. "I never thought I'd get the chance to apologize."

"There is no need for that my love. You have already been forgiven." Saiden bent herself forward, the closest she could get to begging, to genuflection and she could swear that Nakti's warmth embraced her as she crossed through the space where her soul had been summoned.

"Rise child. There is no need for this. In war there is death, that is something we both understand. You did what you believed was right in the moment. That is all I could have hoped for with you."

"Like you did?"

Nakti's face slowly changed, and Saiden saw the moment understanding crossed her features. It had never been hard for them, the understanding. Nakti had raised her after all. Mozare's hand squeezed hers, his strength always within her reach. She loved him for it, at the same time she knew pain was coming for them all, and wanted him to be as far away from it as possible.

"I saw your mother on the other side, I knew what must've become of you. Yet I had continued to hope that it wouldn't come to this."

Saiden couldn't hold back her tears. Couldn't remember crying this much since she'd been a child who'd lost her parents. She had already lost so much, and now the trust that she'd once placed in Nakti, in her morals and her own strength was tarnished by this one memory.

"You visited the Enlightened." They both already knew the answer, knew that Saiden and Nakti were both aware of what this conversation was about, but the words were needed anyway. They solidified things, made them real.

Saiden only nodded.

"Sometimes we don't recognize the strength of the ones we are trying to protect until it is too late." Nakti said in answer. "You were a child then, but I was not much older. It is no excuse, but I did what I thought was best. What good would it have done you to know that your mother lived, and yet was still torn from you?"

"I was a child then, but I was not a child long. You could've told me. How could you keep her from me?" Saiden was yelling, and finally she realized the wind around them was coming from her. A storm inside herself that she could never outrun.

"I love you Saiden, my little warrior. I wanted to spare you the pain." There were tears on Nakti's face, a shine to them that rivaled the brilliance of Ilona's hair. Deaths mark on her, a reminder that their time here was limited.

But was that really different from anything else in her life? She'd always known that death's call sang behind her, carried her through life.

"You spared me nothing but time and trust." Her voice was cold, all the fire gone. How could she reconcile the two versions of Nakti that now warred in her mind. She would never stop loving her, but she barely had time to grieve her, to be angry, to heal. Saiden was starting to doubt she'd ever get to the healing part of this journey.

"Listen to me well child, for there is still a great deal you don't know of this world." Saiden could hear anger rising in Nakti's voice too, matching her strike for strike. She'd already beaten her once, and she was tired of fighting. Her ears rang with the words Nakti had said the day she'd died.

"Every good soldier knows to trust their gut." Saiden threw Nakti's own words, the words she had stolen from her memory, back at her. "You told me to trust my gut, and to trust you. And you kept my mother hidden from me."

"You are my child too. Maybe not my blood, maybe we didn't share what you could have had with Magdalena, but you are mine too. Forged in love and fire, sworn by the blade you still carry. That will never stop. I did what I thought was best at the time, as all mothers do."

Saiden wanted nothing more than to hold her, to have Nakti at her back again, taming the curls of her hair into the four neat, braided buns. She reached out a hand, and Nakti reached back, until she saw the lily.

"Carry a piece of me with you always my love. You are the greatest joy of my life." Their fingers nearly brushed, and then she was gone again. Somehow Saiden knew that was the last she would hear from her, the last piece of Nakti that she would ever be given. The ritual would not work a second time.

Finally, as she settled back into herself, she realized that Mozare's hand had gone limp in her own.

55
LORALEI

Loralei watched the ritual from the top of the mountain, saw the storm gathering around them from whatever feelings were rising in Saiden, and stayed still amongst it all. Saiden had saved them from a gods-damned hurricane, Loralei could deal with a little wind. As quickly as she could, she twisted the loose pieces of her shorter hair back around her head so that nothing obscured her vision of her friends. Nothing would be sneaking up on them today, not when she knew how badly they needed this.

She saw the moment Nakti came to them, a glitter of light from this distance. Loralei recognized the call of her soul, their gifts calling to each other no matter the distance. Nakti had protected her once, had died trying to keep her safe. She bowed from her hiding place, a respect no one else needed to witness.

Slowly, she saw Mozare start to weaken, didn't know how she could see it from her post, but trusted the feeling nonetheless. Torn between what might come for them, and helping him Loralei hesitated to leave her position. She wasn't a soldier, she didn't know how to make the kind of strategic decisions she needed to make the way her friends did.

Loralei was simply a girl, who'd once had a kingdom, and now had only love. The love for her friends, and the love she knew they gave back to her. She descended from her perch, trying to keep her senses open to danger, but still losing track of her surroundings as she honed in on Mozare.

His heartbeat slowed, no longer matching her own. Panic caused the beating in her own chest to run rampant. She could not run fast enough, had not spent enough time amongst the dead of her people to know her way around the cemetery.

She caught him as he slumped to the side, and Nakti disappeared from in front of them. The time it took Saiden to realize she was gone angered Loralei, but she tried to keep it contained. She knew there was no world where Saiden would've asked this of Mozare if she'd known the consequences.

When she did feel his absence, she turned, only to spook at Loralei already there, warmth in her hands as she pressed her gifts into Mozare, seeking out the damage his own gifts had done to his insides. "I've got him. He's going to be fine."

Saiden sent a watery smile her way, and stood, wiping her own tears from her face. "I'll patrol around, make sure no one is coming this way."

Loralei didn't answer her, but Saiden didn't need her to. She needed a moment alone to collect herself, and there were bigger things to focus on at the moment. When Mozare was set right, the two of them could go about figuring out how to comfort Saiden.

Deep into her power she dove, pulling at every piece of herself to find the damage inside Mozare. Even as she healed what was broken, his heartbeat didn't steady, his eyes wouldn't focus on her again. It shouldn't have taken this long for him to come back to her.

Loralei gingerly wiped the blood from Mozare's face with the hem of her dress, doing her best to keep her own tears from falling on his face. Logically, she knew he was going to be okay. She was a strong enough healer now that not much could stop her. Watching him go through that though, had put a pain in her heart that rivaled the moment she had been sure she would lose him in Taezhali.

"No tears." He said, eyes still closed and voice weak. She wasn't even sure how he knew she was crying, except that he knew her so well.

"You're an idiot." She couldn't hide the waver in her voice that came when she was going to cry. And she knew Mozare could hear it too, but while he laid injured in her lap, he had the decency not to call her on it.

"You wouldn't have it another way." He coughed, and a dabble of blood freckled his face again. She didn't like how pale the red made him look. "Imagine if I was the smarter one in this relationship." She laughed and then balked at the idea that he could make her laugh when he'd been sitting on Ilona's doorstep.

"You need to stop doing this to me." She said, and they may have been the truest words she'd ever spoken. "You need to stop trying to leave me behind."

"Wasn't me this time." He said, a healthy color rising to his cheeks again. She started brushing the hair away from his face, the repetitive motion keeping her centered. Outside of her pain, she felt a lot worse than she had the last time he'd almost died, but he was right. Mozare wasn't trying to leave her here, he was helping their friend.

"It's reckless to use that much power in one go."

"I wanted to grant them as much time as I could. They deserved that much."

"And I deserve to not have my love at risk at every opportunity. I cannot bear it."

"So, you love me?"

"Of course that's the only thing you heard in that conversation." She laughed again and pressed her lips to his forehead. They'd survived today, they needed to continue that way, as long as they possibly could. Survive today, and the next day, over and over.

That was how they would win this war. How they would live to love again, in a new world.

56
SAIDEN

SAIDEN WAS GLAD CASSIMIR WAS OUTSIDE OF THE SAFE HOUSE WHEN SHE made her way back, because if she'd had to go inside without Mozare and Loralei to face Rhena she might never have made it inside. She couldn't believe she had been so selfish, asking Mozare to put himself in harm's way so that she could have one last confrontation with Nakti.

Her last words, the new ones he had been able to gift her rang in Saiden's head with every footfall. Cassimir saw her, eyes checking her over for injury again, a habit he might never grow out of. He then took in what must've been the distress on her face.

"Is everyone okay?"

She swallowed hard, trying to summon her voice to answer him, but unable to manage it. She nodded instead, and Cassimir must've seen enough to know that they were fine physically, but she was not fine mentally. She was so desperately not okay, and Saiden was starting to wonder if she ever would be again.

It didn't seem likely.

Cassimir opened his arms to her, and she stepped inside. Her mind still wouldn't let her find peace, even wrapped up in him.

"Let me check in on the others and then we'll go for a walk." He kissed her forehead, and she let him go back into the house, still not prepared to face them on her own. She loved that he gave her that space, that he understood her so well as to give it to her. Even when it kept him from his sister, he didn't share things until she was ready.

She wasn't sure she could love him more than she did in that moment, though she somehow didn't doubt that he would find another way to make that happen. When he came back outside he had another one of Eleni's scarves with him to replace the one she had lost on their way to the temple, and a hooded cloak. They couldn't be too careful, when her hair was a dead giveaway as to who she was.

He helped her into the cloak, and she realized that she was shivering. She hadn't noticed it before, with the chaos in her mind, but her body was reacting to it as well. At least, after all the fighting she'd done earlier, her powers remained dormant inside her. Though, she was sure they would never be far from hand if she really let her emotions get the better of her.

Cassimir slipped her hand into his elbow. She imagined another life where they were two lovers who'd met despite the distance, despite the odds, taking a casual stroll through a city she belonged in. And while it was true how they'd met, Saiden had never belonged in this city.

Instead of focusing on all the overwhelming sensations around her, and the vicious thoughts lashing the inside of her mind, Saiden put all of her focus into her breathing and the sound of their steps on the cobblestones.

"What happened? The full story this time?"

"I've never had a lot of people in my life that cared about me." She didn't want him to feel bad for her, it was the simple truth of her life, the consequence of her birth and the powers she never asked for. "But I had enough. I had Mozare and Nakti. The only reason I'm even alive is because she took a risk on me and basically committed treason to save my life."

"When we went back to the legion, they shunned us both. But she was always a good soldier, and she rose quickly through the ranks. And she took me with her. I had become her responsibility. And she was the closest thing I had to a mother growing up."

The words hurt because she could've had her own mother, if this country hadn't reviled her from birth. And she could've had them both if she hadn't believed in Revon's lies and put him on a throne he didn't belong on. She had been the one who'd ruined her own life, and that was a hard truth to face.

"And I found out that she knew the whole time that Magdalena was in prison. Or maybe not the whole time, but she knew pretty early on, and she never told me. I can't believe she kept her from me." Saiden hadn't told him that the first time. She waited for anger to cloud the concern on his face because she was hiding it from him, but it never came.

"I can't imagine how hard that must've been to find out." She wanted to cry at the words. At his understanding when she'd been so afraid she had hurt him too.

Saiden leaned in closer to him, reveling in the warmth of his words and his body. "I wanted answers. And Rhena made a comment about how it was a shame I couldn't ask Nakti what she had been thinking. I thought, maybe Mozare could summon her, and I could finally get closure. I never thought that would be an option. I was prepared to live with that guilt for the rest of my life."

She knew he understood the exact moment she was talking about; when she'd been forced to take Nakti's life for what she had thought was a good reason. But Nakti had been right. Saiden hadn't known the people she was fighting for, and everyone she loved had suffered because of it.

"Sometimes the challenges life throws at us are more than we can handle alone." Cassimir said, and she waited for him to go on. He paused, thinking over his words before he spoke them, taking care with every one of them. "That is why we need our family, to help us carry the weight when it becomes too much."

The words were eerily similar to what her mother had said the night before Revon had killed her. Saiden was torn between kissing him and crying, but she didn't have time to do either before Cassimir was turning her around, pressing her back to the wall of a house at the entry to a dark alley and pressing his body into hers.

She heard it a moment after him, the sound of approaching boots.

He pulled her hood tighter against her, making sure not a single curl managed to give them away, and pressing his face into her neck, every one of their combined senses focused on the guards coming their way.

To the world, they probably looked like a couple out for a late night rendezvous, and she hoped the appearance of passion between them was enough to make the guards look away.

Then she remembered what had happened outside the temple, and another idea popped into her head. She tucked her finger under Cassimir's chin, turning his face up so he was looking at her, and then she called on Ilona's shadows, and Keir's light, and made them disappear. Even without seeing him, Saiden managed to get a hand over Cassimir's mouth so he didn't make a noise at their sudden lack of visibility, trying to keep anything from making the guards look too closely at her hastily thrown together shield.

She hadn't been sure that it would work anyway, and with her control over her powers being what it was, she didn't know how long it would hold. But as the guards passed her without even a glance in her direction, she breathed a strong sigh of relief.

It wasn't much, but it kept her love safe. She'd only ever wanted to protect them.

57

RHENA

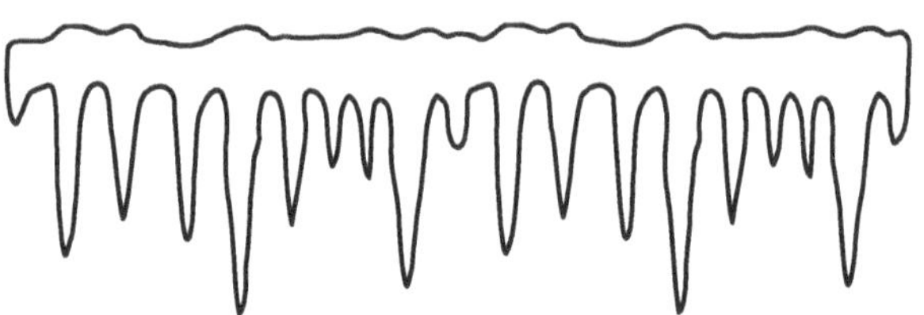

RHENA WASN'T SURPRISED THAT WHEN SHE TRIED TO SLIP AWAY FROM THE group the next morning, Mozare followed her up to the roof. She wasn't sure if it was going to be him or Saiden, but she knew after everything that had gone down in the square the day before, she was due for a sibling chat. Even if they weren't technically her siblings.

Spending time with Cassimir had been peaceful, and he had done a lot to help her process what had happened, but they didn't really know each other yet, so it couldn't take the place of this kind of comfort.

Rhena didn't flinch when he sat down next to her, but she didn't start the conversation either. She didn't know what to say. But when Mozare put his arm around her, she happily cuddled in next to him. She was starting to understand what it must've felt like to be Saiden before the rebellion, where she was constantly looking for threats around every corner.

It wasn't easy to spend so much time afraid.

But it wasn't as hard now that she was with them as it had been when she was alone. They made it easier, not because they made the fear go away, but because she knew they were going to face it with her.

"We need to talk." Mozare said. Normally those words were unsettling. Not knowing was something else to be afraid of. But Mozare's voice was calm, and she didn't have to add him to list of things that scared her. Even if she wasn't exactly looking forward to this conversation.

"I didn't think you came up here for the view." She answered, trying to summon a pinch of his cocky ego. Rhena wasn't really sure she could pull it off. But Mozare tried to laugh anyway, if only to loosen some of the tension building on the rooftop.

"You didn't use your power in the square yesterday." It wasn't a question, and it didn't have to be. If she had used her gifts, Mozare would have felt it, their connection through the goddess so innate to both of them. And she hadn't used them. Hadn't wanted to.

"It's not like you really taught me to kick ass and wield shadows did you?" Rhena tried to joke remembering the first time they had trained her powers together, the way she'd knocked him on his ass when she'd accidentally coated the floor in ice.

Mozare didn't rise to her teasing, and it was probably for the best. As much as she wanted to joke it off, this was a serious conversation and that was what it needed to be.

"Emotions control elemental gifts. That's what you taught me." She started, trying to work out her own reasoning in her head at the same time she was explaining it to Mozare. "In the palace, I was so afraid, so tense all the time, that I could barely walk through the halls without lowering the temperature. It was dangerous. It could've gotten me caught, and yet I still couldn't manage to control it."

Mozare squeezed her in closer, and she finally realized she was shivering. She'd dropped the temperature up here too, and Mozare hadn't even said anything. "Talon helped. He's life gifted, and he can control heat. He'd balance the temperature so we were less likely to get caught.

"And then he did the testing. He made everyone line up, and used those new soldiers of his to see who had the strongest gifts. I made it storm in the mess hall with a drop of their blood. Revon looked like he'd been given a gift of his own when he saw it." She knew now how little talent of his own the king actually possessed. Enough to bastardize the rest of theirs.

"He signed me up for his experiments." She felt Mozare tense. She hadn't told any of them that she'd been on the list of candidates Revon intended to experiment on. "But I was still too young. So he wanted me to prove myself to him. And I tried, if only to keep up appearances."

"You're safe here." Mozare said a reminder to them both, pausing to kiss her forehead. She could feel how much this story was hurting him, but they both knew she had to finish.

"I was afraid all the time, so I pushed my power back inside. If I couldn't control the fear, at least I wouldn't show everyone that I was afraid. If they couldn't feel it, they wouldn't know. But I can't control it either, not really, and it's much harder to control now."

"And I hurt that general. The scar across his face that was me, but it was the last time I felt in control of my power. Because then they locked me up, and they used me as bait and I thought they would do to me what they'd done to Talon or worse." She was crying, everything she'd bottled up in the weeks since she decided to go back to the palace finally freed.

"I can't even imagine dealing with all of that." Mozare admitted, and the realization that even her friend might have struggled in her place helped more than she would've expected it too. "But you have a gift, even if it doesn't always feel like that. And it's important that you remember it's a tool in your arsenal, it answers to you."

"Sometimes." Rhena threw in. He squeezed her again.

"You're still new to your gifts. You can't expect to have it all under control yet. And this is the worst kind of environment to be trying to figure it all out in. When there's so much other uncertainty. How can you be expected to teach yourself?"

Mozare's words were a balm over her wounds. Even without healing gifts, he was helping to mend the injury rotting between her and her powers. "I need more training. I can't fight with you, not when I can't defend myself."

That was a truth she hadn't been prepared to face until now. She wanted to fight beside her friends, but she was more of a danger to them than a help. And they would be so focused on protecting her that they wouldn't be careful enough to keep themselves out of harm.

"There are other ways to fight than holding a blade." Mozare wasn't usually the one who had the right thing to say. But, right now, every word he spoke gave Rhena a small piece of herself back. "Eleni will need help in the medical tents. You can stay with her, tend to the wounded."

Rhena liked that idea. Even if she didn't have healing talents, she could wrap injuries as well as any other person, and there were sure to be plenty of those to deal with.

"I can do that."

Mozare stood, pulling her up from the roof as he went. "But first, we need to call on those powers. They aren't a threat, and they are only a weapon if you choose for them to be. I need to know that you can use them to defend yourself if it comes down to it."

Those words didn't make Rhena feel better, but she understood their logic all the same. She settled into her body, reaching into the well of power, and opened a rain cloud right over Mozare's head. She had forgotten that there used to be a time when calling on her powers felt good, and as she watched Mozare get soaked by her rainstorm, she couldn't stop herself from laughing.

Mozare on the other hand, didn't seem nearly as amused as she was. Watching him, she finally noticed the rings of shadows around his hands, his own power not completely under his control either. But he didn't seem bothered by it in the slightest. Rhena wasn't sure if that calm was for her benefit or his own.

"That's good, but you aren't stopping an enemy with a rainstorm. We fight rain or shine." She buffeted up her storm, but when Mozare continued to stare at her despite the hair stuck to his forehead, she got serious. She pushed deeper into her powers and pulled on the ice that she was so afraid of, forming two long icicles in her hands.

"Now that's a weapon." Mozare praised her. "Do something else."

She remembered the way she had called her ice in the mess hall to keep that drop of blood from getting into her body, and the way she had used it to stop the bleeding when she'd been cut in training. Rhena pressed the icicles to her skin, using her power to shape them into armor. With her magic running through it, she didn't think it would be easy for a blade to pierce through.

Her power could protect her when she let it. Mozare smiled at her, and she finally let the rain stop, pulling the water from his clothes and siphoning it off to the plants Loralei had grown on the rooftop for their privacy. She wasn't sure plants grown by the god's gift needed water, but she figured it couldn't hurt.

And as she and Mozare climbed down the ladder to rejoin their friends, she felt a little lighter than she had coming up.

58

SAIDEN

If Revon wanted to play dirty Saiden was going to make him regret it. There were many ways to take away a person's power and if she had to try every single one of them to get Revon to acknowledge their presence she would. After his attack in the square and lighting the orphanage on fire, Saiden wanted to march right into the palace and cut his head off his shoulders.

But she had enough training to know she'd never even make it to his rooms. Not when every soldier in the kingdom still loyal to him could recognize her by a single lock of hair. She had to be smarter than Revon.

After her time in his rebellion, Saiden had an idea of how he thought, knew that without her expertise, his seat on the throne would never have been won. It was a thought that had long bothered her, but she knew that meant she had a chance against him as well. And she was going to hold on to that.

They had done their best to lay low in the weeks since the orphanage had burned down, focusing on relocating the children to families in the surrounding houses. None of them wanted to draw any more attention to themselves after all the fighting they'd seen recently.

Saiden knew how important patience was in a war. They used the time to track the comings and goings in the palace and to get information.

After spending so much time cooped up, watching Revon's soldiers patrol the streets, Saiden was ready for action. They wanted her to be afraid; she wanted them to feel terrified. She wanted to be in every shadowy corner and midnight nightmare.

Revon wanted a monster, and she could wear that face for a while longer.

But she wouldn't let him hurt anyone else if she could help it. Because she had put him on that throne, and his horrendous behavior was her responsibility. Just as it was her responsibility to see him deposed and punished.

Cassimir and Saiden set off to disrupt the delivery they had overheard soldiers talking about from their rooftop perch. Mozare stayed back with Rhena to keep the house safe, and Loralei took Eleni out to collect more materials for her healing supplies. They were preparing for war, far more thoroughly than they had last time, when Revon had been leading their rebellion. And they were preparing for injury as best they could, even though they were so few people and most of them would need to be fighting.

If anyone could help Eleni get the herbs she needed though, it was Loralei. With even the smallest hint of them, she'd be able to grow more. Aside from the ivy Saiden had grown in response to Loralei's powers during the ambush outside the temple, gardening wasn't a gift that came easily to her.

But tracking these deliveries? That was something she had practice with. She and Mozare had infiltrated so many townships and border cities to the north to do the exact same thing, it felt like returning to her old life.

Except she wouldn't have had Cassimir with her then, and she didn't want to give him up.

It was weird however to see him dressed in black from head to toe. Cassimir was someone who thrived on color and his normal wardrobe certainly reflected that. She missed his bold hues, but it didn't make sense to give their enemies any assistance in hunting them. They would survive one night without his brightness. Especially because she knew she would see it again.

She was dangerously optimistic now. She was going to see this country brought back to glory. She was going to see justice done within its borders. She was prepared to fight until it happened.

Saiden caught sight of soldiers from the palace. She rushed after them, desperate, feverishly prepared for bloodshed. Blade in hand, she grabbed the smaller of the two, pulled their arms behind their back and placed a blade to their throat. Keir's gifts lit up inside her but luckily, she couldn't feel the grime of augmented magic here. She was relieved, until the other soldier pulled down his hood and turned to face her, weapon already drawn.

"It's that Blood-Cursed bitch." It had been a long time since she'd been called Blood-Cursed, and the voice that spoke made her freeze. She had beat Oliver once in a duel, but she wasn't prepared to fight him now. Cassimir's hands hovered over the handle of his chakram at his waist, but this was Saiden's fight.

Saiden released Melana. She knew exactly what the other girl was capable of with a little skin to skin contact. She backed away, putting one hand over Cassimir's to stay him before she turned to face Oliver and Melana adjusting her grip on her own blade.

"Didn't think it was bad enough to plunge the entire country into this shit hole and then abandon it, now you're what? Disrupting its supplies?"

Saiden didn't know how to answer him. And she had to admit, that after days of fighting and too little sleep she wasn't entirely sure if she could beat him in a one-on-one fight.

Then his partner surprised Saiden. She wasn't used to Melana speaking at all, especially not to counteract her partner. "What the oaf means to say is, do you have Rhena?"

Saiden tensed at the sound of Rhena's name. "I will kill you before you ever lay a hand on her."

"So you do have her?" Oliver asked and she couldn't read the tone of his voice.

"She's safe?" Melana asked. "She disappeared. By the time we knew she was missing it was as if she had never existed to begin with. We couldn't do anything to help her."

In her confusion Saiden dropped her guard a little, her blades held more loosely in her hands. "You wanted to help her?"

"What do you think? That we enjoy the current state of the country we've dedicated our lives too? Who do you think got stuck cleaning up your mess while you were gone all that time?" Anger laced his words.

Saiden took a risk and resheathed her blades. If this was some kind of trick, she always had her powers to fall back on, no matter how unpredictable they were. And she still had Cassimir.

"You were protecting Rhena?"

"We protect every soldier we can." Melana answered. "We funnel prisoners out of the palace, reunite families that have been separated, hide the newly gifted before they can be enlisted to Revon's military. Anything we can do to make this city an even marginally safer of a place for people to live."

Saiden couldn't hide her shock. "I've never done anything other than care about this country." Oliver said, and he returned his own weapon to its carrier on his back. "You and I might not have been friends, but we fight on the same side of this war. My blade and my might is yours. At least until you get this shit fixed." Oliver added contemptuously.

At his side Melana nodded her agreement.

"Rhena is safe." Saiden finally said, realizing that she'd never given them that confirmation. And if they cared about her the way she did, they deserved that reassurance. "Can you give us any information about what Revon is doing?"

"Let's go somewhere quieter, another patrol should come through here soon, and we don't want to be seen talking to traitors when they do." Melana said, no hint of malice in her voice. And she was right, if the crown didn't view Melana and Oliver as traitors they couldn't risk being seen together and tipping them off. They needed any advantages they could get if they were going to win this war.

"Come this way." Oliver, despite his bulk, led them to a small alcove surrounded by houses that had been abandoned weeks before by their occupants. Crowded inside the small space they were all sitting knee to knee, but for once she wasn't worried about the proximity.

Saiden was far more worried about what they were going to tell her was happening in the palace. They were aware of Revon's experiments, but Saiden knew he wouldn't stop there. Especially if there were other things he could do to grasp at the power outside his reach.

"What about Talon?" Cassimir asked first, reminding Saiden about Rhena's friend in the palace who she had wanted to protect. Saiden hadn't even considered asking about him, she was still so thrown at being allied, however hesitantly, with Oliver.

"We've been watching out for him. He's already received retribution as a traitor. Revon seems to believe that he's seen the errors of his ways, but we won't let anything else happen to him." Melana answered. Something about her voice, which Saiden had rarely heard before, soothed the tension in the tight space around them.

"Thank you." Saiden said, and she meant it more than she could express. There were too many pieces in motion for her to have eyes on everything, and having more allies was never a bad thing, even tentative allies like Oliver. She didn't know him well, but she knew he had morals. A code he lived by. She could respect that. And, after all, their fight had not been born out of hatred towards her.

"How can we aid you from inside the palace?" Oliver asked, and despite the tension in his voice as he forced out the words, she believed that if there was something he could do, he would find a way to help them.

It was weird how the networks of people she trusted was expanding. It now included people she never thought would fit on that list. It was very strange, but she didn't want to look at it too closely, not when they needed all the help they could get.

"We're going to interrupt the supply to the palace. What patrols should we expect?"

"Around 10 of his augmented soldiers. Possibly a few gifted, but Revon has been relying heavily on the augmented ones. Something about the process seems to increase their loyalty to him. They sit at his feet like dogs and wait for his orders." Oliver sounded unsettled, and the thought bothered her too.

Even with how much the gods had been influencing her life recently, and the way her gifts didn't always respond the way she wanted them too, she was not beholden to them. She had free will, and she didn't like the idea of Revon taking it away, even from the horrible people who'd volunteered for his experiments.

"But the gifted can still be useful to him, even if he doesn't trust them. And some are still trying to prove their worth so they can be part of his next trials. That's what he's calling it."

"No one wants to be part of an experiment." Melana added, "but plenty of his followers will go through trials to earn his favor."

"That's maniacal." Cassimir said, and she knew exactly what he meant. The fact that Revon went so far as to adjust his language to manipulate people into wanting to be experimented on was beyond vile.

"How many augmented are there?"

"It's not always obvious," Oliver started. "But we're guessing about 60."

60. She hadn't thought that many of his soldiers would want that kind of power, but she was wrong. How many of them had been forced? There was no way for her to know.

"How much stronger are they?" Cassimir asked. For someone who didn't grow up with the power they were all exposed to on a daily basis, he handled the middle kingdom like he'd lived there all his life. Gifts included. But, even she was scared about the augmented. And she couldn't blame him if he was too.

"It varies." Melana answered, hand reaching for Oliver's. That was new. "It depends on how strong they are going in. And we think the trials react differently to everyone when they're undergoing them. It's all very convoluted."

Her answer frightened Saiden, so she changed the subject. "You can get in touch with us through the Enlightened." Saiden still didn't want to go anywhere near the temple, but she couldn't give them the location of their safe house either. Not because she didn't trust them, but because there were too many other lives to consider if they brought trouble to their door. "And if you can get Talon out, send him there. Rhena would feel better knowing he wasn't in the middle of this." It was a last ditch effort to save the boy, and to be honest, she wasn't sure he was any better off with them.

"We're going to stop those supplies, whatever they are, but if you need medical care, you can send your wounded to the temple as well. We'll ferry them out to healing tents and help as many people as we can." Cassimir was too good for her. Always thinking about others. She didn't want anyone injured near Eleni until the fighting began, but he didn't want anyone dying unnecessarily. It was the unselfish choice; one she wouldn't have been strong enough to make on her own.

She loved him even more for it.

59
MOZARE

THEY HAD MANAGED TO FIND FLEEING FAMILIES WHO WERE WILLING TO take almost every single orphan from the fire, except for Zeli. She had never really gotten over her attachment to Mozare, and since the family they were staying with didn't seem to mind watching her while Mozare was running missions, he didn't fight very hard to send her away.

To be honest, he was quite attached to the little one himself.

While Saiden and Cassimir were out blocking supply deliveries to the palace, the rest of them were hidden away in the safe house, trying to think of anything they could do to give themselves an advantage in the coming battles.

He didn't know if the others could feel it, but death sang in the wind. He knew that every day brought her closer, and yet he was desperate to keep them as far from it as he could. Holding Zeli reminded him of the future they were fighting to bring back to their country. Of the peace they would finally restore.

Of the peace he could bring himself, when he righted the wrongs that aiding Revon had brought. He didn't know how he had gotten things so wrong, but he was going to see them put right. And he had another reason to fight now, because he wanted to see this little one grow.

He wasn't sure how he had gotten so attached to her. Maybe it was that she cried when he put her down, and holding her was something he could never do wrong. He'd laughed when their hostess had given him a wrap and shown him how to tie the baby to his body. But, she'd slept so peacefully the first time he'd swaddled her in it, that she'd slept there every day since. Even when that meant Mozare slept sitting up on the floor.

He'd slept in worse places. But never with such a small warm body pressed against him.

Sometimes, he'd catch Loralei watching them, her face an unreadable cross of emotions. Until she saw him notice her, and quickly busied herself with some menial task.

Mozare wanted to give her everything he had. All the peace he'd manage to carve out for himself in this hellhole. But he didn't know how to do that. Not when she couldn't bear to be anywhere near him.

When Rhena sought him out later that day, he was more than happy for the chance to get out of the small house. She'd made great progress reconnecting to her powers in a healthy way after all she'd witnessed in the palace. But she had her sword in hand now, so he didn't think that was what she was looking for this time.

"If I'm going to stay behind, to help in the healing tents, I need to be able to protect myself and Eleni. Zeli too, if you decide to leave her with us." Mozare was pretty sure they would leave Zeli here with the couple that let them use their home, but he loved that Rhena was looking out for the baby, as if her presence there were as normal as anything else.

"I'd like another training session as well, if that's not objectionable." Eleni added from behind Rhena. "Not because I think I'll be anywhere near good enough to defend anyone, but to keep my promise to my oaf of a brother."

Mozare wondered if Cassimir could feel his sister making fun of him. Sometimes the two of them seemed to be that connected to each other. He and Saiden were like siblings, they had been for a long time, but they hadn't grown up together. There was something different, no matter how close they were now, to having a shared childhood.

And one that didn't involve so much blood.

"Sure, you can take turns watching Zeli while we train." He didn't bother asking Loralei if she wanted to join them. He figured she'd be glad to be free of him for a while, to not have to breathe in the same space as him.

He took the baby in her sling and carefully handed her to Eleni, trusting the young woman to care for her. Gently, Eleni rocked her, keeping her asleep, and heading to one corner to watch somewhere out of the way. Mozare pulled out his own short sword, a weapon perfectly matched to the gold sword Saiden had commissioned to gift Rhena. He didn't need to use his best weapon, but he needed her to be strong in hers.

This might be all the protection he would be able to offer her. When Saiden gave them their orders, and he knew when it came down to it Saiden would be the one giving orders, it was very unlikely she'd be able to spare anyone to guard the camp.

"Strong position. No one moves you without your permission. You do not yield even an inch to your enemy without gaining something in return." He watched her get into place, adjusting her with small taps of his blade until he was satisfied with the way she was standing.

"Don't watch the blade alone, watch the arm, and the body. Movement doesn't start at the wrist. And leave your senses open to feel for their gifts. Enemies are going to come at you from every angle, with every weapon in their arsenal. Ready?"

Rhena nodded, and Mozare advanced, proud when she stood her ground. He swung his blade, casting his shadows toward her at the same time. This wasn't the place to be careful, to go slow. He needed to be confident that he could leave her behind and she would be able to defend herself. Mozare knew Rhena wanted the same thing.

To go easy on her would have been a disservice. He pushed her, and when she finally moved from her place on the roof, he saw too late what she was gaining with the inch she'd lost. She ducked as he swung, the momentum too strong to stop, sliding under his blade and coming up behind him.

The point of her sword was pressed against the back of his neck before he even had an opportunity to fully turn. He clapped, careful of the blade he was still holding. From the corner, Eleni did her best to clap as well, although her hands were still full with Zeli.

Rhena smiled, then handed Eleni her sword, opening her arms to take the child from Eleni. "Your turn."

"Well. I'm not sure I can live up to that display."

"You shouldn't try to live up to that. That's more training than we have time to give you." Mozare started, but he didn't like the disappointment that crossed Eleni's face at his words. He was used to soldiers, or at least those who were training to become soldiers. He didn't know how to temper his lessons to suit a softer kind of student.

Still, he tried, because she deserved to be able to keep herself safe, and she needed confidence that only training could give her. "A sword is unwieldy, if you carry one, people will assume you are more trained than you are. It is better in this instance to be underestimated." Mozare gently took Rhena's blade from her, sheathing it at his back until he could return it to her.

"You're better off with a smaller, concealed weapon. You'll only be using it in the last possible moment, if everything else has gone to shit." The words were not as gentle as he wished they were, but that was not the world they were living in.

He picked a blade from his own collection and started to pull the sheath free from his thigh so he could hand the whole of it to Eleni. "May it protect you from every harm." It wasn't the weapon ceremony of the legion, nothing like what Saiden had done for Rhena, but it was an honor to give it to her nonetheless.

Mozare backed away from her, and opened his arms wide, using himself for the purpose of his demonstration. "There are some strike points that work better without armor, and some that are better when your foe is wearing it. Fighting any normal person, strike on the center line." He motioned down his own front. "Eyes, nose, neck, sternum, stomach, groin. Sometimes you can manage to hit the instep, but you have be precise to do damage there. I wouldn't risk it. You can only guarantee one strike before they defend, you have to make it worth the risk."

He turned slightly, angling himself diagonally across her view. "In armor the center line tends to be protected. You want to aim into the side of the neck, or the armpits, sometimes the ankle if you have space to run. If all else fails, strike the wrist, a soldier who cannot lift their sword cannot strike you down."

They practiced, Mozare adjusting Eleni's grip and the ankle she aimed the blade towards. When she was tired, when Mozare saw her strength flagging, he let her sit, and he went another round with Rhena. They spent the night like that, preparing for the worst.

60
CASSIMIR

CASSIMIR AND SAIDEN MADE SURE NOT TO PUSH THEMSELVES TOO HARD AS they raced to intercept the soldiers gathering supplies for Revon's army. The entire time, Cassimir's brain had one question running on loop. Why would his uncle have backed this rebellion, and what did he stand to gain from having Revon on the throne?

Originally, when his uncle had asked him to come, he hadn't questioned it. His loyalty to both his family and his emperor blinding him to the possibility of any ulterior motive. But now, after every rotten thing he'd seen in his cousin Akil, and the destitute state of this country, Cassimir wasn't sure his uncle had been right to send him.

Even still, he'd never stop being grateful that this fight had brought him to Saiden. She ran a few paces ahead of him, the glow of her skin telling him that she was using her powers. Possibly to scout ahead, possibly without even realizing it. He didn't have the kind of power necessary to know what she was doing.

It didn't change the fact that he trusted her completely. Even as they ran headfirst into danger, he wasn't as worried as he knew he should be, because she was fighting at his side. And these augmented soldiers, no matter how powerful, couldn't fight Saiden's raw desire to protect the people she loved.

He was fortunate enough to be included in that group.

And she was powerful now. Not that she hadn't been strong in her own right before, she'd beaten him in training too many times for him not to know that, but now her powers were magnificent. He'd witnessed their glory and been brought back from the brink of death by that strength. Cassimir knew she would see them through this darkness too.

When Saiden moved to duck behind a tree, Cassimir followed, and together they watched the two men in the clearing below waiting for their pickup. Their moves were sluggish, nerves radiating off them. Cassimir found he pitied them some, the same way he pitied the version of himself that had believed Revon's lies about a brighter future.

The only bright thing in his future was the life he'd have after this war. A life he hoped to share with Saiden.

"What's your plan. I don't think a bunch of trained soldiers will fall for the same trick the pirates did." Even with all the fear that surrounded the memories of rescuing his sister, he still smiled when he remembered threatening those men with the might behind him. They hadn't known the only one who'd come was Saiden. Even their uncle hadn't been brave enough to fight for Eleni. But Saiden had been prepared to rescue the princess by herself if needed.

"They have numbers on their side. More than the two of us could handle, and that's before we factor in the uncertainty of the augmented and their abilities." He saw her shiver and wondered what thought had passed through her head. "There is no version of this scenario where we aren't outnumbered and under resourced."

Her words should have bothered him, but he knew she wasn't done yet.

"So we need them to think they're outnumbered. This is my plan." Saiden went over everything with him, and he had to admit, she was a genius. Her brain was meant for this, meant for leading troops into battle. Even when he was her only soldier.

Cassimir did what he could to help her prepare, both of them watching the clearing and the space around them for Revon's soldiers. Fear built up inside him, but he pushed it from his mind. He trusted

Saiden, and he trusted that her plan would be enough to give them an edge. Together they only needed the smallest advantage to bring this battle to a successful end. And every small victory led them closer to the days when the fighting would cease.

That was the future he wanted for this country. Peace.

Cassimir and Saiden finished their preparations and then took their spots on opposite sides of the caravan and waited. Saiden glowed slightly, a sight he was sure no one else could make out with the trees, but he would be able to find her anywhere.

He heard footsteps through the woods at the same time her light went dim, and he knew it was starting. All the fear that had been collecting inside him dissipated, leaving room for battle calm to sweep over him.

In two neat lines, 14 of Revon's soldiers marched into the clearing. It was odd, seeing them marching in formation through the brush, it didn't make any sense to force that kind of rigidity on soldiers when they weren't in a city. Or barracks. But he didn't want the strangeness of it to throw him off.

Oliver had been right. Despite the tension that roiled between him and Saiden, he had given them good intel. But Cassimir couldn't tell which of the soldiers were augmented and that fear tried to push its way to the front of his mind.

All he could tell himself was that gifted or not, augmented or not, they were all still flesh and blood. They could die like any other man. At least he hoped they would still die like any other man. He'd have to make peace with those thoughts too, thoughts of how easily men could be killed, but that would come after they'd survived this.

Saiden and Cassimir stepped into the clearing together, blades in his hands, while hers were empty. He didn't like seeing her hands without weapons in them, not when they were suddenly surrounded by enemies, every one of them armed. But he knew what the plan was ,and he wouldn't let his unease give them away.

"Now look at what the shadows have brought us." A woman spoke from the group. "Revon's number one most wanted. The soldier who turned her back on the entire country for what? Some man?"

Cassimir bristled at the way she talked to Saiden, but he knew Saiden could defend herself. He also knew she'd heard a lot worse.

"Sacrificed your own mother for power, and then abandoned the people who protected you when you were useless. Really is a damn curse to be born like you." Those words made him burn inside, and he could only imagine how they must've hurt Saiden. He hadn't realized that in their absence, Revon had told his soldiers Saiden had killed Magdalena to free her power.

He should've known Revon would be that vile, but he still hadn't expected that.

Saiden didn't even flinch, and Cassimir wasn't sure how she managed it.

"He'd take you back, if you came with us." A different soldier spoke, his voice trying to soften the accusations made. "He'd let you serve our cause again, bring you back into the fold. He's forgiven traitors for far worse."

Now that Cassimir didn't believe. There would be no forgiveness for any of them. But for Saiden, there were chains in her future if Revon ever got hold of her. He wouldn't let that happen to her again. He'd never forget seeing the lifeless expression on her face as her gifts had controlled her, forcing her to murder for a man who believed human life had no value beyond what it could do for him.

All her life Saiden had fought for somewhere to belong. Cassimir knew she had found that place with them, with their small broken family. She wouldn't give it up to go back to the man who'd killed her mother. He watched her move her hands behind her back, and pushed forward, slicing his blade across the throat of the soldier closest to him before they could even see what was happening.

Around them, the forest burst into flames, controlled by Saiden's powers. The fake soldiers they'd hastily put together in the shadowy parts of the woods lighting up like they were an army prepared to follow Saiden's orders. At the same time, she lashed out, hiding the use of her power behind the birds that suddenly flocked the clearing diving straight towards their enemies. Even if Revon's soldiers felt her powers, they wouldn't know that she was using them to create an army of decoys surrounding them.

Her soldiers, or the appearance of them, were different from the undead ones Mozare summoned. Aside from the distraction they served, these visages couldn't actually aid them, and he knew Saiden didn't believe she could raise them to do so. All they did was give the two of them time.

Saiden finally pulled her blades, the blue one he'd given her in her right hand, the gift from Nakti in her left. With her birds pecking at them, Saiden sliced deep into the chests of the two soldiers closest to her, not bothering to watch them fall to the ground before she moved on to the next. Four of Revon's men raced into the forest, preparing to face the soldiers that would remain always a step out of reach.

Light was a powerful thing. Not only because it created fire, but because it could be used to weave illusion. Cassimir wasn't sure how she managed to keep so much focus on their deceptions while fighting for her life. He couldn't dwell on it, not when two soldiers jumped him at the same time.

Cassimir ducked, swinging a blade out at the calves of one of the soldiers, tipping them into the second. It wasn't a killing blow, but it should've been enough to disarm temporarily. Except Cassimir watched the wounds heal even as he was cleaving through flesh.

This man was one of Revon's augmented. After that display he was sure of it. Glancing at Saiden, he threw one of his circular blades into a soldier attempting to attack her from behind and pulled the long sword from its sheath on his back. The second soldier struck out, but Cassimir blocked, managing to get both of his attackers in front of him.

At the same time as he threw his remaining chakram at the second soldier, Cassimir turned fully, using the force to decapitate the augmented soldier who'd healed his first injury. Let him try to heal from that.

He pulled his chakram from the felled soldier, and sliced it across his throat one last time. For good measure, incase this one could bring himself back from the brink. He didn't like the feeling of it, but he would do what needed to be done to see they both walked out of this fight.

Two more bodies laid at Saiden's feet, and beyond her, the fires wavered. That wasn't a good sign. If she was burning out, or worse, if she were injured, there were still too many for him to face on his own while he tried to protect her.

Cassimir surprised his next victim, who had ignored him in favor of charging Saiden. A straight stab through the back and he collapsed, joining the others on the ground before he even knew what hit him.

Someone jumped on his back, using their whole weight to push Cassimir towards the ground. Twisting as fast as he could, Cassimir landed on his back before his attacker was on top of him. She pressed her dagger downwards, using gravity to her advantage. Under her, Cassimir was forced to use all his strength to stop the blade from plunging directly into his heart. Her strength lagged for a second and he got one small opening to stop her. He rolled them to the side enough to dislodge her, grabbing her blade and stabbing into her armpit.

She screamed, and he wasn't sure if it was pain, or if she was trying to get help. But her intentions didn't matter because he silenced her scream with a flick of his wrist, leaving her blade beside her dying body and recovering his own sword.

While Cassimir was on the ground, the other soldiers must've finally recognized their ruse. The remaining six soldiers surrounded Saiden, who twirled between them doing her best to stay alive. Cassimir stood, but before he could make his way towards her, power exploded, pushing the soldiers back. Cassimir dug in his feet, resisting the force only because he wasn't as close to her as the guards.

A blade sailed, though he couldn't tell where it had come from, sinking into Saiden's shoulder. The wind around her stopped, the soldiers rising to their feet. Cassimir ran towards them, taking out the two guards closest to him as he tried to get to her. A third saw him kill his friends and attacked, but Cassimir was brutal now, cutting the man down without a thought; gift or no gift. He wouldn't let them get to her first.

Saiden pulled the blade out of her shoulder, blood soaking her shirt until it clung to her skin. He didn't understand why she wasn't healing it. She should've been as strong as the augmented he had killed, but she kept bleeding.

Cassimir blocked a blow coming from another guard, twisting

under their blades and stabbing up with a short sword he'd picked up from one of the fallen augmented. He was quick to pull the blade back out, throwing it into the chest of the soldier closest to Saiden.

With only one hand, Saiden managed to fight off another attacker, slicing into her arms in quick sucession before she was able to end things. And he took out the last opponent, leaving his sword stuck through his chest so he could catch Saiden before she hit the ground.

"What happened? Why haven't you healed this?"

Saiden hissed through gritted teeth. "The blade was poisoned. I don't want to seal it inside, but I don't have enough focus to work such small healing and pull the poison out."

Cassimir could feel his face paling, the blood on his skin going cold. He didn't have any way to fight poison. He didn't know how to help her.

She pressed a bloodied hand to his cheek, forcing him to look at her. "I won't let this kill me. Now let's get these supplies where they're needed and find Loralei and your sister. Between them, someone should be able to help with this."

He leaned down to kiss her forehead, "sit here. Don't move too much."

As quickly as he could, Cassimir wrapped the supplies onto the carriage, moving packages around so that there was room on board for Saiden. It would be difficult to pull it on his own, and he could already feel his strength waning after the fight, but he didn't think she would make it if she had to pull the cart as well, and there was too much on there, too many supplies they desperately needed, for them to risk leaving it behind to thieves or more of Revon's soldiers.

He returned to Saiden, gingerly picking her up, careful of the gash on her shoulder where blood still trickled free. She smiled at him, but her face was wan, the battle flush missing. And she looked tired. Cassimir rested her among the supplies in the cart, checking that everything was settled so he could start pulling.

"Listen to me Saiden, let me tell you a story."

61

LORALEI

LORALEI WATCHED FROM THE SAFE HOUSE ROOF AS CASSIMIR PULLED THE cart of supplies towards their hiding place. Only when they were close enough for her to see his face did she realize that he wasn't pulling the pilfered supplies in the cart, Saiden was also sitting in the back, and she was covered in blood.

Even knowing the way Saiden fought in battle, there was too much blood for none of it to be her own. She pushed out her senses, and found the wound in Saiden's shoulder. As she was about to stitch the flesh shut, Saiden yelled out to her. She must have sensed Loralei's powers probing at her. "Don't close it." Her voice was weak, but Loralei heard her well enough to follow her directions. Even if she didn't understand them.

The cart pulled up to the house, the noise of it enough to pull Eleni out the front door. "There's poison." Saiden managed, but Loralei could see her strength failing her. They didn't have a lot of time. Even with all her healing practice, Loralei had never dealt with poison before. She was out of her element now.

But Eleni didn't seem to be. She raced back into the house, coming out with one of the bundles she'd been packing full of healing herbs and bandages. Digging around inside Eleni pulled out a pouch and a knife. Wasting no time, she cut open Saiden's shirt. Loralei almost felt bad about revealing Saiden's tattoos, until she remembered that everyone here had already seen them.

These were the people Saiden shared her secrets with. And Loralei was one of them. She finally was able to move again, coming up to the cart. "What do you need me to do?" She asked Eleni. She may have been gifted in the healing arts, but that was nothing without knowledge. She could heal simple injuries, could bring herself back from death, but she didn't know how to push the poison back out of Saiden.

"Can you slow her heart? Keep her pulse low so the poison can't spread, but don't let it stop. I'll use the herbs to pull the poison free, but it will take time. Can you manage that?"

Loralie nodded, sinking back into her powers and focusing on Saiden. Everything else around her became background noise, her mind fully wrapped in her power and Saiden's heart. The rhythm inside Saiden slipped into the melody of her powers, and it sounded right. Loralei tried not to think about that too hard.

She smelled Eleni's herb mixture, but didn't realize she was applying it until Saiden hissed. "Damn Eleni. That shit stings." Loralei wasn't sure she'd ever heard Saiden curse.

"That's how you know it's working." Eleni cooed, like she was talking to a baby. Even without opening her eyes, Loralei could feel the glare Saiden was sending the younger woman. But she could also feel the love and the gratitude.

Because that's what they did. They saved each other, over and over, as many times as it would take. Finally, she felt Mozare and Rhena step out of the cottage, and their little family was complete, his worry playing into the symphony in her head as everything finally clicked. Because they were her family too. She had no doubts about it now.

She tuned into Saiden's body, and she could feel the sting as if Eleni had applied the herbs to her own skin. And underneath that, she could feel it pulling the toxins from Saiden's blood, slowly but surely. "It's working."

"If it's this uncomfortable it better be working." Saiden groaned, "or you might as well kill me now."

Cassimir tsked. "Don't speak like that. What would we do without you?"

"Move back to the southern kingdom and live in peace." Saiden said, and Loralei couldn't really tell by the tone of her voice if it was meant to be a joke or not.

"That's not true." Eleni said, indignant. "This is our fight now too, whether you are a part of it or not. And we're going to see it through." She didn't have to be watching this either, to know that Cassimir whole-heartedly agreed with his sister.

Warmth bloomed in Saiden's chest, and by nature of their connection, or maybe because Saiden's powers were finally reacting to the presence of Loralei's healing, she felt that warmth inside her own chest too.

When Loralei could no longer feel any trace of the poison inside Saiden's system, she finally opened her eyes again, pulling Eleni's compress free from Saiden's shoulder so she could clean the wound and seal it. The blood had stopped, but Loralei didn't trust that it wouldn't start again once uncovered. And Saiden was still so pale from the blood she'd already lost.

"That was incredible." Rhena exclaimed from the doorway. After the ambush, their younger friend hadn't really left the house. They needed to work on that, but it would have to wait until things weren't so dangerous. No point forcing her to face her fears so she could develop worse ones.

Loralei understood that on a very personal level.

Eleni met her in the doorway. "Can you teach me to do that too?" Rhena asked her. Although the two were very nearly the same height, Eleni reached over to ruffle Rhena's hair, "of course little one." The sight made Loralei simultaneously want to laugh and cry.

As they all crowded back into the small house, Loralei realized she was left alone outside the door with Mozare. She wasn't sure if her friends had done it intentionally, but she found that didn't matter. She wanted to be with him. Wanted to get rid of the barriers between them and go back to the happiness they had so briefly shared in Taezhali.

"We should talk." Mozare said, not waiting for her to agree, heading towards the ladder to the roof. Over their time here, the roof had become a haven for them. She would need one like it when she finally had a home of her own.

That was a future she could look forward to. She'd never had a home of her own, not once in her life. Now that she thought about it, she realized how badly she wanted one. A place she could cover with flowers and never hide herself again.

And she wanted that future with him. As much as he was a self-sacrificing idiot sometimes, he was her self-sacrificing idiot. It was time for her to fight for him.

She only realized when he turned around that the orphan who seemed to have claimed him was strapped tight to his back taking a nap. It warmed her to see it. Mozare looked like he might explode as she stepped over the railing, and finally got her feet under her. "You belong here. I know you keep distancing yourself because of me, because of what I did, because of our past. But you deserve a family, and they could be that for you. I don't want you to give that up because of me. And I know it's selfish, to insist you do things because of what I do or do not want…"

She cut him off, because she was barely brave enough to say the words, and if he kept talking her heart might very well jump out of her throat. "I love you." It was barely a whisper, but in the silence after, she could've heard the birds flying if they hadn't abandoned the country."

Mozare's face paled. "You what?"

"I love you, you idiot. And your self-sacrificing bullshit. And our little family. I don't want to lose any part of it." She shouted it out so loudly, she was fairly certain her friends inside could hear her too. "I love you, and this family wouldn't be the same without you in it."

Mozare looked at her like he was dreaming, like he almost didn't believe that those words were really coming out of her mouth.

"Forgive me," she started, but he cut her off this time.

"Forgiven. Always."

"You didn't even let me say what I was sorry for."

"It doesn't matter. As long as you love me, it doesn't matter. Because I love you."

She stepped into his space, finally awake, finally whole. And she kissed him, aware of the small child sleeping on his back as she pressed herself to him.

"Say it again." Mozare demanded, pulling back to rest his forehead against hers.

"I love you."

"I love you. I'll never tire of being able to tell you. I've kept the words inside me for so long. I love you." Loralei laughed as he shouted the words out to everyone who could hear them, despite how careless it was. Because she loved him, foolishness and all.

62
MOZARE

EARLY IN THE MORNING, A FEW DAYS AFTER SAIDEN'S CLOSE CALL WITH Revon's soldiers, Mozare was rushing people out of their homes. Revon was trying new tactics against them every day, and Mozare was worried for the people caught up in the crossfire. Today had been all about reducing casualties, and he and Loralei had been sent to evacuate this part of the city because their intel suggested Revon was looking for them here next.

If Mozare could keep innocents from being hurt he would. It was gratifying to see the way people rejoiced to see Loralei alive and well, but he was worried about her. After everything she'd gone through, and her confession the other night at the fire, he didn't want her to think she was only valuable for what she could do for others.

For all that she struggled with the idea of her future, she thrived anytime someone needed her help. She healed any injuries she could find and offered kind words and smiles to the terrified people who were facing the loss of their homes.

He hoped the losses would be temporary, but without more information, they were running out of obstacles to hinder Revon. Fate was not on their side, even if Mozare finally believed they were truly and objectively in the right.

Right now, he was distracted, transfixed watching her, until she'd eventually catch him and roll her eyes, motioning for him to keep people moving. And he'd do what she'd asked, until he saw her bend to help a little girl save her doll, and he'd be stuck all over again.

This was what it felt like to be in love with someone in the middle of a war zone. The constant threat that they could lose everything in a moment. He didn't want to miss a single second with her.

Some people did not want to leave their homes. They wouldn't force anyone, even if they both agreed that leaving people behind was likely a death sentence. If they didn't want to leave, Mozare and Loralei could do nothing without becoming exactly like the regime they were fighting. He sent a prayer up to whoever was still listening that these citizens made it through the coming days unscathed. It wasn't much, but it was all he could offer them.

Suddenly, he heard the thick thuds of boots marching in step heading in their direction. He froze for only the briefest moment before Loralei was at his side, hands grabbing for his elbow.

"Those are his men." Loralei said, "I can feel them. They're coming straight this way."

Mozare didn't need her gifts to know that. Their information had been good, but they had still been too slow. He watched families clutch their children between them, paralyzed by fear. He couldn't let this be the end to their stories. He wouldn't.

"Get them out of here. Find them places in the woods, as far away as you can manage. I'll slow them down."

She held on to him with fingers so tight he could feel her heartbeat through his skin.

He pressed his hand over hers. "Trust me. I will never stop fighting to get back to you." Mozare didn't expect, and he certainly didn't intend to force her into anything with his declaration, but with the same force she put behind every action Loralei leaned into him and pressed a kiss to his lips.

It felt like coming home and saying goodbye wrapped up in one.

"I'm going to hold you to that." She said the words against his lips, taking one last look at him before she ran off to herd the remaining evacuating villagers out of town. A few of the ones who remained grabbed whatever they could find in their homes to use as a weapon and stood in their doorways, ready to protect the lives they had built there.

Mozare respected each of them, but he also knew the truth. The average person didn't stand a chance against a trained and gifted soldier. Those were the facts. If he wanted these people to survive, he had to stop Revon's troops before they made it into the village.

As he walked, he dipped deep into his gifts, and started searching for bodies. He needed soldiers if he was going to stop this attack. He was a good soldier himself, but judging by the way the streets rumbled, even he could not take on the number of soldiers that were marching his way.

He pulled his own weapons from the sheaths on his back, the handles newly carved from Kazian hardwood. Saiden had even managed to use a little of her talent for manipulating things that came from the earth to support the wood further. These weapons could handle a beating.

Which was good, because that was very likely what was coming for him.

But he didn't want the soldiers to see that. He knew that confidence could trip them up as well, so although he had called his soldiers, he sent them into the dark alleys and doorways and waited.

Revon's men thought they were setting a trap, and he wouldn't want to disappoint them. Mozare was very good at being bait.

Every synchronized step on the cobblestones sent his blood rushing, but he sat as still as he could, axes within reach, as he picked at his nails with the tip of one of Saiden's throwing daggers. He wanted them off their guard when they saw him. He'd take any advantage he could get when the odds were so far from being in his favor.

Revon's guard arrived and spread through the limited space, blocking any chance he had of escaping, like he knew they would. He knew exactly what Revon's protocols were. Knew exactly how his mind worked.

"Look boys, if you wanted to see me, I'm sure we could've worked something out. I'm a very accommodating man, I know what the people want."

Not a single one of the soldiers gathered around him seemed to be amused by his joking. He stepped out from his shadows, and they all tensed. He could feel them reaching for their powers, and it felt wrong. He hadn't realized it before, but they all felt wrong.

A burly man spoke for the group. "You can come with us, and submit to the king's justice, or we can put you down like a stray dog. Your choice."

"Oh what a wonderful choice." Mozare said, twirling one of his axes around the back of his hand. "I think I'll go with the option that doesn't end with me dead." Although it was far less dramatic than he normally would have been, he signaled his soldiers with a reach into his powers, and they stepped out of their shadows.

For the first time he saw fear on the faces of Revon's mutilations. He wanted them as afraid as he was inside, and unsure of what the outcome would be. If only to level the playing field a bit.

The soldiers he called back from beyond didn't need weapons, and unless he relinquished his hold on them, they couldn't be killed. Even with the augmentation Rhena told them about, Revon's soldiers didn't understand what was happening.

He let his men tear them to shreds. There was no time in this fight for mercy. Not when he knew what he was fighting to protect. Who he was fighting to protect.

The soldiers who made it through his corpses came for him. He danced around them, death's song in his ears. This wasn't fate. Everything here was under his control.

One life gifted soldier attacked him, aiming his vines at Mozare's wrists trying to keep him from reaching his weapons. Mozare twirled his blades through the vines as fast as the man could summon them, stalling him long enough that one of his undead picked up a spare weapon and stabbed him through the back the same way Revon had once done to Loralei.

It felt like revenge. It felt like justice.

As death claimed those around him, Mozare realized that he could not feel the life leaving their bodies. With the experiments Akil had done, he'd been more in tune with death, but he didn't have time to think about why he couldn't feel theirs. He didn't want his gifts anywhere near what Revon had done to these soldiers.

As strong as his undead soldiers were, even they were not completely invincible. As they crumbled, their bodies continuing to fight, Mozare finally released his hold on them, not willing to sacrifice anymore of their eternal rest.

The last few soldiers were injured, and he believed he'd be able to handle them on his own. He was wrong. Two of them went directly for him, but the others ran into the village. He thought they'd been there to satisfy Revon's need to see them dead, their heads on spikes to remind others what happened when you fought back.

But Revon wouldn't be satisfied with killing him and his friends. He should have realized that was too compassionate a fate for them in his eyes. Whatever atrocities these soldiers were on their way to commit, Revon wanted him to know it was because he had failed.

Mozare threw the other dagger from his thigh into the leg of one of the retreating soldiers before he had to focus on the man and woman in front of him. The man, clearly gifted by Ilona threw his shadows at Mozare as if they had weight, and when they hit him, he realized *they did have weight*. They hung on him like ropes, and his own powers couldn't feel them.

He couldn't use his own gifts to fight back against them. With all the agility he could manage, Mozare tucked, trying to pretend the shadows were knocking him over, and used the momentum to throw his axe into the chest of man who'd bound him.

It was too easy for his opponent to block the axe with a flick of his wrist, shadows slapping against the flat of his blade. A moment of panic hit Mozare as he faced the two of them. Until, to his surprise, the woman turned, pulled her blade and stabbed it through the side of her partner's neck.

For whatever reason, she had helped Mozare, stepping away and sheathing her weapon, even as he bent over to retrieve his blade from the ground, never taking her eyes off him. "This isn't my fight. I don't want to serve Revon."

"How do we stop him?" Mozare took the risk that she wasn't

baiting him into another more elaborate trap. If she wanted to kill him, she wasn't going about it the right way at all.

"With every one of us he makes, he grows stronger. He wants to be a god himself. He won't settle for anything less."

Mozare nodded. "Leave the country. Pretend you're dead. Don't come back until the war is over, or I'll be forced to kill you." She laid her weapons on the ground beside the dead man, and escaped through an alley and out of his sight. He hoped he didn't regret his choice. Or maybe that he lived long enough to regret it.

He didn't have time to think about it though. He turned on his heels chasing after the other two soldiers who'd run into town. One of them he caught fighting the villagers. People were hung on the walls of their houses, trapped by vines that grew where none had been before. Mozare didn't hesitate to remove the man's head from his shoulders.

If he thought he had time, he might've stopped to see if any of the trapped folk were still alive, but he knew the last of Revon's soldiers could be hurting more people, and deep inside, he knew that these people had already been sent beyond this life. There was nothing he could do for them.

But he could stop more death. Exhaustion crept in at the edges of his consciousness, the mix of stress on his gifts and physical difficulty of fighting Revon's abominations was sure to make him pass out any minute now.

When he finally caught sight of the woman who kept evading him, he stopped running. Loralei had already strung her through with vines of her own.

She was a beautiful sight, and his last one, as his back hit the cobblestones, and he finally lost consciousness completely.

63

LORALEI

It had taken Loralei what felt like hours to lug Mozare's unconscious body back to their safe house, with a good dozen stops along the way. She'd healed everything she could find wrong with him, but sometimes the body needed its own time to come to right with things. She wished he had picked a more convenient location to finally collapse. One where she wasn't the only one around to get him back home.

Damn he was heavy. He'd already relinquished most of his weapons, leaving them buried in the limbs of Revon's soldiers, but even without the steel she wasn't sure how he weighed as much as he did. If her powers were not as exhausted as his she might have been able to use them to help, but there was nothing left. This task she would have to do as a mere mortal, like the rest of the people she had lost today.

She'd been too late to save all of the villagers, and yet, somehow she felt that today should be marked as a success. They'd killed at least eight of Revon's men, most, if not all of them augmented. And they had saved so many people with the evacuation. In a war, that was certainly more success than loss.

Loralei couldn't embrace joy, couldn't even find it within herself to be content. She worried too much for Mozare, for her friends wherever they were, to think anything good about the day. As footsteps sounded around the corner, she sloppily tucked Mozare into a corner, keeping one eye on him and the other on the road.

She had a blade in her hand, one of the last from Mozare's collection, ready to protect him to her dying breath. Finally, she understood what Mozare must've felt that day in the catacombs when he'd killed Akil. That desperate need to do anything within her power to stop more pain from befalling her love.

The soldiers simply passed them by, the foul stench of their augmented magic clouding her senses. She let her blade fly, sinking true into the back of the first soldier, who fell without even a scream. Then she grabbed the stolen sword from her back and attacked the second as he turned to face her.

Loralei was no master swordsman, and she was at an even greater disadvantage now that her gifts had been exhausted. But she had something worth fighting for, something worth protecting and that gave her the strength to do what must be done.

The guard swung for her head, and she ducked, catching the pieces of her hair he'd severed as they fell to the cobblestone streets below them. She swung her blade at his leg, nicking the artery at the inside. A dirty move, but she wasn't above fighting dirty. Not for her people.

Not for her love.

The soldier didn't seem to care, barely noticed the slice, treating it like a simple cut as he swung at her again. But she knew better, felt the life draining out of the soldier even as he continued to fight like nothing was wrong.

She blocked his next strike, then sliced down the inside of his arm, letting the blood drip off his fingers. He smelled too acidic, a rotten acrimonious smell that burned the inside of her nostrils. She didn't want to experience it ever again, but she knew the chances of that were basically nothing.

He aimed his sword for her neck, and she moved before he impaled her, then turned, pulled a small dagger from her waist and plunged it through the back of his neck. The soldier hit the ground with a wet thud, his blood burning the plants around him.

Loralei's own fingers burned with the feel of it, and she used the cloth of his own tunic to clean her skin and her weapons before returning for Mozare. She heaved his arm over her shoulder, taking him with her as fast as she could manage with all the added weight.

They barely made it to the safe house. Loralei's whole body shook under the strain of it. Her friends poured out of the house, having returned from their own missions to aid their cause. Cassimir lifted Mozare into his arms and brought him inside while Saiden tended to Loralei, searching the blood staining her dress for any sign it was hers.

It was strange, to be the one on the receiving end of healing magic, but she felt it as Saiden cautiously fed her own power into Loralei's body, searching for any injuries invisible to the eye. Exhaustion finally settling in her bones, Loralei collapsed, but Saiden managed to catch her, to hold on to her, as she fell into sleep.

64

SAIDEN

One moment Saiden had been standing in the small kitchen of the safe house, and the next her mind had left her body again, and she was somewhere in between. A place the gods had not bothered to give form, and that was never a good sign. But this was somewhat different she noticed with a shock, because she wasn't the only ones the gods had called to them.

Inside the nothingness, she could barely make out Mozare and Loralei's faces. She'd never been anything but alone here, and she couldn't help feeling grateful to have them both by her side. Even if it did very little to dull the throb of fear at the base of her skull. She hadn't had a lot of pleasant experiences with the gods lately.

Saiden recognized what had happened immediately, but it was strange, seeing her friends there with her. Of course, they'd been present in the one nightmare vision the gods had shown her, where she'd been the Queen who presided over their execution, but this was different. She knew this wasn't a different timeline, a different possibility for her future. This was them, in all their flaws, sucked into the divine world the same as her.

At least they had been kind enough to send them somewhere peaceful. It wouldn't have been out of the ordinary for them to put them somewhere perilous and make them wait there. Because of course they would make them wait, after pulling them from their lives.

That was how things worked when the divine had to interact with the mortals. It was always on their timeline, and never when it was convenient for anyone else.

Mozare and Loralei huddled behind her, and she tried to remember what it had been like for her the first time she'd been taken to the gods' realm. She'd been a child then, still filled with some sense of wonder, though it hadn't lasted very long. Now, she hated being here, and hated that they were probably taking enjoyment in scaring her friends.

Saiden was starting to believe they fed on human emotion, fear most of all.

"Where are we?" Mozare asked her, a tremor shaking his voice.

In Loralei's voice all she could hear was anger. "Why can't I reach my powers?"

"We're in the gods realm." It had taken Saiden a long time to realize that her first time here. And she'd never even tried to reach her powers, so she couldn't answer Loralei's question. Not that she had time to speak again before their hosts finally deigned to appear before them.

"What use is the in giving you our gifts if you cannot keep a single mad man from threatening everything we've tried to establish in your world?" Ilona answered Loralei's question, and Saiden saw dread cross her face at the idea that her gifts might be gone. "It's bad enough our reach no longer extends past the middle kingdom, but to let that go to ruin as well? It's unthinkable."

For Saiden, this introduction offered far more questions than it did answers. But for her friends, who'd never been here, never born witness, she couldn't imagine how overwhelming it was.

Saiden did her best to hide her friends further behind her, determined to be their shield. There might not be much she could do to protect them here, but she'd be damned if she wouldn't try.

Ilona smiled at her, a vicious predatory smile, all while Keir had remained motionless. Saiden finally took the time to look at them closely, and realized that their normal monochrome colors had been changed. The red that had being bleeding into their hemlines had covered them entirely, the exact same shade as Saiden's hair.

She couldn't tell if that was a good sign or not.

"Why did you bring us here?" Saiden's voice had no tone, left no chance for them to interpret it as rude or wanting, provoking the gods to thrust them into another alternate reality hell.

Ilona did not look like she wanted to answer, and when she faltered, Keir finally spoke. "We need your help, and you need to hear a story. It is one that brings us great shame, but has the power to change your understanding of the world."

Saiden hadn't realized they were capable of human sentiments like shame. Didn't understand how they weren't more embarrassed after what had happened in the brief history of their country. Saiden didn't want to listen to them, but she didn't think they were really going to be given a choice in the matter. And she wasn't willing to do anything reckless while her friends were here and risk invoking divine wrath.

Wrath was an emotion she knew they were familiar with, but as the predatory gleam faded from Ilona's face, Saiden's gut sank. This wasn't going to be a story they enjoyed hearing.

As the sound of Keir's voice surrounded them completely, she felt Loralei grab at her arm, wrapping herself around it. "This is a story we've never shared before." She turned enough to grab Mozare too, his face still frozen as he stared at the gods he'd been raised to revere.

This must've been something completely different for him. To see the power he'd known about, that he always believed dictated everything in his life, given human form. But, she knew that together, they could weather this storm.

"When this world was new, there was no life here, only me." Saiden was surprised when Ilona began the story. She had never been one inclined to speaking. That was usually Keir's role until Saiden angered her.

Saiden didn't want to imagine a world that was only death. Keir took over, "When I came, life could start. Worlds bloomed where before there had been only darkness." Around them the nothingness they had been summoned to exploded in color, but none of them moved.

"Things were good for a time, but it was always separate from us. Until the gifted. We used to have children like the two of you," Ilona pointed to Mozare and Loralei "all across the world."

"But we wanted more," Keir cut in. "And it is dangerous to want. And in our wanting we find our shame."

"Keir and I had two children. Natural children, not gifted ones. Gods like us. They put the world out of balance. But we were selfish, and we didn't care how this affected the mortals we were responsible for. And it ruined everything. In the end our unbalance turned even our children against us. Our children did not believe we should have our power on earth if they could not do the same."

Ilona was emotional, but her anger wasn't the same hot thing it was when Saiden upset them. It was something twisted, something skewed by other emotions. It was completely unfamiliar to Saiden. Loralei's hands was squeezing her arm so tightly she was losing feeling in her fingers, but she didn't ask her to let go. The feeling helped ground her from the overwhelming sorrow.

Keir took over the story. "They rebelled against us, deciding to separate the world so that they could rule in their own lands. But magic is not that straightforward for deities, and it had great cost. For our son, he wanted to rid all the land of our influence and his binding created what you call Gotar, and their history of hatred for the gifted. Our daughter thought we were selfish in only choosing the few to be gifted, believing power should be available to anyone willing to learn. Her influence created Taezhali and the magic your priestess friend harnesses."

"But it destroyed our children. And it bound our influence to the middle kingdom of Kaizia. Your religion stemmed from the belief that you were the chosen people, when in reality you are the prisoners of our greed." Ilona finished.

"What of Saiden?" Mozare asked, his first words in their presence. She couldn't imagine how hard all of this was for him to hear, when he'd spent so long believing in his own worthiness.

"The Anointed were created to try to break us free. A tool powerful enough to end this binding." Saiden felt a rage all her own build inside herself. That they'd hidden that purpose from her, that she'd lost so much because of their own greed

"I have no intention of ever freeing you from the consequences of your own actions." She almost growled, her rage a feral, primal thing inside her. And she knew where that rage came from. Every infant murdered because of their marking, every family member who'd had to face that loss. For her mother, who should have lived a happy simple life together with her father. For herself, who'd had to endure all that loss, because they could not bear their own punishment.

"We know." Keir said, no rage in his own voice. Even Ilona looked resigned to her fate.

"We have a warning." Ilona started, and Saiden swore there was genuine concern in her voice. "The ritual the blasphemer performs, it was never intended for use. It comes from a perverted history and man's own greed. Should he continue to gain power, he will be too much for any of us to stop."

Us. Not you, us. She was worried even their intervention would not be enough to stop him.

"I fear he has already grown too powerful." Keir added, "Unless you, child, come into the full strength of your gifts. Accept them as a part of you, or you will stand no chance of stopping him."

Saiden didn't want that responsibility. She didn't want this fight. She was so very tired of all of it. This was a mess they had made, why was she always the one who had to clean it up?

"Should you decide not to fight, know that it will throw the world back out of balance. It will be the end of everything good."

They didn't even get a chance to ask questions, before they were suddenly back in the kitchen, Keir's words still ringing in their ears.

"What did they want from you this time?" Cassimir asked, and she didn't know how he'd known where they were, or how she would answer. She simply stepped into his arms when he opened them, and hoped Mozare or Loralei could put words to what they'd dealt with.

Mozare was the one who finally summed it up, "basically, we're fucked."

65

RHENA

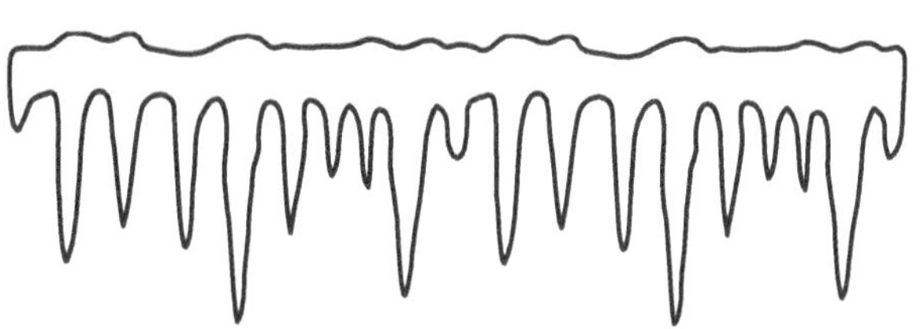

A FEW WEEKS AFTER HER RESCUE FROM THE PALACE, RHENA WATCHED HER friends gear up for battle again. Panic kept her rooted to her spot on the kitchen floor. She knew they had the best plan possible, and they were all strong fighters, but she couldn't help but feel this might be the last time she saw them all. Rhena wasn't sure there was any way the gods would see fit to keep them all alive.

She knew it made sense for her to stay behind, but she couldn't keep the tears from her eyes. There was a very real possibility that they wouldn't all make it out of this alive. And her friends were rushing directly into the fight armed with very little, supported by even less.

Eleni stepped up behind her, a calming presence in the storm of her fear. She wondered if the young healer felt the same panic as she watched her friends prepare for war, but Rhena couldn't read anything on her face.

Saiden came and crouched down in front of her, making her feel small like a child. Protected. And she started crying again. "Be brave my little Maus. I will see you again in a free country." Rhena wanted to argue but didn't dare give voice to the panic in her head. Couldn't risk putting her fear into words and have it come true. She wouldn't poison her friends with her own panic.

"I love you, Saiden." She finally managed, her voice colored by the turmoil inside herself. Saiden pulled her into her arms, and pressed a lingering kiss on her head, and Rhena felt the resolve in her bones. Her sister would fight tooth and nail to make it back to her, of that Rhena was sure. And she had far more faith in Saiden than she had ever had in their gods.

She needed to make sure that she was still going to be around when they came back. Not for the first time, she was forcibly reminded of her own youth, wondering at how she'd managed to get herself caught up in this war in the first place. Rhena wasn't the same girl she'd been when Saiden had caught her following them on patrol, but she wasn't as far removed from that version of herself as she wished she was.

Saiden stepped to the side, checking the straps of her gear and each of her weapons, all the ones Rhena could see and quite a few more that she knew from experience Saiden had hidden elsewhere on her person. Then Mozare was in front of her, and her panic stilled, just a little.

"It's okay to be afraid." He tucked a strand of her hair behind her ear that had fallen loose from the braid Saiden had woven for her. "But the worst of the fighting will be far from where you are. We will make sure of it. Your training is good, so you need to keep your nerves under control. You can rely on your gifts and your blade; they are both strong."

Rhena nodded, taking his words and wrapping them around herself like armor. If they believed in her, then maybe she could believe in herself, at least long enough to get through whatever hell this day would bring them.

He pressed a kiss to her forehead, and she took that feeling with her, the love that these two people, strangers not that long ago, had given her. A seal on her head that told her where she belonged. What she had to fight for.

She was surprised that she didn't hear Eleni come up behind her. But the healer had a way about moving that even the trained soldiers in her presence couldn't manage to duplicate. Silent like the wind passing through the street, light as a leaf hitting the ground.

Eleni reached a hand towards her, and despite the fact that Rhena was fairly sure she was stronger than the older girl, at least physically, she let Eleni help her to her feet. Neither of them spoke as they collected the supplies Eleni had been gathering, or as they left the others behind to head towards the healing tent.

Still, she felt the strength of the other girl permeate the air around them, felt her friends well wishes weave a shield around her. Rhena had to hope it would be enough.

66

SAIDEN

SAIDEN WAITED UNTIL SHE WAS OUT OF SIGHT OF THE OTHERS TO SAY HER goodbyes to Cassimir. She knew the moment would make her vulnerable, and she couldn't let the others see her fear. Couldn't let Rhena doubt her at all. She would make it back to them, or she would die fighting. Those were the only options left to her at this point.

"I wish I were coming with you." Cassimir said, a wistful look on his face that she didn't have the strength to decipher.

"There are a lot of things I wish. But mostly I want to see the new dawn with all of you by my side."

Cassimir pressed his forehead against hers. "I promise I will find my way back to you."

"You can't make that promise. Don't promise me things you can't keep." She'd be heartbroken if she lost him, but a promise made it worse somehow. She didn't want that hanging over them.

"I have already beaten death to stay with you. I will see you again, of that I have no doubt." He pressed himself against her, fusing their souls as he kissed her like it was the last time they'd ever get the chance to do so. A reminder of the future they could have together if they made it through the coming battle.

She turned to leave him, but couldn't bear it, pressing herself against him for one more tear-stained kiss. Then she forced herself to leave, knowing that if she stayed too long she'd never be able to leave him.

Saiden ran towards the temple, careful not to push herself too hard considering she didn't know what tonight would have in store for her. She had to save her strength if she was going to kill the king.

The Enlightened loitered outside the temple as usual, but she could feel the tension in the air around them. She wasn't the only one preparing for the horrors tonight would bring. Aside from their assistance getting messages to and from the palace, she hadn't given them any role in the fighting. She hoped whatever they were itching to do wouldn't be a hindrance to her own plans.

Inside, Oliver and Melana prayed, though she didn't think they were praying to the gods. They knelt facing each other, hands held between them, heads pressed to each other. It reminded her too much of the embrace she'd shared with Cassimir, she had to look away. She was sure her curiosity would demand their story if they all made it out alive.

When Oliver turned to look at her, she had the embarrassing urge to wave, which was very out of character. Instead, she nodded her head and waited for them to be ready. Everyone prepared for war differently, she wouldn't take this time away from them.

They met her outside, and she led them towards the palace without any words. She didn't have anything to say that would be enough to convey the gratitude welling up inside her. At least she wasn't going into this fight alone.

If Saiden's past self could see her going into battle with Oliver and Melana at her back, she never would've believed it. Worse, after everything she'd gone through, she would've thought herself trapped in another life, punished by the gods' own mercurialness. But she had made this plan, and left it with the Enlightened in the hopes that the news would make it to the pair.

Thanks to whatever power still looked after her, they had gotten her letter. She could not thank her gods, not after all the torment they had caused. Not after the mess they made and expected her to clean up.

It was completely unfair, but it did not change the fact that this was her fate. And she was determined to see it through, if only to see her country free again. The country that had not loved her, but where she had found love and family, nonetheless.

The mace in Oliver's hand reminded her of their duel, and though odd, it gave her a sense of comfort to be reminded of it. Or maybe it was more the fact that it reminded her of what a good fighter Oliver was, that even though her partner was not at her back, she was not alone.

Despite all their training, she had never seen Melana fight, but the twin whips coiled at her wrists were not for show, Saiden was sure of that. She never could have dealt with a partner like Oliver if she were not strong in her own right. Saiden had finally learned that strength could come in many different forms.

It had not been an easy lesson for her to learn. But she had learned it all the same.

Like last time, Saiden stepped up to the palace steps, preparing herself for another siege. They were not an arrow this time, but a dart, the three of them against the forces inside dedicated to Revon and his unjust rule.

Melana had assured her that there were fighters inside who did not want to live under the boot of his tyranny, but Saiden knew better than to plan on their help when success was not guaranteed. Fear is a powerful weapon, and there was a good chance they would not be victorious. She could understand why some would choose to hide, rather than embrace that risk; that vulnerability.

Saiden no longer had the benefit of hiding. No matter how her gods had angered her, she could not let Revon join their ranks, could not allow him to gain that much power. He was too dangerous already. She did not know if she was as powerful as the gods believed, but she was very likely the only one who stood a chance at this point.

And Oliver and Melana would help to clear the path.

67

Mozare

Mozare had one task in the battle to come. He would take out as many of Revon's augmented soldiers as possible. He let his powers leak out of him, hiding pieces of himself in every shadowy corner in Norbury and looking for the feeling of their disturbed gifts. Then he hid his soldiers there as well, in case he wasn't close enough to fight them himself. It stretched his power out, but he had better control over his gifts now. He had fought to grow his power.

Every one of Revon's soldiers he could take out was another his friends wouldn't need to face. That might be the only thing he could offer them, but it was a chance he wouldn't pass up. Fractured pieces of his consciousness fought all over the city under his strict orders.

He swore the undead could smell the augmentation on them, because they only struck out at members of the guard tainted by Revon's experiments. Mozare patrolled another block, and quickly ran into a patrol group of his own. He released the newly repaired axes from his sheath and stood his ground, letting them surround him.

It wasn't his best move, but it kept the focus on him, instead of any lingering locals nearby. He could be a decoy, if that was what was needed of him. And he'd fought with worse odds before.

The first soldier who dared to strike at him came from his left. It took Mozare two swings to relieve him of his hands, and a third to send his head rolling. He didn't have time for pretty sword play, or to spare his enemies. Two others approached from opposite sides of him, trying to trick him into being skewered between them.

Mozare waited until his position was the most advantageous, then he stepped out of the way of the soldier behind him, hooked his blade on the collar of the man's uniform and flipped him into another man who had yet to advance, both of them hitting the ground hard.

The soldier in front of him summoned fire at his fingertips, but Mozare didn't have enough power left in him to summon his own gifts to fight, not that he wanted these soldiers to know that. He was doing his best to keep his soldiers from being found. If they were going to be an advantage in this fight, he only wanted them to fight when there would be no one left to report them. Otherwise, Revon's men would all retreat to the palace.

Then the fighting would be far too close to his friends. He couldn't let that happen. To keep this next soldier from realizing that his gifts were already close to spent, he wove shadows around his fingers like brass knuckles.

The woman fought with two blades, a sight too similar to Saiden for Mozare's comfort. For a second, he froze in place, transported to years of duels. He managed to block the soldier's blade right before she attempted to bury it in his shoulder.

The flat of his blade took the brunt of her force and he heard the cracks form. Whatever Revon had done to them, this soldier's strength was far greater than he had faced before. He let his shoulder sag, using her own force against her. As he turned, he kicked out at the back of her knees. He rushed her as she fell to her knees, slitting her throat from behind before there was ever an opportunity for her to get back to her feet.

Two soldiers grabbed his shoulders pulling him to his knees so he landed hard on the cobblestones, his axes thrown from his grip. He heard the one the soldier had damaged shatter, the metal weakened already. Instead of searching blindly for the whole blade, he grabbed the forearm length dagger from its sheath at his waist and stabbed it through the calf of the soldier closest to him.

It made a sickening sound as he pulled the blade free, blackened blood burning his skin where it touched him. The second soldier pressed the advantage, straddling Mozare on the ground and trying to push his blade through Mozare's heart.

Mozare pressed back against him, but things were not in his favor. "Should've bought me dinner first." He gritted out, his humor the only defense to the very real risk that this man was going to kill him right here, right now.

The blade kissed his chest, the pain of it excruciating, and then the soldier slumped forward, his blood seeping into the wound. Behind him, a uniformed man wiped him blackened blade against the pant leg of the soldier he'd killed. "Get up man. Live to fight another day." Mozare didn't recognize the fighter who'd saved him, but he was grateful all the same. The wound on his chest burned, but the pain meant he was alive.

That wasn't nothing. He gave himself two minutes in the shadows to recoup, to get his breath back and shake the nerves from his fingers before he went back out to fight.

68
CASSIMIR

CASSIMIR HAD ONE MISSION, TO GET ANY OF THEIR INJURED PEOPLE TO THE healing tents where Eleni and anyone else who could, would be able to help them. But that didn't mean he wasn't expecting a fight. He didn't know enough of this country to recognize friend from foe and didn't have the gifts his friends had that would help him identify Revon's new bastardized soldiers.

He had only his own faith, and his unending belief in his friends. He knew it would be enough.

Cassimir ducked through alleys that were still not familiar to him, following a path parallel to the main one leading to the palace. He was going to meet Talon, the boy Rhena wanted to protect, and help him to get anyone who wanted to leave the palace, out. Saiden didn't want collateral damage, so the rest of them were tasked to try to keep the loss of innocent lives to a minimum.

Cassimir knew Saiden was happy it would keep him out of the worst of the fighting. If he were another man, maybe he would have been offended, but he knew he was far out of his depths amongst even the gifted soldiers. Trying to fight Revon's augmented on his own would have been nearly impossible.

It was better this way. He followed Saiden and Mozare's instructions, until he heard the heavy sound of booted footsteps behind him. In the time it took for them to find him, he prayed, for swiftness and a guiding hand for his blades.

Luckily there were only two of them, but the odds were still stacked against him. Especially when light blinded him in his hiding spot, leaving him dependent on his other senses to defend himself.

He heard rather than saw, a blade scrape free from its scabbard and sail through the air towards him. A tilt of his head at the last second left him with only a nick to the top of his ear, instead of a hole in the middle of his face. It hit the wall behind him, bouncing to hit him again, but unfocused the blade could do no harm against the thick leather of his pilfered armor.

The god's light still burning in front of him, he closed his eyes, letting himself pretend he was home, the true sun warm on his face, the people he cared about safe. This was the life he was going to bring about, the reason he would continue to fight.

This promise he held on to, that was the reason he knew they would win. Despite his own lack of magic and his own lack of military training in the north, he could beat these men. Because he had something more important than king and country to fight for.

He held his love for Saiden in his heart and listened for the sounds of his opponents around him. A blade aimed for his arm came next, the chafing of fabric alerting him to the movement. A step behind and he twisted in time to hear another blade cross sail past him and accidentally hit the soldier on his other side.

Cassimir felt the warmth leave his face, the cool fall air stinging against the nick on his ear. He opened his eyes to be met with the vision of a soldier pulling the blade from the soft meat of her own shoulder, an unnatural shade of sour smelling blood oozing from the wound.

While she was distracted, Cassimir struck out slicing his own chakra down the inside of her arms. The smell grew stronger as blood spilled from the wounds, the thick curdled strings dripping from the woman's fingertips and sparking as it hit the ground at her feet. He wasn't sure if the injuries would kill her, but theywould keep her from fighting. He could only hope it would also keep her from calling on her gifts.

The soldier behind him, nearly forgotten, reached out and grabbed for Cassimir's shoulder. But, Cassimir was quicker, the ease of which he moved aided by having his sight finally returned to him. Cassimir swung under his arm, copying a move he had seen Saiden use a lifetime ago, to break the prisoner's arm. He saw the soldier begin to call on his own gifts, pulling water from the streets to flood Cassimir's airways in an attempt to drown him.

Cassimir swung his chakram for the soldier's throat and ran as soon as he had breath in his lungs again, listening as the soldier's body collapsed to the cobblestones with a loud, wet thud. He couldn't bring himself to feel guilty, even though he knew he should. He kept running, until he was certain he had left that place behind him, and escaped any other patrols who might stumble upon their dead comrades and want revenge.

In another alley way he bent over at the waist, coughing up the rest of the water Revon's man had tried to force into his lungs. His breathing ragged, he almost didn't hear the footsteps running past his hiding place.

But they had certainly heard him. A group of people crowded into the alleyway in front of him. Armed to the teeth, Cassimir saw the glint of metal before he saw the man carrying it. Although man was a stretch, the soldier didn't seem to be much older than Rhena. It was thinking of her, that finally made Cassimir notice the map of scars crossing every inch of the skin visible to Cassimir beneath this boy's armor.

Cassimir switched both of his blades into one hand, lifting the other palm out in front of him in a gesture of good will. "You're Talon, aren't you?" Every moment they hesitated, they all risked being encountered. At his words, the boy held his blade out between them, sharpened point aimed at Cassimir's heart. He couldn't blame the boy, not with everything he had already gone through.

"Where have you heard that name?"

"We are both friends of Rhena's." He didn't have time for there to be any confusion between them. History would not remember him as a poet anyway.

He didn't re-sheath his blade, but he did have the decency to at least point it towards the ground, instead of straight for him. "Where is she?"

"At the healer's tent, with my sister."

"She's injured?" His hand wavered, tip lifting again, but without the conviction it had before.

"She was well when I left her there. If you have injured among you, go, and my sister can help. She is a skilled healer. And if any among your numbers are healers, they can help there too."

"There are more defectors, more people who need assistance, I couldn't stay behind to help them."

The blade between them was gone, and Cassimir placed a brotherly hand on Talon's shoulder. "I will go. I will help them."

Cassimir gave him the same directions he had already passed on a dozen times this morning. Talon didn't speak, but he nodded as he turned, and guided those following towards the healing tent. That was all he could do for them now. His fight was here in the city, to help anyone else he could find. That was his purpose in this fight, and he intended to serve it well.

69
SAIDEN

SAIDEN WALKED INTO THE PALACE WITH MELANA AND OLIVER BEHIND HER, one to either side. She turned to them quickly, "stay on me, stay in form. We only get through this together." They weren't the people she normally would have chosen to have her back, but she trusted in their strength, and their partnership. She trusted that they wanted to see this country restored to freedom and out from under Revon's rule.

Enemy soldiers greeted them, several lines deep, too far down the hall for her to get a good count of how many were there. "We fight as one."

"Together." Melana said behind her, the crack of her whip punctuating the words.

"We have your back. Get to Revon, end this." Oliver added, cracking his knuckles before he finally pulled his weapon from his back. She didn't know how they could use those weapons to fight in close quarters, but they had all the training she did, so she trusted that they knew what they were doing.

The first soldiers attacked as one, a hive mind of some sort that unsettled Saiden. But they still bled like men as she cut them, leaving any who got past her for her friends to deal with. Not that she let many past her.

Carefully she dipped into the well of her power, using it to build shields, to force the soldiers to pass single file through a block in the hall so they couldn't overwhelm them. It was so different from the last time they'd fought in this palace, when they'd come to rescue Rhena. Outside her shields, she grew vines that would make Loralei proud, pulling soldiers into the walls and keeping them secured.

If the Enlightened were correct, the augmented soldiers would die when she killed Revon, and if they didn't they could come back and deal with them when they were finished.

Blood made her fingers slippery, so although she did not fully trust the power inside her, she sheathed one of her blades. She called a shadow weapon to hand, the way Mozare had shown her, wrapping her fingers around its darkened hilt.

This made Revon's soldiers flinch, a reaction she wasn't expecting, but their hesitation only served to benefit her. She rammed the shadow blade through the first two before they had regained their bearings, leaving splintered pieces of her power inside them. Even that small touch into the deformed depth of their power left Saiden's skin crawling.

Try as she might, she couldn't ignore the doubt in her mind that she wouldn't be enough to put an end to this. Not when his soldiers fought like possessed men, barely noticing the wounds that were inflicted on them. She saw them, knew they would not stop until they were dead, and felt a trickle of fear in her heart that she would not be enough.

Then she remembered everything she had to fight for. This wasn't her fight against the hatred aimed towards her as long as she could remember. This wasn't her defending herself. She had a family, people who loved her and depended on her, and she would not fail them.

Saiden screamed in the hallway, a noise that was more than rage, or fear, or love. It was power, in its simplest form. The sound bounced around her, knocking into their rivals and pushing them against the wall of vines, trapping them. This cleared enough of a path for Saiden and her partners to pass through, slicing at any hands that reached out, while trying to ignore the wet thud as they hit the ground.

She did her best to keep her mind open to Oliver and Melana behind her, to shield them from the blind rage of her power, but she couldn't sacrifice the time to look behind her and check on them. Saiden wouldn't pray for them, not the way she might have once in a different life, but still she hoped that she would see them again in this one.

A man dropped from the rafters directly in her path and Saiden didn't hesitate to raise her blade. The metal one sparked as she blocked the soldier's first strike. The shadow one broke against his blade, so she pulled the pieces of them around her and sent them out, needles flung at high velocity in every direction.

Her control wasn't good, it wasn't well trained, but the brute force of it was effective enough, as one of the pieces pierced the soldier's throat and came out the back side. He almost didn't seem to notice at first, and then his hand grabbed at his throat, as if meager human fingers could possibly keep his life blood from escaping if he held on tight enough.

Saiden's power flickered, the shattered pieces of the blade in her hand returning to shadow. She wiped her hand on her pants, although they too were soaked in blood, so it didn't help will the slick of blood between her fingers. Then she pulled her metal blade free from its sheath.

Ahead of her she could see the door to the throne room, and the group of Revon's men that guarded it fiercely. She didn't need his minions to show her that he was hiding in there, it would have been the first place she checked. Revon was a man in love with dramatics; as much as capable as he was of loving anything.

Saiden tried to use her power again, but they flagged, and she didn't have time to figure out why, not when two of the soldiers attacked her as one. She remembered telling Loralei why she carried the two blades, why Nakti had chosen them for her. In a maelstrom of movement, Saiden pushed into one of the soldiers, only to turn her back to him to block a strike from the second.

She tried to get out from between them, but they were too fast. She could barely get one move in, block one strike, before the next one was coming. Saiden didn't even have time to try her powers again. Wouldn't risk relying on them and having them fail her here.

Eventually she managed to move one of them to the middle, using his own momentum to throw him at the blade of the other, putrid blood spilling between them. Saiden rushed them, slicing her blade across the throat of the soldier who had killed his comrade. She wanted to feel grief, but she would not even tattoo these deaths on her skin. The fault rested in Revon, and she was going to set that to right.

She would not feel sorrow, she would get vengeance. Saiden threw one of the small daggers straight into the chest of the last soldier between her and the great hall. Then she stepped up to the door and swung them open. Inside someone was going to die, and her country would be forever changed as a consequence.

Pulling her powers back into her consciousness, Saiden took her first step into the throne room.

70

LORALEI

LORALEI MOURNED FOR EVERYTHING HER CITY HAD ONCE BEEN. HER HEART was as much a piece of her country as it had been all those years ago when the choosing ceremony had plucked her off the streets and brought her to the palace. Her advisors had told her that her life would now serve a greater purpose. Abandoning her alone in a dark room, only a child. Loralei had embraced the idea that she would be the force of good she had once needed.

Until her friends betrayed her, Revon invaded her home and put a blade between her vertebrae. Clearly, she had a lot of mixed feelings about this city, but nothing would stop her from trying as hard as possible to protect this place from Revon and his wrath. Even if she was mostly motivated by spite.

Each of them had been given a task, and she would do hers. She'd respected the way Saiden had laid out the plans for each of them, and could tell by her directions that her friend had done a careful job making plans for how best to deploy their small army. Because this was the best thing Loralei could fight for, and Saiden had known that.

Despite their best efforts to evacuate those closest to the palace grounds, she noticed quite a few houses still had candles burning in the windows. She tried to keep a mental list of them, tracking the places she thought her city was most vulnerable, as she waited for fate to descend upon them.

The first soldiers to spot her didn't hesitate in their attack. She supposed, since she had spent the last few months terrorizing the king these soldiers were connected to, they might also have a personal vendetta against her. Or maybe they were told to kill anyone on sight. She wouldn't put that kind of blind cruelty past Revon.

Loralei wasn't a fighter the same way her friends were. Her training was limited, split between the little she'd had in her life before, the scraps from her bandit troupe, and the skirmishes they'd had in this new life. Instead of relying solely on her blade, Loralei fought with her powers wrapped around her, striking out with thorns as much as with steel.

The first soldier to reach her used the wall of a house to throw himself into the air towards her, blade aimed for her heart. The move felt rather showy to Loralei, and a deranged part of her wanted to laugh at the ridiculousness.

All she needed to stop his descent was a brief flick of her wrist, a layer of energy like what Saiden had used to protect her and Mozare in the hall of Taezhali, striking out to stop his downward momentum. She didn't hesitate went she punched her blade through the back of his neck right before he struck the ground.

This was not a day for mercy.

The second soldier was not so easily drawn in to the fight. He watched her, a spider weaving his web, as she dispatched his partner with ease, blood splattering across her face. And she smiled at him, letting the madness boiling inside her split the facade of calm she had wrapped around herself.

Loralei wouldn't be the one to make the first move. Not here, not when every second mattered. She wasn't some hotheaded grunt to be baited into a fight.

Inside, she was still a queen, the queen this kingdom had raised her to be. She might not wear a crown anymore, but that didn't mean she would stop holding herself like it was perched on her brow. And queens weren't drawn recklessly into battle the way men were. They taunted and teased and waited until their prey came to them.

It didn't take this man very long to come to her. His face shifted between one moment and the next, patience shedding to make way for vile anger. She smiled at him in return, a mix of glee and madness making her cheeks hurt. She wanted his rage to burn him alive.

He attacked her, every footstep sending cracks through the pavement, which probably should've scared her. It should have at least warned her that his power would be strong and from the earth, but she didn't have enough training or experience to know what to expect.

Suddenly, stones flew at her from every angle, a distraction she couldn't afford as the soldier charged her from the front. For a brief moment Loralei could've sworn she saw tear tracks on his cheeks, but she couldn't focus long enough to know if she was seeing things truly, or imagining pain in his features.

She couldn't afford either distraction.

Bruises formed from each blow, but she ignored those as well, keeping her hand tight on her weapon, her mind focused on her own powers. Looking at him, she saw every place to strike to end his life. The way his blood would burst from the artery in his thigh if she sliced it right. The way she could choke the air from his lungs with a well-placed vine.

In the end, she threw her blade seconds before a large brick forced her to the ground. Loralei saw the blade bury itself deep in the soldier's eye, blood spraying in ribbons from the wound as he raised his hands and pulled the blade free as if it was nothing.

Dust settled in her hair, and clogged the air around her with filth. She knew without understanding, that she wouldn't last long letting the dirt into her lungs. She threw another one of her blades, but she wasn't as well-equipped as her friends, and she didn't want to be caught without any weapons at all. Especially when he blocked the blade with a flick of his wrist.

This wasn't a fight she was going to win from afar. She coughed and did her best to ignore the blood that splattered the stones in front of her. Loralei pulled away, giving herself enough space to finally stand without being directly in front of her opponent.

The buildings around her shook, and she feared for her people, for anyone who might return here to find their homes gone, collapsed beneath the weight of her inability to protect them. She pushed her power out around her, grew vines to hold the buildings together until she could think of something more permanent to keep her city from falling to ruins.

The strain on her power was noticeable, but not unmanageable. She would need to be careful though, not to push herself too hard. The others might still need her, and her strength, when the fighting was over. To save lives, instead of ending them.

A blade pierced through the soldier's chest, too far to the side to hit his heart, but sharp enough to do damage. The only problem was that she had no idea where it had come from. On guard, she stepped forward, walking towards the slumped body, trying to decide if whoever had killed him was her friend, or another threat to her.

Around the corner, a dozen or so Enlightened waited for her, bowing their heads as she passed, reverence clear in their gazes. It didn't sit well with her. Loralei didn't know the Enlightened to be defenders, and she didn't trust anyone with unclear motivations.

Loralei saw another one of Revon's men racing towards them. She called on her powers, grabbed for his ankles with one of her vines, and hung him from the rafters of a nearby house. There was no way she could know what his gifts were, but he didn't seem able to fight the vines cocooning around him. Loralei walked right up to him, and stripped him of his weapons, tightening his leather straps to her own body, carrying his blades as her own.

She thanked him, moments before she drove his own blade through his heart.

People stared at her from their doorways, and she could see the fight in their eyes. The Enlightened pushed through the crowd, blood on their robes. "I am not your queen. I am not your goddess. I am not your path to redemption. Follow me at your own peril." She wasn't a general, she had no words to encourage their loyalty, and yet, as she walked through the streets, she could feel them at her back.

71
RHENA

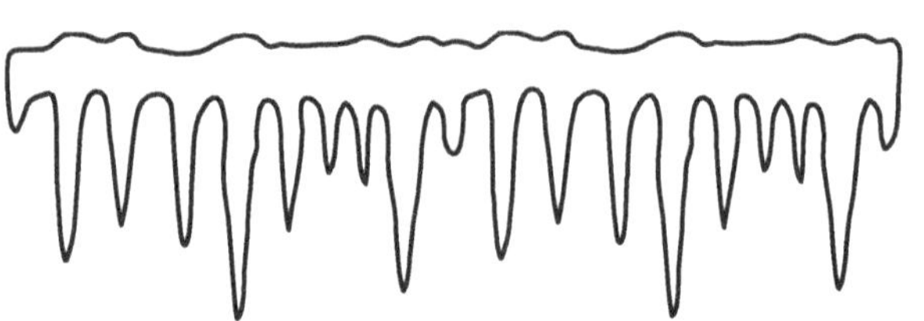

RHENA WAS OVERWHELMED IN THE HEALING CAMP, DOING HER BEST TO care for others and follow the rapid-fire commands Eleni shouted over the wailing of the injured and dying. She felt death hovering over them —a storm cloud no sun could break through. Because she knew, whether through her own gut or her goddess given gift, that it would not be possible for them to save every life in this tent. Not even Eleni's knowledge and her bag of herbs would be enough.

But they would fight for every single one of them. They would do whatever they could to keep casualties down. On her back, Rhena had her own sack, each of the herb packets specifically labeled with their purpose and usage instructions. Eleni hadn't left anything to chance, hadn't assumed she'd be there to give directions.

And she was smart to do that. Rhena knelt at the bed closest to her, and inspected the burn marks that covered a villager's legs, doing her best not to retch at the sight. Eleni was too far away to ask for help. This person, this innocent, who'd been hurt in the crossfire was hers to save.

Rhena would do whatever she could to save him. She searched through her bag, pulling out a pungent smelling salve Eleni had labeled for burns. Rhena set it on the cot, and pulled out some bandages. Taking a deep breath, Rhena reached into her powers, pulling at the threads to call water to her, gently cleaning away whatever flesh was no longer connected. Later, a real healer could help with the rest, but she hoped this would at least stave off the worst chances for infection.

Eleni had given her many lessons on the risk of getting infections. It wasn't something commonly dealt with in the big cities of Kaizia, not when there were always gifted healers. But they didn't have those options in Taezhali, so Eleni had learned other kinds of magic. The kind of magic that had always belonged to humans, that didn't come with strings attached.

She opened the small jar of salve and worked as gently as she could to spread it over the affected areas. The man groaned, but he did his best not to scream as she worked, something she greatly appreciated. Rhena wasn't sure how long her own composure would last if her patients screamed as she tended to them.

Rhena left him with fresh water in a small bowl so he could drink, and tried not to look too hard at his face, in case she'd never see it among the living again. She already knew these days would live on in her nightmares. That was her price to pay.

She moved to the next bed, but before she could treat the patient lying in it, she felt death reach for them. Rhena never even bothered looking at their face. She turned to the next bed, letting silent tears drip down her face.

Bed after bed she went, treating those she could, providing ice and water, instructing those who came to help, or sending them to Eleni for more instructions. Even as others came to their aid, the beds filled faster than they could be tended. Injured men and women, gifted and not, cried out as pain burned through them.

Rhena wasn't strong enough to help them all. She ran, cautious not to go too far, she didn't want to abandon Eleni, but far enough to quiet the sound of tears and agony. She'd never get far enough away.

Above the cacophony of the dying, Rhena heard boots stomping through the streets. She fell back on her training, steadying her breathing and focusing on the sound as it grew closer. There was no limping, no crying, no screaming for help. These were not injured men seeking care. This was a threat.

Rhena ran back to the tent. "Soldiers are coming." She did her best to keep her voice calm. If death was coming for them, she didn't want them to die afraid. Across the tent, Eleni stared right back at her, realization on her face.

There was no way to evacuate, there weren't nearly enough volunteers to get all the injured out in such a short amount of time. She was going to have to fight. For the first time in her life, she felt the battle calm her friends had talked about settle over her. This was the place she'd make her last stand.

She was too young for such a declaration, but it suited her all the same. For every life inside that tent, for Eleni, for her friends fighting gods know where, Rhena unsheathed her sword. The words Saiden had spoken when she'd bestowed it on her ringing through her memory. *May you raise your blade only in the aid of another. May you never draw blood without righteous cause.*

At least she could say she lived by that oath.

And her life would serve to save others. She believed in that truth, and in her own blade. Her powers swelled inside her, but the air didn't freeze. They rose only in her aid, and only when she bid them. Three soldiers turned the corner, heading straight for her.

She didn't know if someone had sold them out, or if these soldiers were on patrol, but she was lucky there were only three of them. That would already put her at a severe disadvantage, anything more, and she didn't think it would be possible for her to fight them.

Rhena had been trained by the best legionnaires in recent history. Every lesson they'd taught her made her stronger. The love they all shared, their little family, made them stronger. But they couldn't win this fight for her. That was up to her, and the strength of her blade.

The soldier bringing up the rear of their group leaned against the wall, and it angered her that he didn't bother to take her ability seriously. At the same time, let them doubt her. She knew the advantage of letting them underestimate her.

She shivered. Not because it was cold, and not because she was afraid, but rather she knew it would feed their image of her. Even if they recognized her from the barracks, they would expect her to be afraid. That was their mistake.

Rhena had been taught that other people's perceptions of you could be a strength, if you played it correctly. She'd seen that enough in her training with Mozare and Saiden. And she was going to play these soldiers, especially if it would help to save the people behind her.

The other soldiers waited, letting the first stalk towards her as they laughed. Rhena flinched, keeping her eyes down, watching his hands. Twin daggers, the blades themselves somewhat vicious, clutched between scarred fingers. The moment he flinched, she was prepared to defend herself. But she wanted to let him get as close as possible.

His toes almost pressed against hers before he finally moved to strike, but she was ready. The shock on his face as she raised her blade to parry his strike was glorious. She reveled in it, matching each of his blows with one of her own. Slowly, she reached into her powers, trying to keep these soldiers from feeling it.

Once she felt the strands, she exploded into action all at once. She encased the soldier leaning against the house in a tunnel of ice, preventing him from coming to aid his companions. She pushed back against the second, and plunged her sword through the first. His blood pooled under her, bleeding across her ice and dying it a macabre twist of colors.

Rhena couldn't focus on that. Inside her tunnel the guard who'd underestimated her chipped away at her ice, she couldn't tell if it was with power or blades, but she knew the result would be the same. She couldn't hold him forever.

The second soldier didn't bother to toy with her. There was no pretending to be afraid when his friend lay bleeding out at her feet. It really ruined the image she had been going for. Instead, she smiled at him, and for a brief second, he hesitated. She must've looked properly insane. The soldier shook his head, and she felt him reach inside the perverted power he'd gotten from Revon.

He struck out with vines, twisted dead things that reached for her arms while he swung his long sword. Distracted by both his blade and his powers, Rhena missed the fist he aimed at her face. The blow threw her off balance, the ringing in her ears drowning out the wounded behind her. But she wouldn't forget who she was fighting for. Reaching into her own powers, she pulled her ice back, leaving the thinnest sheet encapsulating his comrade.

In the air, her ice coalesced into a thousand thin shards, and she threw every one of them at the man in front of her, the rage inside her burning higher. She might control ice, but she was powered by something much hotter.

She wasn't surprised when the last soldier broke free from his cage. She was winded from the fight and the exertion of using so much power. There were no games with this man. He struck at her hard and fast, throwing a dagger with every step he took. Every ounce of her focus and her strength went in to blocking the blades with the flat side of her sword, but her efforts were not enough.

One of the daggers sank into her thigh, and the scream that escaped from her mouth felt like it came from deep within her soul. The second blade cut through her bicep. She froze both injuries, gritting her teeth through the pain, and doing her best to stand her ground.

The man she was fighting didn't falter. This was the truth of battle, one that she had become all too familiar with recently. The person on the other side wasn't going to stop so you could recover. They were fighting because they wanted you dead. Rhena was determined to be the one that emerged from this clash. This wasn't going to be the way her story ended.

Though she wasn't entirely sure how she would manage it. The soldier got close to her, and they fought, her leg unstable and her arm disabled as her blood still seeped through her hasty ministrations. She did her best to block his blows, flipping her blade so that flat of it lay against her forearm, making it easier to block his assault.

Rhena was certain the only thing keeping her on her feet was knowing the injured people behind her needed her to keep them safe.

Using her powers, she laid a sheet of ice at his feet, but it didn't play out the way she'd intended. As he slipped, he fell forward, and she didn't have the strength to push him off her. As she collapsed, her blade slipped from her bloodied fingers. All she could manage was to cross her wrists in front of her face, pushing against him where he was trying to push his blade through her chest.

As the tip of his blade cut through her skin, Rhena couldn't stop herself from screaming. Her arms shook, each tremble giving him the space to cut deeper into her. Tears mixed with blood on her face, pooling around her on the cobblestone streets.

A blade punched through the soldier's throat, and suddenly his weight was pulled off her. If this was death, at least it was freedom too.

In this new life, Talon was staring down at her. That was a sight to behold, the healed over scars on his face tugging as he smiled down at her. "Time to get up now Rhena." He reached out a hand to her, but as hard as she tried, she couldn't get her arms to reach back to him.

In her hazy vision, Eleni's face joined the image above her, but she didn't speak to Rhena. Instead she spoke to Talon in a voice that sounded far away. It didn't make sense for the two of them to be here together, when she knew they'd never met before.

"We need to get her sitting up. I've got some medicine and bandages." Eleni touched her hand. "She's so cold, I'll go see if I can't get her a blanket too."

"I can help with the cold." Talon answered, sitting down next to her and lifting her into him as gently as he could. She knew he was pulling on his own gifts, even if she couldn't sense it. Warmth engulfed her. She hadn't realized how cold she was; a cold that had nothing to do with her powers.

Eleni didn't know about his gifts, but she always trusted her gut. Her gut must've told her Talon could be trusted. Rhena would've told her the same, if only she were able to speak. Blood still trickled down her chest, but she was lucky Talon had arrived when he had, because the wound shouldn't kill her. Especially once Eleni administered one of her poultices. Rhena would probably have a nasty scar, but that seemed to come with the territory.

And she kept reminding herself, these people would live because of her.

72
SAIDEN

SAIDEN MET REVON WITH NO FEAR IN HER HEART. THERE WERE ONLY TWO outcomes to this fight, she would win, or she would die. She was not afraid of either fate. Her friends could survive without her, her country would endure as it had for hundreds of years before her. She would set them on the right path, even if she had to sacrifice her life. Saiden was at peace with that cost.

Revon slouched haphazardly on the throne he had stolen, a blade in his hand sparking as he recklessly sharpened it. Saiden figured it was more for show than anything else. She could feel the fear tainting the space between them. It crackled with a life of its own, but it did not touch Saiden. She was too determined, too resolved, to feel the same fear Revon exuded.

There was a blade in each of her hands, one given to her by the woman who raised her, the other by the man who loved her. Their love wrapped around her, settling into her bones, another kind of armor stronger than any this world could offer her.

"Have you finally come for me?" There was a madness in his voice as it cracked through the silence of the great hall. "Come to take my throne, my power away, from me at last. Done haunting my halls with the memory of you and your betrayal?"

Saiden couldn't tell if these were questions or simple musings he was presenting to himself. She'd never seen the king so out of sorts, couldn't reconcile this image with the man she had first met in that interrogation room a lifetime ago. Wondered if it was the throne, or the experiments or Loralei's own torments that had driven him to this point.

Not that any of it mattered. His madness was further proof he was unfit to be king. The moment he had chosen to kill her mother, he had lost any chance that Saiden might ever again defend him or his aims.

Saiden picked her own words very carefully. "You wanted to find your own power in the world. Did you think it would not have a cost?"

The blade in his hands hit the floor with a clatter, though she could not tell if it had fallen or been thrown. "You talk of power. You stole mine right from under me and then you taunted me with it. You left me no choice but to seek another way. To turn to dark rituals and pull that power from the earth herself. You have caused me to anger the gods, they scream constantly in my ears, never giving me silence."

He stood, and Saiden stepped back, not out of fear, but to center herself deeper into a stance, in case he jumped to attack her. Her blades were balanced carelessly in her grip, though she trusted her own ability well enough to know that she would not miss if he came for her. Shadows pooled behind him, distorting her view of the windows.

"If I kill you, maybe they will stop. Maybe they will give me peace."

"Can you not see that these are punishments for your own actions?" The words were soft, but they carried well enough, the flinch that reverberated through Revon as he heard them worse than if she had struck him physically.

It was the wrong thing to say. Or maybe it was that she continued to talk, to stand in front of him, when he had suggested that her death would solve all his problems. As if she should lie down and offer her life for his peace.

She would not give this man another piece of herself, not to save the entire world, much less to save him from the consequences of his own actions. He waited, neither of them moving as they stared each other down from across the hall. A world seemed to span the space between them, the ghosts of so many dead. Dead who deserved justice.

Saiden broke the frozen tableau first, taking a step towards him, and then another, waiting for the king's trap to fall. His darkness continued to spread, though she couldn't feel it the way that she felt the shadows Mozare summoned. She knew it had to be the result of his experiments, a tarnish on the gifts Keir and Ilona had bestowed upon him.

A sound like raging thunder cracked through the room, and the darkness spread, eternal and unyielding. Saiden could not touch it, could not move the shadow away from her eyes, or twist it to clear the space around her.

"You can die on your feet or at mine, but either way you will bleed just the same."

The sound of breathing was the only thing that alerted her to the soldier behind her. She moved in time to miss being completely impaled, although a blade did slice into her arm, sending a stinging all the way to her fingers.

She blocked the second strike with her own blade, pulling at the well of power inside herself. Instead of focusing on the shadows, she coated herself in Keir's divine light. It didn't offer her a very wide view of the room, but it was enough for her to slice her blade through the wrist of the man attacking her.

His weapon and his hand fell to the floor, but as soon as they did, another soldier struck at her, cutting her across the face, leaving blood seeping, warm on her cheek. Saiden pulled back into herself, letting her mind sink into the calm place she had carved out for herself over a lifetime of training. She blocked his next strike, sank her other blade into his chest and pulled it out again so fast his blood barely grazed her knuckles.

Saiden did not let another blade touch her skin, did not let another anywhere near her. Blades swirling, Saiden fought dirty, slicing at the veins in elbows and cutting fingers off if she could not get close enough to hit center. She gave up any moral high ground, fought in a way that would have made Nakti proud.

She felt that joy radiating through her, almost as if Nakti's hand rested on her shoulder to guide her. She did not know how many of Revon's soldiers she killed, did not even know if they could be killed now that they had undergone his experiments. Saiden would keep fighting as long as she must, to see the damage she had caused this country rectified.

The shadows kept her from knowing how many she faced, or where the next blade would come from. Her own powers, strong as they were, began to falter. Her control over the gods' gifts was still minimal at best, she had no hope of keeping her grasp on it against the constant press of Revon's experiments.

Instead, she pulled the light, her light, Keir's light, close around her. Wrapping his gift around herself like an embrace. She pictured Loralei, using the same gift, the way she had been amazed the first time Saiden had used it, and her friend's love bolstered her gifts.

Saiden turned, using the momentum to aim a small throwing dagger into the space Revon had been standing, flinching when she heard the metal hit stone. Then she continued her own defense, stopping one of Revon's men from taking her head clean off her shoulders.

Between one breath and the next, the remaining soldiers swarmed her, too many and too fast for Saiden to properly defend herself from all of them. She fought as best she could, but she was still only one person, one pair of hands, one set of blades, no matter how well-crafted they were.

Someone pushed her and she stumbled, her feet slipping in the blood that had pooled across the cracked stone floor. Saiden landed hard on her knees, something cracking, though she didn't feel the pain she should have. Around her, the harsh breathing of Revon's soldiers kept her from retreating.

In front of her, the sharp point of Revon's sword hung in her face. Surrounded, there was nothing left that Saiden could do. Death hovered around her, alone on her knees at Revon's feet, she did the only thing she could think of.

Saiden flipped her hands palms up, and she prayed.

73
LORALEI

LORALEI WAS SOAKED IN BLOOD, THE CLUMPED AND TANGLED ENDS OF HER hair dripping on to the stone below. She wasn't entirely sure what had gotten her through the fighting, not when all these soldiers were trained and enhanced. She was too proud to give any credit to the gods, though an inkling in the back of her mind knew it was likely they had a hand in this. She certainly couldn't claim it was her own skills that made the difference.

The control she had over her powers, she could claim as her own. The strength of them knitting the wounds on her skin together, had saved her. Though, she began to wonder if there would ever be enough air in the world to replace what she had exhaled whirling around during the fight. And several of them were wrapped in her vines, though she could see where they had started to die as she stretched herself farther and farther.

For the first time since healing the damage to Mozare's back, Loralei could feel herself approaching burnout. Only this time she didn't have the luxury of a warm bed and a sun-soaked nap. Even now, she could feel the darkness of Revon's tainted magic pouring into the city. Her city.

She'd done what she could to support the buildings his soldiers damaged. She could see the Enlightened racing behind her, using materials far more solid than her magic to prop them up so she could let go of the power that was keeping everything from crumbling to ruins. Without dirt, her flowers didn't survive long once she'd taken her power from them.

Without warning, a burning pain sliced through her arm. With all the blood on her skin, she couldn't see if there was a cut she had missed, or maybe a poison seeping into her system. She didn't think that she would have missed that, but Loralei couldn't deny the pain that was beginning to make her fingers go numb.

Another slice hit her on the inside of her thigh, sending her to her knees. The blade in her hands clattered loudly against the stone cobbles at her feet, and several of the Enlightened turned to look at her. None of it made sense. Her powers didn't feel an injury inside her, there was no poison to chase out.

"My lady," one of them said, finally daring to approach her. She could've sworn she'd growled at them, but she wasn't entirely sure. Pain made her mind race, made her blood pump faster, the sound rushing in her ears. "What can I do for you"

"What the hell is going on? What did they do to me?"

"Any power they might have had over you should've passed when they died. I do not think this is the work of the dark ones."

"Speak plain." Her teeth ground against each other as she tried to keep from screaming at the pain.

"Your magic is bound to the others." Another Enlightened spoke, their voice worn with age. She turned her head, biting down on another scream, to see who had spoken. This Enlightened was ancient, wrinkles buried deep in their skin, the hair on their head thinning and withering away. But what shocked Loralei the most was the cloudiness of their eyes.

Still, Loralei could feel them looking over her body. "I can see it in the power around you child. And when he hurts, you will hurt. Especially with your gifts, that leave you so vulnerable to the pain of this mortal world."

Loralei almost yelled again about the riddled way they spoke to her, before all the pieces clicked into place. The Enlightened didn't use gender without caution, if they were saying that there was a link between her power and a man, it could only be one person.

Mozare.

And that meant that the pain she was feeling was from injuries he was suffering fighting somewhere else.

Loralei wasn't about to lose him a second time, wasn't prepared to let him go, and certainly not to Revon's men. She had lost enough to the false king. Still, she was embarrassed by how much willpower it took for her to push herself from the ground, to stand again on her own two feet and move forward.

"How do I find him?"

"Open yourself, and it will be nearly impossible to stay away from him."

God the way these idiots spoke. Only the pressing reality that Mozare was likely dying right now stopped her from throwing a blade at the Enlightened hovering behind her. Instead, she reached down unsteadily to grab her sword and charged back into the crumbling fray of her city.

There were things about her powers that Loralei knew intrinsically. It took barely a thought for flowers to bloom under her care. But she had no idea how to open herself up to a magical connection that she hadn't even know existed until the blind elder had pointed it out seconds ago. And Mozare had to be close to death for her to be in this position. It wasn't like the Enlightened had offered up the information during their visit to the temple, when she might have had time to train with it.

That would have been far too helpful.

In a tight alley, Loralei hid herself again as a new wave of pain skated over her back. In the darkness, she looked inside herself, and tried to find something that connected them beyond the pain and the nightmares. Then she remembered what he had said about darkness, when they'd been trying to train Saiden in Eleni's garden. There were different kinds of darkness, and some were meant to comfort.

Loralei found the thread of Mozare wrapped inside her by looking into her own darkness, and suddenly, everything around her was touched by him. By his silly smile when he'd told a goddess awful joke, and the stalwart way he had defended her to the emperor. He was there in the way he loved her in the small moments and in the big ones.

Suddenly, there was nothing easier in the world than getting to Mozare. She could feel him all around her like a warm embrace. She didn't think or allow doubt to creep in by letting her mind overpower her instincts. The pain lancing through her became background noise, the sound of Mozare's heartbeats roaring in her ears in harmony with her own, no matter how impossible that should've been.

The first glimpse of him almost sent her back to her knees, all the pain rushing back. The rotten feeling of the enhanced soldier's powers crawled over her skin. Mozare turned, blocking a blade aimed at his head, and then he saw her.

In the end she was his fatal flaw. As he froze to stare at her, a blade went through his stomach, the tip shining red as it broke through the leather covering his stomach. She screamed, running towards him, ignoring the pain that radiated through her. It called her back to the day Revon had run his blade through the vertebrae of her spine, nearly killing her.

Loralei ignored everything except her need to get to him. For the first time in her life, she slipped into that place she'd seen Saiden go to, where she became a blazing ball of power, running on instinct alone. In her hands, the sun flared, catching the soldier whose blade was still through Mozare's body and setting him ablaze.

Madness crowded the edges of her mind, pushing her faster, allowing her to reach further into the well of power stored inside her than she ever had before.

Loralei felled the soldiers as if they were made of tin. They were ants beneath her slippered foot fearfully awaiting the pressure. And she would crush every single one of these monsters as easily. She didn't care if it was by blade, or her magic that they died, only that they hit the ground in rapid succession, giving her enough time to catch Mozare as he pulled the blade from his gut and hit the ground.

He landed in her lap, her knees bruising against uneven stones, but keeping him from hitting anything hard on his way down. The blood pouring from the gaping wound in his chest warmed the skin of her thighs, but did nothing for the goosebumps rapidly covering her skin. Exhaustion blackened the edges of her vision, fear chasing every heartbeat.

"We really have to stop meeting like this." Mozare coughed, and blood trickled down his chin.

"When I have grey hairs, I am going to blame them all on you and your recklessness."

"Unless you have them now, I don't think I'm going to get to see them love."

She pressed a kiss to his forehead, all the blood they'd lost and all the blood they'd shed sealing a promise between them. She wasn't going to let him die today. And if she failed to save him, then she knew she'd follow shortly after.

"After all this time, you still doubt me?"

"Not even the gods themselves could make me doubt you. But we aren't gods."

The words hung heavy in the air, but they didn't stop her from stretching into the dregs of her power, pulling at her own soul for a warm enough spark to send through him. She didn't think it would fix everything, but slowly she watched the skin between the rip of his leather armor begin to reach for itself, stretching across the wound to pull Mozare back together.

His eyes never left hers, his bloody hand holding on to hers, the squeeze getting gradually stronger as the blood stopped escaping from his body.

"Enough" he said, and the words didn't bring any more blood up. But she didn't stop either. She poured everything she had into him, unafraid to give because she knew that he would be there to catch her when she fell.

Only the press of his lips against hers finally threw her back into her own body. The coppery taste of blood burnt her tongue. But beneath it all he was real and whole and Mozare. He was everything she loved. Every good thing in this world wound up together in one person.

Beneath them, the street cracked, the ground releasing an angry rumble that sent them tumbling apart. She didn't miss the way he winced as he hit the ground, as much as she was sure she had a matching expression on her face, buried under the blood.

Mozare met her gaze, and then together they turned towards the castle raised high above the city. The place that had once been her home, and then her prison. Vines cracked against the foundation, stones crumbling, dark and light flashing through the windows at an unsustainable rate.

Loralei heard Mozare's voice echo her own as she gasped. "Saiden."

74
MOZARE

THE ONLY IMPORTANT THING MOZARE COULD FEEL WAS LORALEI'S HAND IN his own. Nothing else mattered. Not the pain, not the cracking streets of the city he'd once protected. They were together and they were alive, and he truly believed that meant they would make it through this.

Maybe it wasn't practical given they were in a war-torn city, keeping their hands occupied with each other instead of grasping for weapons, but he didn't care. He needed the reminder that she was beside him more than he needed his next breath. Loralei kept him grounded, gave him something to focus on other than the pain in his chest and how close he had once again come to dying.

Together, they raced towards the castle, now covered in vines, aging it until it looked old and decrepit. A mausoleum for everything lost. It was more magic than he had ever seen at one time. Far more than any of the most powerful Legionnaires he had ever come across. Saiden's curse wouldn't protect her from burning out, and if she was out of control they didn't have time to waste.

Saiden had saved them all time and time again, now she needed them. And he wasn't going to let her down. He didn't even know how it was possible for him to push his body further, or how Loralei managed to stay awake so close to burnout herself. But, by some miracle they managed, slicing the vines as they got closer to the palace, as whatever was happening inside the palace spread, and tried to claim them too.

Inside, the main hall was blood soaked, a stain that would never come clean. A grief that would coat this place for the rest of time. Bodies were strewn across the floor, left wherever they had fallen. Mozare searched among their faces for people he knew, people he'd trained or those who had trained him.

Mozare wasn't quite sure if it was relief or dread filling his chest when he didn't recognize any of them. He turned, following the path of bodies towards the throne room. It was the first place he would've checked for Revon, even without the corpses leading him directly there. He knew that was exactly what Revon would want, a grand stage for his final victory, a glorious backdrop to what he assumed would be the fight to quell any further rebellion.

An execution at the place of power, where he had gained and lost so much.

The doors were closed, bodies piled in front of it, which would make getting through difficult. He heard a breath, and for the first time, he let go of Loralei's hand so he could pull his remaining axe. One had already broken, he wasn't sure this one would hold after the abuse it had sustained in town, but he wasn't going to give up without even fighting.

As quickly as he'd pulled it free from their sheaths, he found himself returning it there, the quiet click a reassurance in the eerie quiet of the hall.

Sitting against the wall, Oliver and Melana rested against each other. He almost thought they were dead, but their chests heaved, keeping them moving. He couldn't tell amidst all of the blood if any of it was theirs.

Together, he and Loralei approached them. "Friends," he started, not wanting to shock the legionnaires into attacking before they realized who they were. "What do you need?"

He had no healing gifts of his own, and he wasn't quite sure what

Loralei could manage, but if there was any way they could help, he wasn't going to stop until he had.

With a deep breath, Oliver finally answered them, pulling Melana in tighter to his side. "We are well. We will survive this." Mozare was a little shocked when he turned to press a kiss against Melana's forehead. The two barely made sense as partners, but who was he to judge.

"Saiden is not well. Go to her." Melana's voice was weak, and Oliver turned his entire focus back to her, ignoring Mozare and Loralei now that they had given their message. Mozare wanted to thank them, but he had to hope there would be time for that when all of this was settled.

They cleared only the bodies they needed to open the door to the throne room wide enough for them to slip inside.

Inside was worse than anything they had seen coming into the palace. The entire room looked as if it had been reclaimed by a jungle, something he had never actually seen, but had learned about in training. Vines wove together, the floor beneath them barely visible anymore.

All around Saiden, soldiers seemed to be frozen in time; at least those that weren't already lying dead surrounding her. Because of course she was in the middle of all of it, kneeling in front of Revon, palms upwards as if she were praying.

Revon seemed to be the only one left outside of her control, untouched by her power, or whatever divine intervention was taking place in this room right now. He still had the tip of a blade pressed to her throat, as if considering the idea of killing her right now.

That was too far for Mozare. And if he had to guess by the way she'd tensed up next to him, it was too far for Loralei as well. He pulled one of his knives free from the sheath across his chest, and threw it as hard as he could.

The blade sailed true, and it would have landed perfectly, had something, some power greater than the rest of them, not stopped the blade in midair, a breath away from Revon's chest.

"What a shame," Revon said, as he looked down at the blade that should have ended him. "That was such a great throw, but you are nothing compared to the power in this room boy."

"I was once your power, or did you forget your own insignificance?" The words were out of his mouth before he could think them through. Rage burned away all the pain inside him except for the betrayal of this man. "I believed in you. I fought for you." Spit flew from his mouth as he yelled. "I killed for you. Because I thought you were in the right. And you betrayed that trust."

"You were a child, and you still think like one. You have not earned the anger you feel now."

Mozare went to charge him, and suddenly none of them were in the room anymore. The whole world shifted one step to the left, as he and Loralei fell to the floor, unconscious.

INTERLUDE

In the world they woke up in, the palace was undamaged. No marks to show that there had been injury to begin with. It was an erasure of the pain they'd had suffered through. Their bodies felt foreign, as if lifted from another world and pulled through to somewhere new.

In this new world, they felt nothing. No pain or fear. But the numbness was all-encompassing. There was no space for joy or love here either. That should've bothered them.

A child ran in front of them, laughing as he chased a small cat, wisps of shadow trailing behind the small creature. They tried to follow, but the scene changed before they could take a step. The world around them shifted again, a weight that kept them pressed against the ground, forced to observe as the tableau morphed into something new.

This time they weren't in the throne room anymore. Construction riddled the hallways of their palace, something neither of them had seen in real life. The boy looked the same, but this time tears tracked down his face. The little cat swirled between his legs, shadows flickering in and out of view.

Men were yelling at him, but they couldn't hear it from where they were standing. Their ears rang, muddling any sounds around them. They were forced to watch helplessly as a guard stepped behind the child, lifting him as if he weighed nothing, and forcibly removing him from the palace grounds.

The scene changed again as he reached out to help the boy, swirling beyond the reach of his fingers.

The boy was a man now, still unused to the height that came with it, huddled low in the forest. Someone came out to meet the man, a different boy, unused to the hiding their man had long been accustomed to. He recognized himself.

The world blurred once more, and they were underwater, but didn't drown. His lungs filled with water, but it was as easy to breathe as it had ever been. "This is the way we fix this." Someone said, and despite the water, they heard it perfectly clear. A hand grabbed his, and he recognized it somewhere beyond his consciousness. "This is the way I take it all back."

They were falling, he and the person whose hand he was still holding. He hit the floor hard, but pain was still missing. He should have been in agony, should feel the hard stone of the floor beneath him.

This throne room was the way he remembered, Saiden kneeling in the middle of the floor, palms up in offering. With Revon's blade at her throat.

In a rush, Mozare and Loralei came back to themselves, bursting into action.

75
SAIDEN

SAIDEN HAD NEVER BROUGHT ANYONE INTO THE REALM OF THE DIVINE. The one time that Loralei and Mozare had crossed with her, they had been called there by Keir and Ilona. Now, she hoped the unbinding of her curse meant she had enough power to bring Revon along, so she could finish him away from his reinforcements. Whatever the consequence of her decision, she would deal with when he was dead, because she would kill him here.

Her spirit felt lighter here, separated from the injury and weight of her mortal body. That thought scared her for a moment, before fear also escaped her grasp; too mundane of a feeling for her to hold on to. She waited, although she was not sure what for. Sometimes the gods kept her waiting there for so long she'd go numb before they finally met her.

She could be patient far longer than they realized. Ilona and Keir had given her that gift, although she doubted that they had understood it at the time. Now she would take everything they had given her, every gift and every curse, and she would use it to end this.

There was no way for her to know how long it took for Revon to arrive, but suddenly he was standing in front of her. His hand still poised like it held a blade, yet here it was empty. He stared down at his own hand and only once he had fully grasped that it was empty did he startle at his transition here.

"Where am I? What have you done to me?"

Saiden barely recognized her own voice as she answered him. "You thought you were a god. That is what you tried to become. Welcome to the land of the divine. Do you feel the foreignness on your skin? The way you will never belong here?"

Revon hissed at her, and finally she stood. Saiden felt no fear here, a sensation that had started even before she'd left the mortal realm. The only difference now was the detachment she felt from her old life, and from the people who had given this fight purpose.

In her hands, blades formed, their edges a pure white flame wrapping around her knuckles. It should have burned her, should've made her want to drop them, but their touch was as gentle as water flowing across her skin. She pointed her right hand, the one tattooed with Loralei's roses, towards Revon, blade parallel to the ground.

"You wanted your suffering to mean something, your trials to bring you something greater. I am the hand of your gods, I am your final trial. You will not pass me." As she spoke something possessed her, a cold sinking deep into her bones.

"I am more powerful than you could ever be, child." Revon bluffed, though fear had begun to paint itself across his features.

"Then face me." Saiden didn't wait for him to answer. This wasn't a battle to be fought with words, she already knew Revon would twist his to try and save his own life. She'd already met too many men like him. She swung her blade, and Revon narrowly avoided beheading by throwing his whole body off balance to duck beneath the blade.

He took time between her strikes to finally conjure a weapon on his own. It blurred at the edges, unstable, and she hoped that it would finally force Revon to face his own weakness. But there was nothing on his face but rage.

Revon swung towards her, trying to go on the offensive. Saiden couldn't find enough of herself to care. To worry for her own safety. She blocked his blows like she was training him on his first day in the legion. This was child's play to her.

Something shifted in the air behind her, but even she wasn't so reckless as to turn her back to her enemy. Not even with her instincts dulled and the feeling of consequences miles away.

Saiden went on the attack, striking out against Revon with both blades. But, suddenly, Revon wasn't the easy foe she'd thought him. Maybe it was his experiments, maybe it was madness, but his strikes reverberated through her entire being every time their blades clashed.

He came at her without stopping, without breathing between strikes, as if all he needed to cut her down was to keep moving forward. To keep striking at her until he'd chipped away enough of her to kill the rest.

Slowly, her senses began to come back to her, humanity invading the fog her powers had put her in. It gave her fear. But it also gave her purpose. She tried to strike back, but her blades slipped, the white flames flickering out as she lost hold of her own gifts.

Revon shoved her, and she stumbled to her knees. His blade followed after, and she barely managed to catch his wrist as he swung the blade towards her head. Above her and pressing down, even Saiden's strength was no match for Revon. His blade cut into her shoulder, and she screamed, pain finally finding her here, beneath everything.

When Revon's blade freed itself, she assumed death was coming for her with his next strike. But it didn't come. Instead, a hand pressed against her other shoulder, and a blade clashed against Revon's.

"You thought I'd let you die alone?"

Only Mozare would quip when he found himself in the divine realm facing the greatest evil they had ever known. And of course, because it was Mozare and he was here with her, she couldn't help but smile.

Saiden took his hand when he offered it to her and stood, blood dripping from fingers she could no longer feel. In her other hand, she now held her kindjal blade, the blue one Cassimir had given to her before he could say out loud that he loved her.

With Mozare at her side, she could face this man, without having to sacrifice her humanity. She wouldn't become like their gods, separate from the pain of humans. But it didn't matter.

Revon screamed as a blade cut through his mid-section. "Now, how does that feel you fucking prick?" Loralei spat on Revon as his body fell to the ground, and then slowly disappeared from the realm altogether.

At his death, Saiden assumed she'd lose her hold on the divine realm. That they would return home to rebuild and start anew, but they remained. She stepped forward, hand in Mozare's to hug Loralei to her chest.

When she stepped away, Ilona and Keir were waiting. "You failed us once Anointed one, but today you have restored balance. For you, we are grateful."

"I do not want your gratitude." Saiden placed herself between her gods and her friends, prepared to defend them if necessary. She wouldn't let Mozare or Loralei come to more harm at the hands of the divine.

"You do not need to do that child." Keir spoke, his voice coming from behind her, as his hand pressed into the wound Revon had left in her shoulder. She could feel him healing it, yet it was unlike any healing she had known before, natural or aided by a healer's gift. When she looked at the injury, a silvery rope of scar tissue covered the mark, reflecting the light as she turned her shoulder.

"Things do not break here the way they do in your realm. They cannot be fixed the same way either."

"You will return home, and you will live your lives. That is our gift."

She wanted to argue, but they were gone as quickly as they'd come. Together, she and her friends crashed back to the throne room floor, free at last.

EPILOGUE
A FEW WEEKS LATER

Seven chairs sat at the front of the hall as the council session was called to order. In the days following Revon's death, it had been hard to chase the darkness from the streets of their city, but Saiden and her friends had spent every waking moment doing that. And every night when screaming terrors chased her from her sleep, Saiden sat with Cassimir and listed all the good things they would accomplish.

Saiden wouldn't stop until she'd earned her peace.

Today was a good start. It was time for a change in Kaizia, something new. The old ways weren't working anymore, and none of them wanted to live through another rebellion. Something different would give them all a chance to grow, to become something better than what they were.

Saiden wore regalia all in red. It was time for something new for her as well. A time without fear, without hiding. The armored bodice settled over her like a second skin, her reflection in the mirror strong. She ran a finger over the silvered scar on her shoulder, and then quickly covered it with the fabric of the cape that would trail behind her.

Cassimir was waiting in the throne room. He may have been a crucial part of the fight, but today he was representing his uncle at the beginning of this new age, so couldn't stand beside her. Instead, she met Loralei and Mozare in the hallway, hands clasped as they whispered to each other while they waited.

Loralei wore a striking gown in white, the back lowered so that the scar where her life was almost taken from her was visible for everyone to see. They were both proud of everything they had survived, and this was the time to show that they would continue to fight. Mozare was back in his black gear, the fit of his ebony suit somewhere between the military gear they normally wore, and the embroidered decadence of Taezhali fashion.

She smiled at both of them, the warmth inside her radiating through the hallway in a bright light. Someday she would finally get complete control over her power, but she knew there was still time before that day would come. For now, she did not mind that joy shone out from her body, not after she'd spent so long angry and afraid.

Her friends smiled at her light show, both of them stepping up to her and pressing a kiss to her cheeks. Their love, and the love that they all shared for each other was a force to be reckoned with. It wrapped around her, as strong as any armor she'd ever worn.

Together, the three of them made their way to throne room. The blood staining the floor had been covered with new Taezhali rugs, but despite their best efforts, the vines Saiden had grown throughout the room and much of the kingdom had been impossible to remove. They weren't entirely sure why they didn't die when none of them fed power into the vines, but they weren't concerned.

Personally, Saiden liked them. She didn't want to risk people forgetting what had happened and repeating it. Like the vines tattooed on her own skin, these were scars that her kingdom would have to bear, to remind them of the sins of their past.

The three of them processed to the front of the room together, a united front as the crowds of people waited to learn what the future of this kingdom would look like. And for a second, nerves invaded the joy Saiden had felt. That they would make a mistake, that their efforts wouldn't be enough to stop darkness from reaching them again.

Then she saw Cassimir in the crowd, his sister smiling brightly beside him, a blood red prayer scarf wrapped around her head. On the other side of the hall, Rhena stood with Talon, both in their new military uniforms, proud to be at the front of a new army. Her family centered her.

Mozare had tried to convince her that she should be the one to speak today, to introduce their people to the new world, but she wasn't a politician. She was a soldier, and so she stood, spine straight, at the base of the dais as Loralei and Mozare walked up the few steps to address the crowd.

"Good morning my friends," Loralei started, Mozare's hand pressed to her back. "It has been a long time that we have waited for this morning to come. For darkness to be pushed back. I am not to be excused from that. For my time as your queen, I failed to see this darkness as it bloomed throughout our city and in the hearts of those closest to me."

"You see, divinity, or divine choice, does not free us from human error. And so, one person cannot be chosen to rule over all without great risk for evil to bloom again. The man who took this kingdom from us is proof of that. He let wickedness, no" she paused correcting herself, "he encouraged wickedness to spread. He wanted you to see the worst in each other, to see evil in the face of every neighbor. But a people cannot survive that division."

Mozare began his part, the small bit they had given him after it was decided that he was no politician either. "This time, we cannot leave every seat to the gods. Instead, we will have a council, a representative of Keir, of Ilona, and of the Anointed." Saiden had argued against this, as she was the only Anointed choice among the people, but she had been outvoted by her friends. "And four non-gifted representatives, voted for by the people to give voice to their concerns." She had asked the Enlightened if they wanted a seat of their own, but the elder had thought it was unwise.

"Today is a day for hope, for us to come together and rejoice in the spreading of light." Loralei began again, and Saiden couldn't help but shine again at her words, although she hated the attention it brought her. Old habits were not so easy to abandon.

People gasped in awe around her, as light filled the room, giving everything an ethereal glow. And then they smiled at her, at the show of power that had once been a reason to fear her. Freed from her curse, this was the first time in her life that she could've done them harm without taking a single step.

But she wouldn't. Because she was Saiden, the daughter of Magdalena and Nakti. A soldier, a friend, a tool. But most importantly she was herself, master of her own life. She would not be used by anyone, friend or foe. She would serve her people, as she had always tried, and she would love. Because this was her one life to live.

From her place, she watched the people begin to debate, to think about what they wanted to see for their country. But this wasn't a show for her benefit. In the following days, they would pick who was meant to lead them, to represent them.

Loralei and Mozare stepped down from the dais, and together, they left the people to their discussion. Saiden felt her friends leave their places in the crowd to follow her, and she smiled again. Beyond those doors, anything was possible. And it was all hers—theirs, to reach for.

THE END

ACKNOWLEDGMENTS

Thank you to everyone who has seen me through this journey. To my parents, Alex, Max and Catie, for helping me work through this draft when it felt impossible to see the end.

To my friends Jessi, Aly and Jess, who have supported so many writing dreams.

To everyone who's given this author dream of mine support-Jennie, Andy, Mary, Falla, Aimee, Coach Donna, Aunt Laurie and so many more. Thank you.

www.ingramcontent.com/pod-product-compliance
Lightning Source LLC
Chambersburg PA
CBHW020457310726
48979CB00016B/2687/J

* 9 7 8 1 9 6 5 4 3 6 0 6 6 *